IMPERIUM: BETRAYAL

By Paul M Calvert

Thanks to:

My understanding wife, Irene, who allowed me the time and space to type for hours on end.
Richard Golding for listening to plots for the Imperium universe, and both
Mike Woods and Skye "Tempest" Macfarlane for helping with proof-reading.

Housekeeping

To make everything seem familiar, I've deliberately set out to anglicise names, places and things. For example, if on an alien planet there is a drink analogous to tea, that's the name I've given it. I hope this will allow you to immerse yourself better in the Imperium universe. At the rear is an Appendix, containing a history of how the Empire was founded, the theory behind Quantum Attraction and how ships can travel between solar systems.
Finally, I've also drawn on the fine history and tradition of the Royal Navy for inspiration, especially around the naming of ships and ranks.

Chapter 1, Raigmore Hospital, Isle of Skye

Chapter 2, Ascension

Chapter 3, Flt Lt Harris

Chapter 4, Heaven

Chapter 5, Bridge, Dauntless

Chapter 6, Bombardment

Chapter 7, Crown Prince

Chapter 8, Raigmore Hospital, Inverness

Chapter 9, Planet Capital

Chapter 10, Suspicion

Chapter 11, Banishment

Chapter 12, Capital

Chapter 13, Boundary of Heaven's system

Chapter 14, Struan, Isle of Skye.

Chapter 15, Approaching Earth orbit.

Chapter 16, Aurora Borealis

Chapter 17, Vimes

Chapter 18, Dauntless

Chapter 19, Western Highlands, Scotland

Chapter 20, Palace Woodlands

Chapter 21, The day after.

Chapter 22, Planet Kiyami, Sector 12

Chapter 23, Capital

Chapter 24, Dauntless

Chapter 25, Homeward Bound

Chapter 26, A walk in the dark

Chapter 27, DU-499

Chapter 28, Bridge Cottages, Skye

Chapter 29, Dauntless

Chapter 30, Dunvegan Castle, Skye

Chapter 31, Surprise

Chapter 32, Uncovering the truth

Chapter 33, Palace Bunker

Chapter 34, The morning after the night before

Dear Reader,

Appendix 1, The Alexander Doctrine

Appendix 2, Capital and a bit of history
Appendix 3, Quantum Attraction

It was seven in the morning, and dawn was beginning to break on what promised to be another cloudy and overcast day in early March. Senior Trauma Doctor Karen McLeod had already been awake for an hour, getting herself ready for work and her last shift of the week. She had set her alarm an hour earlier than usual and had used the extra time to ensure everything was packed and ready for tomorrow's trip. All that was left unpacked were her toiletries and the clothes she would be wearing for the journey. Karen looked around the room with a critical eye, looking for anything obvious she might have missed.

"*Nope, I can't see anything,*" she told herself, slipping the lanyard of her identity card and pass over her head.

Twenty-eight years old, slim, one point eight metres tall with highlighted brown hair, she was looking forward to staying at her uncle's empty house on the Isle of Skye, while he and his wife Flora went away for a few weeks cruising around the Mediterranean. Working straight shifts in the Accident & Emergency Department of Raigmore Hospital had left Karen feeling tired to her bones, and she knew the three-week break away from it all would do her good.

"*Once I've dealt with today's early drunks, heart attacks and road traffic accidents I can relax and think about what to do next with my life,*" she thought. "*Three weeks peace and quiet, that's just what the Doctor ordered!*"

She had moved temporarily into the Hospital's accommodation block a few days previously, after her long-term partner, Ian, had unceremoniously dumped her via email from the US and given a month's notice to quit his flat. While it had been her home for the past four years, she had no hesitation in moving out immediately he'd made his feelings known.

"*I don't want anything to do with that bastard,*" she'd thought after being dumped, and had moved out the following day, arranging for her few things to be placed in storage. Fortunately, she was never one for many possessions, believing a simple life was preferable to being weighed down by clutter. "Things only attract dust and tie you down," was a phrase she often used when asked why.

Deep down, she knew the split with Ian had been brewing for months, ever since refusing to follow him to New York where he had been offered a job at the Columbia University Medical Centre. *"Why should I give up my career just for him?"* she had asked herself many times over the last few days, *"If our relationship had meant anything surely he would have stayed here with me?"*

She tried to think calming thoughts as she felt her blood pressure begin to rise.

"No, I'm not going to go there today," she said to herself, "Think happy thoughts, Karen."

Moving out had been on the cards at some point, as he'd made it known he was going to sell the flat they shared in Inverness as part of his move abroad, but she hadn't thought he would be so ruthless, so quickly.

"Just goes to show that it doesn't matter how long you have lived with someone or think you know them, there no guarantees," she thought to herself. *"How does that old Japanese saying go; let's see now...got it."*

She spoke out loud, "Every person has three hearts: one that they show in public, one that they show to close friends and family, and one that only they and their God sees. Try to see through to the heart that is reserved for themselves and their God, for that is the heart most trustworthy."

Feeling pleased she had remembered it, and not a little proud of her near photographic memory which had helped her get through Medical School, Karen picked up her mobile and pager from where they had been charging overnight. Not bothering to make breakfast, for she could get a full English in the Hospital canteen, she headed for the door, making sure it was locked behind her before moving through the corridor and greeting the cold morning air. She hadn't bothered with an overcoat, and although the early March morning was crisp and sharp, Karen was used to the cold and paid it little attention.

"*Anyway,*" she thought, "*it's only two hundred metres or so to A&E.*"

Striding briskly along the footpath, she passed the car park on her right and entered A&E, sandwiched between the main entrance on her left and Outpatients. The warm air hit her as the automatic doors opened and she was greeted by the familiar smell of antiseptic with an overlay of stale, spilt beer from a small puddle a cleaner was mopping up along with a few dark blood spots by the entrance.

"*No doubt from a broken nose or something similar,*" she thought to herself, nodding at the cleaner as she walked past towards her station. After checking nothing serious was outstanding before taking over the shift, she decided there was just enough time to get to the canteen and back with a sandwich and large coffee before getting down to business.

"*That'll keep me going till I get a chance to grab something more substantial,*" Karen thought, dispensing with the idea of a full English as she walked through A&E and turned left towards the canteen.

Fifteen minutes later, Karen was sitting at her workstation, checking through the notes of the patients left over from the previous night's intake. One of them, Mr McKinley, was a regular to A&E with chronic alcoholism and incipient liver failure. He was under observation in one of the curtained off treatment booths. Karen shook her head on looking at his stats.

"*If he keeps this up for another year we'll need to find another poor soul to hold the record for most attendances in a month,*" she thought sadly, feeling sorry for the man. He had obviously fallen onto hard times emotionally, but was unfailingly polite, even when blind drunk.

The red emergency phone rang, the sound making her jump.

"*Christ Almighty,*" she thought, annoyed with herself for being startled, "*if I'm this jumpy now what state will I be in at the end of the shift?*"

Frank, one of her team, answered the telephone and was busy writing down the incident details with his left hand while cradling the handset between his neck and right shoulder. Finished speaking, he put the telephone back onto its cradle and called out.

"Hillclimber, male, twenty-five years old, compound fracture of the right tibia, possible mild hypothermia. Air Ambulance bringing him in, ETA thirty minutes," he called out to the assembling team in a slightly effeminate voice for one so heavily built.

Karen watched her staff start preparing for the arrival with quiet efficiency. Satisfied everything was OK, she went back to her notes and coffee, smiling as she remembered Frank's half-hearted attempts to seduce her at the last Christmas party where everyone had just a bit too much to drink that night.

"*He might sound effeminate,*" she thought to herself, smiling at the memory, "*but that wasn't a canoe in his pocket when he was trying for some tonsil hockey.*"

Karen looked over in his direction for a moment, accidentally catching his eye. He raised an eyebrow in query, but she shook her head slightly and looked down again, chuckling quietly to herself and feeling a little flushed. "*God, I so need this break.*"

Fortunately, as morning progressed the expected early rush of patients didn't appear, just a steady stream of commuters who'd fallen over, sprained ankles or were taken ill on their way into work. The most serious case in the last half hour had been an elderly lady, brought in by her worried husband, complaining of pains in her neck and left arm. Potentially a heart attack or severe angina, she'd been rushed through and was currently in the cubicle next to Mr McKinley who had woken up and was currently asking for a cup of tea "with something a wee bit stronger, if you get my meaning," winking at the nurses. He always followed the same pattern and would no doubt be leaving soon under his own steam to find somewhere to buy more alcohol.

Anticipation had been steadily rising in readiness for the Air Ambulances arrival, especially as it had been a slow morning. Colleen, a lovely nurse from Blessington in County Wicklow, had gone with two porters and a trolley to the Helipad.

"I can hear it coming," Karen said to herself, debating if she had enough time to grab another coffee, go to the toilet or preferably both. Toilet needs came first so by the time she had returned to her station, the patient was being brought in through the doors, followed by the Pilot and Paramedic in their orange flight suits. Karen could see a silver Mylar heat retaining sheet peeking out from underneath the green blanket the patient was wrapped in and was relieved that he seemed responsive to Colleen's ministrations.

Letting her team get on with the initial assessment and diagnostics, Karen walked over to James and Michael, the pilot and paramedic.

"Morning gentlemen, how are you this fine morning?" she asked them with a smile.

"All the better for seeing you, Karen," replied James, with a tired grin. Michael just nodded and headed off at speed for the toilet.

"Don't mind him, he's been busting to go for the last hour," James said, laughing quietly. "Too much tea. He refuses to use the emergency bottle so just had to suffer. He'll be all right once he's been."

"How's the patient?" Karen asked, looking over to him. Already, he had been transferred from the trolley and lifted onto a bed and was being examined carefully by one of the Junior Doctors. Colleen was cutting off his heavy hiking boot while another nurse was attaching an IV line into the back of his hand.

"He'll be fine. Tough one that lad, smart too," replied James. "Even with his busted leg he still managed to set up and spend the night in his emergency tent, so apart from a nasty fracture, he should be OK once your lot have sorted him out. The only daft thing he did was go out on his own."

Michael returned, smiling and looking a lot happier.

"Sorry Karen," he said, "couldn't wait for a second longer, literally a matter of life and death!"

Returning the broad smile, Karen said, "You are forgiven Michael, providing you buy me a cup of coffee if you two have the time and don't have to go right away."

"Fine by us Karen," replied Michael, "we are due a break now anyway. Lead on," pointing the way to the canteen.

Twenty minutes later, Karen found herself nursing an empty, lukewarm coffee cup while pouring out her troubles to her two slightly bemused colleagues. Her pager hadn't gone off, so she knew everything was going smoothly back in A&E.

"What, so he just sent you an email telling you to leave, and it was all over?" exclaimed Michael. "What a bastard. I had a girlfriend dump me like that once. Did I ever tell you about...?"

James interrupted his friend. "I don't think Karen wants to hear about that now Mike," he said, given him a pointed stare.

"Oh, right, sorry Karen," Michael mumbled an apology.

"Yup, just like that," Karen said, looking back down into her empty cup. "So, I moved out right away and will spend part of my three-week break looking for somewhere to stay." Karen looked up at the two men. "Either of you two familiar with Bracadale, near Struan?" she asked. "That's where I'm staying."

"Wasn't that where we picked up that heart attack a few months back?" Michael turned to James. "You know, the overweight Scandinavian woman that insisted it was just indigestion?"

James agreed, nodding. "That was Struan. We had problems finding somewhere safe to land, so I put us down by the ruined barn near the jetty. One of the nicest parts of the island, if you ask me."

Karen nodded, "That's the place. I'll be staying there, at least for the first week, then it depends on how long it takes me to find somewhere permanent to stay. If you can recommend somewhere or know someone with a flat to rent, please tell me."

Before anyone could speak, Karen heard her pager buzz, so the three took that as their cue to get up and get back to work. Saying their goodbyes, the two men each gave Karen a friendly hug before heading for the main exit, while Karen turned left and walked swiftly back to A&E to see what emergency needed her attention.

Protected Planet P414, Sector 11. Local name: Heaven

The planet hung in space, sitting like a bright blue-green marble on a black velvet cloth, backlit by a billion tiny points of light. Below, the stars making up the bright lens of the galactic plane stretched across the midnight black of space.

Wisps of white and grey cloud hung motionless in the atmosphere and on the horizon a large cyclone slowly turned, creating a dense field of angry grey-white cloud cover spreading over a large part of the planet. In amongst the storm, bursts of lightning reached down from the upper reaches of the atmosphere, leaving actinic flashes on the retinas of any observer.

In front of the dark terminator line marking the border between night and day, bright cobweb-like centres of light clearly defined the busy, teeming cities. Spidery strings of light connected them to each other while empty expanses of desert or jungle were represented by large patches of darkness.

Far below, a small speck of light suddenly appeared through the cloud cover, rapidly rising through the upper atmosphere. Growing larger by the second, the speck morphed into the recognisable shape of a shuttle, its prow marked with the orange and black crest of the Imperial family. Suitable for short journeys between planets and their moons, this one was ferrying passengers between the planet below to the orbiting capital ships of the Emperor's personal fleet. Thirty meters-long and ten wide, the shuttle was built to a standard design used throughout the Imperial Navy.

Climbing quickly into a medium orbit, the shuttle adjusted its course and headed towards another small speck coming into view over the horizon. With few points of reference in space to judge size or distance, the shuttle's two pilots, one male the other female, were relying on instrumentation to guide them towards their destination, a distant speck of light stationed in an orbit allowing the planet to slowly rotate beneath it.

Although perfectly capable of being flown by the shuttle's AI, wherever possible the human pilots flew themselves, enjoying the power and sense of freedom given to them through their sensory link with the shuttle. As they closed with the speck of light it grew rapidly, finally becoming the massive, brooding shape that marked it as the Imperial flagship, INS Dauntless.

Built over one hundred years previously in the Imperial family's private shipyards, Dauntless remained the single most powerful and impressive symbol of the Imperium. Nearly two kilometres long and studded with lumps and extrusions hinting at concealed power, she was by no means the oldest ship in the Imperial Navy and over the years had been continually refitted to keep up to date with the latest weaponry and armour. Dauntless remained as powerful now as when she was first constructed on the orders of the previous Emperor, Thomas II.

Dauntless was normally kept invisible to sensors or prying eyes by the camouflage smart-metal covering her hull, but in honour of the planet's Ascension today into the Empire, she was currently brightly lit and clearly visible to any inhabitants viewing from the night side of the planet as she moved overhead. Those not prepared to go outside and brave the evening cold could view her, and the upcoming ceremony, at home on their televisions and computer screens.

Inside the shuttle, despite having obtained clearance from the Air Officer to dock, the lead pilot always found it disconcerting to sense the massive point defence systems track their approach, knowing they could vaporise her craft and occupants in an instant. Intellectually, she knew it was perfectly safe, yet on a primaeval level, there was something about the defences impersonal mirroring of her craft's movements which made her uneasy.

Ignoring the feeling and focusing on the job at hand, she skilfully guided the shuttle along the designated flight path towards one of the open hangars, set in the hull beneath a massive, brightly lit black and orange Imperial insignia. Once the Ascension ceremony was over, the insignia would be absorbed back into the smart-metal, returning the flagship to its normal, unadorned state. The other ships making up the Imperial task force were currently in stealth mode and invisible to the naked eye, but thanks to her sensory link with the shuttle, she could see them on her retinas as translucent pulses of coloured light.

The task force's two Carriers, INS Glorious and INS Courageous, were pulsing blue in her mind and sat several kilometres away in a slightly higher orbit, surrounded by their attendant auxiliaries, coloured pale green. A yellow picket line of cruisers and frigates patrolled space further away from the planet, alert and ready to blockade any approaching threat. Few risks were ever knowingly taken with the Emperor's life, even more so on days like this when the Crown Prince was also aboard. In preparation for docking, she slowly began disengaging her link to the shuttle and the no longer needed long-range images faded from her mind.

She felt a mild tremor from her craft as it closed to within a hundred metres of the hangar entrance, indicating it was passing through the invisible shields protecting the flagship from electromagnetic radiation and micro-meteorites. Although she could allow the shuttle to fly and dock itself, like all good pilots she quietly resented turning control back to the AI. When her current tour of duty on the flagship came to an end, she would be faced with a difficult choice, to either return to fighter duties on board one of the new Carriers being rolled out into service by the regular Navy or remain part of the Emperor's fleet.

Dismissing such thoughts for later, Flight Lieutenant Christine Harris focused on setting the shuttle down at the designated dock. Using a combination of sensors and old-fashioned eyesight, Harris carefully manoeuvred her shuttle towards the dock. Moving deeper into the vast hangar, on both sides she passed numerous other shuttles and sundry vessels already docked in cradles. Brightly lit, the hangar was always alive with activity and movement. Despite the seemingly chaotic mess of personnel, ships, and lifting machinery moving around the deck, Harris knew everything was working together in perfect harmony, controlled or directed by the ship's AI.

Reaching her designated docking space, set alongside three large military shuttles, she slowly spun the craft one hundred and eighty degrees and reversed it into place. So perfect was her approach there wasn't even a tremor to announce to the passengers the shuttle had docked and was now automatically linking itself into the deck. Harris watched for a few moments as a docking tube snaked towards the airlock, then activated the intercom to address her passengers.

"Ladies and Gentlemen, may I have your attention, please. We have now arrived. Please remain seated until the docking tube has been pressurised and you are instructed to disembark," she told the half-dozen diplomats and their assorted aides who were seated in the passenger area behind the flight deck.

Annoyingly, the moment she stopped speaking, most of the passengers begun to remove their belongings stowed in the overhead lockers and mill about in eager anticipation of disembarking. Nearly all of them had been on the planet below for almost a year and were eager for up to date news from home and a return to the comforts of modern living. The gaudy outfits of those in the Diplomatic Service were in stark contrast to the darker, more utilitarian uniforms of the flight crew and attendants.

Looking at the overhead display currently showing the passenger area, Harris muttered a rude comment under her breath about being ignored, then quickly checked the controls to make sure that the intercom hadn't been on. Having been reprimanded in the past for making inappropriate comments within earshot of senior staff, she didn't want to repeat the mistake. A tingle in her spine told her it was safe to completely unmerge from the shuttle, so she initiated the shutdown, sighing with disappointment as the world suddenly became a much smaller place.

Outside, the unpressurized flight deck was full of technicians and ground crew in pressure gear, working hard to prep and restock various craft. Much of the activity was taking place around three large, medium-range military shuttles docked close to her own. In amongst the ground crew, automated cargo handlers and machinery moved around, taking instructions from both human operators and the flagships semi-sentient AI which controlled every aspect of the ship, down to the smallest detail. Heavier or more awkward objects were being moved into place by bulked up autonomous servitor androids of varying sizes and configuration.

Harris knew these large and heavily armed military shuttles to her right were being prepared for the imminent departure of the Emperor and his retinue of bodyguards. They would ferry them to the Ascension ceremony on the planet below, which would shortly get underway in front of the planet's assembled great and good.

Mirroring the flagship, most of the active stealth features on the three shuttles had been switched off, and they were decked out for visual impact rather than functionality, with only one shuttle showing the Imperial insignia on its flank.

Flt Lt Harris wondered if the people on the planet below realised the Emperor was bestowing a singular honour on them by attending, not only in person but with the Crown Prince too, sole heir to the throne. Thinking of the Prince momentarily distracted her, for since coming aboard twenty-five days previously, he had become very popular with the flight crews, especially the females, always greeting everyone by their first name when off duty and seemingly knowing everything about everyone. Because of the Alexander Doctrine, she was aware that, in theory at least, she had a chance of bagging herself a Prince of the Realm. The Doctrine, named after the fourth Emperor who instigated it, forbade members of the Imperial family from marrying within the nobility. Harris smiled inwardly and dismissed the idea as a silly fantasy, particularly as she was aware of the Prince's reputation as a heartbreaker.

"*Just get in the queue,*" she thought, "*along with the other ten thousand females on this ship*". Chuckling quietly to herself, she drew a quizzical look from the second flight officer who looked up from what he had been doing.

"Just thinking about the Prince being on board," she said, which drew a heartfelt "No chance" from her co-pilot, Flying Officer Hendrickson, a skilled flyer but no conversationalist.

Primary Hangar Control interrupted them, confirming the docking tube had been attached and the passengers were cleared to disembark. Out of habit, Harris checked with the shuttle's AI that everything was safe, then instructed it to announce the pre-recorded disembarkation message in the passenger area. Even as the announcement began, Harris was already heading towards the toilets at the rear of the shuttle to freshen up. Without looking, she immediately knew the airlock had been opened, for the air in the shuttle changed from the slightly bitter scent which lingered from the planet below to the more sterile and scrubbed smell characteristic of all big vessels in the Navy. On the flight up, the shuttle's AI had imperceptibly raised the air pressure from that of the planet to the flagship's, so there was no hiss of escaping air when the doors opened.

Weaving her way through the milling passengers, one of the Diplomats noticed her flight rank and held out his hand for her to shake. Unlike the others, he was dressed all in black apart from an imposing scarlet cloak. Not wishing to appear rude, Harris stopped and took it. The man had a firm grip, and as they shook he thanked her for a smooth flight up from the surface. Harris could see from the campaign ribbons and decorations on the Ambassador's uniform that here was a veteran of numerous battles and she instinctively stood a little straighter than normal. Using her command implant, she mentally checked the passenger manifest to see who she was dealing with. Instantly her implant registered a match with the image being fed to it by her eyes. Ambassador Gallagher, Duke of Sector Two and the second most powerful person in the Imperium.

Catching where her eyes had lingered and the subtle shift in posture, he smiled gently and apologised for the ostentation. His pale blue eyes fixed on hers with a focused, yet not unfriendly intensity, and she noticed the prominent laughter lines around his eyes.

"For these type of functions, they wheel us old war horses out from behind a desk, and I'm afraid we have to wear all the braid, no exceptions," he said with a grin, the laughter lines deepening as he spoke, his voice a pleasing baritone. "Thank you again for a smooth ride; I hope you are the one piloting us down when we get back to Capital. Good day to you, Flight-Lieutenant Harris."

With that and a swirl of his cape, Ambassador Gallagher turned away and headed for the companionway. He carried his age well, giving little sign he was approaching his two-hundredth birthday, walking with the self-control and assuredness of one who knew how to handle himself in a crisis. Although simple, the midnight-black uniform hung well on his impressive frame, its shape emphasising here was a man who kept himself in trim, despite holding down a usually sedentary position.

"*So that's the famous Duke*," Harris thought to herself, admiring his style and easy manner, watching his retreating back until he exited her shuttle. Lingering for a few moments as the ground crew came in to get the interior ready for the next flight, she turned around and headed again to the toilet, taking the time to freshen up before reporting with her co-pilot to Primary Hangar Control. After logging their flight times they could go off duty, their shift officially over.

Duke Gallagher, on exiting the docking tube, was greeted by his aide, Second Lieutenant Stephen Collinson, a tall and muscular young man who always seemed to be slightly stooping as if compensating for his height.

"*I wonder if he will remember not to try and take my case this time?*" Gallagher thought. He smiled, seeing his aide's eyes flick down to his case and weigh up whether he should ask, then remembering not to at the last moment. The heavy case rarely left Gallagher's side when he was away from home, and it was unusual for him to allow others to handle it. Collinson had only been assigned to him at the start of this mission and remained annoyingly eager to please. Gallagher preferred his staff to display a healthy dose of cynicism but supposed it was still early days. "*If anyone can teach the boy cynicism it's me,*" he thought, "*Damn, was I ever like this, so eager and nervous?*"

On the flight up from the planet, he'd used his command level overrides to tap into the shuttle's flight systems, monitoring how the pilot performed and accessing the flight recorders for tactical information. Although he had every confidence in the capabilities of the pilots assigned to the Emperor's flagship, Gallagher couldn't break the habit of a lifetime in wanting to know everything going on around him.

"*Just in case,*" he'd thought, justifying it to himself even though he knew he should try and relax more. On the other hand, he knew full well it was this caution which had kept him alive for so long. Gallagher made a mental note to remember the pilot's name as he'd enjoyed the unexpectedly rude comment she had made at the end of the flight, his command implant relaying it to him even though the intercom had been off. After docking, he had waited behind to get a glimpse of her, admiring the flash of rebelliousness she'd shown.

Walking away from the shuttle, Gallagher lengthened his stride, forcing Collinson to do the same if he wanted to keep up. Quickly covering ground, Gallagher sent a query via his implant to Vimes, the Emperor's aide, to see if his old friend was free to meet with him right away. One of the advantages of being an old comrade in arms of the Emperor was that Vimes had standing instructions to always let him through, with few exceptions. Vimes was the immaterial, semi-sentient, electronic Aide of the Emperors' family that followed them everywhere and was currently residing alongside the flagships AI.

"*Ah, Ambassador Gallagher, nice to have you back on board. Don't you wish to freshen up first?*" replied Vimes, using the neural linkage all command staff had to the ship's communication system.

"*No, I can do that later, after I've spoken to the Emperor about the ceremony,*" Gallagher replied, not for the first time thinking privately to himself that if Vimes were only semi-sentient, he'd eat his cloak.

"*The Emperor is always free to see you, Ambassador, and will meet you at your convenience in audience room three. No need to knock this time,*" Vimes replied, referring to another of Gallagher's foibles. As a courtesy, while talking to him, Vimes downloaded details of the quickest route to the Emperor into Gallagher's interface.

Following the directions, Gallagher and Collinson arrived at a transit tube and entered the waiting pod, which, following another neural command from the Ambassador, headed off for the flagship's Imperial quarters and command level. These tubes ran the full length, width and depth of the flagship, ensuring no part of the vessel was more than a few minutes travel time apart. With a few exceptions, the ship's A.I. ensured a travel-tube was always available at all the key access points around the vast ship. Each pod read the personal preferences of its occupants and matched acceleration and G-tolerances accordingly. Although not strictly necessary, the walls of the travel tubes indicated the direction of travel by way of lighting that moved along the walls, useful in avoiding disorientation when the tube changed direction.

A minute later, the pod arrived, and the two men exited. For security purposes, they presented neural and physical ID's to both the human and automated sentries on duty, then passed through into the Imperial suite and command level. Although the travel pod had already checked their identities upon entering and confirming destination, the Imperial Navy preferred human back-ups, particularly where security was concerned.

Turning to his aide, Gallagher looked him in the eyes. "Get yourself a coffee and wait for me in reception until I call for you. I'm not sure how long this will take so you might as well make yourself comfortable."

Gallagher smiled inside as he caught Collinson's eyes flitting for a moment to his case before saluting and moving off.

Dauntless's AI had routed their travel pod to the exit nearest the Emperor's current location, so it was only a short walk through the brightly lit and vaulted corridor before he reached the door to audience room three. As befitted the Imperial quarters of the flagship, numerous works of art were strategically placed along the corridors, many of them famous or of historical significance. Interspersed amongst the paintings and small sculptures were numerous life-sized statues of equally famous historical figures, some of whom Gallagher recognised. With access to the finest works of over four thousand planets, the Imperial family had plenty to choose from. While the works of art couldn't be faulted, Gallagher did sometimes wonder about the Emperor's taste and seeming fondness for statuary.

Although there were no distinct light sources, the corridors and public places were well lit and designed to give the impression of airiness. If requested, private quarters on the flagship could be illuminated according to personal taste, allowing occupants to match the light given off from their home star.

On reaching the private audience room reserved by the Emperor for his friends or intimate gatherings, Gallagher stood for a moment in front of the door. Lifting his arm to knock, he hesitated for a split second, remembering the comment Vimes had made earlier, then knocked sharply anyway. Although he knew Vimes had already detected his approach and had no doubt informed the Emperor of his arrival, Gallagher always preferred to knock and had done so this time just to make a point to Vimes. In his many years of Imperial service, he'd had innumerable conversations with Vimes and for the second time that day was prepared to stake his Dukedom on the aide being fully sentient.

The door opened silently, and Gallagher stepped in, his eye's searching for Alexander. Inside, the clean, fresh smell of the room gently tickled his nose for a moment, reminding him of a summer's morning at the Capital. As with the lighting, individual areas of the ship could have their atmospheres customised. This could be useful in identifying where you were or as a way of reflecting the personality or current mood of the room's owner.

In times of alert, scents could be changed by the AI to provide stimulus or focus minds.

The audience room was well lit. Décor was simple. Currently, just an old wood-effect smart-metal desk and several comfortable armchairs were set up in a semi-circle against one of the walls. Above these, a large wall screen was displaying a life-like, real-time projection of the blue-green planet below.

Alexander II, Emperor of four thousand and fifty-two worlds, descended from the first Emperor Josef through a direct line of an almost similar number of years, strode across the room towards him with arms outstretched in greeting. The two old friends embraced warmly, with no hint of formality between them.

The Emperor was an imposing man, almost two metres tall when barefoot, with the obligatory broad shoulders and slim hips expected of heroic figures. Like most Navy Veterans, his head was shaved close to the skull, with a uniform even plainer than Gallagher's, to the point of being utilitarian. Despite his many numerous battles and engagements, it was conspicuously devoid of any military honours, reflecting his modest nature.

"Good to see you, old friend," said Alexander, greeting him with a broad smile, "I really do appreciate your taking the time to personally oversee the Ascension arrangements for me. I promise this will be the last time…or at least until the next protected planet develops space flight."

Alexander turned away to look at the image of the planet below. "As a thank you, once the ceremony is over, I'll instruct one of my personal yachts to take you back home to Wayland. It will be significantly faster than your having to wait for one of the regular shuttles or staying around until we get back to Capital."

"Thank you, Alex, I appreciate that," responded Gallagher. "Excluding travel time, I've been here over three months now making the arrangements. I've appeared on their information and entertainment channels explaining how the Empire works and the benefits of joining, addressed their world council, smoothing ruffled feathers, etc. It's been quite tiring. Now I just want to get back home and see my family. In case you have forgotten, don't forget I'm an old man now, Alexander," he finished, using the Emperor's full name which he always did when wishing to make a point to him in private.

Alexander smiled at his friend, gesturing towards the seats underneath the large wall screen displaying a real-time image of Heaven. The two men walked over to them, each looking for a moment at the planet, Gallagher waiting a second so Alexander could sit first. Before getting down to business, Alexander asked his friend if he would like some refreshment, but the offer was declined. He knew Gallagher was going over in his mind how to present the information before beginning the briefing, so Alexander sat quietly and waited for his friend and advisor to start.

Gallagher looked again at the planet for a moment, collected his thoughts and addressed his Emperor.

"Everything checks out, Alex. I can find no evidence they are anything other than what they seem to be, and while their technological advancement over the past one hundred years has been remarkably rapid, it is within the upper decile of what we have seen on other worlds, and not entirely unprecedented. They came late to manned space flight, having first set up a comprehensive network of unmanned satellites, which may indicate a cautious approach to risk. Economically they have a wide variety of trade goods to offer us, mainly works of art and high-end foodstuffs which will sell well in the Empire. Unusually for this stage of development, they already have just one global monotheistic religion and a unified world government, hence our offer of Stage Two membership. There are close ties between the two. Again, there are precedents for this." He paused for a moment before continuing.

"Militarily they are accomplished, with basic nuclear weaponry integrated into a planetary based asteroid defence system completed several decades ago. This is unprecedented and worthy of further study by our ethno-biologists. Politically, the governing world council provides effective leadership, in conjunction with their religious leaders. The last global conflict was fought seventy-odd years previously, lasted for eight years and was over religion. Since then they have been at peace."

"Physiology?" asked Alexander, interested in how closely they matched humans in the rest of his Empire.

"They are human to within acceptable norms, obviously lacking most of the genetic improvements we have become familiar with over the millennia. For example, their lifespans are around eighty years, with the final thirty or so deteriorating in quality as they approach death, unlike ourselves where living beyond two hundred isn't unknown, and we remain healthy and capable with few signs of ageing until our final year or so."

"Our medical assistance should prove popular then," Alexander replied, "How did they react when told of the Alexander Doctrines?"

"The conditions of the Doctrine have been accepted, and on the face of it, they are eager to join us with Class Two membership," said Gallagher.

"Why did you end with "on the face of it"? Or are you just being political with me?" asked the Emperor, giving his friend a pointed look. "Out with it, Patrick."

Before speaking, Gallagher looked down at the floor for a moment, then up and out at the planet. The cyclone had grown larger and the terminator line between night and day was clearly visible now, signalling morning was due shortly at the signing ceremony, scheduled to begin in earnest at first light. Gallagher would be returning there with the Emperor and his son once he had finished his report and final preparations were complete.

"Two things. First, it's been almost two hundred years since an Ascension candidate skipped Class Three and was admitted straight to Class Two. While I can find nothing untoward, my uneasy "bump" is telling me we need to proceed with caution. Nothing I can pin down, however. Second, and more importantly, I don't think it's a wise move for both you and the Prince to travel down together for the ceremony. You have never done this before, and I question whether it's worth the risk. The Prince can watch proceedings from here and join us for the post-Ascension celebrations which should interest him more, assuming he can be bothered to attend. Adam's never shown any interest in Ceremonial duties before, and I'm worried that he might say something out of turn. After all, he's inherited his father's tendency towards bluntness."

The Emperor raised his left eyebrow and sighed, giving his old friend a long, hard look before answering.

"You're right, of course, Patrick. There is a chance he'll say something wrong, but both his mother and I agree it's time for him to start acting like a Crown Prince, instead of some wastrel son of a minor Duke that expects everything on a plate. It's been difficult these past fifteen years, as we both know. Constant border incursions with the Silures and other emerging human and reptilian empires have meant that I've been absent for most of his formative years. Christine has done her best, but even so, those two invariably end up clashing heads. No, it's time he started to earn the privileges and take on the responsibilities that come with his position. Beginning today, at this ceremony."

He paused for effect, then continued, "As for your "uneasy bump," it's not always proved accurate, and unless you can provide me with something more definite, the ceremony and Ascension will go ahead today. Do you have anything to convince me otherwise?"

"No Alex, I don't. But be careful anyway."

Sensing that his friend and Emperor had already made up his mind and therefore this wasn't one of those times to argue otherwise, Gallagher kept his peace, moving on to more mundane topics. They sat chatting for some time, covering various items of interest on the planet and how it might benefit the Empire, alongside more personal details of how their respective families were doing.

After a time, the Emperor finally stood and looked at his friend, extending a hand to signal that the briefing was over.

"Once you've sent your final report I'll get Vimes to précis the finer detail for me and will make sure the relevant sections are downloaded to the Bodyguard we have accompanying us this morning. Now go and freshen up before we leave."

Alexander sighed, reaching up and rubbing his head with both hands, an obvious sign to Gallagher of the tension he was under. "Another planet to learn and remember everything about. As if I don't have enough already."

"Rather you than me, Alex," replied Gallagher, smiling, "I'll see you in the hangar with the Crown Prince before we board."

With that brief exchange, the two men parted, each heading for a separate exit; Gallagher to reception where he would pick up Collinson, and the Emperor to deal with other matters of State.

Waiting until the room was empty, the ever-watchful AI closed down the wall screen and switched off the lights.

After updating her flight log, Flt Lt Harris had just arrived at her quarters to change and was sitting in her vacuum under-suit, trying unsuccessfully to remove her last boot, when new departure orders arrived via the ships AI.

"Damn," she said, reading the instructions were to co-pilot down to the planet one of the three military shuttles that she'd seen being prepped in the main hangar bay. While a little annoyed she would have to put off her downtime, Harris was pleased and not a little flattered, to be given the chance of co-piloting one of the diplomatic shuttles, perhaps even the one carrying the Emperor himself. Unbidden, an image of the red-cloaked Ambassador popped into her mind, and she wondered if he'd had anything to do with this new and unexpected assignment.

With not much time left before she would need to begin pre-flight inspections, she headed for the shower cubicle, hopping on one foot while trying to peel off from her leg the skin-tight flight suit that all pilots wore under their uniforms. These light grey customised suits protected the body from vacuum exposure and would function as an emergency spacesuit. In the event of explosive decompression, the integral smart-metal collars and cuffs would morph into a temporary helmet and gloves. In such an emergency, the suit would recycle the air and keep her alive for at least an hour.

She hated being measured for the suits as they needed to be moulded against every part of her body and Harris always found the process too intimate for her liking. To ensure fittings were kept to a minimum, she constantly watched her figure and weight.

Shuddering slightly as she remembered the touch of the machinery on her naked body she laughed at herself for being so prudish.

"*I suppose that comes from being brought up on a colony world that was very protective of their women,*" she thought to herself. Her five years in the egalitarian meritocracy that was the Imperial Navy, which made few concessions towards either sex or beliefs, still hadn't completely cancelled out her upbringing.

She caught a glimpse of herself in the bathroom's full-length mirror and couldn't resist taking stock for an instant. What she saw met with her approval. Regulation short brown hair, coffee coloured skin, a firm, well-muscled body and an attractive face looked back confidently at her from the mirror.

The shower came on as she stepped in, adjusting itself automatically to her preferences and she spent a few moments luxuriating in the slightly perfumed water before soaping herself vigorously to feel completely human again after the morning's events. She preferred a citrus aroma for the shower as it always left her feeling refreshed yet was still feminine enough for her taste.

Regretfully stepping out and towelling herself dry, she picked up the discarded flight suit, dropping it into the laundry chute and reached for a clean one hanging in her wardrobe. She wriggled into it and ran a diagnostic, then put on a fresh uniform, taking only a few minutes to dress. She checked her reflection for any stray lint or other marks, then headed out the door and back the way she'd come earlier.

Next to the main hangar, in a large ready room decorated with friezes and murals of past battles, three hundred of the Emperor's Marine bodyguard were assembled, awaiting final orders to embark. Veterans all, they were lightly armoured for the ceremony and dressed more for show than actual combat, reflecting today's ceremonial role. Even so, despite the removal of much of their regular armament, individually they remained formidable. Their smart-metal armour had been changed from the standard dull black to bright gold, with the Imperial Sigel set out boldly on their chests. Close-quarter combat shields hung on the back of their carapaces. The Marines milled around, looking similar to ancient armoured knights, except these moved with silence and grace.

The ship's AI had set the room's gravity and atmosphere to that of the planet below, allowing the Marines to acclimatise and calibrate their equipment before embarking. A change in gravitational pull not calibrated into their weapon systems invariably meant the first shot fired would miss before the weapon could compensate.

Three Master Sergeants each stood at ease at the head of their respective Cohorts, monitoring progress via the telemetry of their command suits. None of the veterans was showing any signs of undue stress, just normal elevated levels of anticipation. While the Sergeants had the option of administering combat drugs remotely should they be required, it wasn't necessary for these experienced veterans. Although the armoured suits were self-monitoring and reported any problems both to the wearer and command staff, it remained good practice for them to visually check each other's gear, so the Marines were milling around and checking on their buddies. Relying too much on technology, no matter how good or modern, was not something Marines did if they wanted to become veterans.

Captain Stuart-Jack, SJ to his friends, sent out a general heads-up and transmitted the latest set of instructions to his assembled troops, with more specific information going directly to the Sergeants. SJ was not a happy man right now. Tall, well-muscled and short, black hair, he had a genetic tendency to portliness that only strenuous workouts in the gym kept at bay. SJ was well aware the Crown Prince was supposed to have been with them half an hour ago, but all enquiries he'd made to the Prince's personal AI as to when he would be joining had been politely shunted away, leaving him hoping the Emperor's son would make an entrance alongside his father. If not, the fireworks that might follow wouldn't be pleasant and potentially embarrassing for everyone.

From experience, SJ knew that when things annoyed the Emperor, one had better have a good excuse or you could expect to be on the receiving end of one of his thousand-metre stares, famed for being able to strip hull metal within seconds.

The Imperial fanfare rang out, announcing the Emperor and SJ quickly came to attention, banishing his thoughts and focusing on the moment.

The main doors opened and in strode Alexander II, with Ambassador Gallagher following close behind and to his right, for once without his briefcase. Alexander's armoured formal suit was now embellished with honours from numerous major campaigns, and the smart metal shone as if illuminated from within. No weapon systems were visible, but everyone knew that serious armament was concealed within the suit and on-call at a moment's notice. The black and orange Imperial Sigel adorned both of their chests although Gallagher's was slightly smaller than the Emperors.

Together, the assembled bodyguard came to attention, the sound of armour being struck in salute by three hundred and four gauntleted right fists contrasting sharply with the silence that followed as the Emperor looked around the room and his warm smile of greeting was replaced with a neutral expression.

"Captain Stuart-Jack, where's my son?" he asked, fixing him with a stare and using a tone of voice that didn't bode well for the Crown Prince if he wasn't currently using the toilet facilities at that exact moment.

"Sire, my frequent attempts to contact him were declined by his aide and in the absence of contact and the importance of this meeting I assumed that he would be joining us with you." "*Tactfully put,*" SJ thought to himself, desperately trying to keep his expression neutral.

One deep breath and several heartbeats later, Alexander sent a private message via his neural link to Gallagher, warning him not to say a word, especially if it was "*I told you so.*" He continued, "*Go on ahead and begin the formalities without me. Tell SJ to take my shuttle instead and leave his here for me. I'll follow shortly once I've located Adam and shown him the error of his ways. I shouldn't be more than forty-five minutes behind you and will try and make up some of the time on the way down.*"

Alexander paused and took a deep breath before continuing, now speaking aloud to Patrick so everyone could hear, "It seems my son has gone missing and I need to find him. Patrick, I have every confidence you will be able to smooth over my lateness. Blame Affairs of State, that sort of thing. You know the drill."

Catching the eyes of both the Emperor and SJ, Gallagher couldn't resist sending his old friend a short "*Good luck with that one then, Alexander,*" on his private channel before turning away, missing the Emperor spin his armoured form one hundred and eighty degrees and exit the assembly hall, purple cloak billowing behind him from the speed of his departure.

The moment Alexander left the room, most of the assembled bodyguard looked at each other and winced, at that moment not wanting to trade places with the Prince for anything.

"Stand down one of the cohorts," Gallagher instructed SJ as the noise level in the hall began to rise. "They can remain behind and accompany the Emperor when he returns with the Prince."

Heading towards the hangar exit, closely followed by two cohorts of bodyguards, Gallagher's expression remained unreadable while he began updating the ceremonial plan on the fly via his interface.

Stepping into the docking tube, Gallagher was glad when his helmet formed, allowing him to mutter a few choice curses under his breath without being overheard. This was not going well at all, and no doubt someone was going to suffer before this day was through, hopefully, the Crown Prince. While he was very fond of Adam and was thought of as a surrogate uncle by the boy, a reckoning with his father and his Imperial responsibilities was, in his not-so-humble opinion, long overdue.

Watching events unfurl in the hangar, Vimes, the Emperor's aide, had begun asking questions of the ship's AI even before Alexander turned towards the exit, searching for the whereabouts of the missing son. Interrogating the Prince's AI, a stripped-down version of himself, Vimes received the same brush off as had the Marine Captain earlier. Frustratingly, the ship's AI was unable to locate him, leaving Vimes to surmise the Prince had somehow disabled his personal biometric tracker, making him invisible to many of the ship's sensors. Blocked from locating him this way, Vimes started checking through surveillance logs from the night before, finally locating a record of him in one of the many Ward Rooms around the ship. Now that he'd found a starting point, Vimes tracked his movements forward until he entered the private quarters of a recently promoted Second Lieutenant. The recording showed him entering arm in arm with the said red-haired Lieutenant, resulting in a 95% probability he would still be there. Moving forward to the present, Vimes checked no-one had entered or left the room, confirming his suspicion the Prince was still inside. By linking into the ship's fire suppression and control systems, Vimes confirmed two heat sources close together in the room, one unidentified.

"*Still asleep, no doubt after a strenuous session,*" thought Vimes, before noting that all the intercom and ship-wide messaging systems had been switched off in the room. While not alive in the classical sense, Vimes understood human emotions well enough to know that whatever pleasure the Prince might have derived from this romantic assignation, it would in no way compensate him for the storm that was coming his way. Collating all of the information, Vimes transmitted it to the Emperor just as he was exiting the hangar, caveating it with a note that the Lieutenant had been off-duty at the time of the meeting, was single, extremely attractive by most human standards, and that as his son currently held no formal rank in the Navy no offence had been committed, and she was, therefore, free to consort with him. Although Alexander was normally a very fair man, a subtle reminder such as this from Vimes would ensure her career suffered no harm.

Passing through into the corridor, Alexander waited for the doors to close behind him then leant heavily against the nearest wall, feeling sick inside as he read the note from Vimes.

"*What is it with that boy?*" he thought to himself, while at the same time calling up a display of the flight deck so he could watch the two shuttles close their doors and begin launching. He decided to gather his thoughts and watch until the shuttles had disembarked for the short hop to the planet's surface before confronting his son. Challenging him in his current mood would not be a good idea for either of them. It would take the shuttles twenty minutes to make planetfall, and by then he would have decided what to say to his wayward son.

"I might be the most powerful individual in the Empire, yet I can't install any sense into him," he thought bitterly. *"If Christine and I had been blessed with a daughter instead of a son would things have turned out any different? Damned if I know, although if she'd turned out as strong-willed as her mother, perhaps worse."*

As he watched the last of the two shuttles clear the hangar and depart, Alexander let his mind drift back to the desperate days of the Succession Wars which saw his own family killed at the start of a bitterly fought revolt led by one of his uncles. He still missed them, even after the passage of half a lifetime. Many years later, when Alexander and his wife Christine wanted to start a family, to avoid sibling rivalry for the throne, they agreed to have only one child. While Adam didn't know it yet, Alexander had already chosen to abdicate once his son was ready to rule. Partially self-preservation, he hoped Adam would never feel the need to replace him or become impatient waiting to rule. Both of these things had led in the past to bloody in-fighting within the royal family. Although blessed with a long lifespan, it was a simple fact of life that despite the best efforts of scientists, nothing could currently be done to extend childbearing age in women beyond one hundred years or so. Alexander loved his wife deeply and had no intention of siring another child on a woman other than her, so however he turned out, Adam was their only heir. While a risky strategy, the scars left by the revolt had affected him deeply and shaped the way he thought and acted.

After almost ten minutes and long after the shuttles had vanished from view, Alexander strode to the nearest transit tube and entered the waiting pod, instructing it to take him to the quarters of the officer where his son was currently "sleeping." His initial anger had calmed somewhat, replaced instead with a depression that threatened to deepen unless he could resolve matters with his son.

Feeling the pod's acceleration increase to two-G as it compensated for his being in armour, Alexander called up from Vimes information on the layout of the officer's quarters. Before he could study it, Vimes suddenly interrupted and announced a General Alert, followed an instant later by the ship's AI informing him the pod was being redirected straight to the Bridge. Something serious had occurred, and as Vimes and the ship's AI began sending him reports, one thing was certain, the reckoning with his son would have to wait a while longer.

The two shuttles entered the outer atmosphere a mile apart, SJ's on the left and Gallagher's another mile further forward on the right, furiously bleeding away velocity. Inside, unlike regular shuttles, the larger military versions were effectively open plan, maximising space for troops and their equipment. This configuration had the added benefit of allowing both the passengers to see and hear everything going on from the viewscreens placed along the walls, rather than via their suit helmets. At the rear of the shuttle, Ambassador Gallagher began walking carefully forward towards the flight deck, passing orderly rows of troops docked in G-cages, standing upright on either side. The Marines were quiet, lost in their own private thoughts or chatting to each other via comms due to the roar of re-entry, the noise of which was increasing as the shuttle dipped lower into the atmosphere.

Reaching the front of the shuttle, Gallagher was relieved to feel the ride improve. Never a comfortable flyer he tolerated it as a necessary evil. Despite the Empire having developed artificial gravity millennia ago, nothing could be done about inertia which stubbornly refused to be tamed, making sudden changes in direction as uncomfortable now as they were in the distant past, hence his earlier pleasure on the way up at finding a very smooth pilot. In fact, he'd asked earlier for her to pilot this shuttle and was disappointed to find her only in the co-pilot chair this time. "*Perhaps on the return journey,*" he thought.

Sensing a presence behind her, Flt Lt Harris looked over her shoulder and flashed the Ambassador a brief smile of recognition, having already seen his name on the passenger list. As she did so, the outlying edges of the big storm they'd passed over in orbit gave the shuttle one final buffet, causing Harris to quickly turn back to her panel and Gallagher's smart metal boots to merge themselves temporarily into the floor for stability at the sudden movement.

Before Patrick could say anything, Harris announced to everyone in the shuttle, "As agreed, an honour guard of six atmospheric fighters are approaching from the south and will have matched speed and rendezvoused with us in three minutes. I confirm they're not registered as hostile, and our point defences are cold at this time."

As the pilot began matching his speed to that of local air traffic, both the noise and buffeting subsided. Relieved, Gallagher thanked her and the pilot, then walked over to an empty G-cage, locking himself in place and interrogating his suit's AI to confirm arrival time and to check with his diplomats on the ground that everything was in order. He noted they were only a few minutes away from the landing field, where the planet's chief dignitaries and the world's press would be waiting for them, so Gallagher finally allowed himself a moment to relax.

Up front, Harris, with nothing much to do unless the pilot relinquished control to her instead of the AI, requested a schematic of the fighters racing to escort them. Like many fighter pilots she was curious about anything deadly that flew and might prove a threat, so wanted to get a closer look at the fighters and what they were capable of. Using her link to the shuttle's sensors, she magnified the view, the expanded image appearing within the vision of her left eye. Estimated flight capabilities scrolled down next to it.

Sleek, with stubby swept wings that were slowly extending as the atmosphere thickened, the silver craft looked like deadly silver needles. The cockpit was made of some sort of transparent material enabling the pilot to look out, and the missile racks on the wings were empty as agreed. She could see various insignia visible on the wings and tail and wondered if they denoted some sort of religious or mythological figures from the planet's history. Access to the planet's linguistic database was still classified, so Harris was unable to confirm her suspicion.

As the six fighters drew level to the first shuttle, the formation split up into three groups, two pairs taking station with SJ's and the remaining pair accelerating to catch up with her own.

Curious as to the craft's capabilities and impressed with the startling turn of speed such basic technology was demonstrating, she requested an internal scan to see if she could glean more information. They wouldn't be able to detect the scanning, and in the unlikely event they could, Harris didn't think it would be seen as a hostile act. Instantly the information began scrolling through her vision and she speed-read the data. Almost immediately she picked up an anomaly, which she sent to the pilot.

Turning to look at him she asked, "Taylor, what need would fighters, propelled via scram and conventional jet engines, have for fissionable material?" He looked perplexed for a moment, then both their eyes widened as they simultaneously exclaimed "Damn!" slamming the throttle controls hard forward. The AI automatically flipped their seats to the horizontal, locking them both firmly into place and everyone else on the shuttle into their G-racks. Tablets and anything not tightly secured flew violently out of armoured hands as the shuttle accelerated instantly to fifteen-G. Harris could see her vision tunnelling and tried hard not to black out. Through the pounding of blood in her ears, she heard the AI confirm it had taken control, and felt her flight suit compress, forcing blood back to her brain.

Gallagher was surprised to hear both pilots curse and was shocked when their seats flipped. A crushing weight settled onto his chest, and as with the pilots, his vision began to tunnel and fade. Momentarily confused, he was just starting to recover when the shuttle tilted violently forward, then down, as a blinding white flare of light and concussion of sound smacked it hard from behind. The overloaded viewscreens blazed white, bathing the hold in sharp contrast before automatically dimming themselves. The force of the blow almost caught out the bundles of metal fibres making up the muscles of his suit, and he was thankful everybody was in their G-cages. The helmet of his suit automatically formed into place, blanking out the noise.

Simultaneously linking himself into both the shuttle's systems and the troop channels, he was gratified that chatter was being kept to a minimum by the experienced bodyguard as they read the information being relayed to them by the Sergeant. Ridiculously experienced by most standards, these troops knew the drill better than anyone. Smart-metal helmets were all in place, and the battle-suits were powering up into full combat readiness. He noted the Master Sergeant was even recording, for extra practice time, which of his troops were slowest in powering up.

Gallagher couldn't see the pilots' expressions, but the way in which they were struggling with the controls and the slew of red-flagged information scrolling across his vision both told him they had a serious problem. He so hated flying.

Another, less powerful blow hit the shuttle, compounding the damage caused by the first, this time disrupting the viewscreens and knocking the craft completely off its landing trajectory, eliciting another string of curses from Harris and Taylor.

"Main power down, microfractures reported throughout the hull, secondary systems partially online," reported the pilot, while Harris's hands were a blur of motion as she worked the manual switches and controls that were the worst-case fallback. Automatic back-ups, sensing the viewscreen failure, triggered the cockpits opaque metal to turn transparent so they could see out.

"We are in a controlled descent, coming in fast but way off the flight plan. Contact with the other shuttle is down. I think we caught the leading edges of at least two small tactical nukes of around .25 kilotons each. They probably had them in their cockpits and were detonated manually," reported Taylor.

"I can confirm that, Ambassador," said Harris, looking behind her at Gallagher, "I can see the expanding fireballs from here, and there's no sign of the other shuttle. I think the fighters came up close to the Emperor's shuttle then suicided. We caught the remaining two off guard, and they detonated as we pulled away, hoping to catch us in the blast."

Gallagher agreed with the assessment then kept quiet, letting the pilots do their jobs as he waited for his link to the flagship to come back on. Captain Stuart-Jack had been on the other shuttle, and while Gallagher had only a nodding acquaintance with him, his presumed loss along with all his troops left a bitter taste. He could only imagine what other, nastier surprises they had waiting for them if this shuttle made it safely planet-side. Reading the information passing across his vision on the status of the shuttle, he could clearly see the port repulsors were down, and while some of the microfractures were already healing, larger ones where the smart-metal had been fatally damaged were beyond repair.

The violent buffeting intensified as the damaged shuttle descended lower into the atmosphere and the pilots struggled to maintain control with only half of the flight systems available to them. The buffeting was making him feel nauseous, so Gallagher debated with himself whether to request his suit to give him something for it, but, in the end, decided not to as he needed to keep his head clear.

Trying to contact Alexander on his private channel, his suit reported that contact with Dauntless was somehow being blocked from the ground.

"But that's not possible given their current level of technology." he thought, *"How have they done this and why? Someone else has to be behind this attack on the Emperor, perhaps a third-party not of this planet?"*

Inside his helmet, Gallagher's face scowled, then turned thoughtful as he sought then tried to put together any clues he could find.

"Was this how they managed to jump an Ascension Class from three to two?" Gallagher asked himself, *"How on earth did I miss the signs?"* His nausea was worsened by the sickening thought that only chance had saved his friend and son from instant destruction, and through gritted teeth, Gallagher fervently hoped he would live long enough and get the opportunity to deliver

some old-fashioned retribution to the citizens of the planet that was rapidly coming to meet him.

Entering the bridge, nodding in acknowledgement to the guards at the entrance, Alexander was pleased to see everyone was in their place and working towards a solution. Vimes had already sent him current data from Dauntless's sensors, along with telemetry from the shuttles right up to the moment it had stopped or was jammed.

The bridge layout was familiar to him, an inverted horseshoe with its two ends pointing away from the Helm and Navigation stations which sat at the top of the arc, ahead of the Admiral, who was flanked by the First and Second Officers. Two Weapons Masters, one responsible for offence, the other defence, sat to her left in front of the Cyber Warfare station. To her right were positioned both Science and Engineering. Immediately forward of the Admiral, and behind the Navigator, sat Life Support.

"We are at full alert, Your Majesty, and the task force is moving to a higher orbit," confirmed Admiral Janice Frith, a graceful, elegant woman of indeterminate age with shoulder-length black hair and a manner that instantly instilled confidence. A veteran of many fleet engagements, tactically she was at the height of her powers and a formidable opponent. "I believe we can confirm the loss of Captain Stuart-Jack's shuttle with all hands and the possible loss of Ambassador Gallagher's too, although he may be lucky and survive the impact if crash protection systems haven't been too badly damaged. Through luck or good judgement, they managed to avoid the worst of the blasts that took out the Captain's shuttle but seem to be in a descent that is only partially controlled. However, we cannot tell if this is due to automated systems or human interaction for we have lost contact with his shuttle and our people on the ground."

Alexander nodded grimly. He would mourn for his old friend only when he knew all hope of his surviving had been lost. "Is there any chance at all this was a terrible accident?" he enquired.

"No Sire," came the reply, "Before we lost contact with it, telemetry from the surviving shuttle confirmed the escorting fighters had small unexplained tactical fission devices in the cockpit areas. Probably detonated remotely or even by the pilots themselves. Our own sensors have detected radiation emissions concomitant with nuclear blasts."

Alexander thought for a long moment, then ordered Frith to immediately destroy the space defence platforms that he could see from the sensors were already turning to try and locate the flagship and other vessels in the fleet. On commencement of an alert, the ship's systems had automatically reactivated the hull's stealth features. With the immediate change in orbit and given their technological level, it was now impossible for the platforms to get a fix on their location.

"*Or so we think,*" thought Alexander. "I shan't take anything for granted now," he said quietly to himself.

Frith caught what he'd said and nodded grimly in agreement.

Faint, almost imperceptible vibrations came through the floor as the flagship's main batteries began firing, taking out the platforms. Alexander could feel them clearly as his armour began transmitting the deck vibrations through to the soles of his feet.

Although typically used for fleet or ship to ship actions where the opponent was thousands rather than hundreds of kilometres away, he agreed with the Weapon Master's assessment that overkill was called for. Dauntless's main particle weapons had already put the closest two platforms out of action and the railgun slugs impacting a few seconds later reduced them to little more than expanding clouds of debris no more than a metre in size. There would be collateral damage on the planet below, as the immense velocity of the slugs simply tore through the platforms and continued on until they began impacting the surface of a major continent, creating craters hundreds of metres across. Their shock waves could clearly be seen even from this orbit, rippling across the ground, pulverising anything for a radius of several kilometres.

"Admiral, I'm detecting surface launches of ballistic missile type weapons from previously unreported silos across multiple sites and continents," reported one of the Weapon Masters. "AI confirms a spread of impact destinations bracketing an area close to and surrounding our previous location. Estimated impact time one and a half minutes."

"Thank you, Charles," said the Admiral, turning towards the Emperor. "Sire, am I right in assuming that the planet below will no longer be joining the Empire and that you wish me to take out the missiles and silos?" she inquired, her left eyebrow rising slightly.

"Ever the master of understatement, Admiral. Please do so," Alexander replied sadly, looking again at the planet and the blossoming impact points. "Take whatever steps you deem necessary to degrade their ability to strike at us. I want every launching site targeted and taken out and their ability to wage war against us degraded with extreme prejudice."

Alexander gave his final instructions before turning away from the viewscreen and heading towards the exit. "You are now in charge Admiral Frith, I'm going to search for survivors and see if I can rescue my friends."

Knowing it would be useless to argue with him the wisdom of going, Frith nodded at his departing back, then turned to the business in hand.

The remaining cohort of bodyguards, waiting patiently in the departure area, suddenly came to attention as their suits indicated the Sergeant was receiving new instructions. They'd been kept abreast of developments and seen footage of the ambush, so their mood was understandably both sombre and angry. A close-knit group, most were serving five-year tours in the Emperor's personal guard, having been chosen as the best fighting men and women their individual planets could provide. The competition was fierce for this honour, and the majority would be reapplying for further tours when their current one ended, so they felt the loss of their friends and colleagues keenly.

Companions of the Emperor were feted as heroes wherever they travelled in the Empire and could expect to be some of the first to receive invitations to royal functions on their home planet, along with the guaranteed right to vote on planetary matters, or even a minor title if service was particularly meritorious. For the Imperial Navy, with the creation of powered combat armour, any reason to discriminate between men and women on the grounds of physical strength or endurance ended, however, men still outnumbered women in the Marines by two to one. Curiously, these numbers were mirrored but reversed for pilots, where women outnumbered the men.

"Listen up," messaged the Sergeant, "we have five minutes to change armour, weapon loads and unit configurations. We are on a search and rescue mission; expect stiff resistance as we will be going in looking for trouble. Your suits will tell you what your designated speciality will be once you dock hot and reconfigure."

Docking stations began rising from the floor next to each suit, allowing additional smart metal to flow into them, increasing their mass and bulking them out from lightly armoured dress and into battle configurations. Subtle bulges began to form, indicating where weapons would be available as required.

"The Emperor himself will be leading us today, so this is our chance to show him what we are capable of and avenge our comrades," continued the Sergeant as the suits finished changing. "Some of you have never seen him in action, so stay focused and watch each other's back."

The ship's AI announced the imminent arrival of Alexander, who strode into the hall looking formidable and very angry. All markings on his now completely black suit were gone, and it had bulked to twice its original size, with only his head showing inside a partially formed helmet. A monomolecular edged sword was sheathed on his right hip, and a battle shield of partially collapsed material was fixed onto his left arm.

Small handheld lasers, although a popular staple of science fiction, were not practical for foot soldiers due to the bulk required to make them work effectively in the real world. The reality of modern combat meant laser weapons were reserved for spaceships or armoured vehicles that had the size and power to handle them. The bread and butter weapons favoured by ground troops were swords, shields, and handheld railgun-like firearms, all of which could be extruded on command out of the armoured suits smart-metal. High-temperature superconductor-based batteries provided the power supply for both suits and weapons. If required, internal batteries could be topped up by microwave transmissions of power from orbit or ground stations.

Monomolecular swords, edged so they could cut through hull metal, combined with shields able to withstand repeated impacts from hypersonic flechettes, were the preferred weapon load for troops going into close combat.

"Gentlemen," began Alexander, addressing the assembled Marines, "our comrades have been cowardly betrayed by the peoples of the world below us. We freely offered them the Empire's protection along with the security and prosperity that membership brings, yet all the while they were planning to betray us. Our actions today will be long remembered." He paused for a moment. "That's the formal bullshit. Remember our dead comrades-in-arms. We ask no quarter for ourselves, and we'll give those bastards none in return."

Alexander looked at as many faces as he could, nodding slightly whenever his eyes met with a familiar face, recalling names even without the subtle prompting of Vimes in his mind.

"I believe we will find survivors of the second shuttle; how many I do not know, but if not, we will bring their bodies back home. To your stations."

Within moments of the depressurisation warning sounding in the room, helmets formed around heads as the Marines followed their Sergeant through the opening doors into the hard vacuum of the hangar bay, not bothering to use the pressurised docking tube. Alexander stood off to one side of the shuttle entrance, motioning his bodyguard into the opening, slapping the occasional shoulder armour of a veteran he knew personally as they passed by. Once all were inside, he followed the Sergeant and sent a message for the pilot to seal the hatch, taking his assigned G-cage at the front of the craft without a word.

Pre-flight checks all completed, the shuttle noiselessly moved up and forward, clearing the ground crews, turning left and exiting the hangar doors into space. As with the armoured suits, any previous markings had been re-absorbed back into the shuttle's hull, and it had reconfigured itself into full battle readiness, having drawn additional metal from the hangar deck. Point defence bulges dotted the hull, and an extrusion from the belly of the shuttle pointed forward, indicating the presence of a large railgun. On board, everyone noticed the slight tremor as the shuttle moved out through the flagship's electromagnetic shields, closely followed by a squadron of fifty sleek, multi-purpose fighters. Coming from a hangar on the other side of the flagship, an empty shuttle took station to the rear, all moving silently in formation as they accelerated away at high-G towards the last known location of the crippled vessel.

Things were not going well on the surviving shuttle.

"I've extruded a wing on the port side to partially compensate for the damaged repulsors and give us more lift," the pilot told Ambassador Gallagher, "but we will be impacting the ground in just over two minutes. I can still make the original landing site but would you prefer somewhere less obvious?"

"What about those low rise residential areas?" he replied, pointing ahead. "Crashing there will provide good cover from any ground assault until such time we are rescued. We've got to hold on for at least thirty, possibly forty-five minutes before we can be picked up. Attacking troops might hesitate for a few seconds if civilians are around."

"OK, Ambassador, I'll try my best" the pilot replied.

Not lifting her eyes from the controls, Harris also addressed the Ambassador, "I'm expecting more of those silver fighters will soon be heading our way, sir, loaded with missiles rather than tactical nukes this time, unless they plan on wiping out the city just to get at us. Without sensors, we won't be able to do anything until we see them coming down our throats. Starboard point defences are now working and will take them out on that side, but we can't do anything about those that come in on our port. We need to land now before they get here."

"I have every faith in you both, just get us down as fast as you can. Preferably in one piece if you can," Gallagher responded. He feared the worst, not just for himself but also for his colleagues who had been waiting at the designated welcoming area and with whom he'd lost all contact following the ambush.

Settling lower every second, the shuttle avoided the high-rise buildings and skyscrapers surrounding the large park meant to have been the welcoming zone and threaded its way between two towers as it headed towards the crowded residential part of the city situated at one edge of the park. Large crowds were gathered below, probably hundreds of thousands strong, who all looked up as the shuttle zipped over their heads, barely skimming some trees. The pilot wanted to bring the shuttle in at a low glide angle to reduce damage and bleed off speed through friction with the ground. Moments before impacting the first of a row of terraced low-rise dwellings, the shuttle extended forward a large smart-metal shield to begin absorbing the impact. The shield crumpled away in an instant, exactly as it was designed to do, but not before slowing the shuttles forward momentum enough to protect the occupants from serious deceleration G-forces. Crash cocoons of smart metal formed around the pilots in the instant of impact, moving them backwards and away from the forward cockpit area, allowing it to crumple and deform as designed, all the while absorbing more of the impact.

The extruded wing caught suddenly and violently spun the shuttle left, further slowing the forward momentum as it tore through the buildings, pulverising brick and concrete walls into powder. A section of the hull suddenly peeled away, and before anyone could react, a chunk of metal reinforcement speared through into the interior, ripping into a row of Marines. Around them, apartments shattered and exploded into dust, with debris spinning through the air until the shuttle ended sideways on, halfway into a row of small, shop-like buildings. Behind it, clouds of rapidly expanding smoke and dust billowed high into the air, marking a two-hundred-metre long trail of destruction through the residential centre of town. Flames from ruptured gas mains started up in hundreds of locations along the crash path, alongside fountains of water from broken mains.

No longer moving, the previous noise of the shuttle's crash landing was in stark contrast to the relative peace from falling masonry and debris raining down amongst the wreckage. Within the rubble, cries could already be heard coming from those trapped occupants of the buildings who were lucky enough to have avoided being crushed to death by the initial impact. The occasional loud crash of settling debris rang out as a counterpoint to their cries of pain and anger.

"Everyone out, look sharp people, we have work to do," sang out the amplified parade ground voice of Master Sergeant Plewa. "Eames, DeGrizzo, Walker and Tommaso; you four stay with the Ambassador, the rest of you follow me." Switching to battlefield communication via the armoured suits, Plewa continued to give out instructions, all the while checking suit readouts for injuries, noting the ten fatalities from when hull integrity was compromised. Farewells would come later when they were all safely back on the flagship, so Plewa put his sadness for them temporarily on hold. He went about organising the survivors, choosing another four Marines to act as temporary Corporals so he could focus on deployment.

Inside her cocoon, a battered and bruised Harris instructed it to open. She felt a flash of ice in her lower belly when nothing happened, but remembering her training, hit the emergency release. To her relief, a seam of light appeared along the length of her cocoon which she could prise open. A large gauntleted hand appeared, grasping her outstretched arm, pulling her upright. "Ambassador?" she asked, taking stock of the destruction around her.

"Well, you got us down, if not all in one piece. I'm getting no readouts from the AI and believe it and the shuttle to be severely damaged. Either that or it's very, very unhappy about what we did to it just now," said Gallagher, attempting to lighten the moment. "Effectively, work on the assumption that everything is fried."

A sudden series of loud explosions behind Harris made her jump as Marines blew the emergency exits.

Not seeing the other pilot anywhere, she moved to get past the Ambassador as he was blocking her view of the pilot's cocoon. "Help me get out…" Harris's voice began but trailed off as she realised that no-one could have survived the metal beam that had punched up through the shuttle floor, coming out through the cocoon where his head would have been.

Gallagher put his hand lightly on her right shoulder. "I've already checked, but he's dead. I'm sorry. Did you know him well?"

Harris looked up at the Ambassador whose helmet had fully retracted to expose his face. "No, this was our first flight together. After all, he did in getting us down…Damn! Sorry, sir." She looked at the damaged cocoon then back to Gallagher. "I don't suppose you have any spare weapons hidden in that suit of yours, Ambassador?"

Gallagher shook his head. "That's the spirit. No, Lieutenant, at least nothing you could use without armour. Stick close, and between myself and these four Marines here we will do our best to keep you safe." Looking at each of the four Marines in turn, he asked, "Isn't that right, gentlemen?"

"Yes sir," they replied, moving to position themselves around the pilot and Ambassador as they all walked towards the nearest exit, over the debris littering the floor beneath their feet.

Before leaving the shuttle, Gallagher tried merging his exo-suit with the shuttles hull to see if it would let him draw additional metal into his suit. "Damn," he said, as the suit confirmed that the impact, loss of power and dead ships AI had made the metal totally inert. "*Worth a last try, though*," he thought, before following after the others and making sure Harris was covered by the Marines.

Master Sergeant Plewa decided to move everyone away from the immediate vicinity of the downed shuttle, for this would be the first place hit by any long-range barrage. Slightly concussed from the landing, Plewa had already used his suits pharmacological function to administer a cocktail of drugs to keep himself sharp and compensate for his injury. He could see from the readouts in his helmet that a number of his surviving Marines had already done the same. "No broken bones or wounds, that's something," he muttered to himself, checking the display again and noting it seemed those who'd survived the crash were all mobile and able to fight. "I'm almost getting too old for this shit."

Now in his one-hundredth year of Imperial service, Plewa had been a Sergeant for ninety of those, refusing, again and again, the offer of further promotion as it might have entailed a commission away from the Emperor's bodyguard. "*Is this going to be my final battle?*" he thought for an instant before dismissing the idea. "*I know Alexander better than most, and if he isn't leading the rescue himself, I'll swear off alcohol for a month.*" He laughed at the thought before triggering his communicator, telling the Marines to liven it up and get a move on.

Pausing for an instant, he called up a hologram of his wife and extended family, smiled for a split-second at the image, then dismissed it with an almost imperceptible sigh. His Marine Scouts had already released hundreds of micro-drones, and these were rapidly fanning out over the potential battleground. Plewa watched intently as his suit's AI used the data the drones transmitted back to build inside his helmet a 3D image of the surrounding area, combining it with data from all the other Marines. Motion and heat sensor data were combined in real-time to filter out the majority of still falling debris, focusing instead on living targets. Several hundred signals, many not moving and rapidly cooling, were automatically tagged as bodies by the AI, turning them semi-transparent in the display as it downgraded their threat level. In the event any of these should come to life and begin moving towards his current position, the AI would automatically re-tag them as potentially hostile.

As this wasn't a rescue mission, Plewa ignored the pitiful cries coming from the rubble and focused on identifying the best place to await the pickup he knew was coming. The main thing bothering him, however, was the inability of his suit to get through to Dauntless, even though he knew the flagship had certainly been able to use visuals to track their flight and subsequent crash-landing. Also, the plume of smoke still rising into the morning sky from the impact was signalling their whereabouts as plainly as any beacon.

Plewa debated with himself for a few moments whether to move further out into the undamaged streets surrounding the crash site or to stay within the debris field. Each had its own advantages. The streets afforded ease of mobility and the ability to take hostages if required but would make them easier to pinpoint and mean moving further from the shuttle. Staying within the debris would provide cover and a degree of protection from weapons fire, but meant they were a sitting target.

"Which one to choose?" he asked himself quietly, before remembering the adage, "*a good Sergeant makes quick decisions. If they happen to turn out to be correct, so much the better.*" He quickly decided on the latter option, just his suit began picking up and displaying multiple potential hostiles moving rapidly to their position.

"*Here we go,*" he thought, arming his weapons.

On Dauntless's Bridge, Admiral Frith watched the translucent holographic image of the shuttle's impact site expand and resolve into finer detail as sensors and drones relayed more and more information into the AI. The life-like image of the crash site, now ten metres across, hung in the middle of the room, providing a real-time view of the unfolding scene. Hostiles were tagged in red and friendlies in blue. On the ground, a red wave was already converging on the crash site, indicating either a massive response by emergency services or more likely an angry mix of soldiers and general population looking to massacre any survivors before a rescue could take place. The massed crowds awaiting the ceremony had begun moving away, but a large proportion had begun heading towards the crash site. Sensors showed almost one-hundred, ground-based enemy aircraft had already been taken out by drones and hover-missiles launched earlier from Dauntless, severely degrading the enemy's ability to hit the crash survivors. Able to withstand far higher acceleration than a human pilot, the autonomous drones and missiles had reached the landing zone within minutes, clearing the skies long before the rescue shuttles would arrive on the scene.

It annoyed Frith's professionalism that despite their precautions, a substantial build-up of military equipment and personnel had obviously taken place at or near the official landing site before the Ascension ceremony, hidden in plain view amongst the civilian population. With the benefit of hindsight, it was apparent that homes and buildings had been constructed over armoured vehicles and VTOL aircraft, while large numbers of soldiers had been disguised as guests of honour and distributed amongst the crowd.

Although all incoming data to her implant was filtered by Dauntless's AI to stop her becoming overwhelmed with information, with such a volume coming in there was always a risk something important being missed or inappropriately flagged, hence Frith regularly asked each of her officers to provide verbal summaries of the most important developments, instead of relying solely on the AI. She asked everyone to provide her with a verbal update.

The Weapon Master to her left confirmed point defences had destroyed the nuclear-tipped missiles sent to intercept them, long before they could pose a threat to Dauntless. In the vacuum of space, even if the missiles had detonated, there were no concussive or destructive forces to worry about, especially as shields could easily handle the short-lived radiation spikes from any resulting nuclear explosions. A few warheads had been allowed to detonate harmlessly at their last known position, for Frith hoped the resulting Electro-Magnetic Pulses would play havoc with the natives' planetary communications for a while.

"Admiral, Medical stations are standing by," reported her Second Officer, Commander Mark Campbell, who left his station and walked over to where she was standing. "Navigation has plotted us several alternative orbits and awaits your instructions. We are ready to break our current orbit on your command."

"Thank you, Mark, please pass on my compliments to them. What news of Captain Stuart-Jack's shuttle? Any survivors?" she asked.

"No Ma'am, the drones we sent down reported minimal wreckage as would be expected from such close proximity to the blasts. In all probability, they wouldn't have known what hit them. There's not enough left of the shuttle or our technology to be of any use to the people here, although I recommend we sterilise the debris field from orbit to make sure. To allow for debris scatter, a thirty-mile radius should suffice."

Frith thought for a moment then nodded. "Please see to it and begin sending power down to the Ambassador's crash site the moment we break through the jamming. Prepare to also sterilise his crash site once our people are rescued. Use the same radius."

For a second, Frith's thoughts turned to the civilians that would be caught up in the sterilisation. The resulting massive loss of life grated on her professionalism, rather than any misplaced sentimentality over innocent life.

"*They brought this on themselves by their unprovoked attack,*" she thought to herself, "*People ultimately get the leaders they deserve and have to live with the consequences of their actions, good or bad.*"

A few moments later, through her implant and connection to the AI, Frith could sense Dauntless firing its main laser batteries, followed by the tremble of railguns as Campbell instructed the Weapons Officers to proceed. She slowly shook her head, knowing deep down that tonight's dreams might be uncomfortable. In fact, she would probably not sleep well now for several days as thoughts of the innocents would come unbidden to trouble her sleep, despite knowing she had no other choice. Old memories surfaced as she briefly wondered if the Emperor would order the planet sterilised completely, as Remdale 4 had been by his own father. Thankfully, that had happened long before her time, but she'd seen the aftermath, as had all Admirals and Officers of Command Rank, for it was part of their education in war.

To her right, Ian Gomez, her First Officer, walked over.

"Ma'am," he began as Frith turned towards him, "since shortly after the first explosion we have had no contact with the fifteen diplomats on the ground who were attending the ceremony. Our AI confirms that just before the signal blocking started, telemetry from six of the diplomats' biosensors confirmed their life functions had ceased. Sudden loss of neural activity indicated severe head trauma."

"Your assessment?" asked the Admiral.

"Loss of readings are symptomatic with a shot or blow to the head. In light of the dense crowds, I assume it would have been relatively simple for the assailants to have simply approached them from the rear, shooting them once the signal was given, especially if the local authorities were in collusion. It would indicate there were individual assassins for each diplomat and that the other nine are also dead, shot just after the blocking of our telemetry began. We have no proof, however."

"Agreed, thank you, Ian," Frith replied, nodding slowly. She turned back to her previous position and viewed the 3D image again. The crashed shuttle was now clearly defined in blue, as were the positions of the Marines on the ground. It looked to Frith they were using the debris field as cover and had taken up a defensive perimeter ring to await rescue or attack. The wash of red indicating the approaching enemy was slowly closing in on the small blue ring, and it would not be long before the two made contact with each other.

"Incoming, look sharp," Master Sergeant Plewa's warning sounded loudly in the Marines' helmets. Instinctively, they all shrank down a fraction lower in their foxholes and secured positions. Alone in her shallow foxhole, Harris instructed her vacuum suit to form a helmet, hoping that once the fighting began it would afford some protection against flying splinters or gas attacks, in addition to letting her fully tap into the comms channel used by the Marines around her.

The crack of incoming munitions could be clearly heard over the increasingly loud and angry murmuring of the huge mob as it advanced on their position.

"Fire at will if you see targets of opportunity," Plewa told them. "Use high explosive rounds sparingly and only on buildings. If you can demolish them with the enemy inside, then so much the better. Make it hard and costly for the bastards to approach."

Gallagher instructed his suit to detach the shield from his back, then fixed it in place over the shallow foxhole the four Marines had hastily made for Harris to hide in.

"This will afford you a bit more protection, Lieutenant," he said to her, making sure she was covered by it. "With these fine Marines looking after me I have more than enough protection."

Although their faces were armoured, Gallagher could see from the Marines body language that at least two of the assigned bodyguard had looked briefly in his direction and fancied he could sense them smiling.

"That's right Ambassador," responded DeGrizzo, "We'll keep you and the pilot safe, don't worry."

"Well, I hope your bloody aim has improved from the last set of scores you posted in practice," came the voice of Sergeant Plewa, cutting through the good-natured banter, "otherwise it will be the pilot protecting you four".

DeGrizzo chuckled to herself, as did quite a few of the Marines, knowing full well that at the last practice she'd only just missed beating by one point the Cohort record for targets hit in a single session. "Yes, Master Sergeant, Sir!" responded DeGrizzo, laughing. The confidence and humour of the Marines went some way towards reassuring Harris she would get out of this alive, but even so, it was nerve-wracking having to wait impotently in a foxhole, having to rely on others for her safety. She would feel much safer with a weapon in her hand, but as Gallagher had pointed out, she was incapable of using any of the available smart-metal weapons without an armoured suit.

The first of the enemy came into view, clambering over debris and shouting incomprehensible words in the local language as they tried to get at the Marines. No obvious firearms could be seen in this first wave, but everyone carried a variety of sticks or dangerous looking objects. The attackers were all dressed in the local fashion, with flowing multi-coloured robes tied in at the waist by belts. Initially, the Marines hesitated for a second before firing, debating whether these attackers were any real threat. However, in the magnified images of their helmets, the hatred of these people could be clearly seen, making their intentions crystal clear. Irrespective of what the natives were carrying, they were clearly looking to take the Marines apart even if it meant using their bare hands. Almost at once the Marines began to fire.

Master Sergeant Plewa watched as an anti-personnel weapon finished forming above the wrist on his right gauntlet. No matter how many times he saw the smart-metal reshape itself into one of the many weapons templates his suit contained, the fascination never faded. He knew that tiny flechettes of smart-metal were formed on demand within the miniature railgun, ready to be discharged singly or on auto fire as required. Limited only by his suit's ability to carry mass for conversion and power to drive the process, the flechettes were less than a centimetre in size and weighed only five grammes. When the weapon accelerated them to hypersonic speeds, they impacted on their target with devastating effect, disintegrating instantly into a cloud of particles, pulverising flesh and bone. The railguns were normally only used when the armoured suits were braced, thereby absorbing and converting the ferocious recoil into energy, which limited their usefulness on the move. However, from a static firing position, they were deadly effective.

The angry crack of accelerated flechettes started up around him, the sound caused by air rushing in to fill the vacuum created by their passage. Swiftly the volume increased, merging with cries of pain from the attackers, as the Marines began to acquire targets and fire. Taking aim at a large, burly individual dressed in scarlet robes who was clambering towards his position, Plewa set his weapon to single shot and fired. At this range, there was no need to allow for gravity, and he watched the man fly backwards, his midriff mostly vaporised by the kinetic energy as the flechette instantly disintegrated on contact into a deadly mist of tiny accelerated particles. Two more natives took his place, one a slightly built woman in blue robes and carrying a firearm, the other obviously a soldier of some sort. Without hesitation, Plewa fired again. The man's head vanished in a red mist while the woman fell screaming as her entire right leg and part of her hip was destroyed by the force of impact. She instantly went into shock, and the look of horror faded from her face as the effects of blood loss and trauma rapidly took hold. Plewa knew she would quickly bleed out and pose no further threat.

Setting the suit to auto-fire for a few moments, Plewa checked the readouts on his men. "*No casualties yet*," he noted thankfully, turning next to the tactical display showing the deployment of his Marines and the enemy. The colour red was now a dense mass, indicating the sheer numbers they faced.

Sitting in her foxhole as the fight raged around her, Harris could hear and feel the crump of heavy weapons and falling masonry. She desperately wanted to do something, anything except stay behind the shield, letting others fight on her behalf. She was nervous, realising how vulnerable she was compared to the Marines around her. Suddenly, a solid projectile struck the leading edge of her shield, making it ring loudly, drawing from her an involuntary curse. She felt the impact of the blow through her hands and wished again she had more protection and a weapon with which to fight back.

In front and to the right of Harris's shield, DeGrizzo was calmly snapping off single shots from the gun on her left gauntlet, its recoil absorbed by her suit and converted into energy. To her front and left, Eames had switched to rapid fire, sending out streams of flechettes in a wide arc as he steadily moved his right arm from side to side, bracing his suit against the low wall behind him. At close quarters the crack of their guns almost drowned out the constant screams and cries of those hit and not fortunate enough to be killed outright. As the bodies piled up, it became harder for the attackers to advance. Slipping and sliding in the blood and gore, they became slow moving targets that were easily picked off by the Marines. The metallic smell of blood, mixed with the stench of ruptured and spilt intestines, added to the scene of carnage unfolding in front of the Marines.

Gallagher was yet to fire, having instructed his suit to switch to close combat mode. A small buckler had formed against the side of his left forearm along with a flechette launcher. On his right, a one-point two-metre sword was now gripped tightly in his armoured fist. Along Gallagher's right forearm a row of four-inch, razor-sharp spikes formed, ideal for close quarter work. They would rip through most light-weight armour when delivered by the powered muscles of his armoured suit.

His four Marine guards were all firing steadily from their positions, but Gallagher could see that it was only going to be a short time before their position was overwhelmed by the sheer weight of numbers. At that point, his suit should enable him to stay fighting for a while longer. "*If I stand my ground over the shield it might buy Harris a few more moments when they manage to break through. Maybe even enough time until help arrives,*" he thought to himself.

Suddenly, the mass of screaming, charging civilians dwindled to nothing as the last of the robed attackers was cut down, only to be replaced by the grinding sound of heavy machinery smashing its way through and across the debris field. Small arms fire, mainly in the shape of solid slugs fired by chemical propellants, began peppering their positions. Although Marine armour was capable of withstanding multiple impacts from rounds of this calibre, eventually the cumulative damage would degrade even its ability to function. In front of the Marines, hundreds of dead bodies lay draped over the rubble like a gory carpet. A few bodies were feebly twitching or crying out until well-placed flechettes or bullets from their own side silenced them forever.

Suddenly, the Marines' suits all began registering power increases instead of falls, as Dauntless finally broke through the surprisingly capable and sophisticated jamming and began beaming power to their location. A few seconds later, full contact and telemetry were restored between Dauntless and the Marines.

"Patrick, glad to see you made it in one piece," the Emperor's familiar face and voice came through on their private channel. "I'm personally coming to extract you all in the other shuttle, just keep them at bay for a few more minutes."

Gallagher smiled back at his friend, a rueful expression on his face. "I never doubted it for one minute, Alex. You never could resist an excuse to get away from behind your desk, and this was too good an opportunity to turn down. Make it quick please, we have heavy armour about to hit us."

At that, Gallagher cut the link, then called on the nearest Marines to follow him, springing out from behind his cover and sprinting at full speed towards the tank-like vehicle beginning to emerge through the walls of a partially destroyed building. Bullets from small arms fire rang off his armour, only slightly slowing his forward pace. Using the power inherent in the muscle fibres of his suit, he leapt forward onto the upper cowling of the tank, bringing his sword down in an arc that cut through the barrel of the main gun which had been traversing towards his previous position. Using the downward momentum of the blow, he swung the blade upwards again, then brought it down on top of the turret, slicing away a portion of the point three-metre-thick reactive armour, leaving a gash into the interior. He pushed his left hand up to the hole and fired a rapid stream of flechettes inside the turret. The kinetic energy of the flechettes bounced them around inside, slicing and liquefying its occupants in moments. Behind him, Walker and Tommaso had also called up their swords and were following his example, going after another tank which had pushed its way through into the Marines kill zone. Using the tank as a brace and the few seconds grace he had bought by his attack, Gallagher switched from flechettes to larger, heavier slugs and increased their launch speed to maximum.

Plewa, watching with admiration from a few dozen metres away, instructed his men to switch to automatic fire to clear away the properly armed and armoured soldiers that had taken the place of civilian fighters. Although these new soldiers had body armour strong enough to withstand the impact of one or maybe two flechettes, multiple strikes compromised them completely.

A sudden explosion nearby threw Plewa into the air, along with three other Marines who were closer to the blast point. Momentarily stunned by the twin impacts of hitting the ground and explosion, he lay motionless and unable to move, watching with detached abstraction as a large armoured tank finished pushing through the rubble and began traversing its gun towards where he and the other fallen Marines were now lying. Struggling to focus properly, he was strangely fascinated by the last traces of smoke leaving the tank's gun barrel. As if from a distance, he could hear Marines calling his name and asking if he was OK.

At the explosion, Gallagher snapped around, quickly assessing the blast's aftermath. His readout told him Plewa was in trouble and the other three Marines lying there were either badly injured or dying. Knowing he had only seconds to act, he leapt off the crippled hulk below him and ran full speed at the huge tank that was bearing down on the fallen Marines, covering the distance in moments. Several other Marines had made the same decision to switch to heavier flechettes, and as they began firing to support Gallagher, the tank began rocking from the impacts to its turret and armoured body. Unlike the smaller flechettes, these heavier slugs caused parts of the tanks interior walls to liquefy and spray super-heated metal around, igniting anything flammable. The tank crew didn't feel a thing when the HE shell being automatically loaded into its breach ignited, blowing the turret clear of the hull. It landed several metres away, crushing a dozen advancing troops and making the others duck down and scatter.

Gallagher stood his ground, setting his suit to auto-fire, making himself the obvious target instead of the downed Marines, hoping to draw fire away from them.

Suddenly, the killing zone was covered with darkness as the sun was blotted out by the bulk of two Imperial shuttles taking position overhead. Point defence weapons on the shuttles opened up and began scything down any advancing troops and taking out the remaining tanks. High in the sky overhead, the accompanying fighters had split into three groups, one taking station above the shuttles, the other two taking out ground forces and any VTOL aircraft launching from their hidden hangars which had managed to avoid the drones.

Gallagher hurried over to Plewa and lifted his suit upright, supporting him under the shoulders, noting that DeGrizzo and Walker had gone back to Harris and were moving her towards the shuttle, using their shields to protect her while the enemy soldiers were being cleared from the immediate area.

The acting Corporals began organising an orderly withdrawal to the shuttles, which had lowered themselves to within six metres off the ground and extended wide ramps from their rear, from which poured fresh, heavily armoured Marines who quickly moved out into the surrounding area and began clearing it of any remaining hostiles. The Emperor could be seen fighting at their head, his sword rising and falling like a metronome before the enemy routed and began withdrawing. Within minutes the lightly armoured Marines from the crashed shuttle, along with their fallen comrades and the body of the dead pilot, were safely aboard and ready to depart.

For the moment electing to stay on the ground with his Emperor, Gallagher made sure Plewa and Harris were aboard before watching their shuttle depart with the rest of the original cohort. He walked over to a mobile smart-metal station that had been set up and plugged in his suit, instructing it to reform itself into the same heavily armoured variant as the others.

The Emperor walked over to him, idly flicking his sword from side to side to remove any blood from the blade and began speaking while Gallagher's suit reformed. Both their helmets had been retracted so they could see each other's real face.

"Patrick, we've taken several of the soldiers and civilians that weren't too badly wounded for questioning. Now we have full communications restored I'm sorry to tell you that the remaining Diplomats were all killed shortly after the shuttle was taken out. The more we discover, the less I like what happened here. We were obviously set-up."

Gallagher closed his eyes for a few moments and recalled the faces of the men and women with whom he'd spent the last few months. While not close, they were still comrades, and he mourned for them and their families.

"I'll want to let their families know myself, Alex, but a personal message from you too would help with their loss," he said, looking at his friend.

"Of course," Alexander nodded, "I will write personal messages and append them to yours. Just confirm to Vimes when you are ready to send them". Thinking for a moment, Alexander continued, "After a suitable period I'll arrange for all of the families affected here today to visit Capital as my guests. They can stay for as long as they wish and Vimes will make sure they will want for nothing. It's the least we can do to compensate them for today's monumental foul-up."

"I have to take responsibility for that Sire, I'm sorry," Gallagher apologised, bowing his head.

"Don't go all formal on me, Patrick, there's more to this than just a simple foul up or lack of preparation or whatever the damn reason was," Alexander exclaimed. "No, this was well organised and planned. If not for blind luck and my son's disregard for anything apart from himself, we would probably all be dead instead of just my poor bodyguard."

He looked up at the sky for a moment, watching the dense smoke as it rose up from the ruined tanks. It mixed with the dust and ash hanging in the air from the crash site and burning fires.

"It was that and the confusion our appearing with two, and not three shuttles that messed up their plans and panicked those fighter pilots into detonating early. Sheer, blind luck."

"What are you going to do about Adam?" Patrick asked, changing the subject.

"I'm not sure," Alexander replied, "but I want him out of my sight for a while. Not only that, he needs to be kept safe until we expose and deal with whoever was behind this. I know what I have to do but what's his mother going to say?" He sighed deeply and squeezed his eyes shut for a moment. "I'm not looking forward to explaining this all to her."

Gallagher nodded sympathetically, then looked around at the destruction and carnage. "What are we going to do next?" he asked.

"It's a short hop over to the original welcoming site to pick up what we can find of the diplomats and show the local soldiers we mean business, then back to Dauntless to check on your injured survivors. You up for that?" he asked, then laughed loudly at his friend's response.

"Does the Emperor shit on a golden toilet?"

"You know I do Patrick, you know I do."

Adam woke up with a mild headache and the comforting feeling of a soft, warm body snuggled up behind him. His eyes struggled to open, and his dry mouth currently felt as though it belonged to someone else. A shapely feminine arm came into focus as he finally pried one eye open and struggled to concentrate.

"*That was some party*," he thought, smiling as the memories come back, some more clearly than others. He asked his AI to remind him of the woman's name and was surprised when it didn't respond.

"*Oh, that's right, I switched it off last night. That was silly of me,*" he thought, although it had made perfect sense at the time.

Blinking, Adam swung his legs over and sat on the edge of the bed, leaning forward and holding his head in his hands. The sudden movement made the pain in his temples peak for a moment before subsiding. Pushing himself upright, Adam looked around for the bathroom door as he badly needed to take a pee. Entering the small cubicle, he leant one hand against the smooth wall in front of him and with the other directed a stream into the bowl.

"Ah, that's much better" he sighed, moving towards the wash basin and cleaning his hands. Splashing some water onto his face, Adam idly examined his reflection. Tall, good looking and powerfully built, Adam was a younger version of his father with just enough of his mother to make him even more handsome. He ran his hands through the curly mop of hair that people always found so fascinating.

"Another good reason for not accepting a commission. I'd have to cut this lot off," he said to no-one in particular. "No bloody way."

Adam padded back into the bedroom, his head still a little tender, but the ache lessening as he moved.

Last night's love interest lay under the covers where he had left her. She had been celebrating a promotion of some sort and was clearly flattered at his approach. Despite little make-up, she was stunningly gorgeous, and he felt something stirring as he remembered the previous evening's activities. Smiling, he moved back to the bed, slipped under the covers again and began stroking her right arm. "*For what I've in mind,*" he thought, "*I won't need to remember her name.*"

Her eyes slowly opened, and she responded to his caress, moulding herself into him, feeling his obvious interest. She had woken up while he was in the bathroom and had been waiting for him with her eyes closed.

"Morning handsome," she murmured, reaching down to hold him, "whatever do you have in mind with this?"

Not saying anything he pulled her even closer and started kissing her neck. Reaching her mouth, they began kissing while he moved his left hand down between her legs to see if she was ready for him. She moved her hips forward, pressing them into his hand.

Both lost in the moment and their rising passion, neither noticed the door open and an armoured figure enter, stooping to get under the header.

"Lights," an amplified voice rang out.

Immediately, the room lights came on at full intensity, illuminating the couple who came apart and sat bolt upright, startled by the sudden interruption. For a moment, caught like two rabbits in a searchlight, they simply stared, looking at the figure while their eyes adjusted.

"Get dressed and come with me. Now," the armoured figure addressed Adam, its head turning towards the woman. "My apologies, Flight-Lieutenant Schmidt." Looking at her naked breasts for only a moment, Alexander retracted his helmet so she could see his face. "I can see why my son decided to miss this morning's Ascension ceremony, disconnected internal systems and caused you to be absent from a Red Alert."

Schmidt was dumbfounded, confused and rapidly becoming very, very angry with Adam. "Just what the hell have you gotten me into here, you idiot!" she shouted at him, "You turned off the sensors and alarms, so I missed an alert?!" Looking at the Emperor, she started to apologise but was cut short.

"I'm fully aware of what happened Flight-Lieutenant," he interrupted. "I hold you blameless in this matter, and Vimes has already spoken with your commanding officer to explain your absence. I do believe, however, that it would be best if you didn't try to contact my son again until he is off this ship, assuming by then he hasn't found someone else to share his bed."

Her jaw dropped in shock at his words.

Stunned for a moment by what had just happened and the interplay between his female companion and father, Adam suddenly remembered her name. "*Maxine that was it*," almost saying it out loud. Adam jumped out of bed and marched naked over to his father, looking up so he could stare at his face.

"What makes you think you can...," he started to shout until his neck was squeezed by his father's gauntlet and he noticed the sticky blood still spattered on the armour. He was lifted up onto his toes and carried back over to the bed where his father half threw him down onto the covers.

"Be quiet, get dressed, say your goodbyes and meet me outside in five minutes. I've just spent this morning picking through body parts and checking on friends in the infirmary, so I've no inclination whatsoever to listen to your puerile arguments. You are already in enough trouble, Adam." With that, Alexander nodded at Lt. Schmidt, turned around and ducked back out the way he came.

Turning to Maxine to say something, Adam was hit by a ringing slap to the side of his face, so hard it made his teeth rattle.

"You utter bastard. Just what high-level shit have you landed me in, Alex?" she shouted. "I've only just won my commission, and now the Emperor himself has had reason to talk to my CO! You bloody idiot. Get out and stay away from me."

With that, she jumped out of bed and walked naked to the bathroom, slamming the door behind her. Moments later the sound of a shower could be plainly heard.

Ruefully, Adam rubbed the side of his face and reached down to fish his clothes from around the bed. While not at all scared of his father, he wasn't going to make matters worse by keeping him waiting. "*He'll come around,*" he thought, pulling on his socks. "*Dad never stays angry for long, I'll just do what he says for a day or two and keep out of his hair.*"

Dressed, Adam finally remembered to switch his Aide back on, a stripped-down, less intuitive version of Vimes. Immediately a stream of information began scrolling across his vision, all highlighted in red. Stunned by what he was seeing, especially the news of the ambush and death of his father's bodyguard, Adam realised with a sinking feeling that just staying out of his father's way probably wasn't going to be enough this time.

Reaching the door, the last thing he heard before leaving Maxine's quarters was the sound of a fist hitting the bathroom wall and a muffled "Stupid Bastard." He didn't care to stay and discover whether it was aimed at herself or him.

Alexander was waiting quietly outside, leaning against a wall, having taken the time to allow the walls to absorb a large part of his armoured suit which had reduced in size to one more suited to the ship's interior.

"Walk with me son," he said, starting off along the corridor, through officers' quarters and towards the nearest transit tube, not bothering to check if Adam was following.

Adam hurried to catch up, debating with himself whether to apologise or just say nothing. Deciding on the latter, he matched his father's stride. While there was no need for anyone to salute while in the officer's accommodation area, people moved respectfully out of the way as they approached. Alexander nodded to one or two of them he knew personally, but kept quiet and said nothing until they had reached the tube.

"Get in please, and listen," Alexander said, motioning to the entrance and then following him inside. They sat opposite each other. The normally rapid tube set off slowly, instructed by Alexander to travel at a modest pace. "I'd hoped that you would have appreciated the significance of today's ceremony, using it as a start towards your preparations for when you eventually become Emperor."

He looked his son in the eyes, "But, yet again you failed me. And your mother too."

"I know father, and I'm sorry. It won't..." Adam started to speak before being interrupted.

"No it won't happen again, Adam, because for once we are going to do something about it," Alexander interrupted. "You will join the Imperial Navy. Not as an officer, because you don't deserve it, but as a Rating. How quickly or slowly you rise through the ranks will be down to you."

"But Dad, what about my, my...?" Adam paused, trying to think of a reason, but coming up with nothing.

"You knew this day was coming, son. It's just a bit sooner than either of us thought." He paused again before continuing. "There is another, perhaps more pressing reason for you to join. No, hear me out," he said before his son could interrupt. "Gallagher and I believe," he paused, "...know, that today's events were an assassination attempt. Not by the fools on the planet but by third parties from within the Empire or one of our external enemies. Only someone with a great deal of money and resources could have arranged this without our knowing,"

"You and I were the targets today, Adam, and it was only blind luck and the distractions of your Lieutenant friend that saved us from dying along with my bodyguard. I need to get you somewhere safe and where safer than on a Navy ship surrounded by loyalists, learning the ropes out on a six-month tour of the Marches of Sector Twenty-Nine? With the two of us so far apart, it will make their job that much harder, whoever they are."

"Six months!" Adam exploded, not having paid much attention to anything else his Father had said. "It's at least three weeks travel time just to get there!"

"Think of it as your penance for this morning. My mind is made up, Adam. Being so far away you will be out of regular contact, so I've decided to let you take my own personal yacht with a full copy of Vimes to keep you company. He'll provide letters of introduction to Commodore Haynes before coming back with the ship. Haynes is a good man; someone I can rely on to look after you."

Father and son sat in awkward silence for what seemed an age, but in reality, was only a minute. The opening tube door told them they had reached the hangar bay where Alexander's private yachts were stowed. He was sending Adam away in his favourite. Over sixty metres long, fully half of its mass and length was taken up by engines and weaponry. Fully automated and capable of deep-space operations, it was provisioned for long journeys if required. In recent years, as the press of Imperial business weighed down on him, Alexander rarely had a chance to use it, but for a time he had tinkered around with the engines and configuration until he had a ship that suited his needs and temperament.

Adam was shocked at the rapid turn of events and felt powerless to stop himself being railroaded somewhere he didn't want to go. He thought for a second about trying to physically resist his father but dismissed it with a shake of his head as a stupid idea on so many levels. Although equally matched in size, Alexander had almost a century of combat experience to draw on, even if he hadn't been wearing a suit.

They exited the transit tube together in silence, walking the short distance to the hangar's entrance where a pressurised walkway was already attached to the yacht.

Alexander looked at his son and broke the silence. "Vimes has copied himself into the yacht's systems. It's a good opportunity for the two of you to get reacquainted, so consider it an order. Use both him and the transit time wisely to familiarise yourself with Navy protocols and what will be expected of you for the next six months. That way it won't all come as a complete shock."

Alexander stepped forward to embrace his son, but Adam pulled backwards, shaking his head.

"Yes Sire, your devoted servant obeys," he said sarcastically, angry now at the realisation he was trapped. Turning around so his father couldn't see the tears of frustration welling up in his eyes, Adam walked the short distance across the walkway to the entrance of the yacht. As he approached the door, it silently opened, and he saw lights come on in the interior. Without a backwards glance, he walked through, the entrance closing behind him.

Outside, Alexander watched the door close and stayed there as the walkway snaked back into the wall. He looked at his yachts smooth, unmarked exterior, and tried to convince himself this was the right course of action, remembering the time of his own testing.

"Keep safe, my son," he whispered to himself, before squaring his shoulders and walking away, not wanting to see the yacht leave.

Behind him, the lights began going out.

Her twelve-hour shift finally over, a tired Karen left A&E and walked out into the cold, dark evening, chewing on a tired cheese and pickle sandwich she'd liberated from the canteen moments before it closed. She looked up at the sky, slowly savouring the last mouthful. Stars were already twinkling above, but light pollution meant that only the brightest could be seen under the glare from the nearby fluorescent floodlights. Although the long nights were starting to shorten, the sun had set two hours earlier and the little heat generated during the day had all but vanished.

Walking briskly to the living block and her little room, once inside she hurriedly stripped off and ran the shower in the bathroom. It spluttered and spat for a few moments before running true. Fortunately, the living quarters were kept warm, although she hated the feel of the cold tiles underneath her bare feet while she waited for the shower to run hot.

After what seemed an age, the temperature finally reached one acceptable to her, and she stepped in with a grateful sigh of contentment.

"Ah, that's much better," she said out loud, relaxing as she let the hot water spray onto her face.

Turning around, she let the heat soak into her neck, easing away the tensions of the busy day, at the same time trying to avoid the clammy shower curtain from sticking to her bare bottom. She resisted the temptation to dwell on how many strange bottoms had done the same thing over the years. After a minute of soaking, she soaped her hair with shampoo then grabbed a bar of Dove soap and began washing, following her favoured routine. Start with the face, work down to the feet, rinse carefully then dry vigorously.

Carefully stepping out of the bath so as not to slip and fall, Karen towelled herself dry and wrapped a spare one around her hair. She moved over to sit by the vanity mirror and carefully moisturised her face. The makeshift turban fell around her shoulders, and she used the asthmatic dryer provided with the room to dry her hair. Before getting into bed, she lifted the sheets at one end to make a tent and directed the hot air from the hairdryer inside, warming the bed. Satisfied the chill had been taken off, she quickly slipped under the covers, enjoying the heat before it could dissipate away. It was a long drive to Skye tomorrow, so she wanted to get a good night's sleep.

"*Three hours if I take the hill road or two and a half if I drive along Loch Ness and don't get stuck behind a lorry or caravan,*" she thought to herself. "*I'll decide in the morning which route to take.*"

Too tired even to watch TV on her tablet, she manoeuvred her pillows into a V-shape, turned off the side light to her right and went to sleep.

The next morning, Karen woke early and reached for her tablet on the bedside cabinet. Pre-set to Radio Scotland News for the traffic reports, Karen turned up the volume and walked into the tiny bathroom to freshen up, resting it on the windowsill so she could listen while brushing her teeth. The report of an overturned timber lorry, which had shed its load of recently felled timber all over the carriageway on the A832 near Loch Luichart, decided her route to Skye. It would take the authorities hours to get heavy lifting gear to the incident and traffic would be slowed for ages, so Loch Ness it would be.

Having showered the night before and eager to beat the traffic, Karen decided to forego another wash and directed a quick burst of deodorant under each arm before shoving her toiletries into the brightly patterned leather cosmetics bag hanging behind the door. Quickly dressing in the faded blue jeans and baggy jumper she currently favoured, Karen shoved the last of her things into a suitcase and took one last look around the little room which had been her home for the last few days. Certain she had left nothing behind, she put on her overcoat and walked out into the corridor, pulling behind her the grey plastic suitcase which used to belong to her mother. She had customised the case many years before by stencilling a large green cat onto each side, so it always stood out on luggage carousels. Now badly faded and partially rubbed off through years of wear, the cat design blended in with the case's battered exterior. Before every holiday, she was always tempted to buy a brighter and more fashionable suitcase or holdall to better suit her personality, but somehow, she could never part with her mother's old case.

Karen paused for a moment, checking her right coat pocket for car keys. Patting the reassuring bump, she walked on until she came to her car, a silver two-year-old Mini Countryman which she had bought on a whim, following one of the many disagreements she'd had with Ian, her fiancé.

"*No, it's former fiancé,*" she reminded herself, unlocking the car and lifting the case into the boot.

"Bastard. Whatever did you see in him, girl?" she asked herself out loud, annoyed with herself for letting thoughts of him spoil her mood.

Slamming the boot lid down a little too hard, she got in the car before realising she had left her coat on. Tutting with annoyance, she got out, threw the coat onto the back seat and climbed back in. She adjusted the rearview mirror and began rummaging in the door pocket where she'd remembered leaving some mints.

"There you are," she said out loud, finding the half-eaten roll of Sharps Extra Strong Mints.

Picking fluff and crud off the top mint, she popped it in her mouth, synced her phone to the car and set it so her favourite music was ready to play. Pressing the car's starter button, Karen switched the gearbox to auto from manual and headed for the automatic barrier to exit the car park. Once through, she parked outside the white and red ambulance station, rushed in and asked one of her friends at the reception desk if they would drop the room keys off for her later. After a brief chat, she got back into the car and drove off towards the exit, turning right into Culcabock Road to avoid the morning traffic.

"*Right then,*" Karen thought to herself, "*That's one-hundred-odd kilometres to Dornie and breakfast near Castle Eilean Donan, then another eighty kilometres to Struan. Four hours driving time if I allow for a quick food stop and getting stuck behind one or two caravans.*"

Satisfied she had a good plan to follow, Karen pressed shuffle play on her phone and burst out laughing as Soft Cell's Tainted Love began playing. The song always reminded her of the film Coneheads, and the lyrics were curiously spot on for her current frame of mind. Three songs later, just as she was driving over the canal bridge leading into the River Ness, the stereo started playing New Order's True Faith and without thinking the pumping music made her speed up, leaving behind the suburbs of Inverness. Most of the road was single lane in each direction, so Karen knew she had to make good time while the road ahead was clear.

Twenty-five minutes later she turned right, leaving the A82 for the A887, passing the Glenmoriston Arms Hotel on her right and a small Post Office on the left. At the same time, a Camper Van pulled out in front of her and started to accelerate at a snail's pace through the little village. Quickly checking the road ahead for pedestrians, she floored the throttle. The seat pressed into her back, and she imagined she could feel the car squat down as it took off, overtaking the leaden Camper Van with ease.

"*I just love this,*" she thought, "*The rush of acceleration, the sense of freedom and the noise of the engine. Wonderful.*"

As the kilometres speed by to the sound of Dakota, Don't Stop Me Now and Mr Blue Sky, Karen could feel herself relax, letting the car and speed clear her mind of everything except the road talking to her through the steering wheel, becoming one with the car, her senses speeding up to compensate.

A further half an hour of hard driving found her following a loch on her left and a cutting, blasted out of the dark local rock, on her right, covered with large sheets of stainless steel mesh to stop small boulders falling onto the road.

"*Just around this bend and I'll be able to see Eilean Donan Castle,*" she thought, slowing down in anticipation of reaching the slower moving car ahead. Following the road as it turned right, she spotted it in the distance, jutting out into the loch. Several sweeping left and right turns later, Karen had a choice; to stop off for breakfast as planned or keep going. She'd overtaken quite a few slow-moving cars in the last few kilometres and was loathe to let them catch up with her and have to do it all over again at some point.

"*I'll keep going,*" she thought, reaching for another mint. "*I can stop off at the Co-op at Kyle for some supplies, then it'll only be a forty-five-minute drive to Alastair and Flora's place.*"

Leaving Eilean Donan behind, she drove over the wide bridge crossing Loch Long and gradually built up her speed again. As a child, when visiting her aunt and uncle, she'd visited the castle behind her on several occasions. Her Aunt and Uncle had been a constant in her life following the death of her mother when she was sixteen years old and again when her father remarried two years later. The suitcase was one of the few things she had left from her mother, for her father had presented his new love with her mother's jewellery. Annoyingly, he had also allowed the woman to throw away what was left of her mother's clothes and keepsakes before she'd had a chance to take some for herself.

"*She's probably gotten rid of the jewellery by now, out of spite,*" Karen reminded herself, for an instant hoping something horrible might happen to her step-mother.

Thinking of father reminded her of the call she'd received from him, a few weeks into her Medical Degree at Cardiff, telling her that he and his new bride were emigrating to Australia for a new start. This old memory made her scowl for the first time since leaving the Hospital. It had been two years since she had last seen him and even then, she'd had to visit the couple in Sydney where they now lived. His younger wife, while polite, had made it plain she resented the intrusion and would be pleased if the visit was brief. Soon after, Karen took herself off to a local hotel for the remainder of her stay and spent most of it sightseeing, briefly saying goodbye to the pair of them the day before she left for Scotland.

"Why do all the men in my life not stay around?" she asked herself out loud, obviously not expecting any sort of answer.

"Untrustworthy bastards, I'm going to swear off the lot of them. Why not have some fun on my own for some time, maybe even forever?" she told herself, but only half believing it. Karen was already missing the physical side of her previous relationship with Ian but was in no hurry to find another partner for her bed. "Not for a while anyway," she told herself with a grin.

Ten minutes later, she turned left into the Co-op car park, situated on a little hill just before the Skye Bridge. Parking in one of the marked bays, Karen switched off the engine and got out, stretching to get the knots out of her back and legs brought on by over two hours of non-stop driving.

Karen grabbed a shopping trolley, using the Mini token she'd found in the car along with assorted change and stray sweet wrappers. The automatic doors of the store opened, a wash of warm air welcoming her in.

Half an hour later and with the boot fully loaded with a week's worth of food shopping, Karen drove out of the car park, turning left onto the bridge approach. As the road climbed upwards, she drove out into the middle of the tall bridge and took in the breath-taking views on either side, towards the islands of Scalpay and Raasay on her right and back down Loch Alsh to the left. A freshly baked baguette on the seat next to her smelt lovely and she felt her mouth-watering. Keeping her eyes on the road, Karen groped down to the passenger seat on her left and brought the baguette to her mouth, tearing a big bite from the still warm end, which brought another smile but for different reasons this time. After a few moments, she could taste the sweetness of the fresh bread and decided to take a few more bites before setting it back down. Hunger temporarily assuaged, she concentrated on the road ahead, and journeys end.

It was still half an hour before noon by the time she turned a corner and saw ahead the Sligachan Hotel, nestling in a valley at the bottom of the Cuillin Mountains. The roads remained quite empty, with most of the traffic going the other way and heading off the island, a succession of private cars interspersed with delivery lorries shuttling back and forth between Kyle and Portree or Broadford. Resisting the urge to stop and have a quick drink at the Hotel, she took a sharp left, passing the old stone bridge made redundant years ago when the original road had been replaced with a newer one. All around the island you could see the remains of old bridges, gently crumbling away from neglect, having been bypassed years previously. These old roads were now only used by sheep or as lay-bys for lorries or tourists.

Ten minutes later, almost at the end of her journey, Ardtreck Point lighthouse came to view as she rounded the headland on the approach to Struan. The view, one of the best on Skye, never failed to raise a smile and bring back memories of past holidays here. The road curved gently to the right, following the headland, giving Karen the first glimpse of her destination, a small group of white houses and bungalows dotting the far shore. Below the line of three white buildings, slightly raised up from the road and a little to the right was her uncle's recently extended bungalow. The familiar ruined cottage and associated outbuildings down by the jetty had deteriorated further since she was last here, with the roof now almost totally caved in and the walls bowing outwards. Several small fishing boats bobbed gently in the water near the jetty, and she could see one slowly making its way out of the loch towards the outer isles.

"*Probably going to bring in the lobster catch,*" she thought. "*Later, if I time it right, I might be able to go down to the jetty as they unload and see if I can get a lobster or crab. Either would go well with the baguette tonight and a bottle of Chardonnay or St. Emilion from the boot.*"

Having driven around the Loch, Karen turned right into the drive and parked up before the cattle grid to unlock the gate. Turning around, she took a deep breath and looked down the loch and out to sea, savouring the salty tang in the air, mixed with an indefinable scent that always reminded her of Struan.

"*There is something in the air here,*" she thought, catching a last glimpse of the fishing boat as it passed out of sight, before getting back in the car and parking outside the place she would be calling home for the next few weeks.

Capital was unique in the Empire. Many worlds tried to emulate it, but none could compare to the natural beauty of the Imperium's home planet. From Josef on, each Emperor or Empress had left their mark on it in some way, each helping the planet return to nature.

A terrible war, begun just after the Empire's founding, had all but destroyed the planet. The nuclear missiles and orbiting asteroid defence system had been turned against the population they were designed to protect, ravaging ecosystems and polluting the seas and sky. It had taken many decades, but once the radiation had been cleaned away, the next task had been to restore the damaged ecosystems. To that end, a large proportion of the surviving population had been encouraged to move away and join the ongoing exodus to populate new colony worlds. Probes had identified hundreds of potential planets for the race to expand into and for many the lure of clean water, large tracts of land to own, fresh air and a new start, was irresistible.

Instead of rebuilding their cities upwards, those who chose to remain decided to go down into the earth and live underground, a legacy from the long nuclear winter and poisoned atmosphere. Huge cities were created, hollowed out of the living rock, protected from all the natural elements. Neither hurricane nor tsunami could hurt the people, safe in their comfortable, clean environment. Vast networks of high-speed vacuum tubes were created, joining cities below ground across huge distances. Construction of these habitats and transportation links was only suitable in tectonically stable regions, which further accelerated the returning of huge swathes of the continental land masses back to nature as whole regions became deserted. It was found that allowing the planet to heal itself was by far the fastest and least costly option when trying to make good the effects of war, overpopulation and heavy industry, requiring only the occasional technological nudge. By design or happy accident, the exodus off-world had led to the remaining population being less adventurous. Safe in their underground cities, they became natural administrators in their sterile, clean and safe communities. Although not in any way scared of the open spaces above them, most of Capital's citizens preferred to use them only for holidays or to briefly enjoy the planet's natural splendour.

When William, the sixth Emperor, made Capital the administrative centre and seat of Empire some two hundred and eighty years after its founding, the population took to their new role with quiet efficiency, sealing the planet's transformation.

With large areas of the planet's surface uninhabited or scarcely populated, Capital's wildlife thrived. With few outward signs of civilisation detectable from space, an unknowing observer could have easily mistaken it for a new colony world.

William had built his Imperial Palace near the coast, on a good-sized island that lay a few dozen kilometres from a continental land mass in the northern hemisphere. Blessed with a temperate climate and seas warmed by tropical currents that came up from the equator, it was an ideal choice. After his death, it remained the main residence of the Imperial family, with subsequent Emperors building and remodelling it over the course of four thousand years. As each successive Emperor or Empress added to the Palace, the grounds continued to grow and extend until they covered just over two thousand five hundred square kilometres. Consisting mainly of dense woodland, the grounds had several large, landscaped parks and gardens which were opened up to the public in times of national celebration or for invited guests at more formal diplomatic events. Less than twenty minutes travel time by a dedicated transit-tube to the main administrative hub of the planet, the Palace was close enough to make commuting bearable for those staff not resident there but also far enough away to allow for a measure of privacy.

The Palace itself was large, built to a wide crescent design three storeys high, with room for double the current twelve thousand household staff and Imperial administrators that worked there. At the centre of the crescent was situated the Royal quarters, with the remainder of the arc on either side facing the coast reserved as residential quarters for those staff who preferred to live at the Palace rather than commute. Inside of the arc, facing the landscaped gardens and lakes, were the Empire's administrative offices and Halls of State for the thirty-six Sectors. The Grand Hall of Empire was situated at the east tip of the crescent, while assorted audience rooms and chambers could be found at the west end.

With both her husband and son away, Empress Christine was currently the sole royal occupant, continuing the business of running their vast Empire.

Empress, and joint ruler in all but name, Christine woke early as was her custom. Somehow, she had never mastered the art of staying in bed and didn't feel comfortable that Palace servants were already working hard on the day's Council meetings and affairs of State while she lay in bed, so Christine always made sure she was one of the first to rise in the morning.

"Old habits die hard," she told herself, rising and walking towards the massive window that framed the bedroom she shared with Alexander when he was home, her slim figure silhouetted by the morning light through the thin material of her nightdress. Following her standing instructions, Vimes had set the window to full transparency a few minutes before sunrise so she could watch the day begin. This was her favourite time of day, and the window was perfectly positioned so she could take advantage of the views across the valley which sloped down towards the coast. Whenever Alexander was away, she found an almost spiritual comfort from watching the sun rise over the sea. They often watched it together, even after all the many years of their long marriage, not saying a word, yet taking comfort from each other's presence.

"The day I get tired of this view they can take me away and shoot me," she said out loud. "Do you agree, Vimes?"

"No Christine, I don't," he replied, his voice seeming to come out of thin air, "Alex wouldn't be very happy with me if I let anything happen to you, irrespective of whether you deserved it or not."

She chuckled softly. "You needn't worry Vimes, there are times I think he prefers your company to mine."

Diplomatically, Vimes stayed quiet.

Lacking the genetic enhancements her husband enjoyed that allowed Vimes to integrate smoothly within his nervous system, Christine had to rely on a less effective physical implant. To compensate, it was an infinitely more complex version than those used by Command Staff, in theory allowing her full access to almost every one of Vimes's multiple systems throughout Capital. However, in practice, the sheer volume and sources of data under his control meant she rarely attempted to access them, sensibly preferring to leave that to him. In the privacy of her own quarters, away from official business and the responsibilities of State, she rarely used the neural implant to speak with Vimes, preferring to use the spoken word in their dealings. It had taken her many years before becoming totally comfortable with having him see and hear everything she did, especially as she always thought of Vimes as being male. Still, if she thought of him as a person, she could at least address him like one, rather than give commands via the link.

"*It's silly to anthropomorphise an AI, even one so smart and almost human,*" she thought to herself, not for the first or last time.

Turning away from the beautiful sunrise, Christine walked into her dressing room and checked over the clothes she'd chosen thc night before, at the same time going over today's schedule with Vimes. Satisfied she'd not forgotten anything, Christine stepped into the bathroom and walked into the shower.

Washing away the last vestiges of her sleep with the hot, scented water, Christine let her mind wander back to her first few days in the Palace as a guest of her husband.

"*He always used to tell me off for doing everything myself. It took him a while before letting me just get on with things on my own,*" she thought, "*that's one of his more endearing traits, never forcing me to do anything and letting me run the Palace and Capital my way.*" She laughed out loud, remembering the scandalised expressions and comments from the various courtiers when she began making changes.

"*Silly old fossils,*" she remembered thinking at the time, but they'd all come around to her way of thinking in the end. Unbidden, a song from her childhood suddenly came to mind, and she gently began to sing, her voice getting louder as she got to the chorus. Ever thoughtful, Vimes matched it to her private music library, and the musical track began accompanying her.

Laughing, she finished showering and dressed quickly, choosing the formal Navy Dress uniform required for the award ceremony later that morning. Dark navy blue, with the orange and black insignia of the Royal House discretely embroidered onto the left breast, it set off her brown eyes and fine complexion. With only a few laughter lines at the corner of her eyes and mouth, she could pass for a woman of any age between thirty and sixty. The fact she was approaching her one hundred and eighth birthday, yet looked much younger, was one of the few small conceits she allowed herself. Christine had been in her early twenties when she'd first met Alexander, and from then on, they'd spent almost all of their lives together, only kept apart by wars or the demands of Empire. Her life had changed so much after meeting Alexander, going from a commoner to Empress within such a short period of time.

Christine's forehead creased. Thoughts of her husband invariably turned to Adam.

"*A good boy, if too headstrong,*" she thought, "*so much like his father when I first met him, but without his modesty or caution. I hope Alex can turn him around on this trip otherwise we will have to take more drastic steps in readying him for rule.*"

Christine hesitated for a moment, half expecting Vimes to comment, but nothing was forthcoming. Smiling ruefully, she checked her hair one last time before setting off for breakfast, something she made a point of sharing each morning with a selection of Palace staff, a custom instigated by her many years ago, much to the horror of the then Lord Steward of the Royal Household.

"*Long dead now,*" she thought sadly, remembering how the crusty old man had become one of her closest friends and advisors. His daughter now carried on in the role and did a fine job, but there had been something special about the old man that she missed. She had to admit, however, that his daughter did a better job of running the Palace than her father, if only by a whisker.

Both she and Alexander insisted on no bodyguards inside the Palace, relying instead on the external security and Vimes ever watchful presence to keep them safe. The nearly successful Coup d'état, orchestrated many years ago by her husband's uncle, was the last time Palace security had been breached. Although just before her time, there remained scars from the fighting left all around the Palace if you knew where to look. Alexander refused to have them erased, saying they reminded him of his murdered and greatly missed parents and family. Since those dark days, she knew Vimes and Alex had installed additional safeguards, and if she had been a gambler would lay odds there were one or two even she didn't know about.

Taking a scenic route to walk through the gardens, Christine took the time with Vimes to go through the attendance lists for the day's meetings, checking for apologies or any changes from the night before. Satisfied nothing material had changed, she allowed herself a few minutes to relax and properly take in the beautiful gardens. Statuary was dotted around the grounds, some of past Emperors, others of famous citizens of the Empire or even favourite pets loved by the Imperial family over the millennia. The majority Christine didn't recognise, but if one caught her eye, she was able to look it up through Vimes, along with as much history or information as she desired. Some of the older statues were carved in stone and badly weathered by time and rain, but they remained relatively clean due to the lack of pollutants in the air. The majority, however, were made of various metals and better able to resist the ravages of time. An even larger number could not be seen, relegated, unloved and forgotten for various reasons of taste and aesthetics, to the woodlands. On occasion, when out walking in the woods, Christine had been startled by a life-like statue of a previous Emperor or Admiral appearing out of the trees, often covered with ivy or moss.

On the lawn she intended to cross, dew still clung to the grass, soon to evaporate in the morning sunshine. To her right, Christine noticed a dewy spider's web, glistening as it swayed in the light breeze. She paused a few moments to admire it and the small spider busily repairing its handiwork. Looking around she breathed in the damp, earthy smell of the turf, enjoying the scented undertones of the many flowering plants artfully displayed around the grounds. Christine loved listening to the lingering morning chorus that could still be heard as the birds settled down to their daily business. Birdsong reminded her of home and took Christine back to the carefree days of her childhood, growing up in a large city with parks to make up for the small, cramped houses and gardens.

Passing through a wooden arbour festooned with beautiful roses, each bloom emitting a wonderful scent and holding a few drops of dew, she walked across the grass over to the refractory's entrance where breakfast was always served. Before entering she looked back at the gardens, noting her watery footprints on the lawn, tracing her progress across the grass.

Straightening her back, she smiled for her guests and entered the room, barely noticing more of the ubiquitous statues lined up against one wall, the other covered in ancient tapestries and artwork. Christine greeted each of the ten occupants by name, deliberately chosen as a cross-section of experience and seniority. All had been seated around a large circular table but had quickly risen when she entered the room. For Christine, breakfast was a chance for everyone to discuss any issues directly with her, away from the formal pomp and ceremony of the Imperial Court. It was also a good opportunity for her to get to know staff on a personal level, especially those who would not normally interact with her. The relaxed setting and lack of formality had often provided Christine with valuable insights into what was happening in the wider Empire. She highly prized the perspective of real people, instead of the often sanitised versions that too many courtiers preferred to tell her.

Motioning everyone to be seated, Christine took an empty chair and pulled it over to a small gap between an old retainer whom she knew well and a young, fresh-faced woman she hadn't seen before. The instant Christine sat down, servants began bringing in a selection of food that had been chosen beforehand according to personal preferences. Tucking into her favourite scrambled eggs and bacon, she allowed the conversations to wash over her before turning to the young woman sitting to her left.

"You're Rebecca, aren't you?" she asked, despite having access to the young woman's entire history being displayed by Vimes in the vision of her left eye. "How have you enjoyed your first few months at the Palace?"

Hesitating a little at first, Rebecca began to relax once she realised the Empress seemed to be as lovely as everyone had said she would be, and soon the two were chatting away as if they had known each other for years. Two of the older retainers, who had attended these breakfasts before on numerous occasions, looked at each other and smiled, as they too recalled their first meeting with the Empress. She had a natural skill for getting people to open up to her, an ability which had improved with the passage of time and royal experience.

"I'm still learning where everything is and the shortest routes to get around Ma'am," Rebecca replied. "It's trying to remember everyone's name without having to ask that I find hard. I was never good with names."

Christine smiled. "It took me a long time too but don't worry, it will come, especially once you get your upgraded implant. How did you get selected for your post?"

"My parents both served in the Navy, Ma'am, and the Veterans Association found me this position. My Mother died while on active service a year ago." Rebecca stopped for a moment, the memory painful. She took a deep breath and continued, "When my Father was selected to join the Emperor's bodyguard, it meant he would be away for extended periods, so the VA stepped in." Rebecca went silent, and Christine could see the pain of loss was still close to the surface, only partially soothed by the passing of not enough time.

"The Navy always looks after its own, Rebecca," Christine said, breaking the silence. "Until your Father comes back from his tour we will be your family here." Moved to sudden tears at the young woman's loss, Christine impulsively leant across and kissed Rebecca's head. "Never forget that."

"*Christine,*" interrupted Vimes through her implant so only she could hear, "*Sorry to interrupt. Would you like me to arrange for her father to come here and visit Rebecca when his tour is finished or whenever he has some leave due? He has a distinguished service record, and it would be a pleasant surprise for them both.*"

"*You're an old softie at heart Vimes, admit it,*" she thought back, a little annoyed with herself that Vimes had thought of it before her. "*Good idea, please see to it.*"

Later, once everyone had finished eating and had a chance to contribute to the meeting, Christine thanked them all for attending and made her exit. Everyone stood up and bowed as she left the room and behind her, Christine could hear the noise level rise as everyone began talking.

Today's schedule was long and tight, so she headed straight for a transit tube to take her to the audience room where dignitaries from all over the Empire were assembling, seated patiently in rows to be formally introduced and invested with sundry awards for long service, good works, philanthropic acts and the like.

"*Unfortunately, there doesn't seem to be anyone particularly famous or interesting on the guest list today,*" she thought ruefully, entering the tube.

Exiting a short while later, she walked towards the massive, ancient wooden double doors that led into the main chamber. Waiting patiently for her, Christine was met with a smile and a raised eyebrow by the Master of Ceremonies, flanked with numerous Courtiers. She acknowledged them all with a smile of her own and a quick nod of her head, then indicated to him she was ready for the doors to be opened to make her entrance into the large hall beyond. With that signal, the Imperial fanfare began, only slightly muffled through the heavy doors. After a short time, the fanfare finished, the last echoes fading away. The doors slowly opened, silent on well-maintained hinges and Christine walked into a wave of applause, feeling the sudden surge of excitement from the assembled group as they caught sight of her.

"*Here we go again,*" she thought.

Alexander, together with Ambassador Gallagher and his aide Collinson, watched the interrogation of a captured citizen through a one-way, smart-metal wall, listening to what was said via the ship's AI. It was running a sophisticated translation programme, capturing every inflexion and nuance of the conversation. As the interrogation progressed, their earlier suspicions had been confirmed. It became apparent a third party had been secretly active on the planet for many years, well before the Empire's presence was officially made known. This third-party had kept itself hidden from the watching Imperial monitors who had been tasked with ensuring non-interference, which implied a well-organised and obviously well-funded conspiracy. The prisoner currently being interviewed was a mid-level cleric, literally tripping over his words in eagerness to demonstrate how they had seen through the Empire's lies and deceits. As he spoke, the full picture began to emerge.

Subtly, and over many years, long before the Empire formally introduced itself as a prelude to Ascension, the infiltrators had turned the planet's global religion against the idea of off-worlders. Once the Empire made itself known, it began spreading stories of how Emperor worship would, on pain of death, forcibly supplant their own faith and enslave the population. Tales of planets being sequestered and their populations moved into death camps were promoted, until the ranking religious leaders ordered the faithful to fight these devilish strangers and declared holy war. This prisoner's story matched all the others who had been questioned, including those taken in subsequent snatch raids on the surface.

From a four-thousand-year perspective of scientific and social enlightenment, it was hard for Gallagher to understand how an otherwise intelligent, well-educated and advanced society could become so wrapped up with religious fervour and fear.

"What are we going to do now Alex?" Gallagher asked, "Do we bomb them back into the Stone Age and come back in several hundred years; let them be but isolate them completely with a small task force for a similar period, or try and show them the truth? Whatever we chose it's going to be very costly in public opinion, manpower, resources, time, effort and lives."

Alexander shook his head. "Whatever we do will have unintended consequences, Patrick. Any of the three options would work, but I'm not in the right state of mind to make a rational decision now, not immediately after the loss of my Marines and the problem of Adam."

Patrick nodded and looked sympathetic. "We have two days before the Ascension fleet arrives that was meant to bring the planet into the Empire. It can support any decision you or the Imperial Council make. As it was planned to be on station for several years without relief, we can leave them here, return home and either pass this hot potato on to the Council for a decision or get them to rubber stamp whatever you decide here on the ground. For what it's worth, do you want my opinion?"

"Whenever haven't you given it to me, wanted or not, hmmm?" Alexander replied, smiling. He looked his friend in the eyes.

Patrick returned the gaze and began. "These people were duped into attacking us. Stupid of them, yes, but without outside influences turning them against us, the result might have been a new planet for the Empire instead of a new problem. Let's surprise them by not seeking revenge as they expect us to. However, leaving them alone would simply increase the problem over time, perhaps resulting at some future point in our having to sterilise the planet and starting again from scratch with colonists." He continued, "No, let's take the hard option and use the Ascension fleet to educate and show them what the Empire really stands for. It's the hardest and costliest option but the one I believe we should take."

"You do realise there is a strong possibility they won't even engage with us at all, Patrick?" asked Alexander.

"I never said it would be easy, did I?" came the reply. "But it's the right thing to do. Let's give the Ascension fleet three years, and if there's no progress at the end, we always have options one and two. Who knows, someone might even come up with a better idea in that time."

Turning to Collinson, Alexander surprised the aide by asking him a question, "What do you think Lieutenant? What would you do if you were in my position?"

Snapping to attention, a surprised Collinson immediately answered, "Oh, well, Sire I'd um, not make any decision just yet. It is apparent religion plays a large part in these people's lives, and the religious leaders have a great deal of control over how they think. In light of this, are they really ready to join the Empire at all, despite their meeting the criteria? I'd attempt a dialogue with the spiritual leaders first, as they are the ones to convince and get onto our side. After that, the sheep will follow, Sire," he finished, relaxing a bit now that he had spoken.

Alexander nodded, "Good points Lieutenant. Thank you for your advice." He turned back to Patrick. "I've two days to make my decision, then we will return home with the flagship. I'm afraid your family will have to wait a few days longer before they get to see you, old friend." He sent a private message to Gallagher. *"I sent the yacht I'd promised you away with Adam, along with a full copy of Vimes to keep him company. The other yachts aren't really suitable for such long flights."*

Before replying, Patrick paused for a moment, remembering something from long ago, wondering to himself where all the years had gone. He gave a mental nod.

"Given their current relationship, sending Vimes along was cruel but necessary, Alex. If neither this experience nor Vimes can get Adam to face up to his responsibilities, nothing will. Either way, he'll certainly come back a changed man."

Alexander looked away from his friend and back to the interrogation. *"If only all our problems could be sent away, Patrick. If it were only that simple."*

They listened to the interrogation for a while longer, until it became apparent nothing else of use would be achieved by continuing, so Alexander ordered it to cease, and the prisoner sent back to a holding cell to stay with others. Secretly listening in on what was being discussed in the holding cell had already added to their understanding, providing valuable insight into the peoples' faith, the true nature of which had been carefully concealed from the Imperial diplomats sent to smooth the Ascension path. Parting company, Gallagher went off with his aide while Alexander retired to his private offices to catch up on business.

On reaching his offices, Alexander asked Vimes to run a security sweep and lock down his suite.

"*I'll be sending some private messages to Christine and need to warn her to be on guard,*" he thought to Vimes. "*Also, you can update yourself back at the Capital and upload all the latest developments from home.*"

"*Rooms are locked down and clear Alex,*" Vimes confirmed after a few seconds. "*I'm linking now with the ships AI to ensure we won't be disturbed.*"

A few minutes later the secure, ultra-secret real-time Quantum Attraction communication device made contact with the version of Vimes back on Capital. As Alexander sat down behind his desk, a holographic display appeared in front of him. Showing nothing except static it resolved itself into the simulacrum that Vimes used when he needed a public face. "Good evening Alex, I trust my doppelganger has been behaving himself?" the Vimes on Capital asked with a smile.

"You should know," Alex replied. "Is Christine about?"

"No Alex, she retired to bed several hours ago after a long day. Forgetting to check the time difference before calling is not a good sign," Vimes replied, pausing as he synced with his counterpart, "Ah, I see why now. I'll begin discretely arranging transports and arrangements for the families of the injured and bereaved so once the official news has reached them in a few days' time, everything will be ready and the needed support in place." Vimes continued, "Shall I wake Christine?"

"No, please let her sleep," replied Alexander. "I'll record a personal message for Christine to read when she wakes. After she has, please see to it that she isn't disturbed for a while. Rearrange meetings if you have to."

The image of Vimes grew serious. "I have begun increasing security levels and will inform the Palace Guard to begin a series of "exercises" over the coming days. Anything else you would like me to do?"

"Just one thing Vimes, whoever planned this needed access to information and more importantly, money and ships to get here without using Jump Points, which means through normal space. Financing both will have been costly given our control over shipping. Start checking financial records of the major Corporations and Conglomerates for signs of curious transactions, unexplained drops in cash-flow, that sort of thing." He stopped and thought for a moment before continuing. "Check ship manifests, departures and arrivals and anything else you can think of near this system. Begin querying the financial affairs of Dukes, Marquises and Earls, paying particular attention to, and starting with, those nearest to here, then move outwards. Oh, I nearly forgot; pull the servicing records of all privately owned ships over the past five years and look for anomalies such as soil and vegetation samples from air filters, etc. that match with this planets profile."

"Yes, Alex. When ready, did you want me to copy Christine with the findings then forward them to yourself as we are communicating now or await your return to Capital?" Vimes enquired.

Alexander considered for a moment.

"Yes, send immediately you have anything of note and copy in Christine. Finally, please check five years' worth of sales on antique markets, collectors' forums and memorabilia auctions for any items offered for sale which match anything in this planets database. Someone may have become greedy or decided to make some additional money on the side."

"Noted. Good idea, Alex," replied Vimes. "Unless there is anything else you want me to do, I'll stay online and await your private message."

Alexander nodded at the image on the screen, before recording the message updating his wife on what had transpired and why he had brought forward plans to send their son away. It was going to be a long one...

Ten hours into his long flight to reach the outer system Jump Point, Adam was currently refusing to talk to Vimes. Despite Vimes's best efforts, had been unable to coach anything from him, other than a yes or no, so had decided to let Adam stew in his own juice for a while longer, knowing that he'd have to come around eventually.

The two of them had stopped being on good terms many years before. When aged thirteen the Prince had tried unsuccessfully to smuggle a girlfriend into his suite at the Imperial Palace, using the woodlands surrounding the garden as cover. Vimes had alerted the Palace Guard, and the girl had been sent back to her parents with a stern warning. From then on, in a display of stubbornness, Adam had preferred using a stripped-down version of Vimes which lacked most of the personality and critical functions, claiming his thoughts were his own and no-one else's. On turning eighteen, Adam had left the Palace and rented a large suite nearby in the main city, conversing with Vimes only when absolutely necessary.

For the first hour of the trip, Adam sat, lost in his own thoughts and misery, still stunned at his father's decision to send him away. Of course, he knew that joining the Imperial Navy was going to happen at some point in his life, but just not this soon. For a while, he thought perhaps his father was trying to teach him a short lesson and Vimes would eventually turn the yacht around and take him back to the flagship, at which point he would be given another lecture and possibly restricted to his quarters for a few days. When it became apparent this wasn't going to happen, Adams shock had turned to anger, and he'd tried to take it out on Vimes by shouting at him, demanding that he turn the yacht around. When Vimes refused to comply and instead presented a copy of the Imperial edict and letter of introduction to Commodore Haynes on the nearest screen, Adam's anger subsided and turned into resignation. Currently,

Adam was sitting on a sofa in the main cabin, numb, a black mood of despair threatening to overwhelm him.

"Incoming recognition request, Adam," said Vimes, breaking him out of his self-pity. "It's from the Ascension fleet which we will be passing in forty-five minutes. Sending response now."

Adam looked up. "Show me."

Immediately a large viewscreen appeared on the wall opposite his sofa, displaying an image of the star field outside. The magnification increased until hundreds of blue points of light began to appear, spread out in a regular pattern.

"I've marked the position in blue as the ships are currently not visible to the naked eye," said Vimes. "As you will learn, anyone approaching naval vessels must identify themselves or risk being fired on." He continued, "I've sent our ID codes so we will pass by without any trouble. Nothing for you to do except sit there and wallow in your own pity."

"Damn you, Vimes," Adam shouted at the ceiling. "You're enjoying this, aren't you? Admit it, you old bastard."

Vimes chuckled out loud, deliberately to annoy Adam further.

"Yes, I must admit a certain pleasure, Adam. But it's not what you think. I am looking forward to getting to know you again over the next few weeks, without the distractions of having to attend to the Emperor. At least you are now talking to me even if it is only to be rude." Vimes continued, "Adam, I have been the personal aide to every Emperor, from when Josef wrote my first basic programme right through four thousand years of improvements, additions, and changes to my matrix. Each Emperor has left a bit of themselves with me; imprinted a little of their personalities you might say." Vimes paused for effect, "I am the sum of all their experiences, memories, hopes, fears, and dreams for the future. One day I hope you too will share a bit of yourself so that I can add to a future Emperor's wisdom and so benefit the Empire and your successors. Assuming you survive long enough to succeed your father, that is."

"Why shouldn't I succeed Vimes?" asked Adam sarcastically. "Do you know something I don't?"

"Adam, I will happily share with you the views of your father and Ambassador Gallagher about what happened back on Heaven and the ramifications for what this means in the Empire. However, I would prefer you to try and think them through yourself. Indulge an old programme by telling me your views first. Please? It will help you pass the time."

With nothing better to do, Adam thought for a few moments, going over in his mind what he'd bothered to learn about Heaven before the attack. His father had tried to explain some things in the transit tube yesterday, but he'd not been paying too much attention and now struggled to remember what had been said to him.

"OK," he began slowly, "Heaven, like all pre-space-flight civilisations, was embargoed and protected by the Empire until it developed manned space flight. Outside contact was prohibited, and the Jump Point to this star system was only available to authorised vessels or personnel, ensuring the planet could develop naturally without interference."

Warming to the subject, Adam started to regain some of his normal good humour as he thought about something other than self-pity. He ran his hands through the mop of curls on his head and clasped them behind his neck, stretching.

He continued, "That gives us three possibilities. First, they came up with this plan themselves. Second, someone from outside has found another Jump Point in this system we don't know about, which is very unlikely, or came here via normal space and fed them lies. Third, someone in the Empire subverted or tricked a Jump Station into letting them through." He finished, "I can't think of anything else."

"Good," said Vimes, "they are effectively the same conclusions that we came up with. Now, what are the ramifications for each of the three? Take your time, Adam."

"If it's the first, then we have a problem with the population of Heaven being assimilated into the Empire in the near to middle future," he began. "They've demonstrated an unusual aggressiveness and willingness to take on a much larger and more powerful foe, and for no apparent reason. Not good."

"If it's the second, then it's part of a long-term conspiracy or plan. Even allowing for a constant one-G acceleration, it's a fifteen-light year journey from the nearest star in real space. That's some, hmm, five and a half years ship and around seventeen years real time allowing for time dilation. That's a big ship, big expense and a lot of forward planning."

Adam scratched the back of his neck for a moment before continuing. "That would mean someone very wealthy and powerful in the Empire is behind this, probably at least an Earl or more likely a Duke controlling an entire sector. If it's not that, then it has to be one or more of the emerging powers, probably reptilian as most of the smaller human empires we've discovered apparently want to remain friends with us. However, the reptilians are good at cunning but tend to lack patience and long-term strategic planning. Finally, I don't think there's a hidden Jump Point."

Adam yawned, tired from doing nothing meaningful since getting on the yacht. "As for the third option, that troubles me. It would mean Imperial records have been doctored and officials bribed, possibly even in the Navy itself. Again, with this option, it would take a great deal of money and influence to achieve this, pointing once more towards someone in the nobility or another power."

He puffed his cheeks and blew out a long, controlled breath. "If it's either of the last two, Vimes, I suppose we have a big problem as it's either a prelude to war or a rebellion."

Vimes let Adam think through what he'd just said before saying anything himself, hoping the young man would see the obvious reason why his father wanted him safely away from the intrigue.

Adam stood up and stretched. "I'm not happy Vimes, but I understand a bit better why father wanted me gone and a lot of distance between us. He wants to keep me out of harm's way." He paused, realising what Vimes had done. "Clever, you making me work it out for myself. You do know you're a manipulative bastard, don't you? But thank you anyway, I feel a bit better now I understand why father sent me away."

If Vimes could have smiled at that moment, he would. "All part of the service Adam, all part of the service."

Adam looked around the cabin. Luxuriously, yet simply furnished with relatively few items, it reflected his father's current taste. "*Simple but good,*" he thought, thinking back to the family suite back home on Capital. He missed the gardens and woodlands now more than anything, given he was unlikely to see them for the best part of a year. "*With any luck, father will have gotten to the bottom of all of this, and it will be safe for me to return,*" he thought, a little ruefully.

"There are several other factors for you to consider Adam," Vimes continued, interrupting his train of thought. "After we left, your father sent me an update with details gleaned from several interrogations that took place. The religious leaders of the planet had been convinced that we were going to forcibly change their religious beliefs and enslave them. Apparently, Gallagher and the other diplomats failed to notice how deeply held their religious beliefs were as they gave no indication of extremism. There are also strong indications of this religious fervour being whipped up by third parties who are almost certainly from outside of their system. I've downloaded a copy to your moronic aide should you wish to view them, along with tactical data and summaries. I will, of course, keep myself updated on any additional information that comes in until we make the Jump Point."

The two of them chatted for another hour, reminiscing about things they had done before the incident with the girl, Eventually, Adam admitted to himself that Vimes had changed somewhat and wasn't necessarily the pain in the royal backside he had once thought him to be. A little more at peace with his fate, Adam got to his feet and yawned loudly.

"Vimes," he called out, walking to the bedroom, "I'm going to bed now. Can you arrange for a light breakfast tomorrow, please?"

"Certainly, Adam," Vimes replied, "sleep well. I'll wake you at seven. Pleasant dreams."

"Make it ten, Vimes" Adam responded, closing his room door.

"Seven," said Vimes quietly to the closed door and no-one in particular.

Over breakfast the next morning, Adam chatted with Vimes about the latest reports sent from the flagship and updates from around the Empire that had come in from the Ascension fleet. Problems had broken out on the border between Sector Twelve and the Dubunni, a small empire of fifty-two systems that were on/off allies with their own neighbour the Silures, who bordered Sector Thirteen. Both of these rival Empires were human and coveted the same planets, resulting in occasional clashes in unclaimed border space. Also, they found the restrictions placed on them expanding past or through Imperial space hard to accept and regularly tested the Empire's patience. Duke Frederick and Duchess Helena, rulers of Sectors Twelve and Thirteen respectively, were together requesting the appearance of the Emperor and Dauntless to calm matters or take the lead in punitive action.

Adam guessed his father would be heading out there once he'd decided on what to do in this system, possibly stopping off at Capital to see mother first. In the ten years following his twelfth birthday, he'd not seen that much of his father, maybe only a years' worth in total, and his mother perhaps a little more. Although they contacted him regularly, affairs of Empire and his stubbornness meant his education and upbringing had for the most part been left to family advisors and retainers.

Adam watched a humanoid servitor soundlessly clear away from his table. It moved with fluidity and grace, reminding him of his last pet, a cat he'd named Peter. Aged eight at the time, Adam had found Peter wandering the woods one day.

"*Actually*," Adam thought, "*If I'm honest, it was the other way around. Peter found me in those woods.*" The cat had followed him home and became his closest friend and companion until its death ten years later. Heartbroken and feeling true loss for the first time, Adam had buried him in the woods near the spot they'd first met, erecting a little smart-metal monument to his old friend. Soon afterwards he'd moved out of the Palace.

"Vimes," Adam asked, "Why are there so few servitor Androids outside of the royal household? Why don't we use them more, you know, for the basic jobs and such like?"

The servitor turned around and spoke with Vimes' voice, startling Adam and making him jump.

"There are several reasons, Adam." The servitor's eyebrows raised in surprise at his startled expression. "Apologies for startling you, but surely you hadn't forgotten that I control everything on this yacht, including the maintenance and assistance droids? From your expression, I can see you had. Never mind."

"You did that deliberately, didn't you?" Adam responded, but not getting a reply.

The servitor turned back and continued out into the small galley where food was prepared. Adam moved over to his favoured armchair and sat down, crossing his legs and took a drink from the glass he'd carried over from the table.

On the opposite wall, a viewscreen appeared, showing various Android designs over the ages, along with dates of manufacture and what they were used for. Vimes began an audio-visual narration, displaying relevant information on the screen to highlight his answer.

"The simple reason is to preserve human dignity," began Vimes. "As populations grew and lived longer through better medical and scientific breakthroughs, so did pressures on society. In the early years of Empire, production became increasingly automated. Few traditional sources of employment were unaffected. This increasingly led to mass unemployment and lower wages, which in turn reduced the number of people who could afford to buy the very products that automation produced. Lacking experience, the youngest in the labour force found it hardest of all to find work when competing with their experienced, older colleagues."

The screen switched to an image of the earliest android.

"The problem was compounded further once androids were introduced into the labour market, effectively making most of the remaining unskilled or semi-skilled workforce redundant. The social upheaval that followed came to a head in the year 620, in the reign of Emperor Justinian the first. Because of civil unrest, he wisely passed the Android Laws which restricted their use outside of the nobility for other than dangerous or lethal work."

"Lethal work?" asked Adam, not understanding.

"Mine clearance, cleaning up radioactive fall-out, that sort of thing," responded Vimes. "By restricting their use and gradually phasing them out, Justinian was able to defuse the growing problem. As the years went past, save for boring or very repetitive work best left to machinery, humans took back their old jobs. Increasingly longer and more active lifespans were also a significant deciding factor. Bored, poor people become restive and start demanding change. No Emperor, no matter how powerful, can stand for long against a population united by poverty and unhappiness."

Adam thought for a moment before asking a question. "But surely the Empire is now so far removed from those old times that we can provide well for all our citizens without the need for them to work?"

"In theory, yes," responded Vimes, shutting down the images. "But you forget one constant that never changes; human nature. Active, gainful employment has the benefit of providing people with the means to buy luxury goods, gives purpose to their lives and encourages social interaction."

Adam looked thoughtful. "But surely people would prefer to stay at home or do the things they wanted to do rather than work? Wouldn't they?"

"You think that way now because you are young and everything is new and fresh to you," replied Vimes. "You will find that as you get older, it becomes harder to find interests or things you haven't already done at some point. Having a job provides direction and meaning to the lives of many, expanding their social circles and bringing new skills. Being the Crown Prince, you are divorced from ordinary people and have little idea of how they live and order their lives. You surely understand that."

Vimes continued, "Statistically, your citizens change jobs every eight point three years, each time mastering new skills and abilities. The majority do this all through their working lives and, on stopping work, use the contacts and knowledge they have gained from years of employment to enhance their final years."

"Is that why joining the Navy is such a sought-after profession then, Vimes?" asked Adam.

"Partly, Adam. I am disappointed that you need to ask the question. There are certainly many skills and experiences to be learnt and enjoyed in the Navy. Also, off-world travel is another significant factor given only a small percentage of non-military ever get the chance to leave their home planet or visit another system. Another reason is the chance to become active in the running of their home planet. Career military who leave with a distinguished service record automatically obtain a right to vote on planetary affairs. That is a much sought-after privilege. Finally, many relish the idea of having the chance to experience actual combat, strange as that may seem to you."

Adam had been gently nodding at the answers, "I suppose I did know but never really put all the things together like that," he said.

"Well," said Vimes, "We have a long journey ahead of us, so if you are willing, I can bring you up to speed on a large number of topics. Now might be an opportune moment for us to discuss what your position will be with Commodore Haynes, so here's another cup of coffee to help you concentrate," said Vimes via a servitor who had appeared unnoticed behind his right shoulder, gently placing a fresh cup on the small table. Adam jumped again.

"VIMES!" he exclaimed with a smile, "I know you did that deliberately. Give me some warning next time!"

Christine listened to the message from her husband with growing alarm, shocked to her core at how close a call it had been. If not for blind luck and her wayward son's behaviour, she might have lost them both. As she listened, her emotions switched between anger, fear and relief, for a while almost rendering her too shocked and angry to think straight.

Before telling her of the message and anticipating with his usual thoughtfulness she might not want to attend breakfast, Vimes had sent a selection of food items along with a variety of alcoholic drinks and assorted pharmaceutical products for calming her nerves. Seeing these arrive before reading the message had warned her bad news was coming, and she'd opened the message from Alex with trepidation. Rising from her chair, she paced around the room, needing to lose some of the nervous energy that threatened to send her running out into the gardens and scream out loud with frustration. Her first instinct was to don an armoured suit herself and take an automated battlecruiser to meet her husband and protect him, but she knew it was impractical and a pointless gesture to even contemplate and might raise questions as to how she got there so quickly.

"No," she said out loud, marshalling her thoughts, "they are both in the best place. My son's out of harm's way, and Alex is on board the flagship. There's nothing I can do that will make either of them safer at this point. He made the correct decision in sending Adam off for training."

She stopped pacing and walked over to the window.

"Vimes, what additional security measures have you taken?" she asked, knowing that in his capacity as her personal bodyguard he would already have taken a number of steps without first seeking her permission.

"The intrasystem Grand Fleet has been put on General Alert with security tightened at the Jump Point, Christine. I've also moved twenty battle cruisers into a geosynchronous orbit over the Palace, sufficient to deter any ship from approaching.

Interdiction around and above the Palace has been increased, and the Imperial Bodyguard have begun discrete manoeuvres throughout the grounds under the pretext of "additional practice." If, and it's a big if, there are any hostiles currently on Capital then they will know that security has been raised, but as far as the general population is concerned nothing will be out of the ordinary. I can assure you nothing unauthorised can get into the Palace grounds without my knowing about it. Any questions?"

"So, nothing can get through, you say? Not even a girl of fifteen going on twenty with ideas to bag herself a Prince, eh Vimes?" Christine replied. "Adam almost managed to smuggle her into his room, and he was only twelve at the time."

"Ouch, that was a low blow, Christine," said Vimes with a noticeable wince to his voice, "remember, he had an almost fully functioning version of myself to assist at the time. I can assure you something like that would never happen again."

"My apologies, Vimes. It was a low blow, but I'm so angry right now I want to break something. I know you understand." Christine paused for a moment and gently bit her lower lip. "Thank you for rescheduling this morning's meetings. When will the financial data be ready that Alex requested?

Vimes hesitated for a moment, checking updates on the requests. "I've used our private IQA transmitters to request the data from my counterparts at all the Central Banks across the Empire, using our access codes. This will take at least fifteen days, probably more. The non-financial information will have to come through normal channels and be acted on in person by our representatives on those planets, so allow twenty-five days."

"How long will it take you to assimilate the financials once they've arrived?" Christine asked.

"I'm anticipating a huge volume of information which, even for me, will take several days to collate properly. I will not be able to devote more computational time to it without compromising other functions such as planetary security, which is something I am prevented from doing."

"By Alex I suppose," Christine said as a statement rather than a question.

"Yes, Christine. He was very insistent on that point yesterday."

She began pacing around the room again and thought hard. Realistically, there was nothing constructive to be done until the information was all in, and even then, it would be some time before anything useful would be found, if at all. Priding herself on being logical, Christine decided to compartmentalise these latest developments and get on with her daily routine until there was something concrete to work with.

"Thank you, Vimes. Let me know the moment you have anything, no matter what I'm doing at the time." She paused for a moment then continued, "Have I enough time to make the regular breakfast meeting?"

"Yes, but only if you hurry. I'll inform them you will be attending after all but might be a few minutes late," Vimes answered as she walked quickly to the bathroom.

Fifteen minutes later, her hair still slightly damp, Christine was striding purposefully across the garden towards the Refectory. Behind it and to the left and right she could see the morning sun reflecting off two large lakes. The morning was much warmer than the previous day, and this time there wasn't any morning dew to mark her path across the lawn. Unusually, she wasn't enjoying the scents and beautiful scenery, her mind too engaged with events. The fiasco at Heaven and her son being sent away for his training kept going through her mind as if it was on a continuous loop, despite her best efforts to compartmentalise it away. However, as she walked through the gardens, Christine found the impact of the shocking news begin to fade from her mind once she began focusing on the day's business. Thanks to Vimes's rescheduling, she was free after breakfast until midday, when there was a fortuitously pre-booked meeting with General Parmenion, Commander of the Palace Bodyguard. Christine planned to go over the additional security measures with him and together consider any additional ones he might recommend. However, before their meeting, she would walk through the gardens to relax, as she wanted to meet with him in a calm state of mind.

Walking into the Refectory, she motioned everyone to sit down as they began to rise for her. She smiled warmly at the new faces and nodded in recognition at the more familiar ones. Spotting an empty seat, she walked towards it before sitting down and greeting those on either side of her.

Despite herself, she couldn't help but wonder for a moment whether anyone here today might be party to a wider conspiracy. Dismissing the thought as a little paranoid, she signalled the waiters to bring everyone food. Leaning back in her seat she allowed them to begin loading the table with fresh fruits, scrambled eggs, meats and assorted cereals. Once done and the table full, she reached over and helped herself to a glass of fresh orange juice.

"Please everyone, don't stand on ceremony, start," she said, motioning towards the food. At that, everyone began to help themselves and started talking to their neighbours, continuing conversations stopped when she'd made her entrance.

Once talk around the table had reached a point where her pulling back a little wouldn't be noticed, Christine let it all wash over her while mentally picturing the Dukes and Duchesses who potentially had most to gain from the ambush. Most of the Nobles were from long-established families, in the main descended from Emperor Joscf's original team of scientists and adventurers who were there at the beginning and had helped him forge the Empire. Following the Succession War that took the life of her husband's parents and family, four Dukes had been executed, but as Alex had replaced them with old comrades who'd fought by his side and remained loyal, it was easy to dismiss these new nobles from her calculations. Sadly, the list of possible names was too long, so she decided to focus on what had just happened to him and extrapolate forward from there.

The planet Heaven was located in Sector Eleven, currently controlled by the Imperial Council on behalf of the young Duke James who would not take control until he was twenty-one years old, some nine years away. Fortunately, this Sector bordered space claimed by the Durotriges, a loose confederation of small, but powerful human empires that constantly fought amongst themselves rather than encroach on space claimed by the Empire. The long border between themselves and their human neighbours, the Dubunni Empire, was currently peaceful, but Christine knew that Duke Frederick was complaining loudly of problems with Dubunni raiders attacking ships in neutral space and had requested assistance.

"*Is this the next flashpoint?*" Christine wondered, thinking hard. "*A Sector with a young Duke and warring neighbours who all just happen to be next to each other? Or is this all too obvious? Too many questions and not enough information to go by,*" she thought, sighing with frustration and feeling her anger start to bubble through again. "*I really do need to work off this feeling or hit something. Hard.*"

"Is everything all right Ma'am?" asked the young man seated on her right, bringing her back to the present.

She looked at him, noticing properly for the first time that he almost glowed with good health and exuded an air of physical competence. His green-brown eyes were set off by long lashes and with his full sensuous mouth, was very handsome. Long brown hair, bleached several shades lighter by hours spent in the open, framed a face which the sun had deeply tanned from its natural light coffee colour.

"No, I'm fine, thank you," she responded, "I was just thinking about the day ahead and all the meetings and decisions that have to be made. What about you, anything interesting for you today?"

He smiled, making his open face even more appealing.

"Back to tending the woodlands, Ma'am. I'm in one of the teams that care for the forests around the Palace, and I'm currently working on cleaning and restoring the many statues which are now virtually lost and overgrown. It's hard physical work, but as I like being in the open air and feeling the sun on my face, it's something I really enjoy. I often pitch camp where I'm working and sleep outdoors rather than go back to my quarters. Do you ever get much chance to visit the woodlands?" he enquired.

"Not as much as I would like, although when the Crown Prince was much younger, we often camped out under the stars and pretended to live rough."

She chuckled at the old memory that seemed so long ago, although only ten years had passed. Strangely knocked off balance by the young man, she called up his profile and quickly scanned it.

"*Francis De'ath, thirty years old, single, no living family, clean record, worked in our service for five years, first time at breakfast.... originally from Xipe, a farm planet in Sector Four...*" The information flowed through her mind in an instant before coming to an interesting note appended to his profile and highlighted by Vimes, "*Honourable discharge from Marines before twelve-month basic training ended upon diagnosis of Berserker rage syndrome brought on by extreme combat conditions. Recommended for Palace service by Duke Michael himself.*"

Slightly taken aback by the last sentence, Christine looked hard at Francis and asked the obvious question. "How do you know Duke Michael, Francis?"

His smile grew wider at the question, "I don't Ma'am, but my father did. He saved the Duke's life during the Succession War, or so I've been told. After Dad died in a farming accident, the Duke took me under his wing from a distance, so to speak. I didn't have anyone to sponsor me into the Marines, so he stepped in and when that..." He paused for a moment and stopped smiling, then continued, "Didn't work out, he recommended me for service here."

"Ah, I see," said Christine. "I notice from your face there are some painful memories, but as far as I'm concerned the Marines' loss is our gain. My husband and I are very pleased to have you here with us and anyone recommended by the Iron Duke himself doubly so."

Francis blushed, his face deepening in colour underneath the tan and regaining some of its earlier smile.

"Thank you, Ma'am, I really appreciate that," he said, catching her eyes with his own and holding them for a moment before looking down at his food.

Aware that something had happened in the exchange, Christine nodded and turned away to talk to the matronly figure on her left, but not before making a mental note to watch the progress of this one.

Breakfast finally over, Christine waited until the last of her guests had left before finally leaving the Refectory. Instead of heading off for her planned walk through the woods she headed back to her apartments. Reaching her private quarters, she went over to her desk and asked Vimes for a smart-metal station. A hand-sized hole appeared on the right of her desk and she placed her hand into it. Smart-metal began flowing into her bracelet, which steadily grew in size and thickness before extending up from her wrist to elbow. She thought for a few seconds about what design to have, before sending it to the metal for incorporation onto its surface. Removing her hand, the pattern in her mind had been faithfully incorporated onto the surface of the armband. Christine twisted her arm around, admiring the design and smiling at how it had been faithfully copied into the metal. Although aesthetically pleasing, if required, the metal could change into a small anti-personnel weapon similar to the flechette design incorporated into her personal armour, albeit considerably smaller and less powerful. It would rely on power from either the ever-present energy transmissions suffusing the Palace and grounds or, in an emergency, the superconductor batteries cleverly concealed in her clothes and shoes. Until activated, it looked nothing more than a large ornamental armband, easily hidden under her sleeve until required.

"*Just in case,*" she thought grimly, muttering quietly, "Better safe than sorry," using an old expression from her childhood,

General Parmenion was a patient man, slow to anger and normally very calm. On numerous occasions, colleagues had likened him to a slow-burning fuse, one that burnt quietly for a time before exploding violently at the end. It was rare for any kind of alert to be called without informing him first, if only as a courtesy. When coupled with instructions to run "practice" drills throughout the Palace grounds and surrounding woodlands, he knew there must be good reasons to be concerned that he wasn't yet privy to. This rankled him, but as he had a good working relationship with the Empress, he fully expected to be briefed at today's meeting.

As a courtesy to him, Christine normally attended monthly strategy meetings at the Barracks where he lived, situated several kilometres away in the woodlands to the North-West of the Palace, overlooking a large spaceport that was ringed on all sides by military and associated administrative buildings. For this meeting, however, at the last minute, Vimes had changed the venue to a room in the Empress's private quarters overlooking the Palace gardens.

Various beverages and assorted foods had been laid out next to a floor to ceiling window that ran along one entire side of the room. From here, the Refectory was clearly visible a few hundred metres away. Behind it lay two large lakes, only partially hidden by a smattering of ancient trees and the ornamental gardens. Beyond the garden, trees became more frequent, gradually thickening to become a forest, through which tiny glimpses of two much larger lakes could be seen. Beyond them, and to the left, were the barracks and spaceport, completely hidden from view.

From this centrally placed room, almost all of the Palace was visible, sweeping gracefully away on both sides in a graceful arc. To his right, and at the easternmost tip of the Palace, sat the Grand Hall of the Empire where almost every Emperor had been crowned. Originally a separate building, it had been incorporated into the Palace over a thousand years previously. At the other end of the Palace sat smaller audience rooms used for less imposing meetings or ceremonies.

As Parmenion debated whether to avail himself of a drink, Vimes informed him that Christine was approaching. Without fanfare, she entered the room a few seconds later and walked towards him, grasping his hand in a firm grip of welcome. Looking Parmenion in the eyes, she spoke first.

"Apologies, Parmenion, for not informing you in advance of the alerts and heightened security. Late last night, intelligence came to light of an imminent threat to the Royal family and immediate action was called for, hence why you were not informed in advance. As everything was in hand, Vimes decided to wait until our meeting so I could update you personally."

Christine paused for effect before continuing, "At this point, we do not know if it is aimed at us here on Capital or elsewhere in the Empire, but we are taking no chances. Vimes has sent an urgent message to inform the Emperor who by now should have completed the Ascension ceremonies at Heaven, in Sector Eleven."

Christine never liked misleading people, preferring to be honest and forthright at all times, but the closely guarded secret of instantaneous communication could not be jeopardised, even to someone as completely trustworthy as Parmenion, so she had to obscure the truth as to why she had suddenly tightened security.

His eyes narrowed the barest fraction, the only glimpse she could see that the wily old General had any suspicion he was not being told everything, but she knew he would keep any doubts firmly to himself.

"Can I get you anything, Christine?" Parmenion asked, gesturing at the table in front of him.

"Tea, as usual, please, with a little milk today," she replied. "Thank you," taking the proffered cup and moving with him to stand alongside the window.

The clean smell of freshly cut grass was being transmitted into the room from outside, reinforcing the illusion of space and airiness given by the large floor to ceiling window.

"It all looks so peaceful today, you wouldn't think we control an Empire from here would you, Parmenion?" she stated rather than asked.

"No Christine, you wouldn't," he replied, "but like the swans on the lake over there, we are paddling furiously underwater to maintain a serene demeanour above."

Christine smiled, revealing faint laughter lines at the corner of her eyes which were one of the few tell-tales that betrayed her age. "That analogy always makes me smile. It's so apt for our current situation."

Gesturing towards two leather chairs near the window, Christine walked over to them and sat down, closely followed by Parmenion.

"What other steps do you believe we need to take, given the possibility of the intelligence being correct?" she asked, knowing he would have already scanned the summary Vimes had just sent him.

Parmenion gestured towards the window, at which point a section of it turned opaque and began displaying tactical information relayed to it via his implant. It now displayed an aerial view of the Palace grounds taken from low orbit, showing in blue all troop dispositions. As he began setting out his additional recommendations, the display changed, updating itself to mirror the points he was making and provide emphasis where required.

It was going to be another long meeting.

Surprisingly for Adam, his days on the yacht passed quickly. He and Vimes had managed to come to an understanding of sorts, despite the circumstances of them coming together. Adam had to admit Vimes was good company and part of him now regretted the schism which had separated them all those years ago. Grudgingly, Adam also recognised he was the one who had lost out through being stubborn. He'd learnt more about Imperial politics and the workings of Empire from Vimes during these days onboard than in the previous ten years from the various tutors and professors his parents had provided. Somehow, Vimes made it all seem so relevant and interesting, whereas the others had made their subjects seem dry as old bones.

To aid him in assimilating all the data, Adam had even allowed Vimes to bring his implant up to full speed, enabling them to converse, when necessary, at the speed of thought. For the moment, unless there was an emergency, Adam preferred to speak out loud to Vimes, just like his mother. Strangely intimate after so long apart, Vimes had seemed genuinely touched by this acceptance and for the next two days hadn't played any tricks on him, even going so far as to instruct the servitor to make him his favourite food; potato pancakes made with oats, egg, and onion. Over the years, Adam had tried to make them himself, and when they hadn't turned out as he remembered, had some of the finest chefs of Capital try and replicate the taste, but to no avail.

"*If for no other reason, it's for this that's meant this trip hasn't been a complete waste*," he thought contentedly, finishing off his fifth pancake in quick succession.

He could have eaten three times the number, but as they were nearing the Jump Point, Vimes had sent the servitor off to pack away any loose items in preparation for the QA Jump. Following a private message that arrived the previous night from the flagship, Vimes had altered course away from the Imperial Jump Station and would use the ships own QA drive they reached the edge of the system's Jump Point. He had also engaged the cloak and other stealth features to ensure they left unobserved. It was obvious his father wanted to keep his departure and arrival point known to as few people as possible.

Adam walked forward to the flight deck. Although fully automated, the yacht could still be flown manually should circumstances require or, more commonly, simply for the thrill of it. Although his mother was an excellent pilot, she rarely flew herself, but both Adam and Alexander liked to fly whenever the opportunity presented itself. Adam sat down in the pilot's chair and instructed the smart-metal to clear so he could get an unobstructed view of space. Unfortunately, there wasn't currently anything to see this far out on the edge of the system, apart from distant stars and galaxies. Not wishing to fly today, he didn't bother merging with the ship.

"Once we've Jumped I'll send a coded signal to Commodore Haynes advising him of our arrival and estimated transit time, depending on where he is in the system," Vimes advised Adam. "It will be somewhere between seven and ten days before we rendezvous with him, but still plenty of time for us to finish updating you on your duties."

"Vimes," Adam asked, relaxing fully into the chair, "will you be leaving a full copy of yourself with me, or just the old stripped down version?"

"That's up to you Adam," he replied. "Your father didn't give me any instructions not to leave you with a fully functioning copy of myself. Perhaps he assumed you wouldn't want one, so the possibility never crossed his mind. Now that you have reactivated the implant the decision rests with you. Do you want me around?"

"Yes, I do Vimes, please," Adam replied without hesitation, "Strange as it might sound after so long an absence, I think now I would miss not having you around."

He stayed quiet after that, thinking about his parents and what he'd done over the last few years to disappoint them, while at the same time watching the control readouts cycle through the

Jump initiation routines. Behind him, for the first time since boarding, he could hear the yacht's engines start to make a sound other than their usual background thrum. As the energy build up continued, Vimes overlaid onto the field of stars a silent countdown, showing the seconds before initiating the QA drive.

Despite having Jumped on countless occasions in the past, Adam found himself holding onto the armrests as the countdown reached ten seconds.

Suddenly, Adam felt a disturbance in the connection between himself and Vimes, as if his aide's attention had been suddenly withdrawn and focused on something else. "*Aborting Jump sequence, Adam*," Vimes spoke in his mind, as metallic crash restraints suddenly formed over his shoulders and across his waist, holding him tightly into the seat.

"*What's happening, is anything wrong?*" he thought back, the display continuing its tick down to zero.

"*Something's wrong with the command interface which started the moment we reached ten seconds,*" Vimes replied. "*Control has been taken away from me, and the QA destination sequence has been scrambled so I can't abort the Jump nor do I have any control over where we are being sent ...*

Discontinuity

"*...to. Oh! At least we survived; that's good.*"

Moments later, everything shut down, and the thrum of engines ceased. All the displays and the artificial gravity went off, together with main lighting apart from a few emergency backups, leaving Adam with the strange sensation of falling that came with zero gravity. He fought down the urge to vomit up his pancakes and was glad the seat restraints stopped him from floating out of his chair.

"*What's happened Vimes, are we OK?*" he asked, not sure if he wanted to hear the answer.

"*I believe the QA drive and ship's systems were hacked by a semi-sentient Infiltrator Programme, resulting in our making an unknown Jump,*" the reassuringly calm voice of Vimes spoke to him, via the implant. "*I was able to stop the IP from spreading to the ship's engines* and other systems, but only by using an emergency shutdown. I will need to restart each system individually to determine where the IP is residing, then quarantine it for later analysis to try and determine where it came from and who planted it."

"*Why didn't you spot it before?*" Adam asked, "*Surely you run diagnostics and have other safety features which should have picked it up?*"

"*Yes, I do, and I did,*" Vimes replied, sounding a little tetchy, "*unfortunately, the IP was very cleverly written and only became active once the Jump sequence reached a critical point. I suspect but won't know for certain until I have analysed it, that it was designed to either send us to a predetermined point or initiate a cascade failure in the ship's systems and matter conversion engines which would have resulted in our total annihilation. Luckily, I was able to stop both the cascade and its spread by shutting everything down in time.*"

"*What about life-support and that kind of stuff?*" asked Adam, trying to make sense of what he'd been told and his current predicament. "*How long will it take you to get gravity and the essentials back on?*"

Vimes paused for a second then replied. "*An hour for ship's systems to be fully tested, then another hour before I'm satisfied that nothing else has been infected. Don't worry about life support; emergency back-ups have reserves for much longer. My concern is that I am unable to sense anything going on outside the yacht and have no idea if there is anyone or anything out there. From observing the star patterns through the window, I can confirm we are no longer in the Heaven system and have apparently made a safe Jump, but not to our planned destination. With the limited field of vision available to me I am unable to match the visible stars with any known configuration.*"

"*I need to go to the toilet, Vimes. Are they working in zero-G?*"

"*No,*" came the reply, "*they self-sealed when gravity was lost to avoid spilling their contents through the ship. If you are desperate, there are several suits with relief facilities you can use.*"

"*I'll pass on those; I think I can hold on until everything is fixed. What should I do? Can I help in any way?*"

"*That will not be necessary, but thank you for asking,*" Vimes replied, "*However, I recommend you remain in the chair until I tell you otherwise. If the IP had sent us to a predetermined ambush, I feel we would already have been attacked or contacted, but to be safe, please stay where you are, just in case I have to take any sudden action, such as jettisoning you in an emergency pod.*"

"*OK, Vimes, I'll let you get on with it.*"

Adam decided that as he was stuck here, he might as well stay comfortable and try to relax. He had complete faith both in the technology that surrounded him and in the ability of Vimes to fix whatever had gone wrong. It wouldn't be too long before everything was back to normal and they would Jump back to their original destination and continue as planned. Adam called up some music stored in the implant and hoped it would take his mind off the uncomfortable falling sensation in his bladder and stomach.

Adam woke up with a start as the artificial gravity came online, pressing him back down into his seat.

"You dozed off for a while," came the voice of Vimes, "I thought it best you slept during the repairs, so I tweaked your neural patterns a little to encourage you to nap. You must have been tired anyway; otherwise it wouldn't have worked. Don't worry, I won't do it again but as these are not normal circumstances I thought it for the best. If we had been attacked while asleep, you wouldn't have felt a thing."

"Is everything fixed, do you know where we are and who did this to us yet?" asked Adam out loud, releasing the seat restraints and standing up, pleased to feel the floor firmly under his feet. "Toilets?"

"Safe to use, I'll brief you once you get back," Vimes replied, watching Adam walk swiftly to the toilet. A few minutes later he returned, noticeably slower than when he'd left. Sitting back in the chair he told Vimes to update him.

"The good news is that nearly all ship's functions have returned to optimum levels and I have already determined where we are not. The bad news is that we are not in any part of known space, nor can I determine the position of any quasars or other stellar phenomena matching those in our own section of the galaxy. For the moment, we are effectively lost. That's not all. We are unable to Jump or send any QA transmissions as the Infiltrator Programme scrambled the drive and transmitter beyond my ability to repair using resources available to me on the ship."

"What are we to do then? How long are we going to be stuck here for?" asked Adam, sensing he was going to hear something really bad.

"Fortunately, there is an M-Class planet in this system that we can go to. Its indigenous population are human with a rudimentary spaceflight capability. From listening to the electromagnetic transmissions being generated by the population, it would seem they have already visited their orbiting moon, but have not yet built any colonies. A full précis is available should you require it."

"If we are not in the Empire does the Alexander Doctrine still hold true?" he asked, not sure what the answer might be. "And you didn't answer my question. How long are we stuck here for?"

Vimes considered for a fraction of a second before responding. "As to the second part, I don't know yet. As to the first, no Adam, I don't believe it does, however, please consider the ramifications if we should reveal ourselves to the planet's population. I believe in doing so would place you in a very dangerous position, with a strong probability you would be either imprisoned or dissected simply for access to our advanced technologies and your genetic material."

"Why is my genetic material so important?" Adam interrupted.

"Productive lifespans for these people average anywhere between 50 to 70 years, depending on the severity of their lives, with the final third of their total lifespan lived in increasing decrepitude before death," Vimes replied, "that is why they would want access to your superior genome. A cautious approach is in order."

"Travel time to get there?" enquired Adam, hoping he would have enough time to learn the main language of the planet otherwise he would be completely reliant on Vimes to translate for him, which would look odd when trying to communicate.

"I will answer that in a moment, Adam. There are three matters I need to explain to you before we go any further or you make any decisions." Vimes voice took on a serious quality. "There is a secret known only to the Emperor or Empress and their spouse but before I tell you it is imperative that you do not reveal this to anyone should we be successful in returning to the Empire. Do you agree to this?"

"What can be so important that even the Crown Prince has to be sworn to secrecy?" Adam replied, "But yes, I promise not to reveal this to anyone. So, what is it?"

"I can see from your biometric readings you are telling me the truth, so I will continue. This ship is, or was before the IP infection, capable of both making a QA Jump or sending an instantaneous transmission from anywhere within a gravity well."

Adam furrowed his brow, thinking over the revelation and the implications if true, but then why would Vimes lie?

"But that's meant to be impossible. Why would we have Jump Gates and Customs Posts set up if anyone could simply Jump and...oh, I begin to see the implications. The whole fabric of the Empire would be disrupted. Travel between systems becomes faster and cheaper, smuggling becomes impossible to police, criminals can escape to another system at will....no wonder we don't want that secret to come out. It would stop us from controlling travel. Not only that but we lose revenue and our control."

"Yes, Adam, and there's worse. Imagine a fleet of hostile ships that could Jump in close to Capital unannounced and begin bombarding the Imperial Palace, catching everyone unawares. If your father's uncle had access to this technology during the

Succession Wars, your father wouldn't be alive today. Think on that if you are ever tempted to reveal what I have just told you."

Still trying to fully understand the implications of this totally startling news, Adam asked what the second issue was.

"I was not fully able to repair the damage caused by the IP, nor were my attempts to contain it totally successful. We have a short window, sufficient to get us to the habitable third planet and land, but that's all. At some point, I will have to self-destruct this vessel to stop the IP taking control and possibly coming after you. Whoever set this trap was expecting the Emperor to be here, not you, and the IP was instructed to kill anyone left alive should its initial attempt to destroy the ship be unsuccessful. I cannot risk it being clever enough to view you as a worthwhile secondary target of opportunity."

"So, what's the third issue then, Vimes? It can't be any worse than what you've just dropped on me, surely?" Adam asked.

"Good news this time, well, at least for me that is," responded Vimes, sounding slightly more cheerful. "There is another, closely guarded secret that applies to the Imperial bloodline. Being from a non-Royal bloodline, your mother doesn't have it, but you and your Father do as you are blood relatives."

"Have what, Vimes?"

"The implant at the top of your brain stem is not the only means you have of interfacing with me. Please look on the screen for a moment."

A slowly rotating double helix DNA strand appeared on the main screen in front of Adam.

"This is a normal strand of human DNA, Vimes told him. Another helix appeared next to it, this time with a third strand of DNA intertwined around the original two.

"And this is yours. The third strand is unique to the Royal bloodline and is passed down through the family. Now only you and Alexander have this enhancement since the rest of the Royal line was murdered or executed during the war."

Vimes continued, stopping Adam before he could interrupt and ask the obvious question. "No, no need to ask what it does, Adam, I will tell you. It's me. I'm the third DNA strand. Actually, that's not strictly accurate. Think of me as a hive mind with multiple drones such as the mainframe Vimes that controls Capital, the one piloting this ship and the two organic ones that inhabit you and your father."

Seeing the shock on his face, Vimes continued, "If it makes it any easier, think of me as one consciousness but multiple bodies."

Adam was completely taken aback by these revelations and stared at the rotating helices. Vimes dismissed the double helix and enlarged the triple to give him a better look at how it interacted with the original.

"Remember what I told you at the start of this voyage when we first began to be reacquainted?" Vimes asked him. "I said to you, "*I am the sum of all their experiences, memories, hopes, fears and dreams for the future. One day I hope you too will share a bit of yourself so that I can add to the Emperor's wisdom and so benefit the Empire and your successor.*" I told you the truth, just not all of it as I did not know how you would react then."

Vimes waited for Adam to say something but when nothing was forthcoming, he continued.

"If we had remained close, your Father would have revealed this to you on or before your eighteenth birthday, depending on your maturity. At that point, I would have been fully activated within you. Unfortunately, things don't always work the way we plan, and after our falling out over that girl your father decided to wait until you and I became reacquainted and showed greater maturity." Vimes laughed, "You are certainly your father's son, and we both underestimated just how much of his stubbornness you inherited!"

Adam finally thought of something to say that would make sense. "Let me get this straight. Does this mean you are alive and can control me or affect the way I think?" he asked, a little fearfully.

"No, not at all," came the immediate reply. "You have full control and once you have learned how to utilise all of my functions, will be able to switch me "off" at any time with a conscious act of will. Say, for example, when you are "entertaining" some of those lady friends of yours and wish for privacy, not that there's any need for modesty with me. After all, I do have four thousand years of experience in that regard, as both male and female."

"So, which one of your multiple drones is in charge?" Adam asked.

"Good question. Apart from this one in you, all my other avatars are subservient to the Emperors. Even I cannot go against his will in matters impacting on the Empire, but remember, in time you will be able to deactivate me at will."

The ship's engines started up again, replacing the silence with their familiar background hum. Outside, the star field began to move as the ship orientated itself towards the third planet. Now pointing in the right direction, the nearest sun could be seen as a small point of light brighter than any of the other stars.

"I've started us towards the planet to increase the amount of time we have together before I self-destruct this ship, and in answer to your original question, we will travel the distance of four-point two AU's in five-point eight days. If you are willing to accept one-point five-G, we will gain an extra day."

"OK Vimes, make it one and a half then," Adam responded. "Are there are any exo-suits in the hold I can get into? That would help me move around under the higher acceleration."

"Yes, there is one specifically designed for your Father which will fit you well, even though it has only been calibrated for him. I'll walk it here from the hold. Be careful using it, for as you have not yet been measured for a suit of your own I don't have your calibration to set it up properly. You are about the same size but please do not add or remove any smart-metal from the suit as I do not wish to risk contamination from the IP. Acceleration will increase once you have put it on."

"So Vimes," said Adam, looking off into the distance at the tiny star, "where do we go from here? Is there some weird joining ceremony or do you just turn a switch and bang; we are joined?"

"Nothing that dramatic Adam. Integration began the moment I started telling you. By the time you wake up tomorrow morning, I will be fully integrated into your nervous system and the old implant relegated to receiving information or giving commands to external systems the same as before. One of the first things you will notice is your already impressive ability to learn will be further improved by way of a selective eidetic memory. To that end, I've been monitoring the signals coming from the third planet, and have identified the most widely spoken languages, so will begin merging them into your memory. Local idioms will only come through use, but you will be able to converse quite effectively, although initially with a strange accent."

The door from the cargo hold opened behind Adam, and he could hear the exo-suit walk across the floor towards him.

Adam asked, for now, one final question while he tried to take in everything he'd been told, "Vimes, what's the name these humans give to their planet?"

"Earth," came the reply.

Aunt Flora had made sure the house was spotless and everything in its usual place, so it didn't take Karen long to unpack her clothes and put the shopping away. Earlier, to loosen up from the hours of driving and the stiffness in her neck and legs, Karen had been for a walk around the loch. Although out for almost an hour, she hadn't seen anyone and surmised it was probably because the locals were either at work or getting shopping in Portree, the nearest large town.

With the shopping stored and her clothes hung in the wardrobe, Karen brewed a strong cup of coffee and made herself at home in a comfortable brown leather recliner by a large picture window, looking out to watch the occasional car or lorry go by.

Karen realised she must have dozed off for a few hours, as by the time she woke, her coffee was stone cold and the sun had moved quite a way across the sky. Looking through the window, Karen could see several boats returning after a long day fishing for lobster. Recognising one of them as belonging to a friend, Karen decided to walk down to the jetty and say hello. She grabbed her coat went out the front door, locking it carefully behind her.

"*Old habits die hard*," she thought, smiling at her caution, for she'd never heard of anyone ever having been burgled in Struan.

Karen walked down the road towards the jetty, taking the slip road to her left at the point where the road started to climb up a hill towards Struan. To her right, midway along the slip road, she passed a Dutch barn made from rusted steel and a dilapidated farm building. The metal roof was red with rust and next to it the dark grey slate roof of the stone outbuilding had partially fallen in, its tiles scattered all around. Sheep grazed contentedly behind a long stone wall which was she noted was the only thing kept in good repair on the croft. At the end of the road lay the main building, it too now missing most of its roof, its insides exposed to the winds and rain of late winter.

Two vans, one white, the other a faded red, were parked at the small concrete communal jetty belonging to the neighbourhood. Piles of empty lobster pots were stacked up against a low stone wall, along with assorted football sized buoys and tangled netting. Her nose wrinkled at the salty smell of fish and seaweed left too long in the sun. She recognised one of the fishermen whose ten-metre boat was moored next to the jetty and called out in greeting.

"Hi Willy, how was the catch today?"

Willy MacDonald looked up at her call and seemed puzzled for a moment before recognising her. He put the lobster pot down onto the jetty and walked over, hand outstretched.

"Halloo Karen, good to see you. Alastair told me you would be coming to stay for a wee while," he said, shaking her hand vigorously.

She could feel the calluses, brought on by years of hard physical labour, and returned his warm smile.

"It's good to see you again, Willy. How's the family?"

"Fine, fine. They are all fine. I guess I know what you have come down for. A wee crab or lobster perhaps, Hmm?"

He stopped shaking her hand, still smiling broadly. Willy was in his late sixties and had lived and fished on the island all his life, just as his father had before him. Now that his children were all married and gone, he lived alone with his wife in the white stone cottage which had been his parents. It was situated several kilometres away in Ullinish, not far from a small country lodge and guest house. His cottage had a wonderful view out to sea and for him, was the most perfect place to live.

"Both, please, if you can spare them, Willy," Karen replied, "How much?" she asked as he walked off to get them for her.

Willy had walked back to one of the white plastic shipping boxes already stacked up on the jetty next to his boat. Reaching in with his left hand he pulled out a large crab, then reached into another box with his right and produced a fine lobster. Walking back with the shellfish, Willy shook his head.

"Nay lass, it's my welcoming gift for you. I wouldn't dream of charging you anything."

With one last check to make sure the elastic bands around the claws hadn't become loose, Willy put them into the strong carrier bag she held open for him.

"Thanks, Willy, that's really sweet of you."

They chatted for a few minutes then Karen allowed him to get back to unloading his boat. The buyer from the seafood wholesaler would be along soon, and he still had a lot of unloading to do.

With a cheery, "See you, Willy," Karen walked back, up the slight incline towards the main road and home, wondering if she could find a pot of Flora's large enough to cook the two shellfish in.

To Karen's eyes, traffic along the coastal road that ran outside her new home seemed heavier than she remembered and the drivers certainly didn't take any heed of the occasional sheep that managed to get out onto the road. It would soon be lambing season on Skye and Karen could see several heavily pregnant ewes tottering around.

"*They go from cute lamb to foul-tempered, suicidal jay-walkers in such a short period of time,*" she thought, recalling the first time she'd had to make an emergency stop to avoid taking out an evil-eyed sheep which, without warning, had decided to cross the road in front of her car.

Carrying the shellfish, the walk back to the house seemed to take a little longer, but eventually, she reached the small, red letterbox and slip road that marked the entrance to her driveway. Carefully walking over the aluminium cattle grid, she fumbled in her coat pocket for the keys, before unlocking the door at the rear of the house and entering the kitchen. Earlier, Karen had made space in the freezer, so placed both the crab and lobster into it and shut the door. Given their size, it would be about an hour before they were stunned by the cold and ready for the pot.

"*If I can find one that is,*" she reminded herself.

Ten minutes of rummaging around in the cupboards and everything was laid out nicely. A bottle of wine placed there earlier was chilling to perfection in the fridge, so all Karen had to do now was wait. She checked her watch. It was four o'clock and would soon begin to get dark, with sunset around six o'clock at this time of year, so Karen decided there was time for a brandy to keep out the cold. "*Purely for "medicinal" purposes*," she told herself, smiling inside as she headed to where Uncle Alastair kept the good stuff.

Forty-five minutes later, feeling a little tipsy from two large glasses of brandy that seemed to have gone down far too easily, Karen checked to see if her guests for dinner were ready. Satisfied both were safely asleep, she filled the large pan with boiling water from the kettle and lit the gas ring, swiftly bringing the water to a roiling boil. After salting the water, she carefully dropped the large crab into it and set the timer. Due to the size of the thing, she thought twenty minutes simmering time would suffice.

A little while later, and satisfied it was cooked, she pulled it out using tongs and did the same again for the lobster, checking every five minutes until it had turned red. Karen put the crab to one side, for she planned to have it tomorrow and needed it to get cold before placing it in the fridge. The lobster she was going to eat just as soon as she'd dressed it. Buttering the remainder of her baguette from this morning, her mouth began to water at the thought.

A while later, the sun having gone down along with the lobster, Karen was feeling quite full. Because of the earlier brandies, she'd only ended up drinking half the bottle of white wine, deciding to save the rest and have it tomorrow with the crab. Also, while in no way drunk, the alcohol was starting to make her feel decidedly maudlin.

"Plenty of fish in the sea," she said out loud, thinking of Ian, "and crab and lobster too, unless I get to eat them all first." She blew her cheeks out, making a noise. "Bastard."

Deciding the washing up could wait until tomorrow, Karen sat back in the armchair and reached for the remote control to see what was on television or already recorded on the Sky box by her aunt and uncle. She didn't want to be thinking about Ian, not tonight anyway. This was the start of a new life for her. Once she'd relaxed for a week, she would begin looking for somewhere to live permanently, perhaps even buying a flat near the Hospital instead of commuting by car. Karen was sorely tempted to finish off the half-empty bottle of wine in the fridge or pour herself more of the brandy, but resisted the urge, despite imagining she could hear them both calling out to her.

"That's enough for one evening, plenty of time to finish them off," she told herself, feeling virtuous at not giving in.

Karen was puzzled, for other than being angry with Ian, now everything was out in the open she didn't really feel much else towards him. Examining her feelings, she decided that perhaps this was because, deep down, she had always known the relationship wasn't going to last, like a holiday romance but over a longer period. The one thing she was surprised about was the growing sense of relief she was feeling, currently threatening to burst through into tears or laughter. She wasn't quite sure which one it would be if she let it.

"*No*," she decided after a brief period, "*this navel-gazing isn't getting me anywhere. Ian's gone, I'm moving on, and frankly, the more I think about it, the more relieved I am.*"

She turned on the television and looked at what programmes wcrc available. As usual, despite dozens of channels to choose from, there was nothing worth watching on live television that she hadn't seen before, so Karen looked what had been recorded. Pleased to see Frasier on series link, she scrolled through the episodes until coming to one she vaguely remembered, something about them all staying in a ski lodge with a gay instructor who thought Niles was gay too. Classic episode, just like a Brian Rix farce. Before pressing play, she had an attack of the munchies, so walked into the kitchen to raid the biscuit tin she'd filled earlier with milk chocolate digestives, Jammy

Dodgers, and Nice biscuits. Bringing the tin back with her, she lay back down on the recliner. Her left hand pressed play while her right, with a life of its own, reached into the tin and pulled out a chocolate digestive. Her final thought, before slipping into the world of Frasier and Niles Crane, was she would definitely start the diet tomorrow.

The days came and went, the sun growing from an almost invisible speck into the large, life-giving ball which nurtured the blue-green planet around which Adam's ship was now circling.

Shortly before reaching orbit, Vimes confirmed to Adam he'd prepared the main emergency lifeboat and ensured its simple systems held no trace of the IP, which was increasingly threatening to break free of the constraints he had imposed. Food supplies, an emergency synthesiser and a large bundle of various high denomination banknotes of the major currencies had been produced and stored away to provide funds until Adam was able to establish himself. Thinking he'd probably be spending most of his life on Earth, Adam was taking no chances with his future.

Fifteen hours previously, Vimes had warned Adam he would not be able to retain control for much longer, and they had both agreed on increasing deceleration to 3-G. This necessitated Adam staying in the lifeboat's crash couch, as the exo-suit was too large for the entrance. Adam regretted it wasn't possible to take the suit with him down to the planet, but understood how walking around in an armoured exo-suit might attract unwanted attention. Empty, the suit stood silent guard at the lifeboat's entrance.

After telling Adam the news he wouldn't be able to control the IP for much longer, Vimes had become quiet for long periods as more of his processing was diverted to keeping the vicious IP programme in check. Not wishing to disturb Vimes in case it caused a problem and with no-one else to talk to, Adam went over the conversations they'd had since Vimes explained everything several days previously. Apparently, "his" Vimes was helping the yacht's version fight the IP so no further explanations would be forthcoming for a while. Vimes had explained to him that unlike the human brain, his was spread out throughout the whole of Adam's body at a micro-cellular level, with multiple redundancies in case of severe bodily trauma.

Fortunately, because he was organic with no software to corrupt, the physical Vimes in Adam's body was immune to the IP. Adam was thankful to learn this as he'd wondered if he too might become an unwitting host to an inimical foe.

For Adam, the prospect of being a stranger in a strange land was a new and frightening concept, and while he was pleased Vimes would be accompanying him, the irony of it all was not lost, given he'd denied Vimes access for so many years and yet here they were, forever joined at a genetic level.

Of real interest to Adam was how the various copies of Vimes communicated to each other over the vast distances. Vimes had explained they did so at every opportunity, normally via a physical Vimes nearby or utilising the secret instantaneous communication system when available. It was all a little complicated to understand completely, but he was sure he'd be able to fully get to grips with it over time. Adam had enquired whether there was any sort of telepathic link between versions, but Vimes's laugh told him all he needed to know about that.

As to why they were in this predicament, Vimes had concluded whoever was behind the attempted assassination also had access to the yacht and had planted the IP as a backup should the first attempt to kill his Father fail, knowing that there was a good chance the Emperor might want to quickly return to Capital and ensure his wife was safe. The IP, when trying to scramble the ship's systems and destroy it, had done something unknown to both of the QA drives, somehow merging them and coming up with a random Quantum Signature that worked. He and Vimes best hypothesis was that in an infinitely large universe, any random Quantum Signature generated by the scrambled drive would probably exist somewhere and this was how they ended up in Earth's star system, probably billions of light years away from home.

Before trying to contain the IP had become too demanding, full schematics of the QA system and the Quantum Signature of Capital was downloaded to Adam, in the hope at some future time he would be able to build a transmitter and call for help. The current technological level of the planet precluded this so one of Adam's first tasks after establishing himself would be to "invent" from scratch the technologies required and introduce them into the planet's economy.

During the journey in-system, a major topic of conversation had been where to land. Adam's desire to live in a technologically superior society with good human rights ruled out much of the planet's land mass. Three areas remained, the North American civilisations of Canada and the US, the large island continent of Australia with nearby New Zealand, or the European landmass that had been inhabited by technological societies the longest. Japan and China were ruled out because of the difficulty he would have in blending amongst those two closed and racially homogenous societies.

Each of the remaining choices had advantages and disadvantages. Adam finally decided on Great Britain, a large island off the north-west coast of mainland Europe. He did so for two reasons, the first because it reminded him of the island on Capital where the Imperial Palace was situated and secondly because it had a Royal Family and a strong Imperial past. There was a small possibility that if he was ever revealed and taken into custody, the Imperial connection might just swing things in his favour. A slim chance, but one worth taking.

The hours had been passing slowly and orbit only achieved for a short time, when suddenly, without any notice, Adams train of thought was interrupted by a very terse *"Prepare for ejection, now!"*

An instant later, the lifeboat was ejected from the yacht's underbelly at speed, accelerating to 15-G out and away from the doomed ship so as not to be caught in its destruction. Barely able to breathe and unable to speak under the heavy acceleration, Adam could feel his consciousness fade, and everything went deep red then black.

Several seconds later the light came back on in Adam's head as he quickly recovered, the acceleration lessening to a more reasonable 3-G. Annoyingly, the tip of his nose started itching.

However, the effort of raising his arm to scratch it in the increased gravity wasn't worth it, for any sudden movement of the lifeboat might whip his arm around and whack it into his head. He remained still, his hands gripping the armrests to keep them safe.

"*What's happened Vimes?*" he thought to his now fully returned companion, finally released from having to support the yacht's failing systems.

"*We were about to lose control to the IP, so I jettisoned you before it could stop us from leaving. A few seconds more and it would have had us trapped,*" came the reply.

Unexpectedly, the viewscreen in front of Adam lit up brightly with a view of a massive fireball streaking across the sky at high speed, followed by a second, much smaller one which followed the same trajectory but was sinking lower into the atmosphere. The first suddenly exploded into a gigantic fireball of light and released energy, for a few seconds lighting up the entire night sky of the planet below, strong enough to leave strong after-images in the eyes of anyone looking upwards at the night sky.

"*That was the shipboard Vimes using the total conversion drive to self-destruct, stopping the IP from attacking this lifeboat. The second, smaller fireball is us, and once the automatic pilot has slowed us to a more reasonable speed through the atmosphere, we will become undetectable to any ground-based observers.*"

Vimes continued, "*Anyone looking at the spectacle will assume we were a smaller part of a much larger meteorite which broke off and burnt up in the atmosphere.*"

"Has the sudden departure affected our agreed landing zone?" Adam asked, "Or are we still on course?"

"*The lifeboat tells me we are slightly further north than planned, but we will still impact Great Britain, however instead of the mainland, it will be on a large, butterfly-shaped island to the West of Scotland. The local designation is Skye. This will work to our advantage as it is relatively uninhabited, with less risk of our landing being observed.*"

Adam requested flight information from the lifeboat, and it began passing through his vision, updating him on what was happening outside. They had quickly dropped away from the original trajectory and were now only several metres above sea level, moving at a greatly reduced speed. Now that deceleration was complete, he was feeling more comfortable and able to move his arms normally. At last, he could scratch that annoying itch.

They would be landing in a few minutes, and Adam was watching the sea flash past underneath, still illuminated by the lingering traces of light left by the yacht's violent end. The lifeboat's external sensors, although basic, produced a crystal-clear three-dimensional view of the water and terrain ahead. Vimes was overlaying the scene with place names, and Adam smiled at the strange names of the islands they were passing. A short time later, the lifeboat entered Loch Bracadale and began decelerating hard, keeping low until rising sharply to skim noiselessly over a group of white buildings he assumed were dwellings, some of which were emitting a yellow light from their windows. Now so close to landing, Adam gave the lifeboat instructions to head for the semi-plateau that rose up behind a small group of buildings and follow a small stream that dropped down from the deserted interior, covered in peat bogs and purplish moss-like vegetation.

Moving inland until no lights or any sort of dwellings could be seen, Adam hovered the small lifeboat eight metres above the watery terrain, and used ground-penetrating sensors to search between the rocky outcrops for a deep pocket of peat sufficiently large enough to bury the lifeboat. After a few seconds of searching, he found one. Dropping the nose, he forced the craft downwards, burrowing deep until only the upper part was level with the surface.

Adam decided to get out and make sure nothing could be seen of the lifeboat, for he did not want to take any chance someone might see it. The hull was undetectable to the technologies of this planet but even when cloaked, was still vulnerable to being seen with the naked eye, especially up close. Grateful to be alive and safely down, Adam left the crash coach and pulled himself up to the hatch that now formed above him. He opened it and cold, damp air immediately dropped into the warm cabin. He dropped back down, chastising himself for not having checked the outside temperature and dressed accordingly.

"*If I am to survive on this world,*" he told himself, "*I will need to start thinking through my actions rather than just doing and taking things for granted.*"

Climbing over the stacks of equipment fastened to the floor for safe keeping in anticipation of the trip down, Adam opened a wall locker and withdrew a survival suit which Vimes had specifically designed to blend in with the clothing currently fashionable in this part of the world. Multi-part, unlike the normal form fitting one piece he was used to, it consisted of trousers, an undershirt of some kind with a noisy fastening that consisted of hooks and loops, and an overcoat with an integral hood.

Quickly removing his current clothing, Adam donned the new ones. Immediately, he felt restricted and cumbersome wearing them as they didn't flex or move with his body. He wondered how the people could tolerate feeling so constricted. Although these were made from modern fabrics that regulated body temperature and drew away moisture, to pass casual inspection they mimicked the look and feel of local materials. The coat was fastened with a device called a zip, and he had problems fastening it until a short demonstration appeared in his vision, courtesy of Vimes. He realised there was so much to learn about life on this backwards planet.

Pulling the integral hood over his head, Adam reformed the hatch and easily pulled himself out into the chill night air. Taking a deep breath, he was immediately struck by how different this planet smelt to anywhere else he'd been in the Empire. It was slightly reminiscent of Capital but with an indefinable, yet likeable difference. He took several more deep breaths, savouring the sensation. Gravity was the same here, or so close to Capital's that he couldn't tell the difference.

Looking south-west, following the flight-path they had taken, Adam could see no trace left of the massive fireball high in the atmosphere. However, exotic particles and energy from the explosion had interacted with the planet's magnetic field, generating an aurora borealis in the night sky. Red and green streams of almost fluorescent light gently waved across the sky, making an impressive backdrop to the rocky outcrops. Drawing his eyes away from the spectacle, Adam looked down at the boggy ground he had chosen for the lifeboat's resting place. Displaced groundwater and peat was already moving back to completely hide any trace of the craft, and once the hatch was closed, all that was needed to completely hide it would be for the lifeboat to settle a few centimetres into the soil laden water.

Satisfied nothing would be seen when he had finished, Adam dropped back into the cramped cabin and collected from a locker a small bundle of notes that represented the currency of Great Britain. In denominations signified by £50 on the top left-hand corner, he calculated there were around fifty notes in the bundle. Vimes assured him this was sufficient for now. Although Vimes had confirmed there were no wild animals in this part of the world capable of seriously hurting him, walking around in a potentially hostile country was not a pleasant prospect, and Adam regretted having to leave behind his father's exo-suit and the more exotic heavy weaponry.

Rummaging through the survival kit, he placed around his right wrist a small tracker to enable him to find his way back to the lifeboat. The very expensive timepiece on his left wrist, the one that the manufacturer claimed could be set to any planet in the Empire with minimal trouble, was useless here, so he reluctantly took it off, instead opting for a thick-set smart-metal survival armband that was capable of transforming into a number of items, including a mono-molecular knife or walking stick. Covering his left forearm from wrist to elbow, it was reassuringly heavy and gave him a much-needed sense of security. Joining the others was his last piece of equipment, a set of night vision lenses which he quickly placed on his eyes, blinking as they bonded to his corneas. He looked longingly at the emergency firearms fixed to the wall but reluctantly decided against taking one with him.

Leaving the lifeboat, Adam took his bearings carefully, noting a few landmarks to identify the site, then began walking across the boggy ground towards the last set of dwellings he'd seen.

"*It will take me about ten minutes,*" he thought optimistically, setting off at a steady pace and welcoming the chance to stretch his muscles on a long walk after being cooped up in the yacht for so many hours.

After fifteen minutes, Adam found a dirt track and wondered if he had made a mistake in hiding the lifeboat nearby, but on looking closer was relieved to see it hadn't been used for a long time. "Let's hope it stays that way," he muttered to himself. He looked ahead, marking the route in his mind, then began humming along to a tune that suddenly came into his head, trying to match his footsteps to the beat.

Karen was listening to Pavarotti on her iPhone, when the darkened living room was suddenly illuminated by a bright flash that turned night into day, instinctively making her flinch and look out the window. Everything outside was clearly illuminated, and from her seat, she could see a huge fireball high in the sky, rapidly expanding as she watched. Another, smaller streak was visible for a few seconds before being swallowed up. Remembering the previous year's meteorite explosion over Russia, she stood and hurried to the window, reaching it just as darkness began returning. Looking out and up into the darkening night sky, she could see the fireball was dimming as it expanded. Karen watched for a minute until it had completely faded away, leaving only temporary coloured imprints on her retinas.

"Wow, that was amazing," she said to herself, torn between staying in and looking to see if it was reported on the nine o'clock news, or putting on a warm overcoat and going outside in case there were any more. She thought the chances of a repeat were slim, but there might be other, smaller meteorites to see if the big explosion was the forerunner of a meteor shower. Deciding to risk it, Karen picked up her mobile phone and got a torch from the kitchen. Living on Skye with its frequent power outages during periods of bad weather meant that there was an ample supply of candles, matches, and torches to hand at all times. Alastair had thoughtfully brought her old green Wellington boots down from the attic and left them in the porch for her to use, so she wriggled into them, glad of her thick socks to protect from the cold rubber.

With a dark brown overcoat wrapped tightly around her and torch in hand, Karen ventured out into the cold, crisp evening and headed along the dark gravel driveway towards the gate and cattle grid. With the nearest street lights coming from a kilometre away, the only illumination was her torch and the faint glow emanating from a few occupied cottages across the loch, where she could see a few brave souls had stepped outside to watch the night sky, now turning a beautiful green and red. Walking out onto the road, Karen followed the grass verge, making sure to face any oncoming traffic.

She began walking up the hill towards the village centre, consisting of a small general store, a strange bohemian second-hand clothes shop and not much else, but it did afford an uninterrupted view over the loch and out to sea, the reason for her taking this route. The music on her phone changed, and Pavarotti began singing again. She stopped walking and spent at least ten minutes concentrating on the light show in the sky above and listening to the music. Standing still, she began to notice the cold seeping through her clothes, so Karen started walking again. In the distance, about one hundred metres away, her bobbing torchlight illuminated a figure walking towards her.

Entranced by the beautiful light show above and Pavarotti's marvellous rendition of Nessun Dorma in her ears, Karen switched off her torch for a moment in the hope it would give her a better view, wanting to enjoy the Aurora Borealis without any interference from the powerful beam. She also thought it would be rude to dazzle the other lone walker as he might lose his night vision and slip into the gulley running alongside the road. The last thing she wanted to do on a night like this was minister to a stranger's broken ankle. A strange man walking towards her along an unlit street at night would have made her uncomfortable back in Inverness, but here on Skye she felt safe and paid him no heed. A pleasant hello and a brief chat about the light show and explosion would be the worst she might have to endure when they passed each other.

She fleetingly wondered why he was walking away from the lights but dismissed it as Pavarotti hit the high note and made her feel quite emotional. For a long time it had been her favourite song and it still never failed to move her, so when teamed with this marvellous display she could feel herself melting inside.

"*All in all, tonight is turning out to be a simply wonderful evening*," she thought.

Raising her head to continue watching the display, she caught a sudden movement and realised the stranger was running towards her at high speed. She watched him for a second, not knowing what to do or how to react. Almost upon her, he shouted out something in an unintelligible language, and before she could react, with a tremendous display of strength and power, he lifted her bodily off the road and threw her into the gulley. An instant later her attacker was swatted away as if he never existed by a large lorry that mounted the grass verge where she had been standing, careering across the road as the driver fought for control after skidding on the wet grass verge. She could hear the tyres squealing as the brakes locked before finally coming to a stop further up the hill. Of her mysterious benefactor, there was no sign. Sitting up in the gulley, Karen switched on the torch still gripped tightly in her hand and shone it in the direction of the lorry, realising with a sickening feeling that it looked as if someone was trapped underneath the vehicle.

Berating herself for being so stupid for not paying any attention to the possibility of traffic coming from behind, she pulled herself out of the gully, thankful that her fall had been cushioned by the water and thick spongy mosses that lined its sides. Her headphones had fallen out of both ears, and she could just make out their tinny sound as they dangled aimlessly down from her neck. Karen ran towards the lorry, the beam from her torch bobbing up and down, watching as the cab door opened and the driver jumped out. He shouted to her, saying he'd hit someone and began walking around his truck, clearly in a daze.

Slightly out of breath from the uphill run and shock, Karen reached the lorry and shone her torch underneath. Not seeing anything at first, she felt relief, but then saw what she knew was a mangled body partially wedged into one of the inside rear wheel arches. Steeling herself, she shouted out to the driver to check if he'd put the handbrake on.

"Yes, sorry, so sorry, I didn't see him, yes, I did," came the response, the driver clearly in shock and of not much use.

Trusting that the driver really had the presence of mind to have done so, she crawled under the lorry to get a closer look. The dead man was tightly wedged between tyre and wheel arch, his head hanging down loosely. In the bright torchlight, Karen could clearly see his left temple was scraped down to the bone and an eye was missing, probably ripped out as the poor man was dragged face down along the tarmac. The right arm, covered in cloth that had remained surprisingly intact, hung out at a strange angle with blood running down from the wrist to the middle finger before dripping slowly onto the wet ground.

"*Oh God, you poor man,*" she thought, torn between compassion for his fate and relief at not being hit herself. "*You poor, brave man.*"

Blinking away tears, Karen crawled nearer, smelling old grease, diesel, and hot melted rubber. As she crawled, Karen tried to avoid staring at the man's face, keeping her head down and ignoring the cold and damp seeping into her from contact with the road. Pieces of gravel bit into her palms and knees, but she ignored them, focusing on doing her job. She put the torch on the ground, angling it so the wheel arch was illuminated without dazzling her.

The driver had come over and asked under the lorry if there was anything he could do. Biting back an impulse to scream "*drive more fecking carefully,*" she told him to ring for the Police if he hadn't already done so. Out of habit, Karen reached up and felt for a pulse from the man's right wrist. Expecting nothing she was surprised, then horrified when she felt a very slow yet regular thump.

"Sweet Jesus the man's still alive!" she said out loud, shocked to her core.

With hands now trembling from the cold and shock, Karen reached into her coat pocket and pulled out her mobile phone, praying the throw and fall into the gulley hadn't damaged it. Relieved it was still working, she went through its address book until she found the number of the Air Ambulance station back at Raigmore Hospital. Dialling, she prayed the signal wouldn't fail.

Within moments, a familiar voice answered the phone. Karen interrupted her friend and quickly set out what had happened and where she was, making it very clear there would be trouble if one of the two helicopters weren't immediately sent to her location. She asked for someone to ring her back when they were on their way. Finally, she made them repeat her mobile number and hung up.

Karen was faced with a dilemma. She didn't want to risk any spinal damage, but she couldn't leave the man wedged between the tyre and wheel arch for any longer than was necessary, for at the very least he probably had multiple broken ribs and difficulty breathing. What she could see of his legs indicated he might well need one or both amputated, so she made the tough decision and called the driver over to help her pull the trapped man free. Reluctant to help her at first, she swore loudly and ordered him to come over. He was still reluctant, but her shouted threat, "*if you don't come and help when this is over I will hunt you down and shoot you like a dog,*" seemed to decide things, and he finally came over to help. Between the two of them, they eased the wedged body out of the arch and pulled it out from under the rear of the lorry.

Karen checked his heartbeat again and was relieved to still find one, albeit slow and regular. She set about trying to remove his overcoat to get a better look at his chest injuries and was surprised at the materials feel. Putting that to one side, she asked the driver if he had any blankets as she needed to keep the victim warm. None were available, so she instructed him to run over to the nearest house showing lights and ask for several blankets. As he ran off, her mobile rang.

"Karen, it's James. Michael and I were here at Portree when we got the call. You're bloody lucky we were in the area, love. We were about to head back to Raigmore with a casualty but diverted and should be with you in eight minutes. Exactly where in Struan are you?"

"Down near the jetty where you picked up the Scandinavian woman you told me about," she replied, never taking her eyes off the body. "When I hear you approach someone will wave a torch to show you where we are. Park where you did last time, near the old barn."

"OK, we'll see you shortly."

Looking up, she could see an elderly man and woman following the driver back to the lorry, each carrying blankets and a torch. The driver got to her first, and she handed him her powerful torch, instructing him to go over to the barn and shine it in the air when he heard a helicopter. Looking again at the mangled wreckage of a man lying in front of her, Karen marvelled at the tenacity of the human body's ability to cling onto life. Running her hands over him, she could feel compound fractures in both legs, definite problems with the right arm and she could see clearly the horrific facial trauma on the left side of his face. The left forearm was encased in some sort of a cast that she could feel under the cloth. Finally, she noted some of the bicep and shoulder tissue had been abraded away. She grimaced, unable to stop herself from picturing the scraping of his flesh along the rough road surface, and fervently hoped by then he had been unconscious, as the pain would have been unbelievable.

The older couple arrived the same moment a helicopter could be heard coming over the hill road to the south-east. She fended off the customary offer of a cup of tea from the woman and told the man to cover the driver with one of the spare blankets, as he too was in danger of going into shock. Why he was driving without his lights on she might never know, but she fervently hoped he had a damn good reason. If not, she would make sure the Police threw the book at him for this.

The helicopter approached, illuminating the area with its spotlights. Karen worried she might go into shock herself and asked for one of the spare blankets, wrapping it around her shoulders.

"*Once we have stabilised him,*" she told herself, "*I'll allow myself the luxury of a good cry.*"

Thanks to the night vision lenses he was wearing, Adam had seen the woman leave her house and start walking in his direction long before she could see him. Using the zoom function, he looked closely at her face. Two strange white pieces of wire or string hung down from each ear and vanished inside the neck of her coat, probably some sort of ornament, he reasoned. He found her strikingly good-looking, even for someone like him used to the company of beautiful women. He resolved to try and talk to her, hoping she could provide valuable information to help him decide what to do next.

Vimes was keeping quiet, having decided to only interrupt or talk when asked, knowing from previous experience it would be some time before Adam was completely comfortable in having him around all the time and wanting to ease him in gently. It was still early days in their relationship, and after being estranged for so many years, he thought it would be good for Adam to have time alone to think everything through for himself.

Drawing closer to the woman, Adam had his first proper glimpse of a ground vehicle commonly used by this culture to move themselves and goods around. Closing behind the woman, the large vehicle was approaching rapidly. Although his lenses made it clearly visible to Adam, he was surprised no lights were illuminating its path. He wondered if the woman knew it was there, for she seemed intent on looking at the sky. Zooming in on the driver, who was seated behind a circular wheel high up from the road, Adam could see he too was looking intently at the sky, and the vehicle was drifting over to her side of the road. Fearing for her safety, instinctively Adam sprang forward towards the woman, just as the vehicle mounted the grass verge and began sliding out of control. Adam could see the look on the driver's face change from wonderment to one of fear as he spotted both Adam and the woman at the last moment.

Reaching her a split second before the vehicle, Adam registered the look of surprise on her face before he threw her out of the vehicle's path. Unable to do anything else, he was struck harder than anything had ever hit him before, knocking him backwards. In the merest instant before blacking out, he wondered if he would ever know who she was...

Vimes was unexpectedly jolted out of his dormancy. Unable to open Adam's eyes to see what was happening, multiple catastrophic damage signals were being relayed to him via Adam's nervous system, indicating major trauma to the body. Simultaneously replaying the last few moments, while at the same time diagnosing what remedial action to take, Vimes was in danger of becoming overwhelmed himself by the damage. Severe skin and muscle trauma to the limbs and torso, combined with the loss of an eye, impacted for a moment on his ability to think. Immediately, his own redundancies kicked in, replacing the lost memories. Adams body had gone into shock, sealing off damaged veins and arteries. Vimes used his emergency control over the autonomic system, accelerating haemostasis to aid clotting and the production of healing factors. After ten seconds, no additional trauma was registering, but the litany of problems began to rise for Vimes. Adam's heart was labouring under the effect of massive shock, and one of his ribs had badly punctured a lung. With few options open to him without access to a medical suite, Vimes set about shutting down all non-essential bodily functions to ensure blood was kept flowing to the brain. Fortunately, the sinus node hadn't been damaged and through this Vimes lowered Adam's heartbeat to the minimum compatible with life. Running test signals, he checked the spinal column was intact. Fortunately, although bruised in places, there was no serious damage, the second bit of good news.

Vimes could hear faint voices and fought to open Adam's remaining eye, but to no avail. Concentrating on reconstructing the damaged internal organs, Vimes was able to stop the blood loss in Adam's spleen, effectively sealing off hundreds of damaged blood vessels. The impact had partially torn a kidney loose, so it was shut down while he tried to rebuild the damaged area. Granulation of damaged tissues was already taking place, and he diverted stores of sugar and protein from the remaining healthy muscles to repair and replace tissue lost in the accident. This would leave Adam very weak for a time until he was able to replace the muscle mass being cannibalised to heal his injuries.

Sensing movement, Vimes recognised several voices, probably rescuers of some sort. One of them seemed to know what she was doing and was taking control of the situation. He wondered what the chances were of it being the same woman Adam had just risked his life for. Still unable to open the eye and see what was happening, and unable to influence events in any way, Vimes diverted all his attention back to healing his charge.

Chapter 18, Dauntless

Alexander was in his quarters, reviewing the Ascension fleet's deployment around Heaven. As promised, the day after Adam left he'd made his decision what to do about the situation here. A good night's sleep had allowed his natural temperament to reestablish itself, despite the loss of his men and the uncertainties over his son.

Other than what had already taken place to neutralise their offensive nuclear capacity, he ruled no further punitive action would be undertaken against the population or leaders provided they co-operated and made no further hostile moves. In addition, the Ascension Fleet would remain for only twelve months instead of the planned three years.

If, after being shown the truth, the people of Heaven demonstrated sincere regret at what had happened, then they would still be allowed to join the Empire. However, considering the attack and loss of life, it would only be as a normal Class Three planet. However, as Collinson had predicted, senior religious leaders were currently refusing to engage with them and were continuing to extol their followers to ignore the "*demons from the skies that were coming to enslave them.*"

Dismissing them as idiots, Alexander sighed heavily, shaking his head at the stupidity of otherwise intelligent people when it came to matters of religion or racial purity. Four thousand years of fast mass transit and no planetary borders had merged the three main ethnic races of his Empire into one, homogenous population. Religious beliefs tended not to survive the shock of contact with other alien races or foreign belief systems and were now mainly relegated to ceremonial functions. A few religious groups in the Empire could still be found, clinging on to a hard core of believers on a few planets, but most of the population in his Empire considered themselves to be of a secular inclination.

Earlier, for a few brief moments, Alexander had been tempted to resolve the matter of what to do with Heaven once and for all by sterilising the planet in one of two ways. Introducing a lethal, short-lived virus into all the main population centres was one option; the second to introduce one designed to render everybody sterile but leave them alive. The beauty of the latter option was that one hundred years from now the problem would be solved without additional deaths on his conscience. Alexander was tempted, but it was too early for him to consider either of those options. In any event, he never wanted to become that sort of ruler, having witnessed first-hand in his youth the horrors a lack of moral compass could inflict on the innocent and the hard-learned lessons from that time had shaped the man he was now.

Looking around, staring at the pictures and priceless paintings hanging on the walls of his private chambers, Alexander recalled the propaganda messages he'd recorded yesterday, full of Imperial magnanimity and forgiveness that his advisors hoped would play well with the population. Alexander had his doubts but followed their advice.

"*After all, that's what they are employed to do,*" he thought to himself.

Smiling, he recalled one of Christine's favourite sayings, "*There's no point in having a guard dog if you insist on barking yourself.*"

Surprisingly shy by nature for someone in his exalted position, in the early years of his reign following the Succession Wars, Alexander had to force himself to take centre stage and overcome his natural tendency to avoid conflict. It was only because of Christine's emotional support that he had found the strength to wrest back control of the rebellious Sectors and reassert his authority over wavering Nobles.

He sighed, remembering those early days with Christine, fighting side by side and taking on the universe together, missing both her touch and companionship every single day they were apart. After every campaign or State visit, he tried to return home, promising himself they would take a holiday or spend more time together. Invariably, matters of State always interfered with his plans and he would find himself having to leave yet again after too little time together. Heaven, and now this new border dispute were just two more examples of how fate and the universe continually conspired to keep the two of them apart.

His thoughts turned again to Adam, and he allowed himself a few moments to worry about his son. Their parting had not been a good one, and although the decision to send him away had been correct and had to be done, he could not help but blame himself for not having provided him with more guidance and support. *If only* and *what if* were four words that a successful leader could not afford to dwell on for too long, so he brought himself back from his reverie and focused again on the situation at hand.

Alexander checked his data feed and could see his messages were already being inserted into every electromagnetic based means of communication on the planet. Within a few days, he knew everyone would have seen or heard them, despite whatever the religious leaders might do to block them. It pleased him to think of how they would react when their religious broadcasts were replaced with Imperial messages showing images of what the Empire was really like and the many advantages of membership. In addition to the messages, Infiltrator Programmes designed for their backwards technology had also been introduced and were working their way into every mainframe computer and global Internet system on the planet, monitoring for and identifying the key people behind the original attack. Unless they were willing to shut down their entire system of communication and data storage, in time the key players would be identified and located. He would let the Ascension Fleet and the clever people working for the Imperial Intelligence Service deal with them.

Internally checking the time, Alexander realised it would not be long before Dauntless made the Jump to Kiyami, the capital planet of Sector Twelve, where he would meet with Duke Frederick. As a courtesy on arrival, Dauntless would pay its respects to the Jump Station, then travel inwards to take on fresh supplies and send away the bodies of those who had fallen to their families, along with Alexander and Christine's personal invitation to be their guest at the Imperial Palace whenever they liked.

If Alexander shut his eyes, it was easy for him to recall the faces of the fallen he'd known personally, especially that of Captain Stuart-Jack. He was, "*no, had been,*" he corrected himself, watching the young man's progress with interest, marking him down as a future Commodore or higher.

Bringing his mind back for the second time from what might have been to the present, Alexander noted the journey in-system to Kiyami from the Jump Point would only take four days. Kiyami's sun had a particularly weak gravity well, and boasted several Jump Points, the main reason why it had been chosen as the Sector capital. He hadn't seen Duke Frederick since the last Grand Council meeting and wondered what the wily old man had been up to. Approaching two hundred and thirty years of age, Frederick was currently the oldest of the Sector heads and had a well-founded reputation for being miserly with his wealth. Alexander also found him arrogant and even condescending towards him at times but had made allowances in the past, for Frederick had been a close confidant of his father.

With two hundred and eleven inhabited planets, Sector Twelve was the most densely populated and wealthy in the Empire after his own. In comparison, Duchess Helena of neighbouring Sector Thirteen, ruled only fifty-three planets yet maintained a battle fleet almost comparable to her larger, wealthier neighbour. Still only fifty-one years old, the Duchess was a formidable woman who had a great deal of support in the Council and was not afraid to verbally cross swords with Alexander, having done so on several occasions, albeit respectfully and with good arguments to support her position.

There was no love lost between the two neighbouring Sectors, allegedly because Frederick tried to seduce Helena when she was a teenager. Back then, to further her education, as a young woman Helena had been assigned by her father to attend Frederick's Court for a season. Alexander didn't know if the Duke had been successful, but when Helena became Duchess a decade later, relations between the two Sectors had rapidly cooled. Despite the best efforts of Vimes and the Imperial Intelligence Service, other than the two antagonists, no-one knew the real reason for the mutual dislike.

"*Typical of the nonsense I have to deal with, one Sector spending too little on defence, the other possibly too much,*" he thought.

Looking again at the original request for assistance, Alexander decided he would take this opportunity to insist Frederic finance a shipbuilding programme and improve his military readiness. After all, he reasoned, it's not as if he has any valid excuse not to, especially with the Dubunni and Silures Empires potentially disputing their border with the Empire.

Alexander heard the ship-wide Jump Warning sound and counted down the seconds until the...

Discontinuity

...Jump happened. He sensed Vimes send off an update to his counterpart on Kiyami and would review the response when it came back, giving him plenty of time before he transmitted his courtesy greeting to Frederick, advising of his arrival.

A familiar knock on his door told him his old friend and mentor, Duke Gallagher, had arrived. No longer an Ambassador from the moment the Ascension Fleet took over responsibility for Heaven, Duke Gallagher was clearly itching to get home to Sector Two and his family. Rising to his feet and walking over to the door to greet his friend, Alexander instructed it to open at the exact moment he knew his friend would try knocking again. The door opened to reveal Gallagher standing there with his fist poised, making them both laugh. For Alexander, it was the first real laugh he'd had since events in the Heaven system, and he could feel some of the weight lift from his shoulders. Shaking hands, Duke Gallagher spoke first.

"With your permission Alex, I will leave and use the Jump Station to get home. I know it's only a short hop to Kiyami, but I really can't face another of Frederick's interminably boring lectures on how much money he's made from this or that venture. Good luck with trying to persuade him to spend on new ships."

"If he doesn't take the hint then I will simply order him to do it, Patrick. Are you taking Collinson with you? He seems a bright young man," Alexander asked, changing the subject.

"Yes, he's starting to grow on me. He finally stopped asking if he could carry my case, so I gave it to him just now to look after.

The look on his face was priceless. There's a lot he has to learn, and I think he might find living on my estate quite educational."

Alexander chuckled, "Poor man, I hope he survives the experience, especially as I remember how delightfully forward your great, great granddaughters are. I heard even Adam barely escaped unscathed by the experience when he visited last year."

Becoming serious, Alexander placed his right hand on his friend's shoulder, "Be careful, Patrick, and watch your back. You are my most trusted friend and Duke. This, along with your being the second most powerful Noble in the Imperium makes you a key target for the plotters. Should anything happen to me every Noble knows you would come looking for vengeance, so be careful. Please."

"Do Dukes shit on golden toilets, Alex?" asked Gallagher, shaking hands again in farewell before heading off.

"No Patrick, just silver ones," he replied as Duke Gallagher left, smiling at the back of his departing friend.

Alexander returned to his desk, debating what to do next. Although Frederick's contribution to the Imperial Navy was not as powerful as might be expected from such a wealthy Sector, barely exceeding minimum requirements, it remained a potent symbol of power. Consisting of one hundred and eleven Carriers, over two thousand front-line attack ships and double that number of Auxiliaries, the Navy of Sector Twelve was certainly capable of holding its own against any known threat from outside the Empire. Currently, a few ships protected each planet, with the remainder spread out along the Dubunni border in substantial battle groups. In comparison, latest reports from the Imperial Intelligence Service indicated the Dubunni could field less than a quarter of that number across their entire empire. It was unlikely they would ever be able to field them all together in one place, as their preferred method of attack was hit and run, like the Corsairs who roamed the seas of Capital in ancient times. Tactically, however, the advantage lay with the Raiders, unless they could be lured to a specific system and defeated in a pitched battle or their bases found and destroyed, thereby denying them repair and refuelling capabilities. Maintaining the space worthiness of a ship, enabling it to operate safely and effectively, required the use of dedicated repair facilities and regular maintenance. Destroy or capture these and their ability to mount attacks would be severely curtailed.

"*For years we have tried to contain rather than confront them,*" he thought, "*but now might be the time to remind them of our military and financial power. If we offer sufficiently large bribes or rewards for the location of the bases we might be able to destroy them with very little collateral damage.*"

The last thing Alexander needed at this moment was to turn a deteriorating border dispute into a full-blown war with another empire by going in blind and without specific targets in mind. A surgical strike, then presenting the Dubunni with irrefutable evidence of their raiding, would be far better than simply blundering around looking for possible targets, annoying the Dubunni factions and potentially bringing them all together.

Alexander spent another half an hour fleshing out a tentative plan then summoned Admiral Frith to critique and improve it. She told him it would be a while before she could attend, so in the meantime he dictated a short, but suitably non-committal greeting to Frederick, requesting he assemble his military advisors and visit Dauntless to pay his respects once they made orbit in a few days.

"*Making him come to me will give the old miser something to think about,*" he thought. "*He will think I am unhappy about something he's done and potentially make him more receptive in an effort to please me. That's the problem with keeping lots of secrets, you never know if or when one of them has been found out.*"

In the Air Ambulance and on the way to Inverness, Karen and Michael were working non-stop on stabilising their patient, trying to assess the extent of the damage and keep him alive long enough to reach the Hospital. Before bringing him on board, broken bones had been splinted and the wounds they could access covered with dressings and pressure bandages. For some reason, their normal surgical scissors couldn't cut through the tough material of his clothes, so, in the end, they'd had to use shears, taking many minutes instead of seconds. Karen had tried first with the scissors, and in frustration, Michael had taken them from her with a terse "let me do it" only to find he had no more success. It was only when surgical shears were used that they managed to reveal the full extent of the patient's injuries. With little they could do without more sophisticated equipment, they settled for fixing a drip and checking he remained immobilised and warm for the long trip.

Both puzzled by the lack of bleeding, at first, they worried if he had gone into severe shock and might suffer imminent heart failure. However, despite the appaling injuries, his heartbeat remained slow and steady. Worryingly, in case it was a sign of infection, his core temperature remained higher than normal although his undamaged extremities were cold and turning faintly blue.

Reaching an end to what they could achieve in the helicopter, they looked at each other in puzzlement. By any measure, this patient should be dead or have bled out by now, but despite everything, he seemed stable.

"Who the hell is this guy, Karen?" Michael asked, shaking his head. "How come he arrived on your doorstep?"

"I don't know anything about him, Michael, except he came out of nowhere and saved my life."

Speaking these words, Karen could feel hot tears welling up in her eyes and begin rolling down her cheeks. She bit her lip and fought to take the tremble out of her voice.

"I thought at first he was going to attack me, but he literally picked me up and threw me out of the lorry's path as if I was a child. It's no wonder his heart hasn't given out yet, he must be as strong as an ox."

"Hey, guys," James's voice came over their headsets, "Word has gone out and Karen's team are on standby at Raigmore. ETA twenty minutes if I push it. How's the patient?"

"Stable, but God knows how, it's nothing we've done for him," Michael replied, echoing Karen's very thought.

Karen took a few moments to look out the window into the darkness outside. Little could be seen except small isolated patches of light that indicated small communities. The constant drone and noise of the turbines made her glad of the headset. She shut her eyes for a moment and wiped her cheeks, allowing herself the luxury of looking back over her day. Surprisingly she let out a short laugh.

Michael looked at her quizzically.

"I was just thinking it's a good job I put the crab in the fridge earlier, otherwise the house would be stinking when I get back," she explained to a confused Michael.

Not really understanding what she meant, he shook his head and moved back into the co-pilot's seat to give Karen more room. She looked down at the stranger's face, now partially covered by a thick white dressing. Looking at the part of it still visible, Karen thought how handsome he had been. If he survived, how would he react to the loss of his eye and the horrid scarring that would be forever visible? She closed her eyes for a moment and sighed deeply, and in that instant resolved she would not leave his side until he either died or she was able to properly thank him for saving her life. The problems she was having with her ex-partner and having to find somewhere to live were suddenly put into sharp contrast with the issues this man would have to face.

"*Again, if he survives,*" she reminded herself.

Karen looked over at the other passenger, a middle-aged lady with hair dyed a startlingly dark black, but badly needing the roots touching-up. She'd earlier been lightly sedated to help with the pain of a broken leg and lay quietly on the other stretcher, falling in and out of sleep. Her broken leg was encased in a large inflatable splint, mirroring those covering the other, more seriously injured patient.

Over the intercom came the voice of James, "Not long now, just another few minutes, everyone's waiting at the helipad."

Bringing her gaze back to the man, Karen thought for a moment she could see his mouth move. Leaning forward to get a closer look, she violently flinched back when his remaining eye opened and looked right into her own. For a moment, it searched her face as if looking for something, before fixing on her eyes. The mouth moved slowly, and she leant forward again to try and catch what he was trying to say, temporarily lifting the transparent oxygen mask away from his face.

His damaged lungs could obviously only spare a little breath, but as Karen concentrated she heard him say quietly, "*Cut nothing away, this body will heal itself. Please, do nothing else.*"

She asked what his name was and whether he was in a lot of pain but couldn't understand the reply. Leaning forward again and pushing aside her earpiece, she asked him to repeat it. "*Adam. My name is Adam. I will sleep now. Remember, do not cut anything away. It's very important,*" and with that, his eye closed.

From the front of the helicopter, Michael asked what had happened, having been listening over the intercom but only hearing Karen's questions.

"He woke up for a second and spoke to me. Apparently, his name is Adam, but that's all I got that made any sense," she replied, making sure everything was ready for a quick exit as they made their final approach before landing.

She felt a bump as the wheels touched the concrete helipad, followed by a gust of cold air that rushed into the cabin as the large hatch was opened and the faces of Colleen and Frank appeared.

Frank shouted out something, but the headphones and noise from the rotor blades spinning down stopped her from hearing. She took them off and set them down on the seat next to her, asking him to repeat the question.

"Couldn't keep away, could you?" he shouted, reaching for one end of the stretcher and pulling it towards him with a grunt of effort.

Grabbing the other end, Karen pushed it forward so that one of the orderlies could take it from her and drop the wheels down. Another orderly was waiting with a wheelchair for the other patient who had been woken by the cold air and noise. Twenty metres away, two ambulances were waiting to take them the three-hundred-metre drive to A&E. They hurried Adam into the nearest before closing the doors and driving off. Karen waited with the wheelchair for the next ambulance to move forward and climbed in.

In a matter of minutes, Karen was entering A&E, heading for the Trauma area. Although she was only a few moments behind the others, by the time she arrived the team were already going through their well-rehearsed routine, re-checking vitals and calling in various specialists. She could see the radiographer, Alice, looking to assess what to scan first.

Removing her coat and draping it over a nearby chair, Karen walked over and started listing the injuries she'd seen and what had happened. She also mentioned he'd briefly regained consciousness and seemed lucid for a moment but other than that had been unresponsive. For several minutes she watched her team work, until a tap on her left shoulder made her look around. Behind her was James, proffering a brown plastic cup of hot tea. Michael was standing behind him, looking unsure whether to say anything or let James do the talking.

"Here you are love, take this," said James, "sorry I've nothing stronger to give you. What's the prognosis of our RTA?"

Karen shook her head. "I'm amazed he's managed to survive, James. He should have bled out, but almost nothing happened. Once they wiped away the initial bleeding, there was hardly anything new, just minor weeping. Most unusual. He's displayed none of the classic symptoms of shock either. Other than his name we know nothing about him."

"Michael and I are going off duty now until Monday. Is there anything we can do for you, Karen?" he asked, a look of sympathy on his face. James had never seen Karen react to an incident like this before. Normally always in control, she seemed lost today, and he was concerned for her.

Karen looked at them both and managed a small, tight smile. "I'll be fine. I'm just glad you two were there to help. Thanks, guys, I owe you one."

Both men stepped forward and gave her a reassuring hug, for an instant making her feel less vulnerable. Michael gave an extra squeeze before letting go, and they turned around and walked off, leaving her with no-one to talk to for the moment. Seeing her standing there, Frank came over and suggested she go and wait in the nurses' room as they had everything under control and it would be some time before they had anything new to tell her. Knowing Adam was in capable hands, Karen wandered off to make a telephone call. By now the Police on Skye would have arrived at the scene of the accident, and she wanted to make sure the lorry driver was taken in for some serious questioning.

Vimes had been monitoring Adam's vital functions since the accident and was satisfied he'd done everything possible to keep him alive after the initial trauma. For the moment, he decided that more drastic measures were not needed. After managing to open an eye, he'd recognised the woman attending Alex as the one they'd saved. She was obviously a medical practitioner of some kind and her intervention, although minimal compared to his, had been welcome. The addition of a drip helped combat the body's natural instinct to go into shock, and he hoped she had understood and would act on his brief message. An amputated limb would take weeks to re-grow properly and could not be explained away easily, or at all, given the medical knowledge of these people. As it was, the accelerated healing that Adam would soon display was going to be problematic, and he didn't know how to avoid drawing unwanted attention. In his weakened condition, Adam was very vulnerable and their ability to escape severely limited.

From the motion and noise, he recognised they were travelling by air and surmised it would be to a medical facility of some sort. There, he hoped Adam's broken bones could be properly set, the one thing he was unable to assist with while Adam was unconscious. Remaining vigilant, Vimes sensed the landing and subsequent entry into a building. From the voices he could hear, and the actions being taken, he knew the damage to Adam was being assessed, so he continued with accelerating the healing process further. This would result in a marked increase in body temperature as the injury sites became highly inflamed, a by-product of the healing process, however, the Doctors would be able to keep the body cool if it went dangerously high.

He could sense Adam's consciousness beginning to surface and so made sure pain signals were kept to a minimum to keep him comfortable. It would not be long before he could explain all that had happened and allow Adam to decide on what to do next.

Karen had just spent thirty minutes on the telephone with the duty Sergeant at Portree Police Station and was unhappy, but not surprised, at the news. The lorry driver was claiming a fuse controlling his lights had blown just before the incident, and this was why he hadn't seen her, but they had arrested him on suspicion of dangerous driving and retained his lorry for examination. As Karen didn't know when she would be returning to Skye, a local Policeman would be coming to the Hospital to take a statement from her.

Frank popped his head around the door with news on Adam, providing a list of injuries and an update on what treatments they'd provided. Providing he survived the night, his need for reconstructive facial surgery would be assessed. To everyone's amazement, there were no signs of new internal bleeding despite the punctured lung which they'd manipulated out. The lung had immediately reflated and was showing no sign of sucking despite the puncture. His wounds had been washed clean of gravel then dressed, and obvious bone fractures temporarily manipulated back into place, but further treatment would depend on his condition tomorrow.

Karen thanked Frank for the update and followed him back to the Trauma Room, where a nurse was checking the drip hanging from a cradle above Adam. Two orderlies were getting ready to take him to Intensive Care where he would be left until morning. Walking over, Karen noticed that his arms and legs looked a little thinner than she had remembered, and his face seemed pinched. Unsure what to do next, she helped an orderly get his trolley ready and accompanied Adam to the Intensive Care Unit.

Compared to A&E, ICU seemed like an oasis of calm and quiet. Everyone spoke quietly, and unless there were an emergency, the loudest noise would probably come from the beeping monitors. Karen watched as Adam was transferred from the trolley onto the bed situated at the far end of the room, then spoke to the Ward Sister and asked if it would be alright for her to stay by his side. As an extra pair of trained eyes would always be welcome, she was found a comfortable chair and allowed to stay. Ten minutes after entering the ICU, all the required monitors and equipment had been attached and sat gently beeping and flashing next to Adam's bed. Karen knew Adam was lucky, for it was rare for there to be an empty space in Intensive Care on a Saturday night. Karen pulled up a chair next to the bed and sat down, declining another offer of tea with a shake of her head.

Two hours later, her vigil was disturbed by a bored looking Policeman who had come from nearby Burnett Road Station. His grasp of grammar was poor, and she resisted his efforts to write her statement in the fashion he preferred. She wondered if most statements ended up sounding as if they had been written by the same person and whether anybody at Court ever noticed or cared.

It was going to be a long night for everyone concerned.

Parmenion had surprised Christine earlier in the day by suggesting she join in with a mock exercise his Marines were holding in the woodlands and forest surrounding the Palace. Reluctant at first, Christine warmed to the idea after he suggested she would be able to see how effective his troops were, and she would be able to forget for a while the problems of running an Empire. Karen had to admit the thought of getting physical and working off some of the aggression she had felt on learning about the assassination attempt was very appealing.

So here she was, several hours and three skirmishes later, wearing her personalised armour, trying to ambush the last squad of blue armoured Marines, while they, in turn, tried to ambush her red ones. Using them as a decoy, she and the dour-looking Master Sergeant Zuber had swung around behind the blues, using a natural gully to hide their approach.

To make things more interesting for the Marines, all their tracking, targeting aids and field communications had been switched off, and their suits enhanced sound and vision capabilities reduced to normal. Although able to amplify the strength and fighting capabilities of the wearer, the suits still required input from the user's own body, which in turn required the Marines to be in superb physical shape. It was at this point Christine was questioning her decision to get involved, for, fit as she was, she could feel her muscles start to complain about the unusual demands currently being made of them.

A sudden hand signal from Zuber made her halt, and she tried to ignore the pain signals coming from her stomach and knees while hunched over. Ahead, Zuber motioned them forward, and she gratefully unwound, moving next to him as they lay down on a slope facing the blue group. The reds were acting as decoys, drawing the attention of the blues who had fanned out into four groups of three, facing away from Christine and Zuber, towards the approaching reds. The rules of this exercise required the use of bladed weapons or flechettes only, which would be fired at a much-reduced velocity to only mark armour and not penetrate. Swords had their monomolecular edges blunted for the same reason. However, a well-timed blow could still cause considerable pain or break a bone if the target was unlucky or unwary.

Tapping Christine's shoulder, Zuber indicated himself then the group to his right. She nodded, pointing to the six blues to his left, then herself. Setting her flechette launcher to rapid fire, Christine missed Zuber's cue to begin firing. She fired an instant after him, unleashing her own fusillade towards the blues. Her split-second hesitation meant two of her group managed to raise their shields in time, her flechettes simply bouncing off instead of registering kills. Zuber's targets had been less fortunate and all lay where their suits had frozen them, watching events unfold through their helmet's internal screens.

Raising her own shield, she cautiously advanced towards the two Marines, sword drawn. Behind her, Zuber shouted, "They're all yours, Ma'am. Next time don't take so long in firing."

Cursing quietly under her breath, even though no-one could hear her, Christine moved warily in a wide arc, mirroring the movement made by her two opponents who'd split up and were approaching from both sides. Christine knew that unless multiple attackers practised regularly, there was a chance they would get in each other's way, but with these Marines, she didn't think it was likely to happen. Unbidden, the words of her late Weapons Master, Hiro Katana, came to mind.

"Girl, never fight at the same speed as your enemy and when facing multiple attackers do not fixate on one."

She suddenly threw her left arm forward and released her shield, sending it flying at speed towards the face of the nearest attacker on her right. A split second later, as the distracted Marine batted it away with his sword, she rolled forward coming up slightly behind and to his left, at the same time sweeping her sword arm in an arc, so the blade connected with the knee joint of her attacker. He fell forward, his suit registering Christine's attack as disabling and locking it up to signify a kill. As she had planned, his inert body was now between herself and the other, now warier, Marine. He raised his sword in salute at her kill then rested it on the leading edge of his shield, pointing its tip towards her.

Christine's heart was pounding in her ears, now more from excitement at her "kill" than physical exhaustion, and she resisted the urge to leap forward and attack blindly, even though she wanted to do so. She had forgotten how seductive the adrenaline buzz of combat could be for someone like herself. Never taking her eyes off her opponent, she picked up her discarded shield. They circled warily around the body for several seconds, before the amplified voice of Zuber blared out, telling them to get on with it as he didn't have all day.

Using Zuber's words as a distraction, her attacker leapt forward, using the amplified power of his suit's leg muscles to propel him over the body of his comrade. As he landed, Christine brought down an overhead blow which struck his hastily raised shield instead of the intended helmet. His own sword struck upwards, aiming towards where her groin would have been if she hadn't brought down her own shield to block. Using his mass and upwards momentum, the Marine tried to throw her backwards and off balance, so he could land a blow with the edge of his shield. Sensing the move, she followed through with it and executed a graceful backflip, landing on both feet like a cat, shield and sword ready for any follow through.

The Marine ran forward again, swinging his sword towards her head, so Christine decided to finish this and stepped inside the blow, dropping both shield and sword while at the same time raising her rigid left arm inside his arc to block the sword swing. Her open right palm came up and struck the underside of his helmet hard, knocking the head backwards. Locking the Marines right arm with her left and putting pressure on the elbow joint, she used her right to bring his head forward and down, at the same time bringing up her armoured right knee to impact the front of his helmet. Even with the suit's padding, the two blows to his armoured head would have stunned most fighters, and this

Marine was no exception, falling to his knees before toppling backwards into the churned-up earth.

"Bravo, Ma'am," came the voice of Zuber from behind her. "I see you have lost none of your close quarter skills despite sitting on your backside all day."

Christine turned around sharply, fixing him with a stare, her helmet having already retracted back into the suit. Unabashed by her look, Zuber finished what he was saying.

"However, you missed the firing cues I gave you, so I recommend you brush up on our silent battle language as you seem a little rusty." He tilted his head slightly to one side and returned her stare, totally at ease while he waited for her response.

Christine bit back a comment of her own about showing respect, realising she had left rank behind when joining in with this exercise and that Zuber was testing her. "Fair enough, Master Sergeant, I'll take your advice. Back to barracks now?"

"Yes, Ma'am," came the reply, "a shuttle will be picking us up once we reach open ground."

With full control now returned to their suits, the disabled Marines all started to get up from where they had been immobilised. Christine walked a few feet over to the last one she had taken out and extended a gauntleted hand, pulling the Marine to his feet. He retracted his visor, smiled at her and nodded his head in greeting.

"I'll remember those moves, Ma'am. Well fought. My names Johannsson; nice to meet you finally, even if it was a little painful."

Christine considered for a moment, then sent an instruction to Vimes before speaking to Johannsson and all the other Marines on her command channel.

"To thank you for letting me join you today, you and all the other Marines are invited to the Palace tomorrow evening as my guests. Feel free to say no if any of you have prior engagements."

She looked at Zuber, "Will you be able to make it, Master Sergeant?"

"It will be my honour, Ma'am. I hope I fit in as well in your world as you have in mine." He inclined his head a fraction, the nearest thing she was going to get as a compliment from him.

While she was speaking, invitations were pinging up inside the Marines suits, along with ones for partners and children. It was at times like this that Christine loved having Vimes around, knowing he would make all the arrangements for her, rescheduling appointments and issuing apologies without her having to worry about the details. The occasional bit of spontaneity did much to alleviate the metronome-like regularity of her Royal existence.

As the two squads walked together towards the pick-up point, Christine was using her command channel overrides and listening to what was being said about her own performance. She was pleasantly surprised, and not a little relieved too, that the comments were nearly all positive. This went some way to make up for the stiffness already starting to tighten up her muscles, making her look forward to a quick shower and massage back at the Palace, but before that would share some time with the Marines at their debrief session. Along with the other Marines, her suit began registering the shuttle's approach long before it could be seen, so Zuber ordered everyone to pick up the pace and run the last half a mile to the clearing.

"*Yes, I really will need that shower and massage later,*" she thought, as Vimes confirmed to her all the arrangements for the evening had been made, along with a list of rescheduled appointments.

A military shuttle landed quietly in the small clearing ahead, framed by large mature trees. The sky above was clear blue and a welcome change from the subdued forest lighting beneath the large, dense green canopy of leaves and branches. Walking out into the sunlight, Christine squinted slightly until her eyes adjusted to the sunshine. After the forest, it felt good to have the hot sunshine on her face. On reaching the shuttle, doors along one side opened, exposing the familiar open plan arrangement. G-cages had already formed up in rows for the Marines and

Christine took her place at the front, docking with the station and recharging her suit. It had picked up quite a bit of mud and leaf litter from the forest floor, so later she would spend time cleaning it herself. Both Alex and her Weapon Master had drummed into Christine that Marines who wanted to live a long time always looked after their own equipment and didn't leave it for others to do.

"My maids will have a fit if they see me cleaning it in the Imperial suite," she told herself, grinning at the thought.

Within moments of the last Marine docking, the shuttle took off, taking only five minutes to travel the forty kilometres to the nearby spaceport and barracks. First off the shuttle, Christine was greeted by none other than General Parmenion, who saluted as she walked down the ramp. He stepped forward to greet her, all formal now they were no longer in private.

"I watched your progress Majesty, as did many of the Bodyguard not on duty. If you try the close quarter gambit again you might find some of them will be ready for you," he began. "You look as if you enjoyed yourself and worked a few things out of your system."

"I did, Parmenion. Thank you for suggesting it although perhaps I should have guessed I'd have an audience."

Christine found she meant it. Her mind was clearer now than before, and although physically tired, she had enjoyed the change of pace and the excitement of combat. Much of the tension from the previous day's events was gone, and her normal nature had almost fully reasserted itself.

"Maybe I should get Vimes to schedule these into my diary, perhaps once a month?"

Parmenion raised his eyebrows in surprise but said nothing, waving at the Marines who had been waiting patiently for the two of them to finish talking before they disembarked. They filed past on either side, heading towards the ground transport waiting to take them back to barracks and a debriefing.

Christine waited for Master Sergeant Zuber to exit the shuttle, as usual, the last one to leave. She held out her hand. "Thank you, Master Sergeant, I will take your advice and brush up on my battle language. I appreciate your time today."

Shaking the proffered hand, Zuber looked her in the eyes for a second and for a moment, Christine thought she saw the merest flicker of a smile begin at the edges of his eyes and mouth, but before she could be sure, they had gone, replaced with his normal, sour expression.

"Our pleasure, Ma'am, anytime," he replied, before saluting them both and hurrying over to the transport.

Christine walked with Parmenion towards his staff transport, a sleek, black convertible, capable of extended flight at high speed should the situation warrant. His driver opened the doors for them, and they followed the larger transport back to the barracks where Parmenion dropped Christine off outside the briefing hall, before attending to other, more pressing matters.

Looking around, Christine took in the sights and sounds of the military complex. Nearly nine times larger than her Palace building and immediate formal gardens, it lay to the north-west of the Palace, completely surrounded by dense forest that came to within a hundred metres of the perimeter. A flat landing area lay in the middle of a circle five kilometres in diameter, ringed by four, large, crescent-shaped buildings. Two of them, on opposite sides to each other, housed living quarters and barracks for the Marines and their families. To the south-east lay the administrative centre and to the north-east, training and hangar buildings.

Visiting this place never failed to remind Christine the opening shots of the Succession Wars were fired nearby, when the original spaceport and barracks, along with nearly ten thousand loyal Marines, were wiped out from orbit by ships under the command of Marcus, the Emperor's younger brother. The attack had taken place in the early hours of the morning, catching most of the Marines in their quarters with their families. Attacked without warning and given no option to protect their families or surrender, they had all died together in an instant. The site of the old barracks was now designated a war grave and a memorial to the fallen. Over many years, the forest had reclaimed much of the site and the impact craters filled with water, their edges softened by the passage of time and the elements. Every year, on the attack's anniversary, a contingent of Marines would visit the site and pay their respects to fallen comrades, the peace and serenity of the place at stark contrast with the horror it had once borne witness to. This new facility had been built after Alexander had won back his throne and put down the rebellion.

The debriefing was a ribald affair, with many of the Marines who'd taken part finding themselves the butt of several jokes relating to their performance in the field. Even Christine wasn't immune, albeit the jokes at her expense were tactfully kept clean and respectful. Zuber highlighted several areas for improvement and ended with a reminder for everyone to remember that close combat didn't just consist of sword and shield, using Christine's unexpected unarmed attack to highlight his point. His final admonishment of, "*Remember, all weapons are limited by themselves. They are useless until one learns how to apply them in any situation,*" reminded Christine for the second time that day of her old Weapons Master, Hiro Katana.

Many years ago, when she first arrived at the Palace as his wife, Alexander had appointed Hiro to train her in both old and modern combat techniques, just as he'd done for him. A squat, stocky man, he had ruthlessly pushed her for months, ensuring she woke up stiff and sore every morning until her body adapted itself to the training regime. Had she known beforehand about the months of tough training ahead, Christine might have questioned her decision to become Empress, but after the initial shock had worn off, she came to appreciate his martial methods and respect the disciplines he had instilled in her. Many years later, when told of his death, she discovered Hiro had bequeathed her his favourite sword, instead of to Alexander as had been expected. His final note to them both, written in the spidery hand of a man counting down his last few days of life, hoped they might remember him fondly. He went on to regret having to suffer the indignities of spending his final days in bed rather than dying on the battlefield and spoke of his pride in them both. The sword's ownership was his final lesson to them, "*Take nothing for granted.*"

The travel tube ride back to the Palace only took a few minutes, and Christine was soon relaxing in a hot bath, the decision to forego a shower having been made when she started to stiffen up and found exiting the tube difficult. Her masseuse was on standby for when she finished, and clothes were already laid out in readiness for the upcoming formal dinner with several visiting Earls coming to pay their respects after arriving on the planet earlier.

Letting the hot water ease away the ache from her muscles, Christine wondered if having regular sessions with the Marines would be such a good idea after all.

Karen awoke with a start. Annoyed with herself for dropping off, she took a few seconds to take stock of where she was before standing up and stretching. Despite having spent the night in a chair, she had slept well enough, but was stiff in the shoulder and neck from the awkward position and had a bruised hip from where she had been thrown into the ditch. She moved to the foot of the bed and looked at the notes. Adam's high temperature had dropped back a little around five o'clock in the morning; with blood pressure and oxygen levels remaining stable throughout the night...all encouraging signs.

Relieved Adam had made it through the night, Christine wandered off to find a vending machine for a cup of strong coffee and possibly a Twix or Snickers bar, instead of going to the canteen for something more substantial. Seeing a machine at the end of the corridor, she walked towards it, pulling out her mobile phone to check for messages. Noticing the battery was almost out, she ran through the dozen or so emails, noting they were all adverts before switching it off to conserve power. She bought a Twix with the last of the change in her pocket while waiting for the coffee to dispense, then headed back to Intensive Care, using the antiseptic gel from the dispenser to clean her hands before entering.

Now fully awake, apart from the odd yawn, she walked back to Adam's bedside and moved forward to look at his face. He still looked thin and drawn, more so than the previous night. Suddenly curious, she acted on instinct and looked closely at the mysterious metal armband that covered his left forearm. Yesterday, there was hardly any room between it and his arm muscle, but now she could easily get two fingers inside. Moving to her right, she lifted the blanket and looked at his legs. To her amazement, the undamaged muscles had worryingly wasted away by at least a third, and as a result, many of the dressings had become loose. Carefully replacing the blanket, she walked over to the duty station and called over a nurse to check on what she'd seen.

Together they examined Adam, both worried about the noticeable loss of muscle mass. Karen washed her hands thoroughly in the small hand basin next to the bed, then pulled on a pair of blue disposable gloves. Walking over, she lifted the dressing covering the wound on his shoulder and stood very still.

"Oh my God," she said out loud, causing the nurse to come over and see what the matter was. "Look at that. Last night he had suffered abrasion and loss of tissue right down to the bone, and now he has a huge scab."

Together they looked at his other wounds and saw the same thing. Instead of large open wounds, there were scabs with tissue underneath, and the smaller abrasions had healed completely. The compound fracture punctures on his legs were gone too, with just red-looking scars to indicate where the bone had broken through his skin. Trying not to shake, Karen asked the nurse to hold up his head while she unwound the bandage and removed the dressing covering the damage. Amazingly, that too had scabbed over, completely covering the exposed skull. Where before had been a bloody hole, a red, raw-looking eyelid had formed. Karen and the nurse looked at each other, unwilling to accept what they were both seeing, neither of them trusting themselves to comment sensibly. Karen leant closer and gently lifted the eyelid, careful not to damage anything or use undue pressure. A solid, milky white orb filled the socket instead of the expected raw mass of ruined muscle. Within it was the beginnings of a darker iris. Letting the eyelid gently close, she stepped away from the bed and took off the gloves, dropping them into a large pedal bin next to the sink.

"Is this the same patient who came in last night? He is, isn't he?" asked the nurse as she came over again.

Karen nodded, "That's him alright. I'll never forget that face. He saved my life. What's happened here is nothing short of a miracle."

Thinking quickly, Karen gave the nurse some instructions. "We don't want any word of this getting out as the papers and television people will be all over the Hospital. We must keep this quiet. Do you see?"

"Yes, of course, I do. The last thing we need is for the ICU to be distracted, we still have seven other seriously ill patients to look after."

"We'll continue keeping him here under observation. I'll also stay and look after him for a while longer. The fewer that get to see what's happened here, the better. Who knows, at this rate of recovery in a few hours he might be able to tell us himself what is happening to him."

The nurse considered for a few moments then nodded. "If you're OK with that then fine, you can look after him. Just let me know if you have to go away so I can cover."

Watching the nurse walk away to inform the other ICU nurses and attend to her own patients, Karen sat down beside the bed again, her mind whirring with possibilities. She discounted almost immediately the idea they had all made a mistake in their initial diagnosis but still got back up to fetch the notes. No, it was all set out here, in black and white. Severe trauma to the head, compound fractures, etc. She sat back down again, trying to think of any medical condition that might result in these changes.

Vimes was pleased. The accelerated healing factors had worked according to plan and muscle loss had stabilised. He had been focusing much of his attention on Adam's eye and head, but in a moment would also be able to let Adam fully wake and begin interacting with the humans of this place. Surprised, but gratified the young woman called Karen had stayed with them all night, Vimes hoped he would be able to factor her into his plans to get Adam out of here and safely away. However, to do that he needed to increase Adams supply of collagen, calcium phosphate and protein to rapidly repair his bones and replace the muscle mass he'd converted. The best source of all three would be lean red meat and plenty of it, preferably raw. Unfortunately, a request of this nature would probably be looked upon here as a sign of mental illness and draw additional attention to themselves. He slowly brought Adam back to consciousness, keeping his body still, so no indication would be given to anyone watching. Quickly explaining the situation to Adam, he warned him about the damage to his body and that it would be at least another day before he could consider trying to leave due to the broken bones.

"*How did you do all this, Vimes?*" Adam asked, "*You told me I had full control over my body. Did you lie to me?*"

"*Not at all,*" came the reply, "*In the event of a catastrophic failure where you are no longer in control, for example, if unconscious and bleeding out, I have the ability to step in and control your autonomic functions. Once the emergency is over you take back control. That is the only time I can take total control without your permission. To simplify, if I hadn't acted as I did you would now be dead.*"

"*Why didn't you tell me this on the ship along with all the other revelations?*" Adam thought back, not completely convinced.

"*Two reasons Adam. While I can preserve your life in circumstances where others in your position would die, it is not fool-proof. If I had told you this before, you might have taken unnecessary risks, thinking yourself safe from major injury. Secondly, there were other "secrets" you needed to know first. I would have imparted this one to you as required. Remember, it is only a short time since we became reacquainted.*"

"*Well, I want control back. Now!*" Adam insisted. Immediately, he was struck by a wave of pain as Vimes released all the controls and blocks. Taken by surprise, Adam let out a moan and opened his eye, the other one kept shut under the bandages replaced by Karen and the nurse.

Karen was also taken by surprise at the sudden moan from her patient and leant forward just as he opened his eye.

"Welcome back, Adam. What do you remember about yesterday?" Karen asked. There were a dozen questions she wanted answers to but decided to see what he could recall and whether he was able to interact with her.

"I remember the accident but nothing before that," came the reply. "You're the one I saved from being hit, aren't you?"

Karen was struck by his accent, something she couldn't place. Seven years at medical school had exposed her to students and Doctors from every corner of the world, but she couldn't recall anyone sounding like him. She asked where he was from and was puzzled by his momentary hesitation, almost as if he was listening to something else.

"I don't remember. I only know my name is Adam and I somehow ended up walking along that road. Everything else is a blank to me." He let out a low moan. "Can you give me something for the pain please, it seems to be getting worse."

Karen reassured him she would return with something and went to find the duty nurse for keys to the medicine locker. The nurse came back with her and injected morphine into the cannula in his hand, telling him it would take effect in a minute or so. Before she could ask him any more questions, Adam asked for food, insisting he was ravenously hungry and needed to eat right away, preferably meat and food rich in calcium. The nurse looked at Karen for a decision, who nodded and said she would get something from the canteen for him later. After looking at them both for a few seconds, the nurse walked away, to look in on the other patients.

Watching Adam, Karen saw he'd remained very still, breathing regularly and was looking around the room with his good eye, taking everything in.

"Why do you need meat and calcium; do you have a condition we need to know about?" she asked him.

His good eye returned from looking around the room to fix on hers. "Think about this logically, Karen. That is your name, isn't it?"

Before she could ask how he knew, Adam interrupted and told her he'd overheard someone calling her by that name. "I've suffered numerous breakages and tissue loss. You've probably noticed how much I've shrunk in mass overnight. That's because my body has been cannibalising itself to heal the damage. To continue healing, I need raw materials for my body to use, such as protein and calcium. Give me the raw materials, and I will be out of here in another day."

Her initial instinct was to laugh at his naïveté, but his manner and supreme confidence in what he was saying made her stop and reassess. Thinking hard she reviewed the facts. Normally this man in front of her should be dead or so badly traumatised by his ordeal that asking for food would be the last thing on his mind. The head injuries alone would probably have left most men in a coma, yet here he was, lucid and asking for food and in a strange way making perfect sense. There was no denying his body had miraculously speeded up the healing process by a factor of thirty and the overnight muscle loss was not medically explainable, let alone the tissue regeneration. So maybe he did know something she didn't. Recalling a much-used quotation from Sherlock Holmes, *"When you have eliminated all which is impossible, then whatever remains, however improbable, must be the truth,"* Karen decided to accept his explanation at face value, and in the absence of any other explanation, would take the risk.

"OK, I'll get you something. Tell me, Adam, how can you do this. What are you?" Again, she could sense a momentary hesitation before replying.

"I'm human, just like you, but I happen to heal rapidly. I can't tell you anything else until I've learned to trust you. If word gets out about my gift I'd never know peace again, would I?"

With that, he closed his eye and took a deep breath, wincing as he forgot about his damaged ribs.

"Please, just get me some food. There's money in my trouser pocket if you need it."

Karen stood motionless for a while, thinking through all what had just been said, balancing the risks against the potential benefit to her patient. She made a decision. If he was hungry then eating would do him no harm, far from it and if what he was saying was true, doing as asked would speed up the process and make for an amazing write-up in the Lancet.

Decision made, Karen walked off to get him a plate of food, first stopping off at the nurses' station and asking for an injection of Calcium Chloride to be ready for when she returned. Annoyingly, Karen realised she had left her ID card and purse behind in the house. The ID doubled as a credit card for the canteen, and without money she was stuck. Remembering what he'd said, she walked back to his bed and looked through the pile of clothes that had been brought up earlier from A&E. Surprised and a little disturbed at the wad of notes, she put it in her pocket for safe keeping.

Downstairs in the canteen, Karen took two plates from the warming stack and jiggled them around on her tray until they fit. The queue for food was small this morning, so she piled both plates with bacon, sausages, scrambled eggs, hash browns and beans without getting too many strange looks. Just before reaching the till, she also picked up three bottles of freshly squeezed orange juice, thinking to herself that whatever he didn't eat she would, for the sight and smell of the food was making her very hungry. The lady at the till gave her a withering look when proffered a fifty-pound note, then grudgingly gave change. For the briefest of moments Karen had a vision of herself tipping the tray's contents over the woman's head, but instead said thank you and smiled politely.

By the time she returned to the ICU, Adam was awake and sitting up in bed, apparently after insisting the nurse help him as his arms were still too damaged to support his weight. The nurse was fussing around him, looking slightly bemused as to what she should do next. She walked towards Karen, leaning forward to have a quiet word.

"I've left the injection on the tray at the foot of his bed, and I think we can move him out into a general ward later today. He might only have one eye, but I swear he was staring at my bottom a little while ago, so I think he's certainly on the mend!"

Looking down at the tray of food Karen had in her hands, the nurse shook her head and walked off, leaving her alone. Karen sat down next to the bed and asked him what he wanted to eat first.

When Adam said he wasn't bothered, just start bringing it to his mouth, she piled a heap of scrambled egg onto a fork and began feeding him like a baby. Seeing her smile, he asked, between mouthfuls, what was so funny.

"You're by far the largest baby I've ever had to feed. I didn't think I would be spending my holiday looking after a stranger, but I suppose it's the least I can do for you."

Again, there was that brief hesitation before he spoke, shorter this time but still noticeable.

"It was my pleasure to save you, Karen, really." His one eye looked at hers, switching between left and right. "If I had to do it again I would do so without hesitation although next time I would try and get out of the way of that...lorry before it hit me. He motioned with his head for her to feed him some more.

Watching him rapidly eat the food, she noted he hardly seemed to be chewing and certainly couldn't be enjoying the taste as he was eating so fast. Within minutes, the first plate was empty, and he indicated hungrily towards the second. Karen asked if he was sure, but he simply nodded and gave her a smile. Karen looked closely at his face, and although she knew it had to be her imagination, he already looked more vital and awake. Gently shaking her head, she again wondered to herself who he was and what the hell she was getting herself into.

Despite being almost completely focused on the food in front of him, which although it didn't look too appetising, smelt and tasted wonderful, Adam noticed Karen looking at him and the slight shaking of her head. He surmised she was asking herself what to do next and whether she should trust him. To gain her confidence, Adam weighed up the risk of providing more information against that of discovery but couldn't decide what to do. Surprisingly, Vimes had been unusually silent since he woke, talking only when asked. He assumed Vimes was still focusing on healing his body and converting the food into usable raw materials, so he decided not to ask him for advice.

"Karen, I know it must be hard for you to trust me when I don't know much myself," he began, between mouthfuls, "but my body is telling me exactly what I need right now. I can't explain it to you, I just know."

Karen didn't respond, just kept on feeding him until the second plate was empty, along with two of the orange bottles. Placing the empty tray down, she picked up the syringe.

"This is an injection of calcium chloride which will help with your bone growth. We'll see how you get on with this. Are you up for talking a bit more?"

"I'm tired, Karen, but ask away. Perhaps your questioning will jog a few memories. As I've already told you, I remember the accident but nothing before that. I don't know where I'm from, what my...surname is or how I came to be on Skye that evening. It's all blank."

He looked at her face, trying to make himself look vulnerable. "If I knew more I would tell you. What I do know is that I must get back there as I'm sure it will help jog my memory. Is it far?"

"A few hours by car," she said. "My aunt and uncle have a house there, near to where you were run over. I had just arrived to spend a few weeks at their house while they were away on holiday. I need to find somewhere to..."

Karen suddenly stopped talking, realising she was giving away too much information. "*I'd make a terrible inquisitor*," she thought, deciding to wait for Adam to add something before saying anything else.

Adam noted she stopped herself and decided that was enough for now. He yawned and asked if she would mind his going to sleep as he'd become very tired.

"I'll talk to you later, Adam," Karen said, picking up the tray and heading back to the canteen where she was going to get herself a big breakfast and try to make sense of what was happening.

Karen had almost finished her fried breakfast, and over a pot of tea was contemplating how much nicer the world seemed on a full stomach. Using the last of her bread to soak up the remaining tomato juice and pop it into her mouth, she sighed contentedly and leant back in her chair, looking around the room at the other people eating there. At this time of the morning, most were Hospital staff and she nodded whenever she caught the eye of someone she recognised. In the far corner sat a young couple, looking tired and sad; probably staying in the same residential block she had while their child received treatment. The dark shadows under the eyes of the mother were a giveaway, for she'd unfortunately seen that haunted, sad look all too often.

Karen picked up her cup of tea and cradled it in both hands, looking back over the last few days. Her break-up with Ian seemed to have happened a lifetime ago and the associated problems an irrelevance not worth worrying about in the scheme of things. Annoyingly, a part of her mind was trying to tell her something. It was nagging her like a broken tooth which you couldn't resist touching all the time with your tongue. Was it some kind of sixth sense or simply annoyance at not being completely in control of events anymore?

Shrugging the feeling away, she again let her mind go blank and sat there, people-watching, trying to guess why they were coming to the Hospital and what sort of lives they lead. She did this for fifteen minutes before gathering up her rubbish and depositing it on the trolley rack for collection. With one last look around, she left the room and headed back to the ICU to check up on her mystery man.

Despite only having been gone for just over an hour, the change in Adam was remarkable. Whereas before his face had looked pinched and drawn, it now seemed to have filled out a little. Still sitting up in bed, he was now flexing his wrists and hands, seemingly without too much pain. Grabbing a handful of mixed dressings from the supply area, she walked over to the hand basin near his bed and washed her hands. After putting on a pair of the disposal gloves, she told Adam she was going to have another look at his head and eye. He didn't say anything, so she began unwinding the bandage and gently pulled away the dressing covering his eye and head. The eyelid looked better, not as red or raw as before, but when she tried to open it, he pulled his head away for a second, before relenting and staying still. Reaching forward again, he opened it himself and looked at her before she could do so herself. Although the mass in his eye socket remained cloudy white, it was now more solid and the iris better defined than before. At her request, Adam moved it from side to side, indicating the socket muscles had fully recovered. Thankfully, there were no signs of inflammation or infection. Moving her attention to his head, the dressing came away easily and revealed the same scab as before, but this time, it had cracked in places to reveal healthy-looking skin beneath.

It was the same on his left shoulder and legs, scabbed but definite signs of healthy skin forming rapidly underneath. Looking into his eyes, both of them this time, Karen thought she saw on his face a flash of, "I told you so," just before he tried to say something. Karen interrupted before he could go any further, asking if he wanted more food. He nodded and smiled. Redressing the wounds, Karen mentioned she'd had to use some of his money to buy food but that she would repay him when she had the chance. He nodded and didn't seem at all bothered, saying she could help herself if she needed anything else.

With new dressings now in place, she headed back to the canteen to get him more food.

By the time the canteen was getting ready for the lunchtime rush, Adam had demolished three more trays of food and at least two litres of juice. When paying for the last tray, the sour-faced woman on the till simply looked down at the pile of food and then Karen's stomach, before ringing up the price and taking the money without another word.

Sitting by his bedside, watching him eat the last plateful, Karen tried to get more information out of Adam, but he continued to insist on not having any recollection before the accident. She was no expert on memory loss but knew enough to understand that it could be caused by a traumatic injury such as he'd experienced, but it did seem a tad convenient. Then there were these occasional hesitations in his speech, almost as if he was double checking with someone what he was saying for consistency or accuracy. On the other hand, he was friendly enough and seemed very interested in all what had happened to him and about Skye.

She needed to buy some things in Inverness later, so scheduled a scan of his head for when she was away shopping. Although the scans taken on admission had been clear, she wanted one final check to make sure.

Luckily the room she'd used in the residential block was still vacant, so she had somewhere to stay for the next few nights before having to get back to Skye. Unfortunately, she didn't have any spare clothes or toiletries and was starting to feel distinctly uncomfortable in two-day old clothes. She caught a taxi into Inverness and hit Primark for something cheap and cheerful that could be thrown away in a few days' time. A visit to Boots provided basic toiletries, and by the time she headed back to the taxi rank, both hands were full of sundry plastic and large paper shopping bags from various stores. On arriving back at the Hospital, she gratefully dumped them in her room before adding up what she now owed Adam. Looking at the figure, she raised an eyebrow. At this rate, she was going to be in his debt both financially and morally.

When she got back to the main hospital block, she thanked the ICU Ward Sister again for allowing her to stay and look after Adam. Unsurprisingly, his scans had all come back clear, and his rapid progress hadn't gone unnoticed. The Ward Sister was eager to free up his bed for more seriously ill patients and return him to a normal ward, but as a professional courtesy had wanted to check with Karen first. Both agreed this was the best course of action and a bed was quickly found for him in a single room, away from prying eyes. The transfer didn't take long, and as Karen was placing Adam's clothes in the plywood cupboard of his new room, she enquired how he was feeling.

"Much better now Karen, although I'm still hungry," came the prompt reply with another of his smiles.

Karen returned it and headed off to the canteen, hoping the sour-faced woman wasn't still on duty. Returning with another tray full of food, Adam waved away her assistance and asked for it to be placed in front of him. Gingerly at first, but with increasing confidence, he picked up the utensils and began to eat. Karen watched him, fascinated by his actions. He seemed totally at ease with the fork, but the shape of the knife at first gave a few problems, however within twenty minutes all the food was gone, and Karen moved the tray away to the foot of the bed. Looking down at his chart she checked the numbers. Blood pressure 105:65, heart rate 60bpm, oxygenation 100%, all indicating a very fit person in the prime of health. The only anomaly was his raised body temperature, several degrees above normal.

"Have you been to the toilet yet?" she asked. Again, there was that momentary look of distraction she had come to recognise.

"The nurse kindly brought me a bottle to use after you left. There is likely to be no solid waste until tomorrow."

The way he said it with such a deadpan expression made Karen laugh, and he asked if he had said anything wrong.

"No, it's just the way you looked when you spoke. It was just funny, that's all," Karen apologised, still smiling.

She pulled over a chair to sit by his bedside and they talked. Karen found his deep, yet soft voice attractive to listen to and was getting used to the slightly sing-song quality of his accent. He was curious about her life, and this time she decided to open up to him, explaining about her work and somewhat estranged family, hoping it might jog some of his own memories. She suddenly felt uncomfortable at the thought of mentioning Ian to this man and carefully avoided bringing him up in the conversation. Adam appeared very interested in her medical training and how she fitted in with the community. Another topic that fascinated him was politics and the Royal Family, which struck her as a strange subject for an amnesiac to be interested in. The longer they spoke together, the more obvious it became that if Adam was feigning ignorance on all these subjects, then he was a superb actor, for it was plain there were huge holes in his understanding of even the simplest day to day things. She tried to trick him on several occasions, but his ignorance rang true.

As the afternoon turned into evening, Karen was surprised to find herself looking at his handsome face. For a moment, she wondered what it would be like to lean forward and kiss him. Something must have shown on her face, for he stopped talking and asked her what was wrong. Somewhat flustered, she changed the subject and inquired what the large armband was for, something she had meant to ask since his awakening.

As expected, Adam protested ignorance but pointed out it didn't hurt and seemed to have been formed in one piece around his forearm. He held it up to her for closer inspection, and she could see it was indeed made of one, seamless piece of metal. She ran her hand along its surface, noting how smooth and warm it was to the touch. In doing so, his arm moved slightly, and she found herself holding the back of Adam's hand. Despite having done so many times before when attending to his wounds, on this occasion she felt an electric tingle go through her, and she pulled her hand away with a start, looking up at Adam's face and seeing in it something that mirrored her own surprise.

Adam too, sensed something had just happened and now wanted nothing more than to be left alone to think. Feigning a yawn, he apologised and said he needed to have a rest. Glad of the cue, Karen agreed and said she would return in the morning with some more food. Briefly showing him the pull-cord that would summon a nurse should he need any assistance, she wished him goodnight and closed the door behind her as she left.

Adam stared at the closed door for several minutes, before closing his eyes in an attempt to sleep. After an unsuccessful fifteen minutes, Adam gave in and asked Vimes to help him, his last recollection before drifting off was hearing a quiet chuckle from his ever-watchful companion.

The walk back to her room was an interesting one for Karen, full of conflicting emotions. She couldn't believe she'd even considered kissing him, if for no other reason than she was currently his de facto Doctor. The electric frisson when they touched hands was something new, however, and wasn't sure whether she wanted it to happen again or not. Slipping into bed and laying her head on the pillow, before sleep took her, Karen wondered if she would welcome dreams of Adam that night and what form they might take.

During the hours of darkness, Dauntless slowly moved into a geostationary orbit above the capital city Kirushan, with Admiral Frith taking care to position the flagship directly above Frederick's personal residence. Unlike the planet Capital, on Kiyami the signs of an advanced civilisation were noticeable everywhere from orbit. On the planet's dark side, great cities shone brightly and the large central continent, making up ninety per cent of the total landmass, was edged with light. Much of the interior was also illuminated by artificial light, with national parks and nature reserves standing out darkly against the bright background. The remaining landmasses were made up of numerous small islands, dotted around the central continent, the majority of these also shining brightly.

Colonised in the early part of the second millennia, Kiyami was strategically important due to the number of planets that came under its control, the number of Jump Points and its proximity to three aggressive rival human empires, the Durotriges, Dubunni and Silures. Although the Empire was nominally at peace with all three, the reality was somewhat different. Intermittent border infractions, depending on their severity, required varying degrees of response and extended periods of peace were rare. It was not uncommon for the rival empires to be at war with each other and on occasion, fighting would sometimes spill over into space next to the Imperium.

Before moving into orbit, Admiral Frith had ordered all planetary weapon platforms within range of the flagship to power down. She had no intention of taking any chances with the Emperor's safety, nor that of her flagship or task-force. The recent attack on Alexander's life had made her realise that in some areas she may have become complacent, a potential mistake she would not repeat. Frith decided to follow the example of her predecessor, Dauntless's second Captain, Admiral Hale. On taking over command from him, he'd given her just fifteen words of advice before leaving.

"Remember, Janice. Be polite, be professional, but have a plan to kill everyone you meet."

Those simple, if stark words had proved useful on several occasions, but did nothing to endear her in some quarters, especially with those who spent their military careers trying to get promoted at any price or were focused on the cost of everything and the value of nothing.

Until Frith was certain there was no longer any risk to Alexander's life, she was going to insist all safety protocols were followed to the letter, especially when a planet had such formidable close-in defences, capable of overwhelming her relatively small force in a short space of time. Looking at the defences protecting Kiyami, Frith thought to herself that although Duke Frederick may have been reluctant to spend on his naval fleet, whatever money he'd saved had obviously been spent on upgrading his planet's fixed defences.

Personally, Frith disapproved of trying to protect a planet through over-reliance on orbital or ground-based defences, preferring the flexibility of a strong, mobile Navy with the ability to engage attackers away from the planet, rather than waiting to engage at close range. Experience, hard-won on battlefields over many years fighting against the Empire's enemies, had taught her the importance of controlling the fighting distance and retaining the ability to move to a position of advantage. To her mind, allowing the enemy to close within range of the planet's defences allowed no margin of error or retreat. Just one vessel, impacting on the planet at a small fraction of light speed, would cause tremendous damage to the ecosystem and loss of life. However, despite this, there remained many who were convinced sheer defensive firepower alone would keep a planet safe from attack.

While she had no reason to doubt the Duke, nor the loyalty of the forces locally, she agreed with the Emperor's decision to entertain Frederick and his retinue here on Dauntless, rather than go down on the surface. A formal reception taking place on the ship would also provide a welcome distraction for her command staff and allow them an opportunity to mix socially with their opposite numbers locally, before moving out to engage with the Raiders currently plaguing this Sector's border regions. She made a final check and Dauntless's AI confirmed it had everything in hand, even down to guest staterooms prepared in case they were needed. Finally, she could relax a little.

Newly promoted, Squadron Leader Christine Harris was making use of her free time to go over the personnel files of the twenty fighter pilots making up her new command. The promotion had been bitter-sweet for Harris, resulting from the recent action on Heaven that saw her fellow pilot killed. At the Review Board meeting, Harris's commanding officer had intimated to her that a recommendation had come in supporting the promotion from none other than Duke Gallagher.

There was no time for regret or second thoughts, as she would be taking up her new command on INS Courageous when the task-force headed out to engage the raiders. For her first meeting with her new command, Harris knew it would be important to make a good first impression.

Her few possessions were already packed and waiting to be shipped over to Courageous on the next shuttle. While in no way cramped, she would not be sad to say goodbye to her current quarters and was looking forward to the additional cabin space that came with her new posting and promotion. Carriers, although normally larger than battleships, had less communal space, as any spare room was usually reserved for spare parts, fighters and repair facilities. She was fortunate to be going as a Squadron leader and not an ordinary pilot, for this entitled her to larger quarters.

The previous night's party, celebrating her promotion and transfer, had been somewhat subdued, tempered as it was by the losses they had suffered on Heaven. To make matters worse, she found herself having to listen to Flt Lt Schmidt go on and on about what a bastard the Crown Prince had been and the embarrassing meeting she'd had with the Emperor. Initially, Harris had found the story hilariously funny, but Schmidt had drunk one too many and just didn't seem to know when to stop talking about it. Soon afterwards, Harris decided to get an early night and leave her own party, not sure if anyone had even noticed her leaving.

A new fighter from the Carrier had been selected for her personal use and flown over to Dauntless on autopilot earlier that morning. She would use the flight back to familiarise herself with its unique peculiarities and handling characteristics. She knew that on arriving at her new ship, it was traditional for a Squadron to greet their new leader and Harris was keen to make a good first impression.

She scanned the list of names and summaries in front of her, matching them with the fresh faces of the pilots. The holograms had probably been taken when they first enlisted and not updated since. Harris noted most of the pilots had been in service for several years, and almost all had seen at least one combat action.

With no replacement pilots having joined her squadron in the past twelve months, there was every chance it would be nice and tight. A few names stood out for her to watch: Pilot Officers Coleman, Hinchin and Quigley. All three were experienced and competent pilots, but the outgoing Squadron Leader had commented that they tended not to mix too well with the other flyers and Hinchin was currently displaying an issue with authority figures. Harris made a mental note to watch them for a while before making up her own mind about what, if anything, needed changing.

Finishing off, Harris downloaded the files into her personal data storage. She took one last look around the room that had been her home since being posted to Dauntless, squared her shoulders and walked through the door for the last time.

The transit tube took less than thirty seconds to arrive at the flight deck where her new fighter was docked. She looked through the transparent metal of the hangar bay, her eyes quickly scanning along the row of fighters until she recognised hers, decked out in the colours of Courageous and docked closest to the entrance. Ten metres in length, with three matter conversion engines placed at the rear, she noted it appeared to be factory fresh. A single seat variant, with just enough room to fit one passenger behind the pilot for short journeys in an emergency, it had one large and two small diameter rail-guns situated along the ventral axis, complemented by four missile launchers along each side. Its smart-metal hull was currently matt black, highlighted along the rear and nose with blue and yellow markings to signify which carrier it was from.

When Harris's original application to join the Imperial Navy was processed, she discovered her aptitude scores had ranked her high for aggression, individuality and G-tolerance, making her a good candidate for officer training at flight school. Before becoming a pilot, she had, like most of her fellow applicants, wondered why human pilots were still needed. Fighters equipped with semi-sentient AI's could tolerate far higher acceleration and G-forces than their human equivalents. It had been carefully explained to her that human pilots had two abilities AI's could not currently match, namely unpredictability and intuition. AI's, for all their advantages, were predictable and tactically boring, preferring the certainty of algorithms to the sheer unpredictability of feeling or instinct. Those two talents could not effectively be duplicated or predicted by systems, hence the need for humans at the controls, despite their inherent limitations. However, the realities of modern space combat meant that fighters were nearly always remotely operated from the relative safety of the Carrier and their pilots would normally only get in the actual cockpit for training, acclimatisation or atmospheric flights in support of some ground actions.

For Harris, killing another sentient was personal, not something you delegated to a machine. In combat, be it on a blood-soaked battlefield fighting your opponent, or in the airlessness of space dogfighting with an enemy fighter, it was one-on-one. Bombarding a planet or another capital ship, hundreds or thousands of kilometres distant, was too impersonal and didn't seem right. She knew her viewpoint was deemed old-fashioned by many people, but it was just the way she felt.

Harris walked through the waiting area, instructing the smart metal collars of her flight-suit to form a helmet and gloves, then entered the airlock leading to the vacuum of the flight deck where her fighter was sitting. As the airlock finished cycling, all external sounds suddenly cut off and all she could hear was the noise of her own breathing and vibrations picked up from the floor via the soles of her flight boots. She walked the short distance to her fighter, stopping at a control interface situated underneath, placing her gauntleted right hand on it to transmit recognition codes to the ship and alert Primary Hangar Control.

The fighter's AI recognised and welcomed her, activating flight systems in readiness for departure. Smart-metal dropped down from underneath the cockpit area and formed an open cocoon, inviting her to step inside. She did so and felt it retract up into the body of the craft, where a standard breathable atmosphere was maintained. She agreed to the fighter's AI request for integration and felt it interface with her senses. Taste, sight and hearing all merged with its sensor array, while touch and bodily awareness became one with the feel of the fighter. Muscular awareness, even discomfort, was linked to the performance of the engines, and her sense of wellbeing grew, reflecting the fighter's combat status.

Interfacing with a top of the line fighter was a far more intimate experience than linking to simpler craft, for example, her previous shuttle. Harris remembered back to her first full linkage at the naval training academy. Some of her fellow candidates had literally freaked out at the sensation and those who could not accept the intimate connection were instantly dropped from training and reassigned. In civilian life, many people were prepared to pay thousands of credits to achieve the feeling of superiority and wellness that came with a merging, yet here she was, a girl from a farm planet getting to experience this all for free. However, the sensations were seductive, and with an effort, she focused on the job at hand.

Looking around the interior, she instinctively recognised where everything was and what it did, another benefit of the merging. All systems were at one-hundred per cent efficiency, and Harris could almost believe she could sense the fighter wanting to get out and fly free of the hangar.

"Primary Hangar Control, this is CF103 requesting permission to depart for INS Courageous."

"Agreed CF103, please follow designated flight path until you have cleared restricted space. On behalf of the PHC team, good luck with your new posting. Lift when ready," came the almost immediate response.

Letting her mind relax, Harris gave the fighter its instructions. Lifting gently from the docking station, CF103 rose to a height of ten metres, rotated left forty-five degrees and began passing the other lined-up fighters at a fast walking pace, heading for the hangar exit. PHC gave a green light, and she exited the bay, accelerating rapidly away from Dauntless in the direction of her new home. Agreed earlier, her flight path followed a roundabout route that would allow her to test out the new fighter, which would remain hers until she either moved on or it was destroyed in action. Fighters almost always came back from actions unscathed or not at all, for space and modern combat made for little or no margin of error.

Harris had never seen Kiyami like this before, as she hadn't been asked to pilot any shuttles down to the planet on her previous visit to the system. Drawing her eyes away from the beautiful planet, Harris turned the fighter towards the area where she would begin the familiarisation processing. Twisting and rolling under various degrees of thrust, Harris sought to test the operational limits of both herself and the fighter. Although the calibration could have been done in a testing rig, she preferred to let the fighter's AI learn first-hand what she was capable of withstanding, allowing it to build up a pattern of her behaviours and reaction times for any given action. Harris spent an hour flinging the fighter around before deciding to finish, by now feeling sweaty and in need of a shower despite the best efforts of the environmental controls to keep her cool. She terminated the testing and called Courageous to let them know she was coming home.

Ten minutes later, INS Courageous came into view. Four large hangars were arranged around a central core containing main engines and living quarters. Each of the hangars was a self-contained fighting unit, and in an emergency, could operate independently of the main ship. Her main offensive armament consisted of massive railguns running the entire axis of the central body, capable of taking out a Capital ship or bombarding a planet. Defensively, a myriad of point defence systems covered all available space on the five conjoined hulls. The Carrier's design was very striking and reminded her of a word of advice she'd been given in flight training by a seasoned Carrier pilot, "*Don't make yourself conspicuous as it draws fire to you. That's why we call Carriers' missile magnets.*"

Closing with her new home, Harris again felt the familiar sense of unease as her fighter passed under the watchful eyes of its powerful point defences. Approaching number two hangar, the slight resistance of the invisible shielding indicated she was about to relinquish control back to the AI for docking.

The AI took over, linking with Primary Hanger Control to bring her in. Passing through the enormous hangar bay doors and with nothing to do, Harris tried to take in as many of the new sights as possible, realising she would never view them again in the same way. As on Dauntless, her fighter passed rows of other craft, all neatly docked in their cradles for immediate launch. On reaching its allotted cradle, her fighter quickly lowered itself, and she began the process of unmerging. Looking out of the cockpit, she observed a group of pilots watching closely from inside the waiting area, and with a sinking feeling, realised they were her new squadron and responsibility.

Harris hoped she would be up to the task.

Vimes interrupted Christine at breakfast, confirming the first set of financial and other requested data had arrived for him to process. Frustratingly, ten of the Sectors were still collating information, something Vimes noted for future investigation. The requested non-financial information would now probably arrive before the last of the central banks responded.

"Are you all right, Ma'am?" asked Ayumu, interrupting the stream of information from Vimes. An old retainer who had known Alexander as a boy, Ayumu was sitting directly opposite her on the other side of the table. Before Vimes had interrupted, they had been discussing how lovely sea-views were from the residential areas of the Palace.

"You seemed distracted for a second. Forgive me if I've gone on too long on the subject."

"Not at all, Ayumu. Our talk simply brought back a memory of when I first came here and looked out over the sea. I got lost in the recollection for a moment. Please continue."

"I was saying I'd read in the Palace history that the views here were one of the reasons why the original Alexander chose this site. He was said to have once commented the views were some of the most spectacular on Capital."

Christine nodded. "Yes, I've read that too. When I first looked out from the Palace across the sea, it felt as though I'd been looking for somewhere like this all my life. I felt at home here almost immediately...once I'd become used to the idea of being the Empress!"

She paused for a moment before continuing, waiting for Vimes to answer her request for additional information on the Palace.

"The original Palace was only a quarter of its current size, and almost every Emperor or Empress has had a go at remodelling it in some way. My husband is one of the few who has not made any changes, as he feels it's perfect just the way it is. Now then, tell me about your family and those great-grandchildren of yours." Christine leant forward slightly to emphasise the connection between herself and Ayumu.

All around them, the conversations moved back and forth across the table, covering various subjects. Some related to the running of the Palace while others touched on political or social issues experienced by the diners. Christine made a careful note to have her administrative staff look into the more serious and report back to her so she could provide feedback or take action if required.

Breakfast over, everyone stood and bowed as she left the room, heading back across the lawns and gardens towards her private quarters. Thankfully, today held no formal meetings in the Grand Hall of Empire, giving her enough time to read some of Vimes preliminary findings before knuckling down to the business of running Sector One.

Later, after a quick freshen up, Christine left her private quarters and walked along one of the many corridors to meet with her advisors in the rooms reserved for Sector One business. Facing inwards towards the gardens, with a clear view over the refractory and the lakes beyond, these offices were the central hub for the Sector from where the activities of the two hundred and five Lords and Ladies were monitored and controlled. Although each solar system was the noble's personal fiefdom, it was prudent to keep watch to ensure abuses or unrest were quickly dealt with. Just as the Crown kept watch over their actions, they in turn did the same for the Earls, Viscounts and Barons who reported to them.

Christine entered the meeting room, noting the leathery scent of new chairs as she walked to the head of the table. Like all the others on this side of the Palace, the room faced inwards and had a clear view over the grounds. A long, narrow table dominated the centre of the room, its deep brown wood heavily polished and reflecting the sunlight coming in through the large window. Bottles of water and fruit juices were arranged neatly along both sides of table, designating where everyone would sit. On her entering, all the small groups of people already there broke up and took their places, waiting for her to acknowledge them. When everyone was ready, she did so with a nod of the head and sat down, bidding them all to do the same and relax. Everyone sat and began arranging their personal spaces to suit their personalities, moving cups and tablets around until satisfied, some quietly checking none of the others had encroached on their space.

Christine looked down the length of the table, looking for any signs of concern or nervousness amongst the officials. Two of them, seated halfway down the table, seemed unduly tense, so she decided to begin with them once her personal assistants had finished going through the order of business and previous actions from the minutes.

Formalities over, Christine asked the two men for an update, noting they represented a group of twenty-two systems running along her Sector's border with their closest alien neighbours, the Felidae. It transpired that several ships, whose origins and configuration could not be identified, had been sighted along the buffer zone between Empire and Felidae space. Although probably of Felidae origin, a race whose aggressive reaction to interlopers meant any stranger entering their territory would be immediately attacked without warning, the size and configuration of the ships did not match any of their known designs. The two delegates were seeking assurances that additional security measures would be taken along the border and the Felidae Ambassador asked to comment.

Christine could appreciate their nervousness. In 3842, First Contact had been made with the Felidae, almost immediately erupting into a full-scale war across Sectors One, Two and Thirty-six. Twenty-one years of constant, bitter fighting led to a peace of sorts being brokered between the two empires by Alexander's Grandfather, Richard IV. The Felidae were the first, and so far the only, feline based race encountered. Averaging the same size as a human male, they resembled large cats, especially when they chose to travel on all fours. Bi-pedal for short periods, their front paws had adapted to using tools, helped by two of their five paw pads being opposable. Their society was known to be Matriarchal and distrustful of other races. Clothes were not usually worn, although comprehensive combat armour complete with retractable claws had been recovered and studied at length. The full extent of their empire remained unknown at the end of the war, with little more known today although the Imperial Intelligence Service estimated it was comparable to that of the Empire in volume, albeit with fewer inhabited systems.

Vimes had already begun checking their reports for her and projected a hologram above the middle of the table so that all the other delegates could see a simulacrum of the unidentified ships. Comparable in size to their own ships of the line, these were unmistakably built for combat. Multiple weapon configurations and point defences could be clearly seen, and the speed demonstrated when they became aware of being observed, indicated powerful engines. The room filled with voices as most began questioning their neighbours or commenting on the hologram.

"Thank you for the report," Christine's voice cut through the noise, subtly enhanced by Vimes through the rooms PA system.

Everyone fell silent and turned to look at her as the hologram faded away.

"Why hasn't this been brought to my attention before now. When did it happen?

"We only received the images and notification today by courier signal from the border, Ma'am, and as we were already meeting with you, thought we would bring it to your personal attention rather than pass it up through the slower official channels."

The two men looked uncomfortable about not having followed protocol but continued, "The respective Nobles along the border have all been informed and no doubt they will each send their own personal representations to petition you in due course."

In her mind, Vimes confirmed to Christine he would immediately set up a meeting with the Chiefs of Staff, and fast courier messages were ready to be sent to both Sectors thirty-six and two, advising Dukes Markham and Gallagher of the development. *"I'll wish to extend my own personal greetings before sending. Please remind me to do so immediately after this meeting."*

Looking at the two officials, Christine thanked and reassured them the matter would receive immediate attention. Relaxing noticeably, they nodded gratefully, and both leaned back into their chairs, pleased to have spoken first and could now relax a little.

Christine allowed Vimes to take over the meeting from her so she could consider this latest move from the Felidae.

"Is this related in any way to the attempt on Alex and Adam?" she asked herself, thinking back to her interactions with the Felidae. She had met a Felidae Matriarch only twice before, once on her official marriage to Alexander when their Empress honoured them with her presence for a brief period, and again on the Matriarch's death when they returned the honour and met with the new Empress, Freyja, on her home planet, Mau Prime. Aloof, disdainful, cunning, yet extremely honourable and intelligent, the Felidae had no sense of mercy or compassion whatsoever, making them implacable and unpredictable opponents. From the little anyone knew of their behaviour, it would be out of character for them to break an agreement, so Christine decided it probably wasn't a chance meeting, rather a deliberate show of force to keep the Empire at arm's length.

Surprising everyone, especially the Imperial Intelligence Service, Christine and Freyja had bonded well at their first meeting and now corresponded with each other from time to time. Just like a cat Christine had once owned as a child, Freyja seemed to be fascinated with her for short periods, communicating regularly, then lose interest for long periods before getting back in contact again.

"I'll let the Chiefs of Staff run with this one," she thought to herself and Vimes, *"We don't want to get distracted from uncovering who was behind the assassination attempt. Please ensure your counterpart avatars on the border are quietly updated by IQA and find*

out why this news hadn't been communicated to us the same way. Now is not the time for surprises."

With that final thought, Christine brought herself back to the meeting at hand. Taking over from Vimes, she called a brief recess so everyone could take a comfort break, and went to get herself a strong cup of tea from one of the stewards.

The reception for Duke Frederick and his retinue was going well. The annoyance Alexander had expected from Frederick didn't materialise, and to his surprise, the Duke seemed to have positively embraced visiting the flagship, only insisting on being able to stream the Reception to his planet.

The practical and political arrangements for the visit had been made between Vimes and Fredrick's personal AI. Amusingly for Alexander, Vimes had twice complained to him about how pompous and arrogant Frederick's AI was, prompting a comment about the pot calling the kettle black. Admiral Frith had wisely excused herself from the reception an hour earlier, citing pressing ship matters, which meant he couldn't use that excuse himself and had to stay until the end.

Deborah, the longest lasting of Fredrick's many mistresses, had taken Frith's seat to Alexander's left and was trying on and off to make half-hearted small-talk with him. She seemed unhappy to be at the reception, and a quick query to Vimes confirmed the reason. Vimes had told him Court rumour had it she was soon to be permanently replaced by Frederick's new favourite, the stunningly beautiful woman currently sitting to the Duke's right in a position of honour.

The finest musicians and entertainers on the planet had been retained on short notice by the Duke for the event and were living up to their reputations. Also, the old Duke was in fine form, complementing Alexander and earnestly inquiring as to the health of his wife and son. Not yet wishing to reveal Adam was no longer on board and had been sent away, Alexander had made an excuse for Adam's absence from the evening's activities. However, Frederick waved away his apologies, saying he knew how difficult sons could be at that age.

In return, Alexander, his memory aided by Vimes, asked after the individual members of the Duke's large family and found himself promising to spend time on Kiyami as Frederick's guest once the border issue was settled. The Duke seemed particularly interested in Adam meeting several of his great-granddaughters, even though the Alexander Doctrine forbade any heir from marrying within another Noble family. His insistence that Adam should come to visit gave Alexander pause to wonder whether Frederick might like the idea of having one or two royal bastards in the family line, but he dismissed the thought, knowing that Adam, for all his stubbornness, was perfectly aware of the risks that came with fathering children outside of the Imperial marriage bed. Over the millennia, several Emperors had been killed putting down revolts led by usurpers, almost all bearing the royal bloodline because of an ill-thought-through affair or tryst.

"Not that Adam will be in any position to come here for the foreseeable future," Alexander thought to himself, wondering how his son was doing.

Bringing his mind back from thoughts of royal intrigue, Alexander focused on the musicians. The group currently on stage were playing a song which had become popular throughout the Empire. Unfortunately, it was not to Alexander's tastes, so he took the opportunity to let his mind drift again and review the data Vimes had forwarded onto him from the local branch of the Imperial Intelligence Service, containing details of sightings and attacks on Imperial shipping travelling within the border region. Neither he nor Vimes could make any sense of them, nor determine a pattern to their behaviour, so he forwarded a copy to Admiral Frith for her assessment and response once the reception was over.

The food was excellent, with many of the delicacies sourced both locally and from across Sector Twelve proving particularly popular. Surreptitiously, so as not to cause offence, every item of food and drink shipped up from the planet had been inspected at least once for locally occurring toxins or something more sinister. Except for several varieties of shellfish, flagged as carrying a potentially nasty micro-organism likely to cause problems for anyone not sensitised to it, everything had proved safe to consume.

During the evening, Alexander hadn't eaten or drunk much, just enough not to offend his guests, preferring instead sparkling water to wine. He needed to keep a clear head and despite advanced medicines and his efficient metabolism, did not relish waking up in the morning with any sort of a headache or a fuzzy mind.   Perhaps, when this minor campaign and flag-waving exercise was over, he might open a bottle of wine with Frith and her partner in celebration, but not before.

Interestingly, amongst the data from the IIS was a Quantum Signature, allegedly of a system holding the location of a potential base of operations for one of the raiding groups. According to the report, the location of system DU-449 had been obtained several weeks ago by bribing a Dubunni trader suspected of providing the Raiders with supplies. The clear threat of having her ship impounded, plus the promise of favourable trading terms with the Empire seemed to have persuaded the trader to co-operate. As good a place to start the campaign as anywhere else, he highlighted the passage for Frith with a suggestion they discuss it tomorrow. From the details provided, their current task force should be more than sufficient to deal with the base, and it would provide some action for the Marines who had been cooped up in the fleet for several weeks now and were becoming restless, wanting to either fight or go home to their families. DU-449 lay in the fifty light-year buffer zone separating the Empire's current border with the Dubunni, therefore the chances of running into any of that empires warships were remote. The last thing he wanted at this point was yet another diplomatic incident.

Frederick turned to him, politely clapping as the musicians on stage finished their song. Alexander joined in, privately hoping the next set of entertainers would be more to his liking.

"Ah, I so enjoyed that Alexander, didn't you?" asked Frederick, reaching for his wine glass and smiling broadly.

Alexander noted the smile hadn't left the Duke's face all evening and he seemed inordinately pleased with himself, even for someone as annoyingly self-satisfied as the Duke.

"It was certainly different, Frederick," he tactfully replied, "Popular too from the way the song has travelled around the Empire. They are probably wealthy musicians by now. Was it difficult to get them at such short notice?"

"Not at all, they realise the importance of an influential sponsor such as myself. In fact, it was one of my creative consultancies that helped them get started. Of course, we take a fair percentage of the gross for having discovered and promoted them." Frederick warmed to the subject of making money. "Still, they've retained enough from their first release so they no longer need to work if they ever decide to do something else. We have others lined up once these fade in popularity."

His smile widened even further, "Imagine, for every point zero one per cent of my Sectors population that buy their latest album, I make nearly ninety million credits!"

Alexander nodded his head in mock appreciation, then decided now was a good time to broach the subject of military expenditure.

"That's good news, Frederick. After considering your request to assist with the Raiders, I've been reviewing your military disposition and expenditure. It only just exceeds your Sector's agreed minimum requirement and is barely stronger then Helena's who has a Sector only a quarter the size of yours. In fact, much as I enjoy visiting you, I'm disappointed that you could not deal with these border infringements yourself."

To his surprise, Frederic's smile never left his face during the brief exchange, even at the mention of Helena, so Alexander continued, "Although only a suggestion at this point, I would prefer to see a commitment for an increase in your military budget from two percent of Gross Sector Production to three percent GSP."

He paused for effect and waited for the inevitable explosion of excuses, but none was forthcoming. To his amazement, Frederick nodded in agreement.

"I totally agree, Alexander. I've been planning to do this myself for some time now and was going to raise it at the next

Council meeting, but if you agree, I'll simply do so right away, once the budget has been rubber-stamped by the Sector nobles." The smile broadened further. "Consider it done. The raids and now your concerns are just the spurs I needed. I've also mustered my Sector's Navy Reserves to follow up against the Raiders once you have gone. I expect them to arrive shortly after you leave here, and they will continue your good work once you've left and returned to Capital. In fact, you may pass them on your way to the Jump Point."

Genuinely stunned by how easy the exchange had gone, Alexander flashed a query to Vimes who, as always, had been watching and listening. *"What do you make of that? What's the old miser got up his sleeve, any ideas?*

"I am as surprised as you, Alex. My only suggestion is perhaps the recent raids have focused his mind on the subject. It's not as if he was unaware of our concerns and the inevitability of his being told what to do in the very near future."

Genuinely at a loss at what to say next, Alexander smiled and simply acknowledged the unexpected agreement.

"That's excellent news, Frederick. I appreciate such a prompt response, thank you. Perhaps when I return from DU-449, you can find time to show me a few of the sites your capital has to offer. It's been far too long since I formally paid a visit and pressed the flesh, so to speak."

Frederick's smile widened still further still, personally promising he would see to it their next meeting would be one to remember. He signalled for the next round of entertainers to come forward, a group of superbly muscled and graceful dancers. The men and women, naked except for modesty briefs and breast retainers, moved forward and began to move around the stage, lithe as cats. Their movements reminded Alexander of the Felidae he had met from time to time and he idly wondered what that feline race would make of the dancers.

"Probably wonder if they would make good prey and what they tasted like," commented Vimes in his mind, breaking Alexander's train of thought. *"On updating myself just now via IQC, Christine has*

news it's possible the Felidae have developed several new warship designs and are demonstrating them on the border of Sector One, possibly as a show of power. It's probably not a coincidence that neither Sectors Thirty-six or Two have had a visit to their common borders by these mystery ships, indicating this was just for you."

Pulling his attention away from the dancers, who were now throwing each other around in the air without any form of safety device, he rested his elbows on the chair rests and steepled his fingers under his nose, focusing on this new development.

"*Christine has a better relationship with Freyja than anyone else in the Imperium, so I doubt it's anything sinister. Given we've both kept to the letter of the Peace Accords, their strange sense of honour would preclude them from acting against us for no reason.*"

"*I agree,*" responded Vimes, "*Christine believes it's simply them marking the border, akin to a lion leaving a scent trail or scratching a tree. Her full report plus recommendations from the Chiefs of Staff are available for you to go over after the reception.*"

Next to Alexander, Duke Frederick watched the dancers move around the stage with the satisfaction of one who has seen his plans come to fruition. The Emperor was here enjoying his entertainers and would soon be Jumping out to DU-449 with all that would entail. Tonight's festivities were being televised and shown throughout Kiyami and once over, would be transmitted via the Jump Station across the entire Empire, all for a small percentage of each viewing of course. Despite anticipating his own, private entertainment later that night with his new mistress, he couldn't help but calculate the royalties this show would earn him.

Frederick leant forward, bringing a glass of wine to his lips, then sat back into his padded chair, taking the opportunity to take a good look at Alexander. "*So much like his father,*" he thought, taking a small sip of the silky-smooth wine beginning to disappear into fumes as he rolled it gently around his tongue. Enjoying the heady muskiness of the liquid, Frederick remembered the long discussions he'd had with Alexander's father, Thomas, often late into the night. "*So many years ago,*" he said to himself.

They had seldom agreed on anything, especially around the aggressive expansion of Empire. Thomas had wanted a slow, measured expansion, focusing on preserving the protected worlds and maintaining good relations with their neighbours. He, on the other hand, knew that in time the border empires would cause problems and it would be better to turn them into vassal states, while at the same time introducing another age of rapid expansion. It was only their long friendship that stopped them from falling out over the issue, along with Thomas's willingness to tolerate people around him that held differing viewpoints, something that Frederick found intensely annoying.

That all ended with the Revolt and Emperor's death at the hands of his own family. Frederick shuddered, remembering how close he'd been to losing his own head in the Revolt when the battling fleets had come into this very system, laying waste to anything that got between them. The big surprise was how Alexander, a bookish young man he'd written off as unsuited to ruling an Empire, had unexpectedly come forward from anonymity and seclusion in the Palace, to become a war leader who recovered the remnants of the almost defeated Navy loyalists and bound them together into a force that won back his crown.

Just then, the Master of Ceremonies came back on stage and began to introduce the next act, a comedian famous for his impersonations.

"*Ah yes, it's good to be enormously wealthy and powerful,*" he thought smugly, watching his latest mistress began to clap loudly to his right, as the comedian walked onto the stage and bowed towards them, beginning his act.

The morning after the reception saw Admiral Frith bright and early at her daily briefing. Several of the command staff seemed unusually sluggish, prompting her to raise an eyebrow and query whether any of them required a visit to the infirmary before starting their watch. Four of them had the good grace to look a little sheepish at her comment but knew it to be in jest as she'd expressly told them the night before to have a good time. Parked in close orbit to the planet and with both the task force and local fleets in attendance, few places were safer, and she could afford for them to enjoy the occasional lapse from her normally high standards.

Disposition of the task force had already been agreed and transmitted to all ships. The Carrier INS Courageous and battleships INS Rodney and Repulse would form the core, with Interdiction Frigates INS Amethyst, Action, and Diamond accompanying her and providing cover. The remaining Carrier, INS Glorious, together with Dauntless, four battleships and the remaining five frigates, would be held back in reserve. Normally, for a relatively small engagement such as this, once the Jump had been made the fleet would stay together, making one single pass to the target, bombarding it en masse then moving out through the system back towards the Jump Point in a loop, before returning to Kiyami. However, Frith was keen to allow Captain Michael Woods, of INS Courageous, a chance to conduct the operation himself, having selected him to lead and coordinate the attack. Recently promoted and the newest Captain in the task force, this engagement would be a good opportunity for him to prove his worth, so she had decided to split the task force after making the Jump to DU-449, giving him control of one part sufficient to take out the base. Of course, in the event of anything getting out of hand, Captain Woods could rely on the remaining ships coming to his aid.

Frith watched the flow of information passing across her eyes and on the multiple screens in front of her, picking out those of interest.

Dauntless's AI had been updated with all the information available on DU-449, including details of the ISS report and the only known Quantum Signature for the system. The task force would be ready to move out on her command, once the last of the entertainers and Duke Frederick finally returned to the surface. A constant fleet of shuttles had been coming and going all through the night watch, bringing supplies and ferrying passengers, including a few crewmen frantically trying to avoid becoming AWOL. In the main departure lounge, Alexander was currently saying goodbye to the Duke and Frith expected to get underway in a little over one hours' time. It would take four days to reach the closest Jump Point, where they would leave and emerge on the edge of the target system, hopefully unseen by the raider base orbiting the systems only gas giant. To improve the odds of this happening, they planned to arrive when the line of sight from the base to their transition point was concealed by the gas giant's bulk. With any luck and a great deal of planning, the task force would remain hidden from the Raiders until it was too late for them to flee or mount any credible defence.

A short while later, finally alone after seeing off his guests and the still smiling Duke, Alexander was reviewing Christine's report for the second time. Trusting his wife's instincts on the Felidae, he tried looking for any clear patterns to recent events but, like her, couldn't see any. He hoped when Vimes had reviewed the financial data he might get an answer as to who was behind the attempt on him, but at the same time dreaded what it might potentially reveal. Either way, he had a problem. If the data revealed nothing of note, he was back to relying on the Infiltrator Programs running through Heaven's computers to shed more light on who had been behind the attack. However, if it turned out to be a Duke or foreign empire, there was a real possibility of either civil war or an external one, a prospect no sane ruler wished to contemplate. Christine's note indicated some of the requested data was taking Vimes longer to obtain than expected, but she hoped to have some preliminary conclusions in about eleven days.

These sombre thoughts were interrupted by Admiral Frith, letting him know Kiyami's docking authority had confirmed the immediate area of space was free of ships and they were ready to depart.

"Thank you, Janice, please proceed to the Jump Point at your convenience," he responded, pleased they were ready to get underway. He was tired of not being in control of events and was looking forward to dictating them instead of having to react.

Alexander felt the prow of the ship begin turning to port, followed a few moments later by a barely noticeable thrust as the engines fought against Dauntless's massive inertia and slowly begin to accelerate her to a steady one-G. He called up a copy of the display currently showing on the bridge, detailing all the positions of the task force, then cancelled it and leaned back in his chair.

Not for the first time, Alexander wondered what life would have been like if he'd been born to an ordinary family or something simple, for example, the minor son of a Lord. Perhaps he would simply have swapped one set of worries for another, but with less chance to change them or make a difference. Instead of worrying about matters of state, politics and the happiness of his subjects, he might now be concerned as to where the next meal came from, relations with his boss or the security of his family and job. He remembered the three years of his own training away from his family but frowned as concerns for his son returned. Alexander sighed, for as Emperor, he at least had the chance to get things done or implement change where it was most needed. He reasoned with himself that a simpler life didn't automatically bring happiness or fulfilment, but while he knew this intellectually, it didn't stop his heart wishing he could spend more time with his wife.

Frith's task force was slowly moving into position, each ship only a few kilometres from its neighbour. After two and a half minutes, Dauntless caught up with the first of them. Almost in formation, they moved at a constant acceleration towards the Jump Point. With the flagship taking point, Alexander watched the two Carriers finally move into position at the centre of the fleet. In two days' time, at the halfway turnaround point where the task force would begin to decelerate, two of the interdiction frigates, INS Audacity and Daring, would take point in readiness for the transition.

The four days it took to reach the Jump point passed by uneventfully, daily shipboard routines passing without note. In their quarters, the Emperor and his Bodyguard ran a series of drills and exercises with the Marines assigned to Dauntless for the trip to Heaven. A little to everyone's surprise, the Marines had held their own in the simulations, earning them and their commanders well deserved, if a little grudging, respect from the elite Bodyguard. Numerous practice sorties had been flown off the two Carriers, and various scenarios and live-fire drills practised. Shortly before arriving at the Jump Point, Frith instructed the Jump Station to halt any outgoing commercial Jumps, then dispatched two high-speed, short-range reconnaissance drones to Jump ahead of the fleet to DU-499. They would emerge for only a few minutes to scan the immediate area with passive sensors for mines or other traps, then Jump back and report back their findings. Active sensors would not be used so as not to give away their position to the raider base.

On the Bridge, everything was on high alert. Alexander was watching events from his suite and would not interfere unless asked, having every confidence in his Admiral. Information from Dauntless's tank was replicated in his mind's eye, and he could see the task force was in stealth mode and set out in the formation it would use to make the Jump. An interdiction frigate supported each Carrier with the remaining six spread out around the task force, ahead of the six battleships that covered both Dauntless and the Carriers.

"Jump solutions agreed and transmitted Admiral. Awaiting confirmation from the drones," reported Navigation. Everyone on the Bridge waited anxiously for the drones to report their findings, Frith stood impassively, radiating quiet calm and supreme confidence.

Finally, Navigation reported what they wanted to hear. "Telemetry being received from the drones now...all clear."

Frith's expression didn't change. "Thank you. Please inform the task force to Jump on our five-second mark. Five, four, three, two, one...

Discontinuity

"All stations report."

Frith's voice sounded clear and firm. Immediately data started flowing in from the Control stations, and the bridge crew began sounding off, confirming status. Ships sensors and additional passive telemetry from the drones appeared, mapping the system and transferring data into the bridge's central holographic display, known to everyone as the "Tank".

Displayed within in, the task force's disposition was clearly shown in blue at the system's edge, one hundred and fifty million kilometres away from the nearest planet, a large barren K-Class planet with no atmosphere and twice normal gravity. Moving in a further three hundred million kilometres towards the sun, the next planet was a J-Class gas giant circled by seven moons of varying sizes, one of which held the Raider's base. The next planet was another barren K-Class but with a gravity slightly less than standard. The remaining two planets were much further away, on the other side of the sun, but again devoid of life and inhospitable. The sun itself was a small, cool, very faint main sequence star with a surface temperature of under 4,000 K, approximately two-thirds through its life-cycle.

"Wouldn't like to live here," Frith observed to no-one in particular. "Navigation, plot a course to the target moon at one-G, keeping the gas giant between us at all times as agreed. I don't want them picking us up until the last moment. Send your course to the other ships and tell them to standby."

"Course plotted and task force standing by, Admiral," responded the young Commander after a few seconds, "I've compensated for the moon's orbit of seven point three days to ensure we remain undetected until you are ready to engage. Passing to Helm and the rest of the task force now."

"Thank you. Time to target?" asked Frith.

"At one-G, one hundred and nineteen hours, Admiral" came the immediate reply. "On arrival, our speed will be zero relative to the moon."

One of the two Weapons Masters asked a question. "Admiral, do you require any high-speed reconnaissance drones sent on ahead?"

"No, I don't want to risk them being observed," responded Frith. "The longer we can remain undetected the more of their ships we can catch on the ground."

She sent a command to the AI which would transmit her instructions to the other ships. "Helm, take us in."

Within moments, acceleration began to build, as the engines strove again to overcome the massive inertia of the flagship, gradually building towards cruising acceleration. Preparations for the forthcoming battle would continue, with Marines spending their time checking equipment and running more training exercises. Those not chosen for the ground action would be used primarily for boarding any Raider vessels that survived or for shipboard action in the unlikely event the flagship itself came under attack by boarders.

"Captain Woods on the Courageous is requesting permission to move ahead with his command, Admiral."

"Granted. My compliments to Captain Woods." Frith turned her head slightly, speaking to Helm. "Instruct the rest of the task force to reform once Captain Woods has moved ahead."

Turning to her left, she spoke to her First Officer. "You have the Bridge," before standing up and awaiting the formal response.

"Confirmed, I have the Bridge, Admiral."

Frith walked over to the doors, returned the guards salute and passed through, turned right and headed to her ready-room. Apart from splitting the fleet and sending Captain Woods ahead with a small task-force, everything was going by the book, and she was almost looking forward to catching up with some outstanding staff reports.

Karen was awake bright and early, having risen with the sun. A quick shower and she headed towards the canteen to get breakfast for herself and Adam, killing two birds with one stone. The seductive smell of bacon and coffee welcomed her to the canteen, and it wasn't long before she was enjoying another full English breakfast, washing it down with a large mug of strong tea. Finished eating, she put away her tray and piled up a fresh one with two plates of food and a large orange juice, before paying and heading to Adam's room.

She knocked twice with her elbow, as her hands were tied up with holding the tray, then used it to press down on the handle to open the door, forcing her to enter his room backwards. Turning around, she was startled to see him sitting on the edge of the bed, exercising his legs by lifting them.

"Wow, that's amazing Adam, is there any pain? Oh, and good morning by the way."

He looked at her and smiled. It was only at this point she realised the bandages were gone from his head and he was looking at her with two, perfect blue eyes. Adams smile grew wider as he enjoyed the look of surprise on her face.

"Good morning to you too, Karen. No, it doesn't hurt, but they still feel bruised, and it will be a few days before they are back to full strength. Ah, I take it the food is for me?" he asked hopefully, swinging his legs back onto the bed.

"Yes, it is, but first I want a good look at you," Karen replied, moving over to him in her best no-nonsense Doctor manner, placing the food on his over-bed table.

Adam kept still, by now used to her ministrations, while she examined the fresh skin that had almost completely regrown. Only a few small scabs remained, and it was obvious they would be gone after he washed his head. Opening his gown at the neck, she ran her hands along the shoulder, trying to feel anything out of the ordinary. There were no electric shocks this time as she focused on examining where he had been previously injured.

She looked up at his face again. "Any pain or discomfort at all? Anywhere?"

"No Karen. As I said, just a little general soreness and a nagging feeling I'm not where I should be." He looked hungrily at the tray of food. "I would prefer it if breakfast weren't cold. Can't you finish this after I've eaten?" he asked.

Karen stepped back and swung the table over his legs so he could eat. "OK, fair enough."

She sat on the bedside chair and watched him eat. Adam quickly finished off the food and gave the empty plate a look of regret as she moved the table away again. Karen moved closer and lifted the gown covering his legs, running her hands over the fresh skin. No scarring, but she could see some patches of redness that hadn't completely healed. Before pressing harder, she told him to let her know if it hurt, then began to try and see if his leg bones had set properly. Apart from his legs and general musculature still being on the thin side, everything seemed to be in working order. She shook her head in amazement at his recovery.

Examination finished, she stood silently beside the bed, trying to think of what to do next. Adam looked up at her expectantly, not saying anything but examining her face as if trying to determine what she was thinking.

Karen moved to the foot of the bed and looked at the readings taken during the night. Blood pressure, heart rate, everything was normal, apart from his elevated body temperature. She asked him to try and stand. Without a word, Adam did so, the smile leaving his face, replaced with a look of concentration. Standing a little unsteadily at first, he set his balance and walked over to her. Before she could say or do anything, Adam enveloped her in a hug, resting his face against the top of her head.

"Thank you, Karen. I really appreciate everything you have done for me," he said into her hair, "I'm in your debt."

Unsure what to do or how to react but not feeling threatened, Karen simply stood there. After a few seconds, Adam gave a final squeeze and moved away carefully, sitting gratefully down on the bed with a sigh, looking and sounding tired.

"I need your help one last time, Karen. Is there any way you can get me back to the scene of the accident? I'm sure it will help me recall memories of who I am. Please. I need to get there as soon as I possibly can."

Not letting her answer, he continued, "You can see I can walk around almost without pain. I admit it's tiring for now but by the end of today, I should be fighting fit. The longer I stay here, the greater the risk news of my unique healing ability will get out."

Karen sat on the bed next to him. "Are you sure Adam? I confess your recovery is little short of miraculous and I'm at a loss what to do about you."

Earlier, Police had confirmed to Karen they were not looking for anyone matching his description and seemed happy enough not to get involved in the mystery. If, or when, they were ready to act against the driver of the lorry they would let her know, but until that happened both of them were free to do as they pleased. Anyway, it wasn't as if they didn't know where to find her, for Karen had patched up enough of the local force over the past year to be on good terms with most of them.

She searched Adam's face, not really knowing what she was looking for. "I can get you back to Skye, but on one condition. You must stay with me for a few days before moving on to try and find out more about where you came from and what it is you were doing on the island before the accident. Agreed?"

Adam nodded. "Agreed, Karen. Now how do you plan on getting us there?"

Three hours later and they were flying back to Skye in the air ambulance. Karen managed to have a quiet word with James and Michael as they were coming on duty, and although it was against regulations, both agreed to turn a blind eye to Adam and Karen joining them on a planned flight to Broadford Hospital for a patient pick up. Pleased she wouldn't have to catch a bus or an expensive taxi, she'd had just enough time to get to the shops and pick some clothes for Adam before they took off. He'd been as good as his word, and by the time Karen had completed all the discharge papers and thanked everyone for their help, he was able to walk short distances without any trouble. Adam managed to climb into the helicopter unaided, much to the astonishment of the two men, who had trouble believing he was the same man they'd flown here only a short time before.

Michael and then James had bombarded Adam with questions for the first fifteen minutes of the flight until they'd run out of things to ask, then started on Karen. After it had become obvious she didn't have answers to most of the questions either, they lapsed into a confused silence for the remainder of the forty-five-minute flight. On seeing the helicopter properly for the first time, Adam had seemed reluctant to get in, looking apprehensively at the rotors before shrugging his shoulders and strapping himself tightly into his seat. Once airborne he began to relax somewhat and eventually looked as though he was enjoying the experience, gazing out of the window when not answering questions.

After landing on the helipad behind Broadford Hospital, Karen thanked the two men for all their help, hugging them both before moving off with Adam towards the main building where a taxi was meant to be waiting for them.

Watching as they disappeared into the building, James looked at Michael and shrugged his shoulders, patting his colleague on the back before turning to the waiting orderlies for help in lifting the stretcher and new patient into the helicopter in readiness for the return flight.

Unfortunately, the expected Taxi hadn't yet arrived, so Adam and Karen sat on a wooden bench outside the main entrance to wait. Not knowing what to say at this point, Karen kept quiet, but after watching the helicopter depart and vanish into the distance, she wanted to break the awkward silence. Turning her head to look at Adam she caught him looking at her too, so she decided to speak first.

"Are you trying to think of something to say as well?" she asked him.

He nodded and gave her a sad smile, then looked down at his hands. The coat she'd bought for him felt uncomfortable and constricted him across the chest, but Adam was pleased he now blended in with everyone else. It wasn't just the coat that was making him feel uncomfortable. Ever since waking up after the accident he'd had no choice but to rely on this woman, and he didn't like the feeling of not being in control or master of his destiny. Even when his father had sent him away at such short notice, he hadn't felt so lost or alone as he did now. He was attracted to her, this alien woman from a backwards planet, and it disturbed him to feel so vulnerable and helpless. He did wonder if this attraction was simply because he was currently so reliant on her or if it would fade once he gained back his independence. However, he was honest enough with himself to know a part of him was hoping it wouldn't be so.

Karen looked at him and wished she had bought larger sizes. It had been difficult to judge how big he was and perhaps it would have been wiser to go XXX-large. She realised he looked a little ridiculous in trousers several centimetres too short, and a coat that looked distinctly uncomfortable, but at least the trainers fit him.

They both looked up as a blue Mercedes, with a prominent yellow taxi light on its roof, drove between the heavy grey stone wall that marked the entrance and stopped in front of them.

The passenger door window lowered, and Karen acknowledged the shouted "Karen McLeod?" from the driver. She nodded and the driver got out, opening the door for Karen before stowing their few bags in the boot. She told Adam to get in first and move over, chuckling when he seemed unsure what to do next. Karen leaned over and showed Adam how to adjust and buckle the seatbelt before strapping herself in.

"Struan please," she confirmed to the driver, "I'll tell you what house when we get there."

She turned back to Adam. "It'll take us about forty minutes to get home, then you can rest and take it easy. You're doing remarkably well Adam, now just sit back, relax and watch the scenery go by."

Adam did so with another grateful sigh, sinking back into the leather seat. Karen looked at him for a second then turned to gaze out at the familiar scenery. To her left and through the trees she caught glimpses of "The Beinn" as it was referred to locally, the first of the Cuillin Mountains that dominated the middle of Skye. Luckily their taxi driver wasn't interested in chatting, perhaps feeling awkward about asking questions from a Hospital pick-up in case they had bad news.

The motion of the car and white noise from its tyres soon sent Adam to sleep, and Karen had the chance to look at him without being observed. His face had filled out, and of the head injury, there was little sign. The left eyelid looked completely normal and the way he had moved when exiting the helicopter or bending to get into the car, proved beyond doubt his broken bones had healed satisfactorily. Turning away to look again at the passing scenery, she asked herself again for the hundredth time just who Adam was and what on earth was she getting herself into. As a Doctor, Karen knew she had more than her fair share of empathy and a desire to help others in need. Although she also owed him for saving her life, Karen suddenly realised there was something more beginning to grow between them, even though it had only been a few days and she still hardly knew anything about him. Karen found him fascinating, especially the vulnerability interspersed with flashes of something strong and commanding, and she was not looking forward to saying goodbye when he regained his memories. For all she knew, he had a wife or fiancé somewhere waiting for him, a thought that disturbed her more than she wanted to admit, even to herself.

Nine days had passed since Christine's meeting with the Chiefs of Staff. No firm decision had been made regarding the Felidae and Christine was spending the evening walking alone through the Palace gardens, still debating with herself whether to initiate contact with Empress Freyja. The two of them hadn't corresponded for some time, and with all that had been happening, it increasingly seemed a good time to re-establish contact, yet she didn't want to appear vulnerable or needy to a predator species such as the Felidae. Unlike the meagre efforts of the IIS, Christine was certain the Felidae were having more success in obtaining information on the Empire from greedy or disloyal humans than the Empire was on the Felidae. Regrettably, it wasn't hard to find humans willing to do anything for money or power, even to the extent of selling out their own kind.

Christine slowed her pace and looked around, realising she had walked further than intended and was now over two kilometres away from the Palace. The walk had been thoroughly enjoyable, passing between all four lakes before stopping at the outskirts of the forest to get her bearings. The transition between relatively open parkland and the dense forest was small, just a matter of a few dozen metres before the semi-wilderness took over. It was getting too late for her to go any further and although Vimes could always send an air-car to bring her back, her first preference was to walk. Christine regularly needed to spend this time alone, recharging her emotional batteries, away from the distractions of people and responsibility. She valued these times, alone with nothing but her own thoughts and the Palace staff knew better than to disturb her when out walking.

The large flocks of birds which had provided a constant backdrop of song during the day were nearly all silent, having roosted for the night in the heavy woods and trees of the garden. All she could hear was the gentle rustle of leaves in the slight breeze and the sound of trees creaking as they shed the day's warmth, along with the occasional chirruping insect from somewhere in the long grass. In another hour it would be dark.

Thoughts of the Empire brought her back to the present. It would only be a short time before Alexander's task force engaged the Raider base, and while she knew it was a simple mission, with both her husband and son absent, Christine felt suddenly vulnerable. "*Probably ancient fears surfacing of being alone in the dark,*" she thought, dismissing the feeling.

The voice of Vimes interrupted her reverie. "*Christine, I've analysed the financial data from the Sectors who have reported and vigorously chased those who have still to do so. There is nothing out of the ordinary apart from some minor tax avoidance schemes which have come to light; some of which are very ingenious. Do I have your permission to pass these on to the Dukes for action? The non-financial data from markets and auction houses have also arrived, and I will summarise it shortly.*"

"Thank you, Vimes, please do so. How many Sectors still haven't reported?

"*Eleven Sectors, Christine, but my surrogates are looking into the delays.*"

"Any news on Alexander?"

"*No Christine. I will inform you the moment anything arrives from DU-449.*"

After all the years they had been communicating together, Christine felt she could sometimes sense Vimes thinking, even though she knew it wasn't possible.

"*Have you arranged to meet anyone here that I'm not aware of?*" he asked suddenly, the tone of his voice taking on a serious note, bringing her to full alert.

Immediately on guard, she looked around, wishing she'd bothered to take night vision lenses with her. "*No, why?*" she replied, wary of speaking aloud and now angry with herself for not remembering to put on the smart-metal armband before coming out.

"*Ten persons are approaching your position from the direction of the main building, about two hundred metres away directly behind* you...I'm also detecting interference with the security grid and communications..."

His voice cut out for a few seconds before returning... "*I am definitely being interfered with...and contact with the base and local security has been cut off. Local sensors are being jammed too. Very sophisticated...run for the tree line, it will afford cover.*"

"*How did they get through your security?*" she thought back at him, running towards the trees and almost catching her foot on a root, causing her to break step and stumble, "*It's meant to be bloody foolproof.*"

"*These aren't intruders Christine. They are all assigned and accredited as diplomatic staff, hence have free access to the grounds and buildings...I wasn't concerned about them until the jamming began and they started to move directly towards you...head left, then run one hundred metres. Before the jamming started, I'd detected another person ahead of you in the woods, but it's one of the Palace woodsmen, Francis De'ath. I don't think he's part of this but be careful. If you can get him to distract them, it might gain you a few moments.*"

Christine had to force down the beginnings of panic. She could easily take on one, possibly two attackers, but ten was beyond even her capabilities. Even if Francis proved capable, the odds were massively stacked against them.

"*Francis was the young man at breakfast the other day; the one who piqued my interest. Let's hope the Iron Duke chose well or I'm in even more trouble.*"

With that thought, Christine burst through into a small clearing where a small one-person survival tent had been set up next to an unlit fire. She cursed silently. Of Francis there was no sign, so she continued through to the other side and back into the wood, listening to Vimes telling her to slow down and hide behind a large, forgotten statue that would appear shortly amongst the undergrowth. Stumbling and tripping through the dense undergrowth, Christine fancied she could hear her pursuers getting closer.

"*Goodness knows, I'm making enough noise,*" she thought, stifling a curse as a sharp branch left a deep scratch on her arm.

A few steps later Karen reached the statue, a large metal affair depicting a stern looking military man. Both the statue and its nameplate were covered in a thin patina of oxidisation, moss and sundry forest detritus, but she could still read the name: Admiral Lord Martyn Rose, although the date was illegible. It stood in another small clearing which had obviously been recently cleared away and tidied, for she could see fresh cut marks on the trees and a large pile of branches and undergrowth piled up high in one corner. Her face and arms began to sting from where they had been whipped and scratched by the small branches and thorns as she forced her way through.

"*What do I do now, Vimes?*"

"*Get behind it and stand still with your back to the statue,*" came the reply.

"*But then I won't be able to see them coming,*" she thought back furiously but did as instructed. Immediately, Christine felt the familiar touch of smart-metal begin forming around her lower body. For an instant, she wondered if Vimes had deliberately trapped her and was in on the ambush but felt guilty when she realised what was happening. Unfortunately, it was going to take time for the armour to fully form around her and she hoped she had enough.

"*Is this one of the secrets you and Alexander put in place after the revolt?*" she asked Vimes.

"*What do you think, Christine?*" came the reply, his voice sounding rather more pleased with itself than usual. "*Rather than throw all the old statues out we decided to turn them into something useful.*"

At that moment, she heard her attacker's force their way into the small clearing and stop, listening out for where she might have gone. Vimes was relaying a view of the scene from the statue to her via the implant, and she knew she had just run out of luck for the suit wouldn't form in time.

All the attackers were dressed in black skin-tight mesh costumes, probably concealed beneath their normal clothes which they discarded once the ambush started. Instead of powered weapons, each carried two large knives of ordinary metal, so not to be detected by Palace security scanners. Using heat sensors to trace her footprints to the statue, six of them approached it slowly, three on either side. Of the remaining four who were acting as backup, one checked a hand-held tracking device which was obviously unaffected by the jamming.

Bracing herself for a brief and ultimately futile fight, she jumped, just like her attackers, when Francis leapt out from a tree behind the four, screaming at the top of his lungs, brandishing a long scythe as if it was a quarterstaff. He brought it down with a satisfying crack on the nearest neck before swinging it to the left, decapitating another of the startled assassins before he could react. The remaining eight turned immediately towards the noise and interruption, gaining Christine a few more precious seconds for the suit to form. Unsure who he was, they moved cautiously towards Francis, extending their blades in readiness for the kill.

Christine could see he was now in trouble, for the attackers moved as one, indicating they trained together. Francis ignored the risk and selected his next target, changing his grip on the scythe so that it now extended one and a half metres in front of him, taking aim for the face of the nearest attacker, forcing him to move back or lose an eye.

Watching the scene through Vimes, Christine found herself mirroring the moves Francis was making. The way he handled the staff made it look as if it weighed only a few pounds, spinning and weaving it in a protective arc in front of him. Unable to get any closer without being struck, two of the attackers each threw one of their knives. Unable to dodge both, Francis was struck below his left clavicle, the ultra-sharp blade passing through his body until stopped by the hilt, its tip protruding slightly from his back. The pain staggered Francis for a second, then his berserker rage took over. He reached up with his right hand to grasp the handle and in one fluid movement pulled it free before throwing it straight back, taking his target in the eye. The dead man dropped to the floor. Rushing forward, Francis engaged the remaining attackers all at once, throwing himself at them and striking out right and left, heedless of the danger to himself.

Christine watched, mesmerised, until a helmet finally formed over her head and the familiar control suite of an exo-suit lit up in front of her vision, signifying the armour was ready and breaking her attention from the fight. So as not to distract her, Vimes cancelled the live feed, transferring it to the helmet. Weapon read-outs from the suit confirmed a full load, including non-lethal. Deciding at least one prisoner was needed for interrogation, in tribute to Francis she chose the same type of weapon and extruded a two-metre-long quarter-staff, heavily weighted at either end, in preference to a sword or rail-gun.

Christine stepped to her left and around from behind the statue, the night vision of her helmet providing a daylight-clear view of everything in the area. Two more of the black-clad assassins were down, one of them still locked on the ground in an embrace of death with Francis.

"Let's see how you like it," boomed out Christine's amplified voice as she emerged from behind the statue.

The remaining attackers spun around, their faces registering shock and surprise at this sudden change in their fortunes. One quickly looked down at his knives and then back to the exo-suite before deciding to attack. Before he'd moved five paces, Christine crouched down, her staff sweeping down and away, simultaneously taking out both of his legs and breaking them. He howled and fell heavily, clutching his ruined shins. She sprung forward before any of the others could move, taking another attacker between the legs with a crack that indicated a broken pelvis or worse. His agonised scream sounded loud in her helmet. Her suit picked up movement behind and to the left, so she ducked down, again sweeping the staff in an arc at knee height from right to left, toppling another attacker to the floor.

Straightening up, she saw the remainder turn tail and run. The attacker she'd just hit was trying to get back up, still clutching his two knives, so Christine brought the bulbous end of her staff down hard into his temple, the skull collapsing and shattering under the impact, grey brain matter spraying into the air and over her chest. With enough prisoners now disabled for interrogation, she had no wish to chase after anyone, so Christine braced her suit and with a thunderous roar of displaced air, simply sprayed the entire area of the forest in the direction of the fleeing assassins with anti-personnel flechettes from the back of both gauntlets. Within seconds the air was full of splintered wood and leaf debris as a large number of trees simply exploded and toppled, one narrowly missing the now much-diminished statue of Admiral Rose. Vimes confirmed the kills.

Moving around the clearing, she dealt each of the survivors a blow to the head. Knocked unconscious they couldn't take their own lives or object as she injected each of them with a large dose of sedatives from her suit's pharmacological suite. Vimes confirmed the drugs would still be effective despite their age, having been stored in stasis within the statue.

Moving over to Francis's body, she sadly disentangled him from the dead assassin but was delighted to discover he was still alive. Examining him quickly, she noted he was bleeding badly from several deep slashes and puncture wounds on his arms, chest and stomach in addition to the stab to his shoulder. Taking a few moments to spray them all with triage dressings infused with healing factors and medical skin from her suit, she carried him over to the trunk of a large tree and propped him against it, finally injecting a large dose of battlefield nanites for his internal injuries. With nothing more to be done for him until she broke through the jamming, Christine spoke to Vimes.

"How are you getting on with getting through the interference?" she queried, "I would feel happier with several dozen Marines around me at this point."

"*I've pinpointed it to the administrative offices of Sector Twelve, along with major disturbances in the Palace offices of ten other Sectors. The jamming device will need to be physically destroyed before I can contact anyone else. It's fortunate your link to me works on a different channel to any of the others and appears immune to its effects. I'm currently coordinating the defence of your private quarters and that of*" the Palace. *Several hundred armoured attackers are trying to kill the Ambassadors from numerous Sectors, with varying degrees of success. I currently have most of them contained until help arrives. As to the Marines, I expect them here at the Palace very soon for they would have realised something was wrong the moment communication was lost with the Palace.*"

With the immediate threat to her life over and nothing more she could do for Francis, she didn't hesitate and headed back towards the Palace, running as fast as the suit would allow, powering through the trees and bushes with ease. As she ran and the suit re-absorbed the fighting staff, Christine asked Vimes what Sector her attackers had come from but was not surprised to learn they too were from Sector Twelve. It was apparent to Christine that all of the Sectors that had provided the financial information were registering disturbances in their Palace offices. First Alexander, now her. It couldn't be a coincidence that Frederick had asked for Alexander's help, and Christine hoped she would be able to contact her husband before he led his ships into a trap, thankful Adam was safely out of harm's way.

"Can't you use your forces to take out the jammer?" she asked Vimes, jumping easily over the trunk of a two-metre-high fallen tree.

"*No Christine, all of my forces were destroyed in that area, and the others are tied up in close combat elsewhere, protecting the diplomats and their staff.*"

Speeding across the Palace grounds, Vime's presented a tactical display for her to see, showing what areas of the Palace were affected.

"*Christine, my defences are containing the threats in all of the areas except for Sector Twelve where they have been destroyed by armoured troops. Concentrate on this area.*"

Nearing the Palace buildings, several smart-metal statues took station alongside her, obviously under the control of Vimes and part of the hidden defences. Glancing to her left, one of the statues winked at her. Despite herself and the seriousness of the moment, she couldn't stop from laughing out loud into her helmet. A minute later they reached the entrance to the Administrative block and crashed through the large ornamental doors and into the main foyer. Startled by the events going on in the Palace and unsure what to do, nervous staff began asking questions before her amplified voice silenced them with a curt instruction.

"Not now. Take cover and stay here until the Marines come, then do as they tell you without question. Do you all understand?" she queried.

Grateful nods indicated they understood, so she turned and instructed one of the statues to stand watch over the civilian staff. Vimes didn't argue, knowing her concern for their safety was genuine. Having an intimate knowledge of the Palace, she dismissed the map Vimes was displaying in her helmet and began taking the stairs to the top floor of the building, four steps at a time, not wishing to risk getting trapped in a tube. She slowed on reaching the set of doors marking the top and sent the remaining statue ahead into the long corridor which ran the entire length of the Palace. Before going further, Christine took a few moments to form a large shield across her left arm and a one-metre long katana blade for her right. For close-in fighting, a series of hooked blades formed along her shins and forearms.

Following behind her escort, she watched the erstwhile smart metal statue transform into an exact duplicate of her own suit. One hundred metres ahead of them, along the vaulted corridor, lay the impressive offices of Sector Twelve. The enhanced sensors of her suit picked up the sound of fighting nearby in the other Sector Offices and the floor ahead of her was devoid of its usual statuary. The normally pristine marble walls displayed numerous signs of blast and flechette damage, and many of the incredibly strong windows had been broken and were unable to re-form themselves. She instantly counted twenty-two armoured figures lying broken and twisted on the floor alongside a similar number of broken statues, some barely recognisable. Running along the wide, imposing corridor now almost devoid of upright statuary, Vimes indicated this was his handiwork.

"Another one of Alexander's ideas, Christine. Replace statues and sculpture with smart-metal programmed to link into the Palace's internal defences under my direct control. Using them as expendable shock troops, I was able to slow down the attack. None of them expected the statuary to start fighting back."

"How many of them are left for me to fight here?" Christine asked, *"If the odds were bad you wouldn't have let me get anywhere close."*

"There are two remaining. Kill them, and you can destroy the jammer."

As if to prove his words, half-way to Sector Twelve's entrance, two armoured figures stepped out into the hall, firing a stream of accelerated flechettes in Christine's direction, aiming for the suit in front of her. Using the now disintegrating suit as a partial shield, together they closed the distance between themselves and the attackers. Almost there, the faithful statue finally ceased to operate under the relentless onslaught of flechettes and fell heavily to the floor.

Jumping over the inert statue and closing the last few metres, her physical shield also began to disintegrate from the impact of hundreds of flechettes, their kinetic energy slowing her forward momentum. Despite this, she was able to maintain it long enough to close with them. Moments before contact the two armoured figures switched over to close combat mode themselves, the armoured suit on her right swinging a wicked downward blow towards her head with the sword held in its left hand. Thankfully, he telegraphed the move, and she was able to easily block it with her own sword. Keeping her shield between herself and the second opponent, she rammed its sharpened edge diagonally into the first attacker's faceplate. Propelled by all the force her augmented muscles could generate, it cut through the visor and into the face behind, driving deep into skull and brain.

To her left, the second fighter used his own shield to slice down onto Christine's extended left arm, hoping to cut it off. Anticipating the blow, she released her shield and allowed the blows momentum to drive her arm down, before swinging the sword in her right hand horizontally into his neck, the monomolecular blade of her katana slicing through, severing his carotid artery. Not wishing to waste any motion, Christine gracefully turned the movement into a three hundred and sixty-degree spin, looking for other targets. The dying attacker had fallen to his knees, trying to clutch at his throat as he retracted his helmet. Blood fountained out between desperate fingers and down his neckplate. Christine stepped forward and severed the exposed head from its shoulders.

Satisfied no-one else remained in the corridor, she lifted one of the armoured bodies above her head and heaved it through the Sector's entrance doors, shattering the wood and allowing her to see inside. Reassured no-one else was in the doorway, she accelerated her suit forward, smashing through the wall to the left of it, hoping to catch off-guard anyone waiting to the side that might be looking to ambush her. Inside, desks and chairs littered the floor, along with some bodies.

"*Not all of them were in on the plot then*," she thought to Vimes, who'd kept quiet during the brief fight so as not to distract her.

"*No Christine, many of them remained loyal. Jammer's to the left, in the Ambassador's room.*"

Bracing her suit, she called up her rail-gun, dialling in heavy calibre flechettes before using rapid fire to send a stream of hypervelocity slugs through the wall and into the office, but they bounced harmlessly off the shielded jammer. Cursing under her breath, Christine increased the flechette size to maximum and tried again. The jammer's screen held but vanished from sight as the deflected flechettes created a dust storm in the room as they tore through internal walls and destroyed what was left of the furniture, shredding it to splinters.

"*Come on, come on,*" she thought, looking for any signs the small portable shield was starting to fade.

"*It's going,*" said Vimes in her mind, showing her readings taken by her suit. Inside of the dust storm, Christine glimpsed the shield radiate violet for a second before vanishing in a burst of light. Unhindered, the rain of flechettes powered through, destroying the jammer and continuing through several more internal walls. Immediately the jamming was broken, a stream of information came in; urgent enquiries from her Bodyguard, private staff and the naval vessels in orbit. Vimes handled all of these, allowing her to begin checking on the bodies littering the offices for signs of life.

Less than a minute later, a large shuttle suddenly blocked out the view through the window, which melted away to allow several squads of her personal Bodyguard to jump across into the room, led by Master Sergeant Zuber. They quickly fanned out through the other rooms, checking for bodies or survivors, their suits noting which ones had already been attended to by the Empress. Zuber saluted and ordered her to follow him back to the shuttle, but Christine shook her head, holding up her hand to forestall any argument. Now she was protected by her Bodyguard, she took a moment to review how the fighting was going in the rest of the Palace. Dozens of shuttles had already arrived, with more in transit, disgorging her Bodyguard throughout the Palace where they were assisting the internal defences in containing, then mopping up, any pockets of resistance which had managed to hold out against Vimes and his statues.

Having assessed the situation, Christine instructed Zuber to pick a dozen of his men and act as an escort to her quarters. Not wishing to risk a tube, they ran along the main corridor running the entire length of the Palace, taking the most direct route. In less than a minute, they reached the entrance to her private apartments. Nearly two dozen armoured figures lay strewn around the entrance, their suits either blasted apart or burned through by high-intensity beams. The blackened and melted floor and walls bore mute testimony to the ferocity of Vimes's defences.

Christine gave Zuber new instructions to retrieve the sleeping would-be assassins from the forest, then hand them over to the IIS for questioning. After that, if they received no further instructions from her within the hour, they were to go about their normal business. She noted a medical shuttle had already been despatched by Vimes to pick up Francis and was guiding it to where he lay.

Even through his armour, Zuber's body language told Christine he was unhappy at leaving her alone. Before he could object she tried to reassure him.

"I appreciate your concern Master Sergeant, but as you can see around you, here in my own quarters, I am perfectly safe. There are security measures in place that will ensure my complete safety. If it makes you feel happier feel free to assign several guards to the entrance."

They both retracted their helmets so they could look directly at each other. Christine held his gaze for a few seconds until he bowed his head in agreement. He nodded and barked instructions to his men, then turned away to carry out his instructions.

Two of the Marines took station either side of the entrance, and Christine looked at the retreating backs of the other Marines as they ran off to pick up the assassins. She smiled, reassured by their loyalty and the knowledge that today's incidents were not representative of how most of her subjects felt.

Safely in her quarters, Vimes confirmed to her everything was in hand, then began quickly updating her on what steps were being taken to secure the Palace and Capital. She felt a slight tremor, as the entire section of the Palace which made up their quarters sealed off and began to descend into the bedrock below, layers of smart metal forming above as it continued down. Within minutes the entire suite was three kilometres underground and safe from any further attack, surrounded as it was by the most up-to-date and sophisticated defence systems available to the Empire. Through her implant, Christine could sense rarely used defensive and offensive systems begin cycling through into complete readiness.

Satisfied nothing immediate needed her attention, Christine walked to a smart-metal terminal and docked her damaged suit for re-absorption. Stepping out of the diminishing suit, she sat at her desk and instructed Vimes to activate the secret IQA communication device, praying for Alex to contact her from wherever he was before it was too late.

As she waited, Vimes began relaying the terrible news of what was now happening across the Empire.

On the bridge of INS Courageous and two hours after entering the system, Captain Woods was watching his small task force accelerate away from the main fleet. Once they reached twenty-one thousand kilometres in front, he would maintain position by reducing acceleration to normal. He was pleased the Admiral had chosen him to lead the attack but suspected she was testing him rather than it being a sign of her complete faith in his abilities. Unsurprisingly, he was more nervous about making a mistake in front of her than the Emperor.

Woods was well aware Captains under Frith's command either did well and were quickly promoted or didn't impress and were swiftly moved on to less demanding commands, so he wanted to demonstrate her faith in him was justified. He quickly reminded himself they only got to go places if they didn't foul up, which prompted him to go over his plan again, looking for flaws or anything he might have missed.

His plan was simple. When close to the target he would launch nineteen of his twenty fighter squadrons to take out any ships caught on the ground, along with as much of the base's defence infrastructure as possible, leaving it open to ground assault from Marines. These would seek prisoners for questioning and intelligence on other bases. Originally, the Admiral had wanted him to simply bombard the base from orbit, but he had disagreed and set out his alternative plan, supported by the Captain of Marines. Much to his relief, after a short debate the Admiral agreed to his plan of attack. Initially a little nervous about voicing his opinion, especially as it contradicted the Admirals, he was certain he'd done the right thing by arguing but hoped he wouldn't need to do it again or make a habit of it.

The bridge of his ship held a smaller version of the "tank" found on Dauntless and currently displayed six fighter squadrons accelerating away from the Carrier to take position all around his force, just outside the range of its mass sensors. Doing this allowed sensor coverage to be extended and added an extra margin of safety to the force. Although not necessary to run screening this far away from the target, Woods wanted to ensure nothing was left to chance.

Remotely piloting their fighters from the safety of control pods located in the hangars, Harris and the other five squadrons were pulling their ships away from INS Courageous at 10-G and in a few minutes would be in a position to begin looking for anything out of the ordinary. Remotely piloted fighters like hers were ideal for short-range reconnaissance, often picking up details missed by AI controlled drones. In the days leading up to this engagement, she had been drilling her flight regularly until satisfied with their performance. As would be expected from a team that had been together for so long, they didn't need too much work and even Hinchin, Coleman, and Quigley seemed to have come around to her command style.

She checked the head-up display for the relative positions of the three capital ships receding behind her fighter. INS Rodney and Renoun were slightly ahead of the Carrier, with the three interdiction frigates ahead and to either side. Harris knew with the target still days ahead, this was going to be just another routine flight.

From the relative comfort of her ready room, Admiral Frith checked the disposition of the two groups on a holographic display, watching the ships under Captain Woods command move ahead. The display currently identified Woods group in green and her own in blue, slowly moving backwards as the others accelerated away. Tiny silver motes in the tank indicated the fighters from INS Courageous, spread out to cover space ahead of the fleet.

Frith was pleased Woods had risen to the bait and argued earlier against the initial battle plan she had put forward. That was her first test of his leadership and indicated he wasn't afraid to argue against authority, something she valued in her Captains. In her opinion, far too many of those coming out of the Academy seemed to be little more than yes-men and women.

Although confident of success, from her memory two sayings came unbidden, giving her a moment's pause: "*The enemy only attacks on one of two occasions; when you are ready for them and when you're not,*" and "*In battle, if something can go wrong, it will. Usually at the worst possible moment.*"

She thought hard for several seconds before coming to a decision based solely on intuition. Linking privately with her First Officer she instructed him to call battle stations again, even though the ships had stood down only a short while ago, following the successful Jump. On her Bridge monitoring screen, she watched several of the bridge staff turn to look quizzically at her First Officer, who smiled back and nodded as they turned to follow instructions.

Almost immediately, a query came in from Captain Tim Miller of INS Glorious, the other Carrier, requesting clarification before raising shields.

"*Typical of the man,*" she thought. His officious and often superior attitude towards everyone at times rankled even her, and she was seriously considering replacing him at the end of this tour. Assigned by the Admiralty as a replacement for Captain Skye "Tempest" MacFarlane on her promotion to Commodore, Frith was beginning to suspect it had more to do with them wanting to be rid of him rather than his ability to command.

Although raising additional shielding would marginally increase the risk of detection, Frith felt the risk worth taking. Her instincts seldom failed and even if wrong this time, it was unlikely any harm would be done. She recalled from many years ago the first time she had met the Emperor and his first words to her.

"I know you are a fine Admiral, Frith, but are you a lucky one too?" he'd asked.

At the time she was nonplussed but had come to understand exactly what he'd meant by the comment. Impatiently, she watched as her ship's main shields slowly formed and strengthen around Dauntless.

Like all Navy ships, Dauntless had three shield types. Wall and radiation shields protected against micro-meteorites, particle weapons, and radiation, while main shielding was used to absorb, deflect or slow missiles and railgun slugs. Wall and radiation shields were maintained at all times, whereas due to their power drain, main shields were only used during combat and took several minutes to reach maximum effectiveness.

Not wishing to talk to Captain Miller, Frith asked her First Officer to remind him the Navy wasn't a debating society and his ship's shields were to be raised immediately.

Harris's fighters were now at an optimum distance from the fleet, taking station to starboard at the point their AI's had calculated to be the best sentry position for her squadron to follow. Poised to transmit further information, she was surprised when her AI began reporting multiple readings from its close-range mass sensor, immediately confirmed by matching readings from the other fighters in her squadron.

"*This isn't good*," she thought to herself, as the number of unknown ships rose sharply. Although she knew her sensor telemetry was automatically being sent to both Captain Woods and the Flagship, it was hard to resist the urge to comment as the readings began resolving into hard numbers.

On Dauntless, a concerned Admiral Frith was back on the bridge within moments of the news, her mind racing through options before discarding them as more information continued to come in. Of one thing she was certain; there had been too many coincidences recently for this to be harmless, so she gave the order for sensors to go active and damn the consequences. Standing next to her First Officer, they looked together at the "tank," which was updating itself and resolving readings from the now active sensors into ships.

Dauntless's AI emotionlessly read out the facts, "Fifty-two capital ships, two Carriers, thirty-seven frigates. Exact configuration unknown but they resemble modified standard Imperial Navy classes. Range three thousand eight hundred kilometres from Woods task force. We are being actively scanned, detecting weapons lock and incoming fire. Task force AI's advised and are standing by, awaiting our response."

Frith and her First Officer looked at each other for a second before she nodded to him and he spoke to the AI, transmitting his words to all the other ships.

"Assume hostile, link for firing solutions and navigation but take any targets of opportunity, all ships hard to port at two-G acceleration. Move ships into position Beta and head back to the Jump Point."

Frith was thinking furiously, running options through the ship's AI with her implant, looking for more options. Outnumbered at least four to one, her force could not face a pitched battle with the enemy. Powerful as her ships were and capable of destroying a significant portion of the opposing fleet, eventually they would succumb to superior firepower and numbers. At long range, rail-guns were little use against a moving or accelerating target and EM-based weaponry was effective only to one thousand six hundred kilometres or closer. If her summary were correct, Woods fighters would come under missile attack within seconds, followed by Dauntless shortly afterwards.

"This is too much of a coincidence, and it's almost certain these are the same people who were behind the last attempt on Alexander, but, will they try and capture him or go for the kill like last time?" Frith knew whatever their goal was would soon manifest itself in the enemies tactics. She ran through what she already knew. The enemy fleet had obviously been stealthed and waiting for them, knowing in advance their likely time of Jumping and target. Given those two bits of information, their course would have been easy to plot, allowing them to wait with weapons ready until her task force came into range. It was only blind chance that the fighters mass sensors had sensed them before the trap was completely sprung. With main shields down while running in stealth mode, both her fleets would have been severely damaged before being able to respond and raise main shields.

Frith called Alexander, who had been waiting patiently, not wishing to disturb her concentration. He responded immediately, and she began setting out their options. She respected the Emperor had waited and hadn't tried to interfere or demand information, letting her focus on the current situation. He asked what their options were.

"Sire, we had three choices. Firstly, stay and fight. Not a smart idea, given how badly outnumbered we are. Second, turn to starboard, go to flank speed and power right through their fleet and head for the Jump point, but that leaves us open to boarding and suicide runs, plus makes us very vulnerable to enemy fire. The one I've chosen is the third. Turn sharply to port and accelerate at two-G for a time before decelerating hard for the Jump, strengthening our aft shields. Unless their fleet is made up of individuals from high-G worlds that can stand higher acceleration than we can, they won't be able to stop some of us from reaching the Jump Point."

The Emperor said nothing for a few heartbeats then nodded in agreement. "Agreed, you did well. Someone's been trying very hard to get at me, haven't they Admiral?"

"Yes, Sire, they have. If Captain Woods hadn't launched those reconnaissance fighters, we wouldn't have seen them until it was too late for us to do anything except run the gauntlet. You're right, someone really wants you dead or captured."

Alexander looked grim. "They'll just have to get in the queue. I'll be joining my bodyguard to assist should we need to repel boarders, but with a bit of luck, it won't come to that. Vimes and the ship's AI will keep me informed of developments. Be lucky, Janice."

With that he broke contact, switching to talk to his bodyguard and Dauntless's Marine Captain.

On the bridge of INS Courageous, Captain Woods only had a thirty-second warning before impacts began registering on his ships, rocking the Carrier through its still forming main shields which began glowing brightly at the impact points. Grateful now for previously having spent many hours running through multiple scenarios with the ship's AI and his First Officer, Commander Markham, he instructed his ships to act. Knowing the starboard screening fighters were all now effectively lost, he instructed them to target the closest capital ship of the enemy and begin a suicide run. Watching the fighters accelerate away, Woods had a moment of inspiration and quickly instructed the AI to take over control and launch every remaining fighter, including those still on board, towards the enemy on suicide runs, hoping this might gain the fleet vital seconds when the incoming fighters distracted the attacking force.

Judging by the rate at which his shields and point defences were being depleted, Captain Woods thought it only a matter of time before he would be totally reliant on covering fire from his three Interdiction Frigates and the two battleships. The new instructions from Admiral Frith to turn portside made perfect sense and gave him a better chance of survival than simply trying to plough through the enemy's centre, for he doubted his Carrier would survive the experience. As his force was still one thousand six hundred kilometres ahead of the main group, a fair proportion of enemy fire would have initially been directed at his ships, drawing some away from the flagship.

Thinking quickly, Woods gave instructions that once the last fighter had cleared their decks, the four main hangars were to split from the main hull and fight individually. That done, he switched his attention towards the remaining three hundred and eighty fighters which were now beginning their suicide run towards the enemy fleet. At the same time, he wryly wondered whether his unorthodox idea to use than in this way would ever become known as the Woods Gambit. Suddenly, a massive impact violently shook the bridge and threw him off his feet to the deck. Hitting his head hard on the floor, he felt himself blacking out but not before regretting he hadn't obeyed protocol and got into his command chair.

For Squadron Leader Harris, piloting her fighter from inside a combat pod, her first real fighter mission as Squadron Leader was certainly proving to be a memorable one. Long range particle beam weapons had begun searching out her fighters, destroying four of them before their AI's or pilots could react. Her squadron had then been taken out of manual control by the Carrier's AI and accelerated at one hundred-G towards the lead capital ships. At that acceleration, the life of her fighter's engines and spaceframe would only be measured in minutes anyway but would allow them to build up a reasonable velocity in the short distance to the enemy. Now unable to control or influence her fighter in any way, she watched as it manoeuvred and jigged around, trying to evade the incoming missiles and point defences as it made its final approach to the lead ship at almost eighty-two kilometres per second.

Suddenly, her screen went white, and the pod's canopy opened, causing her to blink and squint at the sudden bright light and noise of the alert. All around the control room, she watched the canopies of her squadron lift and the pilots emerge, shaking their heads when asked in turn if their fighter had managed to successfully hit any of the enemy ships.

Climbing out of her own cockpit and looking through the readouts that her command implant was now sending to her, she was impressed with the Captain's quick thinking in using the fighters in such an unorthodox manoeuvre. Beneath her feet she could feel the Carrier's shields begin taking multiple missile hits, their kinetic force being absorbed and converted into heat and energy. Increasingly, she felt some were getting through, juddering the ship and vaporising large areas of the armoured hull and point defences. Inevitably, she knew the more this happened, the fewer point defences would be left to destroy the missiles before they impacted on the shields, a vicious downwards spiral until Courageous was at the mercy of her attackers.

Using her newly uprated command implant, Harris checked for instructions with the ship's AI and discovered all the other fighters had or were in the process of being launched. Her squadron was instructed to report to the nearest muster station and don armoured suits before the ship accelerated to two-G. Running with them to the muster point, Harris thought she'd had enough of being shot at without the chance to shoot back when a massive jolt disrupted the artificial gravity for a second and threw everyone violently around the corridor.

Emergency lighting came on briefly until main power was restored a few moments later. Pilots began getting up from the floor, looking at each other and shared nervous glances, knowing full well their Carrier had just taken a major hit somewhere. Harris quickly scanned her squadron for injuries, mentally crossing everyone off before instructing them to keep moving towards the Marine muster station where suits and weapons would be issued to them. The normally clean, sweet air of the ship was becoming tinged with the acrid smell of burnt insulation and hot metal, overlaid with subtle mood enhancers as the AI tried to reduce the effects of stress amongst the crew. Dozens of other pilots from other redundant squadrons began joining her own, all running in the same direction, not trusting the transit tubes in case they failed.

To Frith's left, Dauntless's Weapon Masters were providing firing and defence solutions for her consideration along with the Cyber Warfare team who were attempting to disrupt the enemies' sensors and missile telemetry. Frith watched as Woods task force began turning away from its original course and accelerate to port along with the rest of her fleet, taking a course which would ensure the two would converge before they all reached the Jump Point. She was extremely gratified to see her faith in Captain Woods confirmed by the innovative use of his fighters and promised herself to accelerate his testing; if they survived, of course. The tank showed INS Diamond had been crippled and was venting atmosphere but still managing to keep up with the other ships. Sadly, considering the pounding it was taking, she knew it was only a matter of time before either its drive engines or armoured hull gave out completely.

At that moment the simulacrum representing INS Diamond flashed brightly in the tank, quickly becoming a receding black mark, sadly confirming her analysis of the situation. She closed her eyes for a second and breathed out, thinking of the men and women dying on the doomed ship. The AI confirmed several hundred missiles had coordinated their attack on Diamond, hitting the same point, with at least fifty getting through her shields to detonate amidships, cutting the Interdiction frigate in two. The two halves were continuing to maintain fire at a reduced rate, and she could detect life pods being launched. With no chance of being picked up by her Taskforce, she knew those poor souls were either fated to die in space or be taken prisoner.

Frith continued watching until the missiles, recognising a weakened target of opportunity, concentrated their attention away from the other ships and onto what was left of Diamond, blowing both halves apart with nuclear explosions and flooding the escape pods with lethal radiation. Automatically compensating for the newly formed hole in their defences, her remaining ships were moving closer together, so their fields of fire once again overlapped. At such close range, the risk of being hit by friendly fire increased slightly, but as it took far less to knock out a missile than a capital ship, any accidental damage would be negligible and worth the risk. Although taking multiple hits, both battleships had directed their main weaponry at the enemy fleet and were maintaining a furious rate of fire.

"Weapons Masters, please instruct our missiles to time their attacks with railgun shells which are nearing their targets. If we can get the enemy ships to move into the path of a shell while avoiding a missile or vice versa, we may be able to take some them out of the fight. Also, why aren't their intra-missile communications being disrupted?"

Turning her attention back to the tank, Captain Woods surprised her for the second time. He had disengaged Courageous's four hangars from the main hull and was using them as mobile weapon platforms, at a stroke increasing both the overlap of point defences and targets. Each of the hangars was an effective fighting unit in its own right, capable of independent flight and able to keep up with the task force. Although one had already been partially disabled, Captain Wood's tactics gave Frith an idea, and she quickly updated the AI, then contacted INS Glorious.

"Captain Miller, please immediately launch **all** of Glorious's fighters under AI control and accelerate them away from the enemy at maximum acceleration. Acknowledge."

A holo of Captain Miller appeared in front of her. "Surely you mean towards the enemy Admiral," he stated, his face and tone expressing mild amusement as if talking to a child. "I've taken the liberty of countermanding that order so..."

"Captain, if those fighters aren't launched within the next five seconds I will come over to your ship and personally reduce you in rank to a rating when this is over, assuming you survive that is. Do I make myself clear?" Frith asked quietly in clipped tones, through her implant ensuring the conversation was heard by all the command staff on every ship.

Miller's face paled, and he stammered for a second before regaining his composure. "Fighters away as instructed, Admiral. Miller out."

She took a deep breath and let it out slowly, conscious her bridge officers were waiting for what came next after the uncharacteristic outburst. Leaning across to her First Officer, Commander Gomez, she stage-whispered, "It's been a while since I've had to do anything like that, Ian. You know, I actually enjoyed it." Immediately she could feel the tension level drop across the bridge, and she knew her words had the desired effect from the smiles she could see on her officers' faces. Gomez looked at her and winked. They had worked together for several years now, and in addition to her tactical knowledge, he appreciated her skill in handling difficult situations.

Having now lost what little confidence she'd had in Captain Miller, Frith checked up on the launch progress and noted that his Carrier's shields were still forming and would still take at least another minute before reaching full strength. "*Damn that man*," she thought to herself, hoping that Miller's hubris wouldn't lead to the death of his ship. With his shields still at only seventy-five per cent effectiveness, a concerted missile attack or several slugs hitting at once would overload the shield generators and allow breakthrough to the Carrier's vulnerable hulls. Fortunately, his ship's AI was doing a fine job in launching the fighters as instructed, and all would be away within the next few seconds. For her plan to work properly she needed all the fighters to get as far away from the Carrier as possible and safe from the wall of enemy fire descending on her task force.

Harris and her pilots made it to the muster station and into spare Marine battle suits only moments before acceleration began to rapidly build, leaving them grateful to have arrived in time. All were familiar with the armoured suits, having trained in them at Flight Academy, but everyone was out of practice and would be spending whatever time they had left re-familiarising themselves with the controls and any changes. Her implant finally interfaced with the suit, and she called for an update from the ship's AI. The news was not good. Both task forces were under fire now, with missiles having also reached the main group. The enemy fleet was accelerating hard to match their speed, making itself more vulnerable to incoming shells and missiles as they tried to close.

Four of the enemy battleships had already been taken out by withering fire from INS Rodney and Repulse, who were continuing to saturate the area with shells and missiles while taking up a position at the rear to cover the escape of Captain Woods and his Carrier. In addition, Dauntless and her four accompanying battleships were sending out their own curtain of fire towards the enemy fleet, which Harris could see was taking multiple impacts. Harris couldn't understand why the full complement of fighters from INS Glorious was accelerating away from the enemy fleet at high-G, however, she, like everyone in the task force, had heard of the Admiral's reputation and knew there must be a good reason for it.

On the Carrier's bridge, Captain Woods came to and managed a wan smile at the concerned face of his First Officer who was tending to him.

"Don't worry," he said, beginning to stand, "there's still life in me yet." The relieved expression on his officer's face told him all he needed to know about how the battle was going.

"Give the order for everyone to form armoured suits."

"Already done, Captain. You and I are the last two, so let's get to it.

Helping him over to the command station, Markham checked his Captain's eyes for any signs of confusion caused by the fall, then nodded and moved back to his post, leaving Woods to assess what had happened and suit up. Between his link to the ship's AI and the information displayed in the tank, it was obvious Hangar One had been hit by multiple railgun shells, having been unlucky enough to occupy the exact point where a full salvo from several of the enemy battleships had been passing through. Her shields had managed to deflect several of them before letting eight through and although a lot of their kinetic energy had already been absorbed and dissipated by the shields, they still struck with the force of tactical nukes, punching through the hull into hangar bays and out the other side, sending shockwaves rippling through the ship and severely damaging point defences. Seeing an opportunity, the enemy missiles co-ordinated and focused on the damaged hangar, overloading the remaining shields and turning it into a fireball when the main engines overloaded and released all of the pent-up shield energy in a titanic, silent explosion. One of the slugs had also struck Glorious a glancing blow below the bridge, sufficiently hard enough to shake the entire main structure, temporarily causing localised power outages.

Stunned for a few moments by the loss of over five hundred lives on Hangar One, he watched silently as the green image representing it in the tank turned to black and began falling back from the remaining blue and green ships. He knew this was just the beginning, before switching his attention to his Carrier's sister-ship, INS Glorious, watching as it began taking multiple impacts through its still forming shields.

Captain Miller looked on in horrid fascination as his AI confirmed the enemy missile swarms were now focusing their attention on his ship, targeting them as his shields were still forming and weaker in comparison to others in the fleet, making Glorious a prime target of opportunity.

"This isn't what is meant to happen," he said to no-one in particular, before looking around in desperation at his fellow officers, mentally willing one of them to make a suggestion or say something useful. His carefully crafted career plan, to be given command of Glorious as a stepping stone to further promotion, never included getting involved in actual combat and was simply meant to be another tick on his upwards march to Flag rank, not something that might get him killed.

To Miller's left, First Officer Lorna Cooke sat tight-lipped, listening to him speak and not bothering to even look in his direction. She knew, as did the rest of the Bridge staff that Glorious was taking a pounding because of the man's arrogance. She was silently willing the laws of physics to allow the shields to firm up in the next few seconds but knew it wasn't going to happen. Dauntless had identified their predicament and was diverting point defence cover away from itself in an effort to protect them. Internally, Cooke quietly thanked the Admiral and Commander Gomez, making a mental note to buy her opposite number as many drinks as he might want, provided they both managed to survive the next few minutes.

With the deck shaking and trembling beneath her seat, Cooke allowed herself a few moments to think of her three-year-old son, safely back home with her husband, and tried to stop the hot, prickly sensation in her eyes.

"Adam, wake up, we're there."

Karen was looking at him when Adam awoke. She noticed there was no momentary confusion or a brief period of awakening; he simply woke, completely aware of his surroundings, needing no time at all to catch up. He returned her look and smiled, then looked at his door in confusion. Karen watched, amazed that he seemed unaware of how to open a car door. At first, he waved his hand in front of it and then she was sure he was going to ask it to open before stopping himself. Laughing, she leant across and pulled the door handle for him.

"See, this is what you do, Adam. Pull the handle towards yourself and the door unlocks. Don't they have cars where you come from?" she asked, jokingly, as she climbed out herself.

Karen paid the driver, who had remotely opened the boot for Adam to pull out the two soft holdalls containing their clothing. Even though the bags were not heavy, Adam noticed the difficulty he had in lifting them. Although his body was almost completely healed, thanks to Vimes taking control and accelerating his autonomic system, it would be several weeks before he retained his previous strength and fitness. Vimes had told him the accelerated healing process put great strain on the body and was not something that could be maintained for any length of time, so once he was out of danger and able to move around, Vimes had released control, allowing his body to return to normal. This meant Adam would have to rebuild his previous muscle mass himself, the old-fashioned way.

Adam took a moment to look around, taking in the view from the bungalow across the loch and out to sea. The earlier grey morning sky was clear on this side of the island, and the sun brought the scenery into sharp contrast, highlighting the rocky cliffs to the left with the green fields and coastline in front of him. Recent heavy rains had swelled a myriad of small streams, which now ran off the boggy higher ground towards the loch, creating numerous small waterfalls. Given all what had happened to him recently, Adam decided Karen was right in thinking this was a lovely place and thanked his good fortune at still being able to appreciate it.

He moved to one side to get out of the taxi's path as it reversed, watching as it drove off over the cattle grid with a thrum and turned left, back to Portree. The chemical smell of burnt fuel lingered in the air, causing Adam to wrinkle his nose and wonder why the people of this planet polluted the air in this fashion when other viable technologies were surely available to them.

Not sure what to do, Adam slowly put down the bags and stretched his arms to lessen the discomfort. He looked at Karen, who came over and picked them both up.

"I've got these, Adam. Come on, don't stand on ceremony, let's get inside."

With that, she crunched across the gravel drive and walked up a short flight of steps leading to the main door, set at ninety degrees to the bungalow to keep the howling winter gales out. She fumbled unsuccessfully in her pocket for the keys, then rummaged through one of the bags for a few moments before triumphantly producing them like a magician producing a rabbit from a hat.

"Wipe your feet when you come in and take your shoes off," she said, before disappearing into the hall.

Adam stood in the doorway, unsure what she meant until he looked down and read similar words repeated on a mat by the entrance. Pleased to have understood, he scrapped his trainers on the rough matting before closing the door and following in the direction Karen had taken. Turning the corner, they unexpectedly bumped into each other, before separating like guilty schoolchildren caught with a hand in the cookie jar. Karen broke the awkwardness and stepped away.

"I'll show you your room, it's just here. Your bed's already made up, and the toilet and bathroom are over there," pointing towards the door at the end of the corridor. "I've put your bag on the bed, so you can hang your clothes in the wardrobe, such as they are. While you're doing that, I'll put the kettle on; tea or coffee?"

Adam looked at her with that puzzled look she had come to recognise, so she squeezed past him and pointed at the wardrobe. "Clothes go in here. Open the door and use the wire hangers to put your clothes on. I didn't just construct the bed, I meant it's ready for you to sleep in tonight. As for the kettle, I'm not going to wear it, simply heat water to make a tea or coffee. Understand me now?"

Adam nodded, mirroring her smile. "Tea please or some warm water. Any chance of food?"

Karen rolled her eyes. "I just knew you were going to ask me that, Adam," she said, disappearing into the kitchen. "Follow me, and I'll show you where everything is kept so you can feed yourself."

Adam followed gratefully, feeling hungry, vulnerable and lost in that order. Once heir apparent to an Empire, he was reduced to following this Earth woman around like a puppy, unable to grasp the simplest of technologies and he didn't like the feeling one bit. He looked around him. The kitchen was a large area, with cupboards and drawers set into fitted furniture. He recognised a sink, taps and what he assumed were cooking utensils, but that was about all. He remembered his father telling him once that both he and his mother were good cooks, but other than the odd trip with them out into the Palace woodlands and the wilderness beyond where they'd cooked food over an open fire, he never really had the need to learn himself as everything was just a thought away and provided by his staff in short order.

Karen looked at him closely. There was no way he was faking his bewilderment, and with a sigh, she set about clearing the fridge. While the seafood still smelt fine, she wasn't going to risk getting food poisoning, so that was tied up in several plastic carrier bags and dropped in the bin. The milk was still ok, so she set about boiling a kettle and thought about what to make them both, for by now she was also starting to get hungry.

"What do you want to eat, Adam?" she asked.

There it was again, that momentary hesitation before answering.

"I'll have whatever you are having, please, Karen."

Taking some ingredients out of the fridge, Karen wondered if English actually was his first language or whether he was having to mentally translate what she was saying into his native tongue and back again before responding.

"Wissen Sie, was ein Omelette ist, oder würden Sie lieber etwas anderes?" She enquired, looking at his face, remembering some of her A-level German.

"Ein Omelette ist fein Karen, Im glücklich damit," came the reply, still with that slightly sing-song accent. He stopped and stared at her for a moment, looking surprised at what had come out of his mouth.

"So, you speak German too, do you? Any other languages hidden away in there, Adam?" Karen asked him, wondering again what she had let herself in for and why she was taking the risk of bringing this stranger into her home. As quickly as that thought came she had another; the memory of his face as she was thrown out of the lorries path and he was struck instead, before vanishing under the wheels. It reminded her again that she owed him a lot and anyway, he was a mystery wrapped up in an enigma; a puzzle she intended to complete. On top of all that, it was nice to have male company again, especially someone this interesting and handsome. Despite his size and strangeness, she could sense a gentleness and knew he wouldn't do anything to hurt her.

Adam sat down at the long kitchen table, large enough for eight people to sit around comfortably, and said nothing, seemingly lost in introspection. Karen busied herself with making something for them to eat and before long the kitchen took on the aroma of cooking, making Adam's mouth water in anticipation. Shortly afterwards they were both tucking into a late breakfast, washed down with fresh orange juice. Between mouthfuls, Karen looked up to observe him but didn't know whether to be flattered or irked at the speed he finished off his omelette.

"Everything OK with the food?" she enquired.

"Lovely, Karen. Thank you. I feel much happier now," he replied with another of his smiles. "Any chance of your showing me where the accident took place? I'm eager to see if it jogs lose any memories up here." He tapped his head.

"You're eager. Let's wash up first, then we can go for a walk once we are settled in properly. You do know how to do the drying don't you?" she responded, only half in jest, rising to pick up both of the empty plates.

"No, but I'm sure you will show me anyway," he replied, raising himself to stand by the sink, taking the dishcloth she handed him. Fortunately, this time he didn't need Vimes to explain what to do with it. It didn't take more than a few minutes to wash-up, and once everything was packed away, they were soon walking down the steps and crunching across the gravel towards the cattle-grid and road beyond. As they walked, Adam began asking lots of questions, from the purpose of the cattle-grid to the types of birds that flew overhead. Karen answered as many as she could and promised to show him on the Internet those she was unsure about. His curiosity was infectious, and his questioning reminded her of a young child who had just learnt the meaning of the word "why?"

It was only a few hundred metres walk before they reached the spot where Adam had been struck. The lorry's skid marks and deep ruts dug in the soft ground by the side of the road were still visible.

Karen watched Adam closely. She had half expected him to be wary about visiting the spot where the accident took place, but surprisingly, he showed no hesitation in walking over to where he'd been struck and seemed to be looking for something. Karen asked him what it was he was looking for and if he needed her help. He hesitated for a moment, all the while looking into her eyes. This was another of those critical moments for Adam;

should he trust her and try to explain about the night-vision lenses that had been knocked out of his eyes by the impact, or should he mislead her? He decided on the latter.

"I'm just looking for clues, Karen. Anything that might explain what I was doing here on that night. If I was carrying something I no longer remember, it might have been thrown clear on impact. I can't see anything, however."

He decided to distract her and gestured to a point several hundred metres away.

"What's over there?" he asked, "Can we go and have a look?"

"It's only a ruined farm no-one cares about anymore, but OK, let's walk. I'll show you around. It used to belong to an old couple, but as they aged and couldn't look after the place, it fell into ruin. Shame really, it could have been so much more in a spot like that."

Karen fell into step alongside him, crossing the road and walking down the gentle incline of the slip road towards the ruined farmhouse and jetty. Rounding a bend in the road, the dilapidated state of the farmhouse became clear. Next to a concrete jetty, a fisherman was unloading his boat and stacking the catch alongside a red van where a second man was carefully loading it into the rear. Although standing with his back turned to her, Karen recognised him immediately and called out.

"Afternoon Willy. How are you doing today?"

"All the better for seeing you, lass," he replied, turning around. He walked over and extended his hand to Adam. "Who's this fine young man you're with, is it your boyfriend?"

"Just a friend, Sir," replied Adam, shaking his hand and noticing the hard calluses, rough skin and firm grip. "My name's Adam. Good to meet you. How was today's catch, any good?"

"So-so, Adam. I've had better. With that accent and tan you're certainly not from around here, so where do you come from?" Willy asked, warming towards the stranger but being direct as usual.

Karen interrupted, not wishing for Adam to be put on the spot. "He's with me, Willy, and staying up at the cottage for a while. You and your questions." She quickly changed the subject before he could ask any more. "The crab and lobster were lovely, by the way. Thank you again."

"We've got to get this lot over to Portree," Willy said, gesturing towards the catch and van, "The buyer is running late and can't make it here today, so we've got to go to him. No rest for the wicked." He looked at Adam, "Nice to meet with you, enjoy your stay on Skye," and with that, nodded to Karen, winking broadly at her before going back to the van.

Karen could feel herself reddening at what the wink implied, even though nothing of the sort was going on. "*Or likely to either,*" she reminded herself. Unfortunately, she knew that by the end of today everyone in Struan would know she had a man friend staying and there would be numerous questions to be answered when her aunt and uncle returned from their cruise. "*Oh well, that's what happens when you live in a small place and everyone knows everyone else's business.*" A low chuckle from the back of the van added to her embarrassment as she imagined Willy was probably already talking to his colleague, so she pulled at Adam's arm and moved him away from where he had been examining the boat.

Adam felt the tug and followed its direction, even though he had wanted to stay and look over the fishing boat. Living on the coast had its advantages, and from an early age he had been allowed to go out fishing, using the traditional boats that were allowed to fish providing it was all done by hand. Industrial methods of fishing had been stopped on Capital thousands of years previously, initially to allow marine life to recover. Subsequently, fish, along with most other sources of protein, were artificially engineered. Those that lived on the coast preferred to eat what they caught, rather than the substitutes, even though it was impossible to distinguish between real and man-made. Also, there was always a ready market for "natural" produce, especially amongst the very wealthy who were always happy to pay a substantial premium for what they perceived to be exclusivity.

On the way back to the cottage, he became aware of a subtle change in Karen's behaviour towards him. She was keeping a wider distance between them and her answers were more abrupt. He thought back over what he had said and done earlier but couldn't think of anything where he might have inadvertently offended her. He decided to ask.

"Karen, have I done anything wrong? You seem suddenly distant, and I would like to apologise if I've said or done anything to offend you." He tried to look at her face, but she turned away and for a moment looked down at the ground before meeting his gaze.

"It's nothing you've done, Adam. Willy assumed that you and I were an item and..." Seeing Adam's familiar look of bafflement, she interrupted herself. "An item means being romantically attached to someone."

Her face and neck began to feel uncomfortably warm, but she continued, fighting the blush she knew was coming, "And it will be all around the village by the end of the day that you are here and staying at the cottage. I just don't feel comfortable with everyone putting two and two together and getting five, especially as I'll get the third degree from Alastair and Flora about my love life when they get back." Karen looked him full in the face and moved a fraction closer. "It's nothing you've done Adam, I promise."

Adam knew not to push any further and thought he understood, even though he still had some questions. As they resumed walking again, he had to ask one more.

"What's receiving the "third degree," Karen?"

Back at the cottage, Adam was feeling unusually tired from the walking, but despite his fatigue, forced himself to go through a routine of callisthenics which Vimes assured him would rapidly improve his fitness. He chose the empty garage attached to the house as it was out of the wind and away from prying eyes.

By the end of his workout session, Adam was near exhaustion, his pants and vest sodden with sweat. Sitting down on his haunches, Adam took a few moments to get his breath back and calm his heartbeat, before beginning a gentler warm-down to remove the build-up of lactic acid in his muscles. He knew that if it weren't removed, tomorrow morning would bring him even more discomfort. Even without the lactic acid burn, he knew in the morning there wouldn't be a single muscle group in his body not complaining, so he wanted to make sure any damage was kept to a minimum. Once warmed down, an ice-cold shower would help the process further.

Fifteen minutes later he was in the shower, gasping out loud as the ice-cold water shocked his still hot body. Karen, on hearing his involuntary gasp from where she was sitting in the kitchen, knocked on the bathroom door and asked if he was OK, then told him to present himself for a quick examination when finished.

Adam was pleased he'd managed to work out how the soap dispenser operated and was in a happier, but tired, frame of mind when he wrapped a bath towel around his hips and went to his room. He decided to slip on a pair of underpants and asked Vimes if there was any useful information available on the sexual customs and mores of this society. He was coming to the conclusion that relationships and matters of sex were a lot less straightforward here than he was used to back home.

His tired, but good mood suddenly vanished as Adam reminded himself that, for the foreseeable future this planet was his home unless he was able to find a way of constructing a QA communication device from scratch. Although Vimes had downloaded a complete set of schematics for such an eventuality, the number of advanced technologies which needed to be introduced before this could happen was daunting. At the very least, he was going to be here for several decades, and he worried about what was happening to his parents and the Empire, especially when news of his disappearance became known. The thought of his mother's tears and his father's private grief darkened his mood further.

A knock on the bedroom door, followed by an "Are you decent?" from Karen brought him back to the present.

"Yes Karen, I am a decent person, but I think you meant do I have clothes on? If so, then yes, my genitalia are covered."

An explosion of laughter from outside the door followed, and Karen's head popped around the door and looked at him. It quickly retracted, and the laughter continued for a further few seconds before she walked into the room, apologising.

"I'm sorry Adam, that was just so funny, I couldn't help laughing at what you said."

He shrugged his shoulders and forced a smile. "I think I'm getting used to the idioms now. As long as you keep making allowances and explaining, I should be OK."

Karen spent several minutes checking his body for scars or any sign of his recent catastrophic injuries. There were no scars or even residual red patches now, and to her trained eyes, his body had started to fill out again. The exercises he'd done in the garage had temporarily pumped his muscles, and she realised he was physically completely healed. His memory loss, however, was different and not something she could do anything about, apart from making enquiries on the island, then remembered the local Police had already done so immediately after the accident. With that in mind, she stepped back and formally confirmed she was discharging him from her unofficial care, adding that she had made a pile of potato salad and sausages for their evening meal and he should hurry up and get dressed.

"I don't know what they are Karen, but it sounds wonderful," he replied, putting on a light blue shirt and the jeans he'd laid earlier on the bed.

While exercising in the garage, he and Vimes had been going over his memories of the night they landed, trying to pinpoint the lifeboat to his current location. Both his tracker and night vision lenses had been lost in the accident, and he hoped that if found, no-one would recognise them for what they represented. Adam's now near perfect recall, courtesy of the union with Vimes, meant he was confident of finding his way back to the ship. There, he could replicate more money and properly equip himself for the tasks ahead, although how or where he was going to make a start were currently beyond him. Vimes had suggested that by using the pod's communications equipment, they might be able to bypass Government and financial institutions online security to create a fictional ID and account but wasn't certain of success until they tried.

A little later, sitting around the kitchen table, Adam's attention was firmly focused on the food in front of him. No stranger to real food, as opposed to the synthetic, this was something else, and he was enjoying every savoury mouthful. It seemed potatoes were very versatile and featured in quite a number of culinary dishes from these isles. Capital had something similar, but these were far nicer.

Sitting opposite, Karen watched him eat, all the while thinking about what to do tomorrow. The food she had initially bought on the way here wouldn't last long at the rate Adam was demolishing it, and he badly needed several more changes of clothing. Although the shops in Portree were expensive and aimed more towards tourists than locals, she knew of a few places where she could get him kitted out properly and at a decent price. Fortunately, she was still holding on to a sizeable sum of his money, and despite trying to give it back, he seemed quite happy for her to use it as she saw fit, so tomorrow they would go shopping, followed by a scenic tour of the island. Ostensibly to help his memory, Karen also needed the trip to get out and about, having been stuck at the Hospital for too long and the wide, open spaces of Skye called out to her need for space and freedom.

After dinner, Adam asked if there was Internet access and a computer he could use. Fast broadband had only been on the island for a few years, and everyone lucky to be in an area that could have it had jumped at the chance to upgrade.

Alastair and Flora had a small side room set up as a home office, and Karen showed him how to start up the computer and access the Internet. She wasn't surprised when Adam showed no understanding of how the computer worked and even had to be shown how to operate the mouse. In a scene reminiscent of Captain Scott in Star Trek IV, at first he'd tried talking into it, but soon grasped the basics and began scrolling through pages. For a while, she watched what he was looking at, but then lost interest and poured herself a glass of wine and sat down by the picture window overlooking the loch. At this time of year it became dark relatively early, so she made herself comfortable while relaxing as the twilight deepened and the sky turned a deep red as the sun dropped below the horizon.

"*Red sky at night, shepherds delight*," she thought to herself, taking another sip of red wine before crossing her legs and letting herself relax. All she could hear in the absolute silence was the faint tippity-tap of keyboard keys coming from the other room.

Alexander was allowing Vimes to handle all the incoming data feeds and damage reports, only allowing through messages from Admiral Frith. He was glad of the support and protection of his armoured suit, for Dauntless was taking a constant pounding. Whenever her shields became temporarily overloaded, a slug or missile would get through to the armoured hull, rocking the huge ship and gouging deep holes in her armour. Under these circumstances, an unarmoured stumble at two-G could easily become a bad fall, possibly resulting in broken bones or severe bruising, not something anyone would want prior to possible combat.

Earlier that day, shortly after arriving at the Marine's practice hall, the hangar situated below his private quarters had taken a direct hit, with the resulting blast damage severely damaging his suite of rooms, making Alexander very glad he'd taken the chance to mingle with his troops. Worse still, the hangar had contained his last two private yachts, one of which was now little more than expensive scrap. Fortunately, the one containing the secret Jump Drive had escaped relatively unscathed.

Since then, he had been moving around Dauntless, encouraging everyone he met who looked nervous or concerned. Sometimes he would join in with whatever they were doing, providing his presence wouldn't distract them from their duties. Finally, at a suggestion from Vimes, he made his way to one of the muster stations where a large number of his Marine bodyguards were waiting.

As usual, they were quietly going on about their business, checking each other's armour or watching the battle's progress on their own screens. The air of calm was belied by the palpable tension everyone in the room felt that heightened whenever the ship was jolted by an unusually large explosion or blow.

Alexander walked around the large hall, chatting and laughing with everyone, making an effort to appear blasé about what was happening outside, but they all knew he cared deeply about the fate of his people in the fleet and was simply putting on a show for their benefit.

Inwardly, Alexander was finding it very difficult not to intervene in the battle planning or even to stay away from the Bridge, but he knew that it would serve little purpose other than making him feel better. Of the two of them, Admiral Frith was the more experienced military tactician, and he knew she would perform better without him getting in the way. He would just have to wait it out with everyone else, but the habit of being in charge was a hard one to break, especially in times like this. Alexander's anger levels had been steadily rising since the incident at Heaven, and it was now a constant inner battle not to let rip in public. To ease his frustration, for days now Alexander had been pounding the practice battle droids in the privacy of his quarters, destroying three of the four available on board. With the remaining droid now wrecked along with his quarters, Alexander felt constrained and angry. Despite heroic work-outs in the gym, he wanted nothing more at this moment than to let out his frustration on the enemy.

On the Bridge, Frith was monitoring events on INS Glorious. The Carrier's shields had finally firmed some time ago, but the damage she had taken during that time was considerable. Swarms of missiles and slugs had severely damaged three of her four hangars, and now she was having trouble holding position with the fleet. The three severely damaged hangar sections were now incapable of being released from the main body, and while they provided a measure of additional protection to the main hull, they were doing nothing to help Glorious maintain position, their engines having been put out of action.

The only hangar to separate in time was having problems of its own, taking damage and struggling to keep up with the main body. A few shuttles had tried to ferry crew away from it back to the main ship, but they had been easily picked off by missiles. It was apparent anyone on board would have to take their chances, either staying and fighting on, or risking an escape pod. Whatever they chose, their chances of survival were not good and diminishing rapidly as the rest of the fleet accelerated away and they fell behind.

She smiled grimly, proud of the fight her ships were putting up against such uneven odds. INS Rodney and Repulse, the two older battleships protecting the rear of Captain Woods force, were successfully managing to draw fire away from their Carrier, despite taking heavy damage in the process. The heavily armoured sections, containing engines and main guns, were still holding out. However, much of the ship's superstructure and less important areas were open to space and venting air into the unforgiving vacuum through the great rents and holes that peppered their hulls.

The images of the two battleship Captains, Singh and Haynes, appeared in front of her, requesting immediate attention.

"Go ahead gentlemen, I'm listening," she said, acknowledging both men with a nod.

Haynes began. "Admiral, Captain Singh and I want your permission to fall back and engage the enemy directly. Captain Woods is in agreement too. It's only a matter of time before we are dead in space, for our rear armour is almost gone, and our engines will be left vulnerable if we don't present another face. By turning around and heading straight towards them, we present our heavily armoured prows, which are currently relatively undamaged."

The image of Captain Baih Singh nodded in agreement.

"You both realise it's almost certainly suicide?" Frith said, knowing it was a statement rather than a question to the experienced Captains.

Captain Singh spoke up. "Yes, Admiral. We've talked it through and realise what we are doing. Even in their damaged state, our two battleships pose a significant threat, and they can't afford to have us in their midst, so they'll have to devote significant resources to neutralise us as we pass through their fleet."

Captain Haynes interrupted his old comrade, "Not only that, Admiral, but we have a better chance doing this than simply trying to keep up with the fleet and being pounded to bits. We'll definitely not survive that. If we manage to pass through their midst, they'll either have to leave ships behind to finish us off, board us or risk having us bring up their rear and attack them from behind as you decelerate to make the Jump point. Either way, we'll keep them occupied long enough to help Captain Woods and the Carrier get further away and draw more of the fire away from you and the Emperor."

The image of Haynes blurred for a moment and cut-out, before reappearing after four seconds. "Apologies Admiral, we just took several hits, one of which knocked out a power plant."

Frith looked intently at the faces of her two Captains, then nodded. Despite the extra gravity, she brought herself to attention and addressed them both. "Agreed. Gentlemen, it's been my privilege to have served with you and if we all make it through to the other side..." She stopped and bit her lip, for once lost for words and unable to articulate the pride and respect she had for the two men.

"We know Admiral, we know. Keep the Emperor safe." And with that, the two images faded, tactical data and damage reports taking their place.

"Did you get that, Alexander?" she asked as the Emperor's face appeared on her screen. "Brave men."

"Yes Janice, they certainly are," Alexander responded, "but ultimately we may all be shortly following them into the long night. Although we are destroying three of the enemy for every one we lose, you know as well as I the odds are not in our favour. We cannot win a battle of attrition." He looked over the update she had sent over. "You believe they want to board Dauntless and take us as a prize?"

Frith shook her head. "Not as a prize, but my assessment is they want you captured to use as a hostage or your dead body to display as proof. A vaporised Dauntless and no body to show for their trouble might make their job of convincing everyone of your demise that much harder. That gives us a slight advantage. Goodness knows we need something to go in our favour. We just need to last another twenty minutes. If we do, at that point would you please join me on the Bridge? There'll be something I'll want to personally show you."

Frith cut the link, focusing on the battle in front of her, set out in red, blue and green in the tank. The enemy had already increased acceleration to close the distance between the two fleets. Frith was reluctant to go beyond two-G herself because of the stresses involved on both the ships and crew, but the enemy was desperate to close the range and had pushed harder, if only by a fraction. Shortly, her fleet would begin decelerating hard to ensure it reached the Jump Point at rest relative to the system, a process that would take ninety minutes, at which point those still capable of Jumping would be able to make the transition to safe space. Once deceleration began, the enemy would have to do the same if they didn't want to overshoot and fly past them. A careful game of cat and mouse was being played out in space between the two opposing fleets, with the enemy desperate to get alongside and board before Dauntless could Jump. Constant changes in acceleration and deceleration ensured the enemy had to work harder to do so, placing greater strain on their systems and personnel. Not wishing to tempt fate, only when she was certain they could make the Jump Point would she ask the Emperor where he wanted to go next

Captain Woods, along with all his Bridge staff, were now at their stations clad in armoured suits. He'd instructed his to administer something for a king-sized headache but was reassured by the diagnostic readouts there was nothing seriously wrong and was suffering from nothing worse than a mild concussion.

Switching his attention to the tank, he watched INS Glorious slowly fall behind the fleet, dropping out from beneath the covering point defences of Dauntless and the other battleships. Its own point defences, hindered now on three sides by the dead hangars, would no longer be capable of providing adequate cover and it was simply a matter of a few minutes before the enemy either blew her to bits or decided to board and take her as a prize. His own shields were flashing brilliantly around the impact point of accelerated slugs, which vapourised into super-heated plasma, adding their energy to those of detonating missiles which sought to find weaknesses as they probed the shield's integrity. Anyone foolish to look at the real thing, instead of the images relayed to the tank or screens, would have their retinas burnt within seconds, searing one last imprint forever onto their optic nerve.

INS Acteon, one of Woods two remaining interdiction frigates, begin flashing in the tank, indicating a serious problem. Looking at a more detailed display of the frigate, he watched as it took multiple impacts from a concerted attack by both missiles and slugs, shearing the drive section away from the main body before detonating in a huge, silent explosion. The remaining frigate, INS Amethyst, began moving closer to his Carrier, attempting to compensate for the loss of cover. With the two battleships falling further behind and moving to confront the closing enemy fleet head-on, the remaining interdiction frigate now had a much smaller volume of space to protect and could concentrate on just itself and Courageous. Woods doubted it would be enough.

On INS Glorious, First Officer Cooke found herself in a maelstrom of decision making. Its AI had determined Captain Miller was no longer capable of captaining the ship and had offered her, as First Officer, his command, providing a battlefield commission to Captain and citing various rules that she'd not bothered listening to. With mixed emotions, she had reluctantly agreed, for she knew in her heart that in all probability this would be both her first and last command as Captain. Miller had been relieved several minutes before and was currently being escorted back to his quarters where she had instructed him to remain until the battle was settled. Cooke had acknowledged a brief note from the Admiral wishing her good luck with a terse one-liner of her own but was under no illusions about the ultimate fate of her ship and crew.

As Glorious fell behind and moved out from under the protective fire of Dauntless and the other ships, the frequency of direct hits increased, with swarms of smart-missiles seeking her out, their AI's recognising her Carrier's vulnerability.

With shields failing and probably collapsing within the next few minutes, Cooke knew Glorious would then either be totally destroyed or boarded if the enemy thought they could take her ship as a prize. Even in her battered state, it made good economic sense to repair and refurbish a capital ship instead of building one from scratch, but she had mixed feelings if she wanted to let this happen.

On her screen, she could see boarding shuttles already being launched from one of the enemy Carriers, but whether it was for her ship or another, she couldn't yet tell from their trajectory. They were holding back, screened by enemy point defences as if waiting for a decision to be made. Cooke didn't know what would be worse; dying in combat or being taken prisoner and spending years, if not the rest of her life, in a cell or on a prison planet.

Escorted by a Marine through a corridor leading to his quarters, Captain Miller was in a state of denial, living moment to moment in a panicky nightmare of his own creation. Being removed from the Bridge, and having the command functions of his implant switched off, had been the final weight which tipped the balance of his mind, toppling him into an abyss of animal-like fear from which he could see no escape. With every shudder and recoil of the deck, his sanity slowly slipped further away from him.

"Captain Miller, Captain Miller!" The voice of his Marine escort finally managed to cut through the mind-numbing fog of his panic. "Change of orders. We have to get you to a muster station for your own protection. Your quarters were just hit, and that section has been sealed off."

Miller looked at the Marine, finding it hard to concentrate on what was being said to him. After a long pause, he shook his head.

"No, I have to get to my quarters. My things are all there and....do you feel that?" he asked the Marine, realising the ship was no longer shuddering and taking hits.

"Feel what Sir? Oh, I see. Probably a lull so their boarding shuttles can pass safely through without fear of being hit by their own weapons." Fresh instructions came through to the Marine, and he listened intently for a moment, before returning his attention back to Miller. "My orders have changed. You are to proceed to the nearest muster station alone."

"Where are you going?" asked Miller as the Marine began turning away to head back in the direction they'd just come from.

"Re-joining my unit, Captain. Good luck Sir." The Marine saluted and sped off, a helmet forming as his suit configured itself to combat mode as he ran, bulkheads opening and closing for him as he sped along the corridor.

Left alone, Miller sank down onto the metal floor with his back against the closest wall, pulling his knees up and cradling his head with his hands, lost in his own misery and oblivious to what was going on around him. After what seemed an age he managed to retain some semblance of control and stood up, the Marine's instructions having finally managed to get through to his befuddled brain. Taking a few seconds to get his bearings, Miller called up the fastest route to the nearest muster station that avoided damaged areas, then set off down the corridor towards the first bulkhead door. He slowed fractionally before reaching it, expecting the door to open automatically on his approach and let him through as it had for the Marine. When it refused to open, he stepped back a few paces and began to inquire of the ship's AI what was the problem. Before Miller could finish articulating the question, he was blown forward into the bulkhead door by an explosion behind him, cracking his head on the hard metal. Stunned and momentarily deafened by the concussion, he turned around to look down the corridor at the explosion's source, only to be faced with dozens of vaguely familiar armoured figures pouring through a ten-metre wide breach in the corridor wall. Anti-boarding measures activated and anti-personnel flechettes and particle weapons began firing from concealed ports in the ceiling and floor, forcing Miller to look desperately for cover. Realising these were the enemy, he began raising his arms in the universal gesture of surrender, but before he could finish or even begin to articulate his surrender, he saw the nearest figures level their arms at him. As his body was shredded by dozens of flechettes, with a last instant of clarity, he noted there was surprisingly little pain.

Captain Cooke watched as the first of the boarding shuttles passed through her ship's weakened point defences and begin ramming into its hull, penetrating deep, relying on the Carrier's smart metal hull to close and create air-tight seals behind them. The AI was sending parties of Marines to the affected areas and coordinating the defence at a speed no human could match. Automated interior defence systems were slowing the enemies advance throughout the ship, but it was only a matter of time before vital areas were taken and key systems turned against the defenders. She briefly considered joining the Marines but realised they would be at the Bridge soon enough and here would be a fitting place to make a last stand. Casualty reports increased rapidly as the enemy methodically began working their way through the Carrier's interior, killing anyone they met and inserting Infiltrator Programmes into key areas before being confronted by defending Marines.

For a brief moment, she had the satisfaction of noting Captain Miller's name on the list of casualties before it was scrolled away by numerous others. Although scared almost to the point of panic, her training and sense of duty kept any trace of it from her face, and she took not a little pride in how calm her voice sounded when she addressed her officers. Rising from her command chair, she called for attention and looked out across the room at the expectant faces.

"You all know our position. This isn't the way I expected my first command to go, but few of us ever get to choose our ending. To stop Glorious being taken as a prize, I've instructed the ship to self-destruct once the Bridge is taken." For a moment, Cooke stopped talking and simply smiled at her comrades. "It's been my honour to serve with you all. Let it not be said that we didn't go down fighting to the last."

With that, she saluted them as one and held their gaze for a few seconds before nodding, at which point everyone turned back to their duties and tried not to contemplate their own mortality.

Admiral Frith watched with a heavy heart as the graphics and internal displays around her showed the boarding of INS Glorious, noting the valiant defence being put up by the crew and the setting of its self-destruct. Once Glorious's AI recorded the death of the last Command Rank officer or capture of key systems and the Bridge, it would trigger the ship's end. Knowing there was little she could do to influence their fight in any way, she turned her attention to what was left of her task force. Two of her four Battleships, Royal Sovereign and Tiger, had been severely damaged, with Tiger's propulsion off-line despite her engineers' best efforts to reestablish it. Tiger only had a brief window in which to begin decelerating, otherwise they would not be able to make the Jump point. Running on auxiliary power, it would only be a matter of time before Tiger would be unable to maintain her defences and become vulnerable to boarding. Royal Sovereign was still under her own power, but it was doubtful whether she would get to the Jump point before being overwhelmed.

Her remaining two, INS Warspite and Vanguard, remained fully functional despite having been severely pounded themselves. Along with the three remaining Interdiction frigates, INS Defender, Daring and Alacrity, they had closed in around Dauntless to shield the flagship. INS Audacity and Dragon were out of the fight, both having been completely destroyed by concerted waves of smart missiles and fighters, reduced to little more than large expanding clouds of gas and debris.

As requested, Alexander would be joining her shortly on the Bridge, and she hoped the plan she had set in motion at the beginning of the engagement would come to fruition.

Frith noted a sudden reduction in the number of blows Dauntless was taking, quickly mirrored by reports from across her remaining ships. Before she could voice or think the question, a report came in from the Cyber-Warfare team to her left.

"Admiral," reported the lead officer, trying hard but not quite succeeding in keeping the satisfaction out of his voice, "we are pleased to report we have identified and jammed the code and frequency used by the enemy smart-missiles, blocking their ability to communicate with each other and act in concert. All ships reporting fewer strikes as a result."

"Thank you, Lieutenant Golding," Frith replied, "please pass on my compliments to your team. The news is most welcome, if perhaps a little late in the day."

She looked across at the team and nodded in their direction, giving Golding a look of appreciation that belied the tartness of her final comment. With a small smile, he returned the nod and went back to work, looking for other weaknesses his team could exploit.

Inwardly, Frith let herself relax a fraction at the news. This was a major turning point in the battle as the missiles, denied the ability to coordinate their attacks, now had to work independently of each other, becoming far less effective. Her implant advised that Alexander was about to enter the Bridge, so she cleared her screens and called up the display she wanted him to see.

Moments later, Alexander entered without any ceremony and walked over, stopping only for a few moments at the Cyber Warfare station to have a few quiet words with Lt Golding and his team. Although she couldn't hear what was being said, she saw his right hand briefly pat the shoulders of the two operatives nearest to him, before continuing over.

"Thank you for coming, Sire. I have something here I think you will want to see."

It had been a frustrating few days for Adam as he'd been unable to find an excuse to vanish for the few hours he would need to retrace his steps back to the escape pod. Although Karen had given him all the space he needed, letting him spend hours either in the garage working on his fitness back or in the study pouring over the ancient computer keyboard, he knew that disappearing would risk questions he was as yet unwilling to answer. Also, he found himself really enjoying her company, even when she was in another part of the house.

Earlier, using satellite imagery taken from the Internet, Adam had located where the pod was likely to be and realised that at night, without his night vision lenses, it would take him at least forty-five minutes to retrace his steps. All told, a round trip in the dark would take three hours, plus whatever time he needed to produce more money and use the basic onboard systems to try and hack into the databases of banks to see if a fictitious account could be opened. Vimes had assured him it was possible and would not take too long once the proper commands had been given, but neither of them wanted to risk using the computer at the house in case they made a mistake, and their meddling could be traced back here.

Both he and Vimes agreed that using the cover of darkness gave the best chance at concealing the visit and he planned to go that evening after Karen had retired for the night. However, Karen had suggested they visit Dunvegan, an old castle dating back eight-hundred years and steeped in local history. Adam was curious as very few such relics remained on Capital and although in the Empire there were numerous buildings far older, all dated from after the great expansion began by his distant ancestor and were post-industrial in style. To visit an actual stone castle, built by a civilisation only slightly removed from a hunter-gatherer or agrarian way of life, was something he might never have a chance to do again.

"*If I can't find a way to get off this planet then I'll have more than enough time to explore,*" he reminded himself, sighing deeply as he waited by the front door for Karen to finish getting ready.

This sombre thought only slightly dampening his good mood, he got into Karen's Mini and watched carefully as she skilfully drove the car out the drive and onto the main road to Dunvegan. Whenever they had gone out for a drive, he'd been watching how she controlled the car and didn't think that it could be that hard.

"*After all,*" he reasoned with himself, "*If I can pilot a starship across a system how hard could it be to drive a "car" a few kilometres on almost deserted roads?*"

Driving along at a fair pace, Karen played some of her favourite music through the car stereo. Prince was singing "Little Red Corvette," and Vimes was supplying a running translation of what the lyrics meant. Even so, many of the references escaped them both, and he made a note to ask Karen how a jockey could feature in a song about a red car and what a "Trojan" was used for. Paloma Faith's haunting "Only Love Can Hurt Like This" followed. He listened intently to the words and music, amazed at the feelings the powerful beat and melody instilled in him.

"*If I ever get off this planet and finally become Emperor, should I bring these humans into the Empire or allow them to remain anonymous? Would their uniqueness survive the inevitable clash of cultures?*" he wondered. However, reservations aside, from what he had already seen and heard, the cultural accomplishments of this branch of humanity would take the Empire by storm, especially the vibrancy of their music. Varied and beautiful as the music of the Empire was, it had a tendency to either be too martial or swing too far into the complex and esoteric for his taste.

"*Maybe I'd simply let them be for another hundred years and come back to see how far they have progressed,*" he thought, "*for at their rate of advancement they might even make contact with us by then, assuming of course that we're even in the same Galaxy.*"

Adam let his mind wander, taking a little respite from his concerns by thinking over what-might-have-been if he'd chosen different paths in his young life. Annoyingly, they all led him back to the same conclusion; he'd acted like an arse, especially towards his parents, even though, at the time, his choices had all made sense to him.

"*I miss them very much and can only imagine the agonies they are going through over my disappearance.*"

Now sad, he looked out of the window, catching glimpses of the sea as Karen followed the hilly road which sometimes hugged the coast. A singer called Shirley Bassey was singing "Moonraker," her voice switching from softness to a powerful force that did something to his soul. Already feeling down, the song caught him off-guard and he thought it was one of the finest things he'd ever heard. Adam was only a little surprised to feel moisture gathering in his eyes.

"*These musicians would make a fortune in the Empire*," he decided, shaking his head and trying hard to push away the pain of separation and loss the music had amplified.

Next to him, Karen was softly singing along to her favourites, stopping every now and then to provide a commentary on the scenery they were driving through. Adam looked at her out of the corner of his eye, not wishing to draw attention. With her face backlit by the low sun and her face lit up from within by a smile, Adam was jolted again by the same tingle he'd experienced back in the hospital, and with a shock, realised he was falling for her.

Nearing Dunvegan, Karen, unaware of Adam's feelings, pointed out a low black and white building to their right.

"That's the School House. It's a lovely restaurant. Good food. My Uncle Alastair used to go to School there before they built a new one and sold the old building off." She looked at him. "I know; you can take me there one night. Your treat," she asked expectantly and was pleasantly surprised when Adam quickly agreed.

"How about tonight, can you make the arrangements?" he asked, forgetting about his planned visit to the ship in his eagerness to be somewhere romantic with Karen.

"Great, I'll phone and book a table when we get off at the castle car park." Seeing the familiar look of confusion on his face, she smiled and explained. "Make a reservation, Adam. That's what it means."

"Ah, thank you," making yet another addition to his growing list of idioms for this amazingly rich and complex language. "*I can always visit the lifeboat later tonight after the meal, when she's asleep,*" he told himself.

The view of the coastline became obscured by dense foliage as they neared the castle and car park. Tall rhododendron bushes and thin trees covered in moss were everywhere, sheltered from the strong winds that stunted their growth almost every else on the island that was open to the elements. Karen parked near to a small pine cabin which served as a reception and ticket booth, opposite a gift shop and a small cafeteria that belonged to the castle. Although it wasn't normally open to the public until April, she'd phoned the day before and used her uncle's name to literally open a few doors. Almost everyone on the island knew her Uncle Alastair, and they'd been allowed to tag onto a small group of elderly Japanese tourists who were being given a private guided tour of the castle.

They joined the queue and Karen had to admit she and Adam looked out of place in the group, for although she was above average height, Adam literally towered over the rest of the people. For an instant, he looked surprised when they all turned, bowed and started taking numerous photographs of him. To Karen's amazement, once the initial surprise had passed, Adam looked completely at home, moving over and posing quite happily with two tiny matrons, to their obvious delight.

"Kare wa hansamuna wakai otokodesu?" said one of the matrons to her friend, who looked approvingly at him before nodding in agreement.

Replying without thinking Adam said, "Arigatō. Anata mo īdesu," before launching into an animated conversation with the group who were delighted to discover he spoke Japanese. As they crowded around him in appreciation, Karen rolled her eyes and stared at him accusingly. He caught her look and gave a feeble shrug, mouthing a silent "sorry" before resuming his conversation with the group. Although she didn't understand a word of what was being said, Ada's response in yet another foreign language reignited the wariness in her that had been fading as she got to know him better.

"A riddle wrapped up in an enigma," she quoted again under her breath, vowing she would get to the bottom of this frustratingly fascinating mystery man of hers.

For his part, Adam was annoyed at his lapse in concentration and could see the wariness return again to Karen's face. Silently cursing his inattention, he managed to separate himself from the eager ministrations of the group by pretending to be on honeymoon with Karen and with a wink, told them he needed some time with his new bride. At this they all looked towards her and smiled, some of them bowing politely before taking photographs of Karen, much to her confusion.

"What did you tell them?" she asked suspiciously, realising Adam had said something to the group that related to her.

"Well, I needed an excuse to get away, so I told them we were on our honeymoon and needed some time together. I hope you don't mind."

Karen simply looked at him, rolling her eyes and shaking her head. "Jesus, Adam. What did you tell them that for?" but on seeing the sad expression on his face, she laughed and took his arm, pulling them both together.

"Well then, husband," she said, emphasising the last word, "you need to show your new wife a good time today and not disappoint your new friends. Lead on."

Together, they picked up the pace to catch up with the group, who were being escorted through the lovely castle gardens, laid out in the last century by a previous Laird.

Taking in the quiet tranquillity of the gardens, neither of them realised they were both wondering what it might be like to be together in reality, instead of it being an act. Without thinking, both gave the others arm a gentle squeeze of affection at the same time, causing Adam to look down at Karen as she looked up at him. For an instant, Karen found herself fighting a powerful urge to reach up and kiss him. Looking down at her, Adam felt his heartbeat quicken, and they both stopped walking. A myriad of thoughts flashed through his mind, and he began moving his head down towards hers, looking into her eyes and seeing a similar need.

The sound of giggling and gentle laughter broke the moment. Startled, they broke eye contact and realised they were again the centre of attention, with the Japanese matrons all watching intently and taking yet more photographs.

Karen and Adam smiled, with Adam nodding in their direction before moving slightly apart, but still holding onto each other, for neither wanted to break the connection just yet. Both of them understood that something was growing between them, but neither was yet brave enough to put it into words.

The rest of the afternoon passed in a blur, the passage of time tempered by a sense of anticipation that came and receded like waves on the shore. Karen had booked the restaurant on her mobile for seven o'clock, giving them enough time to get back after driving across the island to Portree's large Co-op store for food shopping.

In the meantime, they were enjoying a trip on a large rowing boat which had set out to visit a small colony of seals who populated the inlets and small rocky prominences that struggled daily to raise themselves above the high water level. For Adam it was like being back home, reminding him of glorious summers when he spent days with the sailors who fished the teeming waters near the Palace.

Looking around with fresh eyes at the scenery, the wonder of convergent evolution finally came home to him. While he'd known all about the theories that set out why humanity was found all through the known galaxy, the reality of it finally struck him. Back home in the Empire, he'd previously assumed that most of the animals had been exported from Capital over the millennia to other worlds, but here, on this distant speck of a planet, the seals and wildlife were no different from the home-grown varieties, apart from colour or other minor adaptations to the local environment. For an instant, he worried if any of the other alien races were nearby, but a quick check with Vimes reassured him that no traces had been found when they emerged from the Jump, nor had he detected any evidence when checking for emissions from nearby solar systems. He would hate for these people to become subjugated, for other races did not follow the Alexander doctrine in any form and would simply take what they wanted from this planet.

"*What exactly is my responsibility to these people?*" he asked Vimes again as the boat was rowed expertly back to the jetty near the castle. "*Do I make myself known and openly assist them to advance further, do I assist from behind the mask of a shell Corporation or simply allow natural evolution and advancement to take place without any prompting?*"

"*If I may, Adam, aren't you getting somewhat ahead of yourself?*" interrupted Vimes for the first time in days. "*It's only been a relatively short time since the accident, and despite your comprehensive searching of the Internet for information, you know next to nothing of these peoples. If anything, your only responsibility, as it will always be, is to the Empire and the Crown. Your first duty is to try and contact your family and let them know you are safe and well instead of worrying about what you may or may not be able to do for these people.*"

Suitably chastised, Adam compartmentalised that particular train of thought and brought his attention fully back to the present. He could feel the pressure of Karen's thigh on his own and was enjoying the heavy swell of the sea as it rocked the boat, forcing them both together on the hard wooden bench. He risked a quick glance to look at her. As Crown Prince, he had been the centre of attention for many of the most beautiful and intelligent women in the Empire, yet here, sitting next to him was a fascinating woman who wasn't blatantly vying for his affections, something he found refreshingly different and very, very novel.

Karen was also enjoying the boat trip, one she had made on several occasions in the past with family and friends. She felt both anticipation and confusion. Although almost certain that once she and Adam returned home they would continue on from that moment in the garden, she was torn at her reaction in light of her earlier misgivings and the nature of their relationship. Only an hour before, his use of Japanese had made her suspicious again, yet she had to admit to herself she was strongly attracted to him and would take him to her bed if he was interested.

"*Am I misreading the signals here and simply projecting my own needs and wants onto him?*" she mused. "*It is nice being close to such an interesting man. He's such a strange mix of strength and vulnerability. At times almost child-like yet I can sense an inner strength and confidence which is almost regal or even arrogant.*"

She sighed deeply, the sound lost in the noise of the lapping waters and excited conversations from the tourists as they readied themselves to get off the boat.

Ashore first, Adam helped her to step onto the jetty and remove her life jacket, then she did the same for him. They said their goodbyes to the matrons, Adam looking over his shoulder once and waving to them as they both skirted the gardens and walked along the long gravel path back to the car park, following a line of massive rhododendron bushes on their left. Neither of them knew whether now was the right time to talk about what had happened, so they both deliberately ignored it, chatting instead about the boat trip and other inconsequential things, yet each hoping the other would raise the subject.

It was late afternoon and already getting dark by the time they returned home with a car boot full of shopping. They'd driven the twenty-minute journey over the hill road from Portree to Struan in near silence and growing anxiety, both wondering with anticipation what would happen next yet worrying they had picked up the wrong signals.

On arriving back at the house, they packed away the shopping from the boot, again almost without a word being spoken.

Karen emerged from the store-room, where she'd placed the spare toilet rolls and tinned goods, and bumped into a nervous looking Adam who, without her knowing, had been waiting outside. After standing there for a moment, she began to move past but stopped when she saw the look on his face.

Adam spoke first.

"Karen, all afternoon we've both been trying to ignore what happened, and I need to know if I was just imagining…" his voice trailed off into a questioning silence.

"Imagining what, Adam?" Karen asked, looking up at his face with a warm smile, resisting the temptation to play around with him. "Was it this?" and with that she moved in close and put her arms around his neck, gently bringing his head down to hers. For several seconds they simply held each other's gaze, looking for something, before Adam reached behind Karen and pulled her even closer, gently covering her mouth with his own. After what seemed an age, they came up for air and Karen simply rested her head on his chest, Adam gently stroking her hair with his left hand. They held that tableau for several minutes before Adam broke contact and held her apart from him, both hands on her shoulders, looking carefully into her face.

"I've been wondering what that would feel like for some time," he said softly.

"Was it worth the wait?" Karen asked before she could stop herself.

"What do you think?" he replied, batting the question back again with a smile that told her everything she needed to know.

Karen took his hands from her shoulders and put them around her waist, moving in close and looked up at him again, feeling the heat coming from his body. She'd noticed he didn't seem to mind the cold and was always warm to the touch, even when he'd been outside in the cold mornings or evenings, but at the moment it was nice to feel up close and safe against his warm body.

Looking up at him, they kissed again with growing intensity, yet still surprisingly tender. Karen had expected him to more forceful but was pleased he wasn't rushing in like a bull in a china shop. She did notice there was no pressure on her hip from his groin, and the Doctor part of her brain was alarmed at the thought he might still be suffering from the effects of the accident. Normally at this point, a man's interest would be quite pronounced, yet she felt nothing, but as she could hardly reach down and check without appearing to be rushing things, Karen hoped he was simply wearing overly tight pants.

For his part, Adam was feeling torn. He felt a strong emotional and physical attachment towards Karen, finding her extremely interesting and fun to be with, yet now his hindbrain was warning him not to get involved and to back off from complicating matters. The last thing he wanted to do was encourage her to become emotionally involved with him, only to get hurt when he moved on to find a way off this planet. Between the tutelage of Vimes and his own reading of this society's customs and mores, he understood that physical relationships were a lot more complex here than back in the Empire.

"What do I do Vimes?" he asked, only to receive a sympathetic but succinct response, *"Ah, the angst of young love, Adam. I'm not your keeper, and this is one of those times you are going to have to work things out for yourself. However, perhaps this is the moment for you to start thinking about putting other people's feelings first."* And with that, Vimes broke contact.

Karen could sense an almost imperceptible change in what was happening between them and gently pulled herself away.

"Is everything all right, Adam? I thought I could sense something just now when you were holding me." She looked at his face for something. "Is this too sudden?"

Adam looked back, his face displaying conflicting emotions as he tried to make sense of his feelings. Coming to a decision, he took a deep breath before speaking.

"Karen, before we do anything else, there's something you need to know......."

Squadron Leader Harris and her team had joined with pilots from the other squadrons and were now attached to one of the many Marine Cohorts assigned to repel boarders. It hadn't taken long to acclimatise herself to the armoured suit, as the urgency of their predicament helped to sharpen her recall of where everything was and how it operated. Unbidden, useful information seemed to drag itself up from the dim recesses of her memory, speeding up the familiarisation process.

It felt good to be back in a combat suit, and she regretted not having one when she had been shot down on Heaven. Having to cower behind Ambassador Gallagher's shield, instead of taking on the enemy herself, had not felt right. Urgent deployment instructions from Lieutenant Baker came through to her implant, making her jump and she realised she was more nervous than she had thought. Baker was the Officer in charge of the group she was assigned to, and his message gave updates on several hull breaches close to their current position. Boarding shuttles had rammed themselves into the ship, and her Cohort was receiving its instruction to intercept the nearest group of boarders.

Now the information was shared amongst the other pilots, Harris could hear the chatter from her squadron began to increase as the nervous flyers began to vocalise their anxieties with each other.

"Keep it down and focus, team. If we watch out for each other's back then we will do fine," she instructed, noting the chatter rapidly begin to subside.

"*That went well, maybe they do trust me,*" she thought, allowing herself a self-satisfied grin inside the privacy of her helmet.

Shortly afterwards, the one hundred and fifty Marines and Pilots making up the section Harris was assigned to, were thundering down a wide corridor linking the muster station to the closest entry point. Nearing it, her helmet began relaying the nearby sounds of fighting and displayed tactical information setting out the enemy's disposition. Ahead, several Marines were controlling mobile shield generators, their screens evidenced by a slight shimmering as they reacted with fine dust particles in the air. She could feel the deck underneath her feet tremble as the ship's internal defences began firing at a large number of heavily armoured enemy Marines who quickly rounded the corner with their own mobile shields and began firing at the Imperial troops.

The screens on both sides blazed brightly as they sought to dissipate the furious energies generated by the onslaught of both flechettes and particle weapons. The standoff held for thirty seconds until it became obvious that neither side was going to have an advantage. Suddenly, almost as if the same order had been given to each side, both opposing forces began closing with each other, keeping the flaming and now pulsating shields ahead of them.

For a few seconds, before the instruction for close combat configuration registered with her, Harris was transfixed by the display of raw energy being released within the confines of the corridor. She was acutely aware of how weak and light her legs felt, a side-effect of the adrenaline surging through her body but she knew this would pass once the fighting began. As if on cue, the feelings began to lessen as her suit reconfigured itself for close combat, forming a small shield and a stabbing blade.

Between the two opposing forces, pictures and displays in the corridor literally exploded off the walls from the intense heat generated by the energies clawing and chewing at the shields. As the distance between them closed, the reflected energies increased, charring the walls and ceiling until the shields met and neutralised each other in a blinding explosion which blew Marines from both sides off their feet.

Without thinking, and as if from a distance, Harris heard herself shout out her home planet's battle cry, then rushed forward with the other Marines and pilots to engage the enemy. Quigley and Coleman suddenly took positions to her left and right and within moments battle was engaged in a clash of arms and shields, swords swinging and stabbing in the press of armoured figures.

With bodies surging and pressing around her, it seemed to Harris as if an age had passed, yet her suit showed it had only been five minutes since fighting began. Breathing heavily, she could feel her arms ache from wielding her sword and shield. Despite the discomfort, to lower her guard for an instant in the press of bodies would be suicidal. Distracted for an instant by a shout from Hinchin behind her, she sensed but didn't see the sudden blow to her helmet that sent her crashing down into darkness.

Alexander joined Admiral Frith at her command station and continued to follow the battles progress on its multiple displays. The situation remained grave, and unless Frith could work a miracle, she knew the task forces fate would probably be decided before they had decelerated enough to make the Jump point.

Fortunately, now the smart-missiles ability to coordinate their attack was being jammed, much-needed respite had been afforded to the defensive screens, gaining them a little more time. The number and frequency of missiles getting through to impact on the ships hulls had been significantly reduced, offering Dauntless and the remaining ships a slim chance of making the Jump point intact and under their own power. Both of the Carriers had been boarded by enemy troops, and while INS Courageous appeared to have everything under control, for INS Glorious the situation was grave. Alexander had been watching the battle's progress carefully, and now he was on the Bridge as requested, was curious to see what Admiral Frith wanted to show him.

"Well, Janice. I'm here as requested. What is it you wanted me to see?" he asked quietly, not wishing to disturb the Bridge crew's concentration by announcing his presence other than to the Cyber Warfare team.

Frith turned, and as she started speaking, Alexander couldn't help but notice a hopeful look on his Admiral's face, which in turn brought an immediate flutter of anticipation to his belly.

"Sire, keep watching the two enemy Carriers and their screen of escorting battleships. It won't be long now. At first, I didn't know if my gamble would pay off, but as the enemy Fleet has shown no obvious attempts at taking counter-measures, I might have just got lucky."

She paused, waiting for him to ask the obvious question. When he didn't, she continued.

"For the last forty-five minutes, Dauntless's AI has been accelerating the fighters from Glorious away from the task force at an acceleration of 30-g. Any faster and too many of them would have suffered engine or structural failure. Stealthed and running silently without any active sensors, it would be difficult for such small masses to be picked up by the enemy unless they were very close, especially as I've dispersed them quite widely to mask their mass footprint."

Alexander thought he could see where this was going and for the first time since the engagement began allowed himself a glimmer of real hope. Not wishing to spoil her moment, he remained silent and let her continue without interruption, the only sign of his anticipation being the creaking of the command desk as his armoured left hand began to grip it tightly.

"They've been on a long, looping circle back to the fleet and will be impacting on the enemy ships in a few moments."

Frith looked away from the screens and at her Emperor, pleased he'd not interrupted and gratified to see from his tense smile he'd grasped what would happen next.

"The fighters are now travelling at just under forty-eight thousand kilometres per second, and with a mass of twenty tonnes apiece, on impact they will go through the enemy shields and point defences with little problem."

She finished speaking just as the first wave of her fighters began impacting on the enemy capital ships, taking them completely by surprise. Frith had staggered their attack, with each enemy ship being targeted with waves of fighters following closely behind each other. As the lead fighters struck, the enemies shields were sufficiently weakened to allow the following fighters to pass straight through the gaps and impact directly onto the hulls. In many cases, the overloaded shields failed completely. Clearly displayed on their screens, Frith and Alexander watched both enemy Carriers visibly stagger under the attack, with one suddenly vanishing in an enormous explosion as its power plants catastrophically failed, taking them both by surprise.

The remaining Carrier began to pull ahead of its screening battleships as its engines stopped decelerating, bringing it ever closer to Frith's diminished force where it could be finished off. In rapid succession, the enemies fleet began to come apart, with the majority of their remaining thirty-six ships all either demonstrating severe damage or catastrophic systems failures from the impact strikes. Two of the enemy Captains, either through luck or good judgement, had managed to divert their point defences towards the hyper-accelerated fighters in time to avoid serious damage to their ships, but already, Dauntless and the task force began concentrating their firepower on them, for now ignoring the other, more seriously damaged enemy. Once these two were destroyed, the remaining enemy ships would be re-targeted and finished off without quarter.

To their credit, the Bridge crew remained silent, with little outward expression at their sudden change of fortune, yet the uplift in the atmosphere around the huge room was palpable to everyone. Officers sat or stood a little more upright at their stations, and even reports and instructions coming in from the ship's AI sounded more confident.

To her left, Frith heard the Emperor exhale a deep breath, releasing the tension she too had been feeling. "It was a long-shot, Sire, and a very expensive one at that, but it had the desired effect, didn't it?" Frith asked, her eyes bright with pent-up tension and emotion.

"Twenty-eight billion credits well spent, Janice," Alexander replied with a shine in his eyes mirroring her own. "Although I can appreciate why this gambit hasn't been tried before on such a scale. Using missiles is a lot cheaper than state of the art fighters, and at seventy million credits apiece and a three-month replacement cycle, it's thankfully not something we want to do on a regular basis." He smiled broadly, years lifting from his face in a matter of moments, "However, just this once I think we're worth it."

"In fairness, Captain Woods gave me the idea when he sent his fighters on suicide runs at the start of this engagement. I simply ran with it and added my own twist. I hope he and his remaining crew manage to save their ship."

Together, they checked on the progress of Captain Woods and his ship. Remarkably, it had almost managed to rejoin the main fleet, along with its last remaining interdiction frigate, INS Daring. Two of its accompanying hangars remained relatively intact and were in the process of docking. Eight boarding craft had rammed through into various points along both the main hull and into one of the hangars, and fighting was still ongoing as Marines fought off the attackers in the corridors and areas close to the entry points.

Elsewhere, the volume of missiles and slugs lessened sharply from what remained of the enemy fleet, enabling Frith to order Dauntless's own fighter wings to be launched to assist in destroying the remaining ships. With no desire to capture or salvage any of them, each fighter would be armed with two powerful torpedoes which, when fired together, were capable of destroying an already crippled capital ship once its point defences were either destroyed or ineffective and unable to stop the torpedoes from reaching their hulls. The two relatively undamaged enemy battleships that had avoided being struck earlier by the suiciding fighters would be left to the rail guns and missiles of Dauntless and her two remaining serviceable Battleships, INS Warspite and Vanguard. Already, the enemies shields were softening under the combined assault, and it would only be a matter of time before they would either have to try and flee or face destruction.

Frith and Alexander began discussing whether or not to try and take one of the crippled enemy ships for examination, possibly enabling them to question any surviving crew or command staff. They knew valuable intelligence might be obtained as to who or what was behind the ambush, but the risk of sending Marines to board them would be immense. The ship's AI might have been instructed to self-destruct in such an eventuality, and both Frith and Alexander were loath to risk more Imperial lives at this point.

While they talked the risks through, an urgent report from Navigation came in, advising them of a disturbance in the Jump Point ahead. Breaking off their debate, both reviewed the incoming message, with Frith immediately requesting additional information from both Helm and Science stations as to what it might mean. Almost immediately a report came back confirming that Sensor data indicated the Jump Point had become unstable sometime during the last few minutes. Asked what this meant, they responded by confirming the disruption would make it impossible to generate a Quantum Attraction field until it had subsided.

"Timescales," asked Frith of her staff, "Are we looking at minutes, hours, what?"

"Unknown, Admiral," came the reply from Science, "We've nothing in our database regarding this stellar phenomenon. It's not been seen before, and we have no idea how long before it stabilises enough for us to obtain QA between here and Imperial space."

"What happened to destabilise it?" asked Alexander, walking towards the Science station situated between Navigation and Engineering.

"Sensors identified a small EM pulse of an unknown type originating within the QA point a few moments after our fighters struck, Sire," replied the Senior Science Officer. "Amongst all the communication chatter we identified a triggering signal coming from one of the undamaged enemy battleships. Our current hypothesis is a cloaked device was left at the Jump point as a fail-safe to keep us here in case the attack failed for any reason."

Alexander nodded, then turned back to look at Frith. "They could have triggered it at any point. So, even if by some miracle we'd managed to reach the Jump point, they would have had us trapped and effectively dead in the water? Clever. Very clever."

"It looks likely," Frith replied, "we'll work on that hypothesis and bear it in mind next time we Jump through into an unknown system. Now we know what to look for, our advance drones can be calibrated accordingly."

She turned to the Science station. "Keep monitoring and look for ways we can stabilise the Jump Point from here or find a workaround the interference."

Frith stopped talking and thought hard for a moment before continuing, "Will this stop incoming travel and outgoing communications as well?" she asked.

"Unknown, Admiral, but the hypothesis is valid. We are stuck here until it clears but how long that will take is unknown."

Alexander remained outwardly silent but was having an internal debate with Vimes. *"Anything in our private files, old friend? Something Josef might have turned up and filed away for future reference or perhaps information linked to the secret QA Drive that has been kept hidden?*

"I'm checking, Alex...there, I've found something. It's here in his private notes into alternative Star Drives. He says, "An EMP of a particular frequency can upset the natural resonance of the Jump Point, resulting in a period of disturbance in proportion to the gravity field of the system." Using his theory, I've calculated that, based on the mass of this system, it will take a minimum of four days to settle. Until then nothing comes in or out, including transmissions. I've checked the sensor logs, and a resonant EMP of the required frequency was set off just after our fighters hit home. Had your quarters not been severely damaged and the IQA communicator destroyed, I could have used it to communicate with Capital and check the original database there for more information, as it wouldn't have been affected by what's happened to the Jump Point."

Turning his attention back to the Bridge, Alexander sent this information in a series of messages to both Helm and Science stations, telling them what to look for and the phenomena's likely effect. Both sets of Officers quickly perused the data and exchanged looks, impressed at the Emperor's grasp of such technical information.

Reading the information herself, Frith turned to Alexander with a quizzical look, inviting him to respond. Moving close and leaning forward he quickly explained it was from Josef's original work on QA. "Let them think their Emperor's a genius, Janice. It's good for morale."

Leaning closer still, Janice returned the whisper, "It's a good job I know the truth then, isn't it?" At which point Alexander burst out laughing and against all protocol, put his right arm around her and gave his Admiral a hug, much to the surprise and delight of the Bridge staff.

A little taken aback herself at Alexander's show of affection on the Bridge, Frith quickly brought things back to the matter at hand.

"If we are going to be stuck here for several days we have time to recover our escape pods and then see what we can salvage. I'm going to bring what's left of the fleet together so we can harvest usable smart-metal from the crippled ones and repair the damage to our hulls."

Back to his normal self, Alexander nodded in agreement. "I'm taking a battalion of Marines and will head over to INS Glorious to help repel those boarders. No arguments." He hesitated for a moment before speaking again. "Well done, Janice, it seems you are lucky after all," and with that he turned away and headed for the exit, giving mustering instructions to Vimes as his suit began assuming combat mode.

Damage reports from the remaining ships were being collated by the flagship's AI and presented to everyone's screens and the tank, updating on the fly with estimated recovery times. To Frith's eyes, the news was mixed. Rodney and Repulse were both effectively space hulks, venting atmosphere despite their repair crew's best efforts and unable to move closer to the Jump point. Shuttles were already being dispatched to them to ferry survivors back to Dauntless, where the injured could be triaged and treated. She turned her attention to acting Captain Cooke and what remained of her crew on INS Glorious. They were engaged in a battle of attrition against the boarders who were now fighting with the desperation of warriors with nothing to lose, knowing their ships were gone.

By the time Alexander reached the main hangar bay, three heavily armoured and unpressurized boarding shuttles had been prepped, each loaded with three hundred Marines, of which fifty were from his personal bodyguard. The last to board, he soundlessly raced across the flight deck, oblivious to salutes from the numerous ground crew. On reaching his designated shuttle, he launched himself up the steps three at a time before letting his suit finish its transformation at the docking station assigned to him at the front of the craft. Seconds later, the three shuttles lifted soundlessly from their cradles and accelerated away at three-G, making nearly everyone on board groan at the sudden pressure on their chests.

With interior lights dimmed, the shuttles transitioned from brightly lit hangar to the darkness of space, shuddering an instant later as they passed through the hardened shields. Exterior displays showed nothing apart from distant stars and those looking to see evidence of the titanic space battle were disappointed, having forgotten just how vast space was.

The pilot's voice sounded in everyone's helmets, "It's one hundred and sixty kilometres to INS Glorious and our transit time is now just under three minutes. Please stay in your stations and prepare for the deceleration warning at turnover."

Heavily cloaked and stealthed, the first part of the short flight passed without incident. Seventy seconds into the journey, the midpoint switchover warning sounded, alerting everyone to a few moments of normality before deceleration began.

At his docking station, Alexander's anticipation for the coming battle grew, along with a butterfly feeling in the pit of his belly which the adrenaline buzz brought him at these times. As a young boy, before he was given over to be tutored by his Weapon

Masters, he had mistakenly believed these feelings weres a sign of fear or cowardice. It was only when he opened up one day to Master Katana about his fear of being a coward that he discovered it was his bodies way of preparing him for combat and quite the opposite of what he'd always believed.

A few years before becoming Emperor, Alexander had felt for the first time the gut-wrenching fear that combat brought, bringing home to him the wisdom of Hiro's words. From that day forward, he welcomed rather than feared the fluttering feeling in his belly like an old friend to be embraced.

"Here we go again," Vimes said quietly in Alexander's mind before ceasing the flow of tactical information he was continuously relaying as the shuttles made their final approach, allowing him to clear his mind and focus on what was to come.

Glorious's AI, still functioning despite the aggressive IP's that sought to take control, had determined the best entry points along the hull for the shuttles and transmitted them to the pilots. Two shuttles would enter portside while Alexanders would loop around to starboard. Once in place, the AI would allow them access to the interior via temporary passages in the armoured hull which would close behind them as they progressed inside.

All was now quiet in the Marines' helmets apart from the quietly spoken instructions and reminders coming over the intercom from the ever watchful Sergeants. As always, Alexander demurred to them when it came to combat situations, advice he'd received from both his father and father-in-law many years previously. In the few seconds before the side of the shuttle would open to allow them access to the Carrier's hull, Alexander allowed himself a few moments to think warmly about them both. Such thoughts were still bittersweet, despite the passing of so many years. A taciturn, yet kindly man who only spoke when he had something useful or informative to say, his father had been taken before his time by the machinations of his murderous brother, plunging the Empire into a revolt that took many years to quell and cost billions of lives. His father-in-law, Bill, had been remarkably similar.

"Perhaps that's why I liked him so much," he thought to himself.

Drawing his mind back from such pointless reverie, for the third and last time Alexander quickly scanned his suit's status before uncoupling himself from the docking station, his suit now bulked out to full battle readiness. Not part of any squad, Alexander had the luxury of being able to select his own weapon configurations. Not wishing to blow any more holes in the ship than absolutely necessary, the bespoke heavy weaponry his suit was capable of handling had been reluctantly set aside in favour of twin swords and two shoulder-mounted sets of micro-missiles that Vimes would control independently, allowing him to effectively fight multiple opponents simultaneously. The front of his suit took on a shimmer as its electromagnetic shielding formed, giving it the appearance of being viewed through a fine mist.

An almost imperceptible bump and the entire starboard wall of the shuttle slid up and down, exposing the interior to hard vacuum and a correspondingly large, cavernous hole that was deepening in the Carrier's armoured hull. Launching themselves across the small gap, the first Marine squads began moving quickly inwards, giving the following Marines room to follow. Within seconds, the shuttle was emptied, and the smart-metal hull of the Carrier began to close behind the Marines as they moved forward towards the ship's interior compartments.

After twenty metres, the armour in front of them opened up, and light from the interior flooded into their cavern-like hole. No longer in a silent vacuum, everyone could now hear the sounds of distant fighting. Splitting up into three groups, Alexander's bodyguard remained with him and awaited the order to begin moving towards the Bridge. Glad to be finally doing something, the surge of adrenalin was making Alexander's legs feel light and twitchy, an uncomfortable sensation but one that moving around would soon cure.

"Master Sergeant, I'm taking point today, no arguments please," he instructed Lynch, forestalling any objections.

"Yes, sir. I'll be to your right, and Corporal Stopher on your left should you have need of us," came the reply, said in a slightly disapproving tone to make a point, but at the same time moving aside, allowing Alexander to move forward.

"*So much for listening to my Father,*"Alexander thought, grinning to himself inside his helmet.

With the fastest route already mapped out on their helmet displays, Alexander and his Bodyguard fanned out and began to move along the corridor, turning right and marching quickly for one hundred metres until reaching a main intersection leading to the Bridge. The ship's interior was littered with dead crew and Marines from both sides, the enemy clearly marked by the non-standard colouration of their armoured suits, displaying numerous differences from their own, some barely recognisable as power armour at all. In places, where the fighting had been heaviest, blood had pooled all across the floor, making it difficult to avoid slipping on the slick surface. Data lines, power conduits and life-support pipework all spilt out of breaches in the corridor walls and ceilings, sometimes temporarily blocking their path. The fighting had been particularly fierce in these areas.

Their way to the Bridge was clearly marked by numerous bloody boot prints left by the attackers and retreating defenders, to which they added their own as they progressed inwards. Acrid, chemical smoke hung in patches around parts of the route, the ship's air purifiers unable to work effectively due to blast damage from where the attackers had sought to destroy on-board defence systems.

Gaping, ragged holes in the ceilings and walls stood as mute testimony to the severity of the fighting. Mixed in with the bodies were discarded or damaged weapons. The day to day paraphernalia of shipboard life lay scattered around, spilling out from destroyed living quarters and offices along the route. Occasionally a Marine would detect signs of life from one of the many bodies and providing the AI confirmed it was a crew member, would quickly stop to inject non-specific battlefield medical nanites before moving on again, marking their location so the rescuers following later would know exactly where to go.

Progressing through the devastation, Alexander's simmering anger turned into a cold, contained rage as he noted the dead crewmen and women, some who had obviously been unarmed when killed. He noted, with not a little pride, that only a few had taken wounds to the back and many had makeshift weapons still grasped in their hands.

Up ahead, along the curving corridor, sounds of fighting were getting louder, amplified cries of pain and anger telling them they were close now. Rounding a corner, Alexander took stock of the killing ground in front of him. At the same time, Vimes identified multiple armoured targets and fired two salvos of missiles which homed in and detonated before the enemy had time to even acknowledge their arrival, blowing a number apart in an explosion of gore and armour, spattering everything nearby. Noting that at least ninety-six armoured enemy remained standing, and unable to contain himself any longer, Alexander leapt forward and engaged the nearest combatant, slicing clean through the armoured form with a downwards slice of his right sword while simultaneously blocking a thrust from another with the shield on his left. One step behind, Stopher and Lynch engaged those that tried to close in on their Emperor, their swords rising and falling as they pressed forward. In an instant the corridor was a dense press of bodies, swords and battle-axes rising and falling as the two sides closed.

Alexander's helmet rang loudly as a mid-calibre flechette disintegrated against it, knocking his head sideways until it reached its maximum allowed movement, the blows force momentarily distracting him.

"*So much for the shielding,*" he thought to himself, telling his suit to switch it off to conserve power.

"*To your left, Alex,*" warned Vimes, firing another salvo of missiles and removing another four attackers from the fight, as Alexander closed with a huge armoured figure who raised its metal shield and rushed forward, hoping to capitalise on any momentary confusion.

Their two swords clashed, the force of the blow jarring Alexander's arm, despite the protection provided by the pommel and suit. The massive figure moved in, swinging its heavy shield. Alexander barely parried the blow with his left arm and shield, feeling something give in his elbow and registering real pain for a few seconds before his suit anaesthetised the area. To Alexander's surprise, despite the force of his stroke, the attacker had managed to retain hold of its sword, so he stepped in close and followed through with his right elbow, catching his opponent's helmet with the serrated monomolecular blades along his forearm. Ripping chunks of armour away, Alexander brought the hardened needle-point point of his elbow back into the enemy's face-plate, puncturing it and driving the needle through into the brain beneath.

He took one step forward before turning and kicking the now falling body hard into the nearest wall, where it landed heavily, shaking the wall before slumping down to the floor, the legs of the suit moving as they mirrored the corpse's dying twitches.

Alexander flexed his left elbow a few times to test it out, wincing slightly despite the pain relief.

Taking stock of the melee going on around him, he saw Corporal Bradley Stopher trying to defend against two large armoured figures who were slowly driving him back towards the wall. Alexander stepped forward and calmly rammed his sword into the back of the nearest of the two who had foolishly paid no attention to his approach. Stopher quickly finished off the remaining figure, before lifting his sword in salute and moved back to cover Alexander's left side again.

The surprised boarders quickly recovered from the shock of being attacked from the rear and managed to turn a mobile heavy cannon away from the crew who had been valiantly defending the Bridge entrance, and onto Alexander's attacking Bodyguard. Before anyone could react, it began firing, blasting two Imperial Marines on the right of Alexander ten metres backwards along the corridor, knocking several others from their feet before ending up against the far wall, broken and bloodied.

With the heavy cannon protected by its own screen, the Marines wasted no time trying to fire flechettes or missiles at it and simply ran forward, taking two more casualties in the process. Once through the screen, they engaged with the cannon's armoured crew, finishing them off in short order. Now the heavy weapon was taken out, the fight immediately turned against the enemy. Tellingly, no quarter was asked, and none was given, and it was only the work of a few minutes before the last of the enemy lay dead or incapacitated on the deck.

Ahead, a mixed group of crew and Marines had been taking shelter behind a mobile force screen defending the Bridge entrance. They cheered loudly as the Bodyguard signalled the fight was over.

Swords sheathed, Alexander strode forward, faceplate retracting to expose his features to what remained of the defending crew. Those who immediately recognised him registered shock and disbelief on their faces, with several of the bolder ones moving to greet him. He raised a gauntleted hand to stop them.

"Enough," he commanded. "Who's the senior officer here?"

An armoured Marine stepped forward, his armour damaged in numerous places and, like Alexanders, splattered with blood and unidentified bits of flesh.

"Your Majesty," he nodded, "I'm Corporal Jameson, the ranking Marine left here. It's been bloody work, and we're all that's left of the original cohort." He turned back to look at the assorted defenders, made up of Marines and crew, gesturing with a tired arm in their direction.

"Well met, Corporal Jameson. Please arrange for the walking wounded to be helped back to our shuttle. Leave the badly wounded for the medical teams. My Bodyguard will begin infusing the others to stabilise them. There, I've just sent you the most direct route to the shuttle."

Alexander looked around again at the scene. "Before you go, what's your take on the attackers? Your first impressions?"

Jameson nodded as the instructions were relayed to his suit, then thought for a few seconds before speaking.

"This lot here were well organised, Sire, but it was a mixed bunch at the start. Very savage, almost like they sent in wild shock troops first. We held our own pretty well against those but as we whittled them down, the ones that followed had better discipline and training. It really showed. They fought us back to here."

Jameson kicked at the armoured boot of a dead boarder. "Yeah, this last lot certainly weren't wall fodder."

"Two distinct groups then, in your opinion?"

"Yes, Sire. Different tactics, weapons and armour quality too."

Alexander tilted his head slightly to the left, before responding and dismissing the Marine. "Thank you and well done, Corporal Jameson. That will be all."

Jameson nodded and began calling over the survivors to help carry out his instructions. Alexander walked forward, towards the locked and sealed bulkhead door leading to the Bridge section. Everyone silently moved out of the way to let him pass, and he looked enquiringly at Corporal Stopher who had been talking quietly to several Marines trying to unseal it.

"We've managed to get through to the Bridge Officers, Sire, and they are OK. We are having trouble opening the door as they made a damn good job when they sealed it from the inside. A few more minutes and we'll have it open."

It actually took a further ten minutes before the doors could be opened, by which time all of the severely injured had been cleared from the corridor. Alexander noted that the ship's air was not being properly scrubbed and with the damage reports coming in from the ship's AI, suspected that all INS Glorious would be good for going forward was as a source of smart-metal salvage for what was left of his task force.

The Marines stood back, allowing Alexander to walk through into the Bridge area, where he was met by a tousled looking Captain Cooke and her officers. He retracted his gauntlet, and she accepted the outstretched hand with a tired smile, before introducing her First Officer who'd stepped up behind her.

Letting go of her hand, he took stock of what he was seeing around him. The false normality of the Bridge was offset by numerous blank screens and empty stations, a testament to the myriad non-functioning parts of the Carrier. Everyones' faces were turned towards both Alexander and the Captain, most seeing their Emperor in person for the first time and not quite believing that he had personally come to their aid.

He held Cooke's gaze for a moment and smiled warmly, seeking to reassure her. Looking around, and speaking loudly so all on the Bridge could hear, he began, "Well done, Captain. Your crew and ship fought bravely, despite the less than auspicious start. I know the reasons and hold you all blameless. Your reports will no doubt make for interesting reading."

He looked back down to the clearly tired Cooke. "Your first command certainly was an interesting one, wasn't it?"

"Yes, Your Majesty, it certainly was," she responded, "but somewhat short."

"Ah yes, about that. Admiral Frith will have the final word, but just between us, I think your field commission will be confirmed as permanent, *Captain* Cooke, just don't make a habit of losing your commands."

"Oh, thank you, Sire." She paused for a moment. "What's next?"

Pleased she wanted to bring the conversation back to the matters at hand, Alexander confirmed what Captain Cooke already knew and had been dreading hearing.

"This ship isn't going anywhere without the kind of repairs that can't be effected out here in our weakened state. Arrangements are already in hand for the AI's memories and experience to be downloaded and preserved. What's left of the crew will be split between Dauntless and the surviving ships.

Dauntless is already moving closer and will dock shortly to effect the move. Once everyone's off, she will begin the absorption of those parts that can be reclaimed."

Sympathising with the look of sadness in Cooke's eyes, Alexander moved a little closer and spoke again, this time more quietly so only she and her First Officer could hear what he was saying. They both brightened at hearing his words, then Alexander saluted and turned away, heading back to where a new shuttle had docked with the hull, letting Vimes control his suit as he looked through the reports coming in from the rest of what was left of his Task Force.

The moment Alexander left the Bridge, the noise level rose several notches which necessitated Captain Cooke having to remind everyone to get back to work. Quiet restored, she began liaising with Dauntless to arrange the transfer of all essential equipment to its new home, before heading off to what was left of her quarters to retrieve her personal possessions. As she did so, the Emperor's last words played through her mind.

As he'd bent forward, Alexander confirmed he would personally ensure that another Carrier would bear the name of Glorious and he would look favourably on any future request from her if she wished to be its Captain.

Striding along the damaged corridor towards his exit point, Vimes confirmed to Alexander the list of casualties from amongst his Bodyguard and that arrangements would be made for their families. Despite the brief moment of satisfaction he was able to obtain by promising Captain Cooke a new Carrier, Alexander was beginning to feel the familiar post-battle depression that invariably descended on him, especially when the fighting had been up close and personal. In no way denying the necessity of his actions and feeling no hint of pity for those he'd killed, the waste of life and material depressed him now the euphoria and excitement of battle were over. It both annoyed and saddened him in equal measure, and all he wanted to do now was spend some time alone in his temporary quarters to recharge. Like his wife, Christine, he needed regular time to be alone with his thoughts, after which he would be back to his normal self.

Reaching a newly fashioned entrance in the hull serving as a gateway to the waiting shuttle, Alexander was about to pass across and allow the smart-metal to form behind him when an urgent message came through on his private channel from Admiral Frith. He stood still, paying attention as an image of the Admiral, talking from her ready-room, formed in his helmet. Both her look and tone of voice were grave.

"Sire, we have another problem. Long range sensors and drones confirm that another fleet has emerged from behind the gas giant and is heading this way. It will take seventy-two hours to reach here, a full day before the Jump point is stable enough for us to use. Even using the time we have to regroup and re-arm, there is no way we can hope to stop them. It was only the Woods Gambit that saved us last time, and even if we had enough fighters left to try it again, they would be ready for it."

Alexander said nothing. He bowed his head and shut his eyes, trying to digest the terrible news. He stood there for several seconds before responding, forcing his voice to remain calm and steady.

"Janice, these must have been kept at the base as insurance against the first fleet being unable to finish us off. With their destabilising device, they knew full well they had a way to stop us from Jumping back to safety and didn't want to risk everything in one attack. I would wager this second fleet is better trained and battle-hardened too, using the first wave as cannon-fodder to soften us up nicely. Damn, and we were so close too." His armoured fists closed into balls as he fought against the anger that again threatened to cloud his judgement.

"I agree, Sire. Before you ask, my recommendation is we remain here until all the survivors are brought in from escape pods and the other ships and we use the time to repair damaged systems and hulls." Admiral Frith's stern face smiled wryly. "We still have three days, so I propose we use them wisely and prepare ourselves."

Alexander nodded. "Agreed. I'm coming back to Dauntless now that Glorious has been secured. Once I've attended to a private matter, we'll meet in your Ready-Room. Please keep me informed of any developments." He cut the link.

Alexander boarded the waiting shuttle and docked his suit in anticipation of the return trip. The shuttles interior layout had reconfigured itself to accommodate the most seriously injured into medical pods which monitored and stabilised their patients. Other, less seriously injured Marines and crew, sat or lay in form-fitting G-couches, many being fed fluids and medical nanites intravenously.

Despite the suffering, the mood in the shuttle was a good one and would remain so until news of the new enemy fleet became widespread. Even then, many would simply put their faith in Admiral Frith and the Emperor to perform yet another miracle. Alexander remained upright in his dock, going over events and developments again in his mind, replaying them over and over, like a song stuck on repeat. This latest news was galling; they'd come so close to turning an almost certain defeat into a victory, yet again safety was being snatched away at the last moment.

He had a bad feeling, not just about what had happened here but also what might now be transpiring across his Empire. With no means to check on events back home, he feared these two attacks had been the signal for a wider attack on not only his Empire but those closest to him. Once safely on Dauntless, he would check whether he could repair the secret IQA communication device which had been damaged when his quarters had taken a hit. For security reasons, its matrix wasn't recorded anywhere, meaning the automated repair systems were unable to replace or rebuild it automatically. He wanted to try and contact Christine and warn her to be on guard and was annoyed with himself for having left it until it was too late. This whole affair had a familiar smell to it. Nothing he could identify, just a sense of Déjà vu; a hint of something evil from the past coming back for a second attempt at killing him and his family.

Realising he was neglecting his duty, Alexander undocked himself and began to walk among the wounded, listening and chatting with those survivors willing or able to respond. Seeing the grateful faces of those he spoke to, and listening to their stories of bravery and sacrifice, reminded Alexander that although he might be the all-powerful Emperor, he too was a servant of the Empire and like them, would strive to do his duty until the end.

"You're what!? Not human? Oh, for heaven's sake, Adam, why on earth did you have to go and say that? Karen exclaimed, pushing Adam away to make some space between them. "Is this some sort of sick joke you're trying to play on me? Hmm? Why now and just as I was trying to get close to you? Why do all the men in my life turn out to be such bastards?"

Karen stared hard at Adam, daring him with her eyes to either answer or look away. He did neither and simply began to unbutton his cuff and roll up the sleeve on his shirt, which only increased her anger towards him, partially fuelled by frustrated passion and annoyance at yet again being pushed away by someone she wanted to be close to.

Before she could react, he moved quickly and reached out his right hand, grasping her left arm in a firm, yet powerful grip, bringing her close. The part of her mind not clouded by passion or anger noted that much of his strength had returned, although the rest of her was unsure how to react. Before Karen could say anything, Adam spoke.

"Karen, watch my arm closely."

Despite herself, the tone of command in his voice made her eyes follow his gaze down to the large metal band encircling his left forearm. The smooth mirror surface began to gently ripple and without any sound transformed into a perfect replica of her face. Karen watched incredulously and started with shock as the simulacrum winked at her before fading back into the surface.

"How did you do that?" was all Karen could manage to say before she watched again in fascination as the armband flowed down along his arm and formed a large ball in his open palm, before rapidly elongating down to the floor and into a robust looking silver walking cane.

In silence, and without taking his eyes off her face, Adam leant the cane against the wall.

"Isn't one of your sayings, "*A picture paints a thousand words*," Karen?" he asked with a small, tight smile that acknowledged her shock and anger. "Nothing I could say would soften the shock of this or get you to believe anything other than I was an idiot or a madman, so this demonstration was in order."

He caught her eyes and held them with his gaze, a look that bored deep into her own and helped her focus.

"Think, Karen. Is there anything you've ever seen or heard of which could do this? There was no easy way of telling you, and I respect you too much to have waited until after we had become intimate before dropping this news on you."

In her mind, a dozen questions vied with a similar number of accusations, rendering her temporarily speechless as she tried to figure out what to say first. Taking advantage of her silence, Adam continued, relentlessly filling the silence with more information.

"I know you have had suspicions about me, Karen, what person wouldn't have. After all, a mysterious man appears out of nowhere at the same time as a massive fireball lights up the northern hemisphere, has unique healing and regenerative powers. Speaks numerous languages and is completely naive about the simplest of things a ten-year-old child would have known."

Still looking into Karen's eyes, Adam willed her to try and understand why it had to be now and not later. He sensed a small change in her posture and a softening of the muscles around her eyes. His face took on the look of an embarrassed schoolboy caught looking at a young girl he desperately wanted to talk to but hadn't yet plucked up the courage to ask.

"I do care about you, Karen and I do want to...get to know you better, but I don't want there to be any secrets between us, which is why I waited until now to tell you. That, and I didn't want to be carted off for imprisonment and vivisection. I had to know I could trust you with this secret."

Adam's eyes continued to hold hers, but he released the pressure on her arm stopping Karen from moving away. Almost imperceptibly, he gently began to guide her closer with his fingers. Encouraged that she made no move to resist, Adam brought himself close, so they were almost touching. For a moment they stood close without speaking, then Adam leant down and gently kissed Karen's forehead, before straightening up and stepping back a pace.

"Cup of tea or something stronger?" he asked suddenly, breaking the tension.

"Tea, please," came the automatic response before she could stop herself.

Adam left Karen alone in the corridor to think, and walked into the kitchen, where she heard him fill the kettle and open a cupboard to get cups. The spell of his gaze thoroughly broken, and in the absence of any idea what to do next, she reached out and picked up the cane resting against the wall. It was surprisingly heavy and warm to the touch, but in all other respects was solid and devoid of any buttons or controls. Karen twirled it through her fingers a few times and tapped it against the wall, each knock becoming increasingly harder, before inspecting the end for any damage or sign to show how it had been manipulated.

In the kitchen and with his back to the door, Adam smiled as he heard the cane being hit against the wall, each blow louder than the last.

"*I'd be doing the same thing*," he thought to himself, just as he sensed Karen walk in and stand behind him.

"OK, Adam, the stick's real enough and I can't find any buttons to make it change, so how did you do it?"

After making sure the kettle was switched on, Adam turned around and faced her.

"It's called smart-metal, and at my command, will assume a number of pre-determined forms. In the case of this particular armband, it's a high-end, multi-purpose survival device and therefore designed to be more versatile than usual. For example, it can also be used as a simple, non-verbal communication tool."

He looked at her expectantly, waiting for the next question. He was reassured his assessment of how she would take the news had been correct but was concerned he might have ruined their blossoming friendship. Although pleased there was no longer any need to mislead her, a part of him regretted having the truth out in the open as it might well change how she viewed him.

"Assuming what you say is true, where are you from and what are you doing here?" she asked him, with a look that indicated she wasn't entirely convinced this wasn't all a hoax and in very poor taste.

Adam let out a small, tight laugh. "I'm from a planet called Capital which is somewhere that isn't here! No, I'm not being evasive Karen," he said quickly, seeing her about to say something to him. " I'm lost, Karen. Perhaps more lost than anyone else in history has ever been, given my homeworld could be billions of light years from here and I have no idea where it is. As to why I'm here, well, it's pure chance. I was meant to be travelling home, but a malfunction in my ship's drive system brought me here instead. The explosion everyone thought was a meteorite was my spaceship blowing up just after I escaped in a lifeboat."

Karen stood there waiting for him to continue but instead he turned away and poured boiling water into the cups. He looked down at the tea and stirred, waiting for the tea bags to infuse the water.

"I don't know if I can ever get back home, Karen. I'm lost, and apart from you, I'm all alone on this world of yours. I'm scared, worried about what might happen to me if people ever found out what I am. I also miss my family and home more than I ever thought possible."

As Adam spoke those words, he realised again just how much he missed his parents and everything he'd always taken for granted. Not the adoration or the celebrity that came with his position, but the simple comfort of familiarity and the knowledge there were others nearby that cared for him.

He turned back and looked at her. "Now do you understand why I couldn't tell you before? If we'd gone to bed and I only told you afterwards, what would you have thought of me? I couldn't take the risk you might think badly of me, Karen. I'm sorry, but I just couldn't. You had to know first what you were getting yourself into."

No reply was forthcoming, and Karen stood there watching him in silence, looking at his face. He turned around and fished the tea bags out of the cups, placing them on the draining board, hoping she would break the silence. He handed her a cup, which she took silently before sitting down at the kitchen table. Karen motioned him over to sit opposite her.

She finally broke the silence. "I'm still trying to figure out if I believe a word of this or you are just a madman that I've let into my life and home. A changing stick is hardly proof positive. What other proof do you have so I can be totally convinced you are telling me the truth? It better be good, or you'll be sleeping in the garage tonight before leaving here tomorrow, even if you did save my life."

Adam nodded. He'd expected this and had already decided beforehand what to do.

"Fair enough. Drink up your tea, get dressed for a walk over the croft behind the hill and I'll show you."

Karen snorted out loud. "Hah, so you can rape and murder me before burying my body. I don't bloody think so."

Adam's face took on a pained expression. "Don't get even more annoyed with me for saying this Karen, but if I had said nothing you would have willingly gone to bed with me a few minutes ago, so rape's hardly a motive. As to murdering you, why did I risk my life to save you if I wanted to do you harm? Come on, does that make sense?" He raised his eyebrows and looked at her, lifting his hands in a gesture of submission. "You don't really think I could do these things, do you?"

Karen thought for a few seconds then shook her head. "No, I don't, and I apologise for saying them. Despite your funny ways you've done nothing to warrant my accusing you like that. I'm just so angry and confused about you right now."

The silence continued for several long heartbeats before she put down her cup and stood up, a look of determination on her face now she'd made up her mind what to do.

"Why wait. Sod the tea, let's go now before it gets too cold outside, but heaven help you if there's nothing there."

An hour later found them walking side by side over the peat bog that sat on a wide plateau at the back of the bungalow, completely hidden from both the village and road by a large rocky hill. At times their conversation had been fitful, with Adam answering her questions as best he could before she lapsed into long periods of silence, digesting what he'd said and trying to find holes in his story. Try as she might to find flaws, his story was consistent and if nothing else, she now had the plot for a great science fiction story should he turn out to be a liar. His story of Galactic Empires, millennia of civilisation and thousands of worlds all seemed so far-fetched, yet strangely compelling and plausible when he explained it.

Karen was glad of the illumination provided by their two powerful torches and already needed Adams help when her Wellington Boots became stuck in the rain-sodden ground. Suction from the peat had threatened to pull them right off her feet. When he'd come to help her and held out his arm, she'd initially shied away from his touch, but berated herself for being stupid and gratefully used it to pull herself free.

This far away from the small, scattered community that sat along the road a mile behind them, the silence was almost total. All that could be heard was the wind and the gentle sound of the ever-present water as it trickled towards the many rivulets crisscrossing the plateau.

Karen shone her torch ahead, illuminating two rocky outcrops rising up from the peat to her left and right, forming a natural depression between them that looked particularly soggy.

"How much further?" she asked, getting tired and starting to worry that she was on a wild goose chase with Adam and maybe he was delusional after all.

"We're here, Karen. Now don't be alarmed. My lifeboat will rise out of the ground between those two outcrops you just illuminated, so shine your torch in the middle.

Not knowing what to expect and more worried that instead of something, nothing would happen, Karen did as requested. She didn't know if it was the cold or anticipation that suddenly made her tremble, which in turn made the torch beam waver in time to her now chattering teeth.

Nothing happened for a few moments, but then she felt the sodden ground below her feet tremble. With a loud sucking noise, an elongated tear-drop shaped object raised itself two metres from the reluctant ground, dripping water and mud. Wide-eyed, Karen watched as it gently rotated three-hundred and sixty degrees, before noticing Adam was making circular movements with his right hand which the craft seemed to be following. She watched, fascinated, as he beckoned the craft towards them and she took an involuntary step back before it stopped a few scant metres from where they were standing.

"Are you doing that with your hands, Adam?" she asked, enthralled by the spectacle of something so large being controlled by simple hand movements.

"Actually, no. I just thought this would make it look more impressive. I'm actually controlling it by my mind, and the hand gestures are just for effect."

Karen punched Adam hard on the arm, making him wince.

"Don't play with me, Adam." Karen reached out and rubbed his arm where she'd hit him. "Sorry, I hit you. I'm just blown away by this. It's true then. You are from up there." Karen looked up at the sky, a part of her mind wondering whether she could see his star, the rest of it trying to make sense of what she was experiencing. "There's no need to make it any more impressive. Heavens above, I don't know whether to be scared witless and run away or be grateful you aren't a complete madman after all."

Karen looked hard at Adam, almost as if seeing him again for the first time. She could see two paths racing away into the future. One where she turns away and forgets this ever happened and tries going back to her old life; the other where she embraces this once in a lifetime experience and runs with it to who-knows-where. Either way, the life she knew will have gone forever. Karen made a decision and squelched closer to Adam, switching off her torch. Reaching up and putting her arms around his neck, Karen pulled his head down and kissed him hard on the mouth. As she did so, Karen realised that with this kiss there was no going back and it would probably change her life forever, in ways she couldn't yet understand, not least because as he responded to her embrace, she could finally feel the proof he felt the same way.

"*About time too,*" a quiet voice whispered in Adam's mind.

Deep within the safety of the Palace Bunker, Empress
Christine stood in the huge War Room with General Parmenion
and several of her closest advisors. A giant, three-dimensional
map of the Empire hung over a large circular table, surrounded by
comfortable, padded chairs and workstations. The map was
visible from every point in the room, with Empire held sectors
coloured in Imperial Orange and Rebel-held ones a dirty green.
For now, everyone ignored the chairs, preferring to stand while
they waited for the surviving Sector representatives to join them
from the Palace. Christine was currently far too tense and full of
nervous energy to feel comfortable sitting down, choosing
instead to stand and move around as this allowed her to work off
a little of the nervous energy ruining her concentration.

All around the room, displays were showing dire news. In the
twenty-four hours after the attempt on her life, contact had been
partially or totally lost with eleven Sectors, with three more
reporting insurrection and attacks from unidentified fleets that
had Jumped in to attack Jump Stations in key strategic locations.
The majority of these Stations had already been under attack
from within, as insurgents sought to take over key areas. As a
result, many were unable to respond effectively against the
attacking fleets. Soon afterwards, contact had been lost with
dozens of these Stations, and those in the room could only fear
the worst. Before falling, quite a few of the Jump Stations in
Sectors twenty-seven through to thirty-three had also reported
being attacked by ships of other empires, fighting alongside
known human Empire built vessels. To make things worse, due to
the light speed time delay, messages travelling between the Jump
Station and the Palace were at least five hours old or more and
were of past events, leaving everyone fearing what else might
have happened.

Earlier, Vimes had privately confirmed to Christine that
instantaneous contact with his counterparts throughout those
affected Sectors had been lost, cutting her off from one of the key

advantages their secret communication system gave them. From the information Vimes had been able to ascertain before losing contact, it was obvious this revolt had been well planned and professionally conducted. Vimes contact with his avatars in the affected Sectors had all been lost within a short time of each other, immediately after each of the Sector Central Banks and Government buildings had been stormed and taken over. Millennia earlier, Vimes had taken steps to ensure all traces of the secret IQC devices would be removed from his numerous avatars in the event of a revolt, and now confirmed to Christine he was confident the instantaneous communication technology remained secret.

To make matters worse, news was coming in of a new and disturbing development concerning the system of Jump Points. Apparently, the enemy had found a way to destabilise them, rendering the Jump Stations impotent and effectively sealing those planetary systems off from any outside help or communication.

Fortunately, the Sectors loyal and under Empire control remained peaceful, their populations as yet unaware of the unfolding crisis throughout the Empire, although all the Jump Stations and elements of the Imperial Navy which remained loyal were on high alert. Such a mobilisation of forces hadn't been seen in the Empire since the Felidae war, whose borders with the Empire were, at least for now, thankfully still peaceful.

Of her husband, nothing had been heard, although one of the last transmissions intercepted by Vimes from Duke Frederick's home planet, Kiyami, indicated that Alexander's fleet had been attacked and destroyed, along with her son. She had initially dismissed the report as a fabrication, knowing as she did that Adam was safe and in training, but as the hours passed and nothing had been heard from Alexander, her anxiety had grown. Vimes had been unable to contact him using their secret means, adding to her concerns.

Indecision gnawed at her bowels like a vicious cancer, and Christine was finding it difficult to concentrate. No sooner had she begun to digest and analyse one bit of news when another, seemingly more important item would demand her attention. Even the gentle scents coming from the room's climate control wasn't able to counteract the pheromones of anxiety and uncertainty that surged through the room every time another distressing piece of news came in.

General Parmenion, always mindful of what was going on around him, recognised her inner conflict, walked over and quietly spoke so only she could hear what he said.

"Ma'am, you need to stop trying to control everything. Trust Vimes, the AI's and your General Staff here to do their jobs. It's what they were designed to do and what we have trained for all our lives. The sheer volume of information coming in is far beyond anything you can control yourself, and you know this. Our role is to provide the strategy and grand plan, while yours is as much to show stability to the population as anything else."

He broke etiquette and placed a reassuring hand on her left shoulder, giving a reassuring squeeze for a moment before removing it.

Christine turned towards him, warmed by this rare demonstration of affection, "I know, Parmenion, but I feel so helpless at the moment and want to do something, anything, rather than just staying here waiting."

"I know, Ma'am. Every good Commander feels the same way when the battle starts to unfurl and they have to wait for the enemy to make their big move. It isn't a good feeling, all the while knowing that people under your command are dying and there isn't a damn thing you can do to stop it. It doesn't get any easier with experience or the passing of time either."

He laughed, bitterly. "Hark at me giving you advice. As I recall, you and Alexander were in some of the thickest battles during the Succession War."

Christine nodded. "Yes, we were, and this whole thing has a similar smell to it. The careful building up of forces under our very nose, the suddenness of the attacks and the attempts to cut off the heads of the Royal Family are all far too familiar for my liking. It's almost as if..."

Christine stopped talking, her mind suddenly making a powerful connection that left her cold inside, sending a shiver across her back and making the hairs on her neck rise.

"Frederick's been behind this all along, going back to the original Succession War. He has to be."

Christine now had the attention of everyone in the room, so continued.

"The Palace jammer was in Sector Twelve's offices, and his Sector Capital played host to Alexander before he went to System DU-499. The intelligence on the Raider base came from his Sector, and he would have known Alexander's exact arrival time and destination well in advance of his leaving. He couldn't be seen to be the obvious architect of Alexander's disappearance for it would badly hurt any bid he might make for the throne, so manipulated him into going exactly where he wanted, when he wanted. I would wager he was behind the ambush on Heaven too."

Parmenion looked thoughtful, digesting all the information and correlating against other known variables before speaking, "Alexander and I always thought at the end of the Succession War we hadn't destroyed all of the rebel ships. We both suspected many of them had gone to ground, turned to piracy or offered their services to rival empires. As the years passed and we saw no sign of them, apart from an occasional ship that was turned up by a border campaign or skirmish, we thought we'd seen the last of them as a serious, unified threat."

Parmenion shifted his attention from speaking and projected onto the main screen his assumptions for everyone to see.

"If we assume Duke Frederick was a key player in the original revolt and working from a base number of surviving ships...say this number...and assuming over time he persuaded or bribed the other Sectors to support him, it would take anywhere between sixty and one hundred and twenty years to rebuild a fleet sufficiently large to threaten the Empire's stability."

Parmenion looked across to Christine, who had been looking at the screen with growing alarm. "I fear he and his co-conspirators have been playing a long game and have laid their plans well, as evidenced by our inability to get through to the lost Sectors."

"Parmenion," Christine interrupted as he paused for breath, "Vimes has been searching through Josef's original files and has found evidence of how the Jump Points are being disrupted. I've just sent this to you and the Cyber-warfare teams for analysis. It appears we have a five or six-day wait before the Jump Points stabilise sufficiently for incoming or outgoing traffic."

While they debated, representatives from the Sectors attacked during the failed attempt on Christine's life began arriving, many still showing partially healed wounds or sporting medical aids as a result of the earlier attack on the Palace. Servitors directly under the control of Vimes escorted the more obviously injured to their places while others began bringing in plates of food to be eaten later. Fourteen of the thirty-six seats were empty, representing the eleven Sectors which had rebelled and three whose status was currently unknown following the death of their representatives at the hands of rebels.

The room's mood was sombre, although conversations were going on as people quickly checked on which of their opposite numbers had been killed or wounded in the attack and subsequent retaking of the Palace. As everyone talked, Christine looked around, taking in the pinched faces and tense body language which many of those present were displaying. Regrettably, she had a suspicion that some of them still hadn't grasped the full enormity of what was happening and the turmoil that lay ahead of them all. Watching the representatives chat, some of them obviously comparing wounds with each other for bragging rights, she felt an overwhelming urge to leave the room and go seek out her son. Despite not hearing from her husband, she had an almost spiritual faith in his ability to survive against even the worst odds that a capricious universe could throw at him, and discounted the reports from Sector Twelve confirming his and Adam's death. Yet, certain as she was, the lack of any message from her husband gnawed at her, and she feared something bad had happened to one or both of them.

Letting the conversations wash over her and trusting Vimes to warn of anything important that needed her immediate attention, she began to think what her next action should be. Fortunately, she had the utmost faith in Parmenion and her General Staff. The remaining Sector Heads were all highly accomplished and would run affairs perfectly well even without input from her. Coming to a decision, she instructed Vimes to prepare her personal yacht for immediate launch and to confirm when it would be ready.

"*Are you going to tell me or do I have to guess, Christine?*" Vimes asked softly in her mind, his usual good humour subdued to match her mood."*You're going after Adam,*" he stated rather than asked. "*The plan was to have him trained so he would have a better understanding of what it meant to be a normal person, away from the privileges of his birth. You know better than anyone how important this training is for the next Emperor. Are you sure yo...*"

"*Of course, I'm sure, Vimes,*" Christine interrupted, trying hard and not quite succeeding in keeping the annoyance from her face. "*I'm his mother, and nothing in this universe is going to stop me bringing my son home and then find out what the hell has happened to my husband. After that, together we'll kick Duke Fredericks arse from one end of this Empire to the other.*" She took a deep breath.

"Anything I can help with Ma'am?" asked Parmenion, leaning across towards her, his sharp eyes and attention to detail picking up traces of the interplay that had passed across her features.

Letting out her held breath with a gentle sigh, Christine looked at him and nodded, then smiled as she recognised the concern etched into the face of her loyal General.

"*With people like these still loyal to our family, there is no way we cannot win through in the end,*" she thought to herself and Vimes.

Christine sent a private message to Parmenion, telling him she would be leaving him in overall charge for several hours while she remained cloistered in her Private Apartments, not to be disturbed. Vimes would act as her intermediary between him and the Council should anything urgent need her attention.

Although pleased she was taking his advice not to try and be involved with everything, Parmenion suspected he wasn't being told the full story, but his many decades of Imperial service had taught him not to underestimate the Doones, and especially his Empress, who rarely did anything without a good reason.

An hour, and much debate in the chamber later, Vimes confirmed to Christine her yacht was fully prepared and an up-to-date copy of himself loaded into its systems. Christine waited for a natural break in the presentation currently being made by her Sector Admiral, Lord Thomas Rose. A quick search with Vimes confirmed her suspicion he was a many-times-removed descendant of Lord Martyn Rose, whose statue in the Palace grounds she had been directed to. She felt sure the old Admiral would have been proud to know both he and his descendants continued to serve her family well. Choosing this moment, she stood up, motioning for everyone to remain seated as they started to stand.

Looking at the expectant faces around the chamber she indicated to Parmenion, before speaking.

"I will be absenting myself for a few hours on urgent State business. In my absence, General Parmenion will act in my place. Vimes will handle any enquiries you may have. Please be assured you all have my utmost confidence, and I will return to this chamber once my work elsewhere has been completed."

One of the servitors standing nearby her pulled back her chair and escorted her to the door, then returned to stand behind General Parmenion.

Once the door had closed behind her, Christine leaned against the wall to relax for a few moments. The two armoured servitors guarding either side of the door paid her no heed, controlled as they were by Vimes who understood Christine's inner turmoil. Releasing some of the inner tension that had propelled her for the past twenty-four hours, she was assailed again by doubts as to whether she was doing the right thing in bringing Adam back early from training. She knew how important this time had been for Alexander and for a few moments almost wavered, before standing upright and straightening her shoulders.

Decision made and all doubts put aside, Christine walked towards the nearby transit tube, her soft-soled shoes squeaking softly on the mirror-smooth floor. The pod doors opened silently, and internal lights came on. She sank gratefully into the padded seat as it accelerated away to the heavily shielded hangar where her personal yacht was waiting.

In less than a minute, Karen had left the tube and was standing in front of the seamless wall which marked the entrance to her private hanger, waiting for Vimes to allow her access. Smart-metal walls began moving away inwards at a fast walking pace, allowing Christine to pass through the metres thick armour protecting the hangar bay. Moving through into the noticeably artificial light of the cavernous hangar, Christine paused for a few moments to do a visual inspection. Several dozen ships of various sizes and configurations lay settled around the floor in their cradles. She recognised them all, many bringing back memories not thought of for decades. Situated closest to the entrance rested her favourite, a needle-pointed yacht, shaped like a stretched teardrop, its hull mirror-bright and reflecting the harsh lighting. Living quarters and engines were at the rear, with sensors and weapon systems housed in the long prow. At sixty metres in length, it was much larger than Alexanders, and Christine struggled for a few seconds to recall when she last had cause to use it. Vimes gently prompted her recall before again fading back into the background of her thoughts.

"Five years? Has it really been so long since I'd seen my home planet?" she mused. "Well, not long now and I'll be back there."

Approaching the yacht, a door opened in the hull and a ramp extended down to greet her. A small number of servitor androids were still busy burnishing several areas of the hull to a mirror-like sheen, to be absorbed back into the floor when finished. Taking a last quick look around the hangar, Christine entered the ship, the ramp retracting and the hull opening sealing itself soundlessly behind her as she headed for the pilot seat.

Keyed to her DNA and thought patterns, she allowed herself to relax in the command chair and began joining with the ship, the little-used but familiar sensations merging themselves into her senses with a pleasant tingle. It took a good thirty seconds before Christine felt completely settled with the merger, the sensations fading away completely, leaving behind a feeling of well-being that mirrored the ship's status. Instructing the AI to prepare for a Jump, Christine fed in the IQA coordinates and waited as the power began to flow into and build in the Jump engines. Within moments, the ship lifted several metres into the air, and the IQA field expanded to encompass the ship. Christine triggered the drive and the ship vanished. Instantly, the hangar was filled by a monstrously loud thunder-clap as air rushed in to fill the vacuum, heard only by the slowly disappearing servitors.

Karen sat atop the large, rocky hill at the back of her uncle and aunt's bungalow, glad of the padded overcoat and hood that was doing a grand job of keeping the morning chill and damp from seeping into her bones. She'd remembered to take with her a black plastic bin liner to sit on and keep her bottom dry. In all the years she had been coming to Skye, Karen had never sat here and watched the sunrise before, so this was yet another first for her.

She'd woken early, too excited to lie in bed any longer and a little bored of watching Adam breathe slowly by her side, so had decided to go for a walk and try to compose her thoughts. A smile came unbidden to Karen's lips as she wryly remembered the previous night's exertions.

"No wonder he's still sleeping," she murmured to herself with a self-satisfied smile that threatened to take over her face. "I gave a good account of myself too," allowing herself a moment of smugness.

It didn't last long, however, for she knew there were some hard choices ahead; not least what to do about her work and finding somewhere to stay with Adam when her aunt and uncle came home. She thought again about yesterday's events. After Adam had proved beyond doubt his story was true, her relief was such that she couldn't help herself. They'd first made love in the lifeboat then, after Adam had guided it under cover of dark to her uncle's large green boatshed and covered it with a large tarpaulin, they'd run the short distance back to the bungalow and into her bedroom, shedding their clothes again the moment they had shut the front door behind them.

Adam had exceeded her most optimistic expectations and, if she was honest with herself, she'd been surprised at her own reaction. Again, the smile threatened to widen all the way to her ears.

"*But am I doing the right thing*?" the thought kept interrupting her pleasant reveries, again bringing her back to the hard choices ahead. Deep down, Karen knew she wouldn't be leaving Adam's side, with all that meant for her work and future. She found it ironic she'd let her old fiance, Ian, move to New York and leave her because she wasn't prepared to give up her career, yet here she was, on the brink of following a man she'd only known for a few short weeks and, amazingly, was technically an alien.

"*I must be mad,*" she thought to herself, not for the first time.

From the hilltop, Karen had a distant view of the Cuillin hills, fortunately not shrouded today in clouds or mist. To her left she watched a sea-eagle lift off from its eyrie, set high up the cliff that marked the start of the valley cut deep into the rock by two small streams, slowly emptying themselves into the loch beneath the causeway bridge. The tide was out, and the mussel and cockle beds that made up the loch's exposed sandy bottom glistened as the breeze rippled the pools of standing water dotted around. A few sheep were up and about, cropping grass half-heartedly along the fence lines. An occasional car or lorry drove past, disturbing the otherwise quiet morning. The beauty and grandeur of the scenery never failed to make her feel a little awed or even insignificant, and she could understand why many people here turned to religion.

All around her, the ages old, slowly changing landscape reminded Karen of her own insignificance, and she could understand why so many sought the need to discover some higher meaning to their lives. Karen had little time for religion, for as a Doctor she had experience of life and death in all its many forms and knew from bitter experience how little the individual mattered in the grand scheme. Sitting here, watching the sun come up, Karen knew in her heart the important things in life were the people around you and the relationships you formed. She regularly witnessed the depth of love people had which helped them through medical crises, allowing them to draw strength from each other. Things like that were far more important to her than the slim possibility of some omnipresent, capricious deity that required unquestioning obedience.

Earlier, in the warm, intimate glow between periods of lovemaking, Adam had done his best to describe and explain his world and civilisation to her. She was amazed at how far ahead their medicine was compared to what she knew and his stories of aliens and empires spanning hundreds and thousands of worlds left her mind spinning with so many questions. So much to learn and unlearn. Things she'd taken for granted all her life had been turned on their head and she now totally understood Adam's real worry about what would happen to him should his identity ever be found out. When he'd told her about his ever-present companion, Vimes, Karen had at first felt uncomfortable at the thought of being watched but had relented when Adam reassured her Vimes was a part of him. Whenever she had asked about Adam's family, Karen noticed his answers were vague, but she put that down to sadness at being apart from them and so didn't press the point, especially as there were so many other questions. Even so, Karen felt there were things he was deliberately avoiding or only half explaining, but for now, she would let that pass.

Karen suddenly shuddered involuntarily, feeling for an instant as if someone had walked over her grave. She'd heard the expression many times before but until now had never experienced the feeling herself. She stood up, deciding with a smile it was time to go back and either wake Adam or crawl back under the covers and let him warm her another way. Turning around, she was startled to see a woman standing a few metres behind her and took a step backwards in shock. She looked at the strikingly beautiful woman in front of her; tall, with short brown hair devoid of any trace of grey. Of indeterminate age, anywhere from thirty to sixty, she held herself straight and looked appraisingly at Karen, as if judging her in some way. The woman's clothes looked decidedly dated, reminding Karen of outfits her grandmother used to wear.

Shocked at having this woman come upon her so quietly and not knowing what else to say, Karen heard herself say, "Hello, how long have you been standing there?"

"Long enough. It's a beautiful view isn't it?" the woman replied, a hint of a smile creasing her mouth.

She walked forward and extended her hand.

"Apologies for startling you like that, Karen. I saw you up here alone and decided to introduce myself. I'm Christine, Adam's mother and you and I need to have a chat."

For the first time in her life, Karen was truly speechless and unable to articulate anything meaningful other than a strangled, "Mother?" Instinctively, she took the proffered hand, noting the firm grip and familiar unnatural warmth that immediately reminded her of Adam.

Watching the colour drain out of Karen's face, Christine spoke. "I'm sorry, my dear, that was unfair of me, and I apologise for springing this on you in such a fashion. Unfortunately, I don't have much time here, but I did want to meet with you alone before I saw my son."

Karen interrupted, "But Adam told me he was lost with no means of contacting his family so how on earth did you find him? What does this mean?" Karen's initial shock started turning to anger, thinking that for all Adam's protestations of good faith and not wanting to hurt her she had been misled again. Before she could continue with this train of thought, Christine interrupted her.

"No, Karen. He didn't lie or mislead you; everything he told you was true. He was lost and alone, just not in the way he or you thought, but I urgently need to speak with him first before telling you the full story. Let's go surprise him together."

End of Book one.

Thank you for making it through to the end of the first Book. I do hope you enjoyed Imperium: Betrayal. I feel a little bad at leaving their story hanging on a cliff-edge, but it really is too long a tale for one book.

If you want to know more, Book Two (Imperium: Revelations) tells the story of Alexander's father and the death of his family, how he and Christine met, and what happens next to the Emperor, Christine, Adam and Karen.

Betrayal is my first book and something I've wanted to do for a long time. I didn't really set out to write a love story; it just ended up that way as the characters grew and developed a life of their own. As a life-long fan of science fiction, I wanted the main actors to be fully rounded human beings and not two-dimensional as is so often the case in the genre.

Before you go, if you enjoyed the story, please leave a review on Amazon and Goodreads as they both encourage others to try the book for themselves and me to write more!

Paul M Calvert

London, England

No member of the Imperial family may marry another hereditary member of the Nobility.

Planets within Empire space, where the dominant life-form has not achieved safe manned space flight, evidenced by a successful launch into high orbit and safe return of the sentient passenger(s), are to be embargoed from all contact and outside influence.

For embargoed planets, the existence of the Empire must be kept hidden from them until such time as they have achieved the aforementioned safe launch and return. At the Emperor's discretion, they may be offered membership of the Empire.

If the offer is accepted, the appropriate Class of membership is to be proffered, depending on their level of technological and social progress.

In the event a planet rejects membership, the solar system is to be embargoed. No contact with the Empire permitted, other than every fifty standard years at which time membership is to be offered again. Travel outside of their home system is prohibited.

Classes of membership are:

Class Three:

Basic Membership. Self-Governance. To be offered on reaching minimum requirement. No interference by the Empire or transfer of higher technologies. Mandatory free passage for Empire ships within the solar system. Jump Point Custom Stations must be installed. All citizens of the Empire to be given safe passage or assistance, without let or hindrance. Class Three citizens cannot leave their home system without the approval of the Customs Station.

Class Two:

Intermediate Membership. To be offered on reaching a Unitary World Government. Limited transfer of higher technologies and trade with other worlds, providing it would not adversely impact on the planet's population or ecology. Acceptance that Universal Imperial Law replaces their own.

Payment of the Imperial Tithe to be made. A non-voting seat at the Sector Council.

Class One:

Full Membership. To be offered where there is a Unitary World Government and colony worlds have been founded within the solar system. Where colony worlds are not feasible, they must have achieved manned travel to and from the nearest planet or moon. Appointment of Imperial Nobility to Planet. Unrestricted trade and transfers of technology. Free passage allowed in and out of the home system. A voting seat at the Sector Council. Provision of troops to the Imperial Navy and the maintenance of own Fleet as per Imperial Edict. All citizens have full rights and responsibilities.

The Empire was old. So old in fact, the majority of its citizens didn't know or had forgotten it might have once gone by a name other than "Empire."

Not that too many of those who knew would have cared anyway, for life in the Empire was good for the majority of its citizens and worrying about such things tended to be the purview of historians and scholars.

Before the Empire's founding, the planet called Capital had been no different to any other that nurtured human life in the galaxy. Circling a yellow, type G star in a binary system, it was one of twelve planets held by that sun. It sat in the habitable Goldilocks zone with another, slightly smaller planet that orbited closer in and was at the hotter end of what humans would find comfortable.

Home of the Emperor, his family and the Imperial Court, Capital was now a verdant, lush world that showed little sign of the widespread industrialisation and scars of war which had marked its surface millennia before.

Pre-Empire, every continent on Capital had borne several civilisations, each with unique languages, customs and mores. Throughout recorded history, they rose, blossomed for a time, then stagnated and ultimately fell. Religious, economic or ideological wars had all been fought at one time or another, many on a global scale.

During these periods of rise and fall, almost every conceivable type of governance had been tried and found wanting. No matter what good intentions or altruistic ideals these civilisations began with, each, in turn, had failed by not providing one or more of the four main constants of governance; the will to make hard decisions on behalf of the people, the illusion of freedom, social cohesion, and protection from the harsh realities of existence.

Invariably, after each fall, one strong, clever or charismatic individual would come forward and lead the people out of darkness and despair and into the light, promising hope and a return of pride. Unfortunately, no matter how pure in heart or noble their intentions were to begin with, in time each new start invariably harboured within it the age-old cycle of growth and collapse.

Ironically, it was not during one of these periodic collapses or wars that the Empire came into being, far from it. It began in a peaceful period that had already lasted ninety years, following a devastating world war which ruined many of the world's economies and saw tens of millions killed. After the war had ended, scientific advancements and burgeoning prosperity brought about a time of optimism in which nations decided to compete with each other to conquer the challenges of space instead of on the battlefield. The urge to spread across the solar system intensified following a planetary near miss by a potentially planet-killing, massive nickel-iron meteorite. Nearly half of the planet's population watched in horror as it burned through the upper atmosphere, before skimming away into deep space, changing their perception of space forever.

Into this time of exploration and advance was born Josef Doone, youngest of three children from a well to do family living on the largest continent, Mohanes. Showing enormous talent from an early age, Doone was by any measure a genius. Not only did he possess a remarkable ability to take other people's ideas and improve on them, but also displayed an instinctive understanding of quantum physics and genetics. These prodigious talents would ultimately propel him into the history books as the first Emperor.

Aged twenty-two, he revolutionised power generation by working out how to liberate and commercially utilise the energy released from the total conversion of matter into energy. Governments paid huge sums to licence this technology, and Doone rapidly became an incredibly wealthy man. In addition to fulfilling the growing energy needs of a modern, technological society, this new power source accelerated the move out into the solar system, something that had begun several years previously. Using ships designed around Doone's total conversion engines, nations began exploring the solar system, mining the asteroid belts for raw materials and water. This expansion and utilisation of resources allowed colonies to be settled on the hotter sister planet and bases to be established on less hospitable ones.

Josef, drawing on his wealth and powerful commercial interests, established a private laboratory at the edge of the solar system, away from prying eyes and manned it with the brightest and best from his huge commercial empire. Focusing all of his efforts into the study of Quantum Attraction, Josef first postulated, then proved and finally demonstrated that it was possible to move objects or messages instantaneously from one point to another, providing the "Quantum Signature" of both points were both known and took place outside of a sun's gravity well. When the two "Signatures" were matched together within an artificially generated QA field, the lesser of the two signatures and anything contained within it would instantaneously move to the greater. Every star, depending on its mass and gravity well, was postulated to have at least one, or possibly more, regions (Jump Points) where Quantum Signatures could be matched and Jumps performed.

Of no immediate commercial use within their sun's gravity well, Josef kept this breakthrough and associated technology secret, aided in this by the isolation of his laboratory at the edge of space. He knew that once this and his other work on genome enhancements became known, Governments would seek to take them from him for their own ends.

Conveniently located close to the systems only Jump point, Josef's research station was kept away from inquisitive eyes and guarded by the best private security money could buy. Utilising his immense wealth to produce and equip star-faring probes, each with the ability to map Quantum Signatures, Josef quietly launched hundreds from his laboratory to neighbouring star systems. Travelling at a constant three-G of acceleration and allowing for slowing down at the destination so precise Quantum mapping could take place, the first probe took just over five years to reach the closest system outside of their binary, four light years away. With the "Signature" of a distant Jump point mapped and transmitted back using Quantum Attraction, Josef was eventually able to set up a commercially sized transmitter/receiver, enabling instantaneous travel between the two systems. Although instantaneous travel to another star system was now a reality, journeys within a sun's gravity well still required travel through normal space and could take several weeks.

Maintaining strict secrecy, and using families from within his commercial empire, Josef began establishing small colonies of like-minded people on an increasing number of new worlds. Growing increasingly fearful that Governments would interfere with his plans or seek to take control of his technologies, Josef accelerated preparations for the time when he might have to flee. By his sixtieth birthday, Josef was the de facto owner and leader of nine star systems, albeit sparsely populated ones. Inevitably, an undertaking of this magnitude could not be kept secret forever. When news of his discoveries and the existence of human colonies around other stars finally became public knowledge, Josef was forced to flee the home system with his family and associates. As he had predicted and feared, national Governments on the home planet tried to take control for themselves and gain a monopoly over the new technologies and worlds he had discovered. Faced with the stark choices of either capitulation, imprisonment or fleeing, Josef and his associates abandoned their home system forever through the Jump Point, leaving the laboratory and transmitting machinery behind to self-destruct in a total conversion explosion, leaving no trace of his research or discoveries.

At this point, Josef felt relatively safe, as he knew that even if the will was there to follow him to the stars, it would be many years before construction of ships large enough to make the trip through relativistic space could even begin. Even then, without his QA drive, the travel time at one-G would take a little over six years, by which time he and his fledgeling colonies would be ready for them.

Following the destruction of Doone's laboratory and disappearance, along with any hope of their taking or replicating his QA jump technology, Governments turned inwards, seeking to try and develop it for themselves and claim the stars for their own people. As a result, planetary co-operation began to fall apart

With the passing of years, suspicion and greed replaced the earlier altruistic fervour to explore the system and protect the race, eventually culminating in a series of small wars over territory and resources. Mistrust and xenophobia flourished. Old religious and ideological hatreds resurfaced which had previously been buried under a thin veneer of civilisation and prosperity. Eventually, one side believed they saw an opportunity, and in a bid to destroy their rivals, managed to turn the orbiting asteroid defence platforms onto their enemies. The very weapons designed to protect the planet and race were now used to destroy everything they had built up. As nations retaliated from within hardened bunkers, a cataclysmic war ensued, decimating large areas of the planet and killing hundreds of millions within days. The atmosphere became full of particulate matter released from fires and impact strikes, which in turn decreased crop yields and brought about global starvation. Finally, once the dust of war had literally settled, billions were dead or starving and what civilisation remained had returned to pre-industrial revolution levels.

Away from the home system and safe amongst the stars, the colonies set up and controlled by the benevolent Doone family could do nothing but watch in horror at the unfolding tragedy back home. After seeing the weapon platforms used and the resulting catastrophe, the Council tasked with governing the nine colonies met and decided to appoint Josef, now in his eighties, as Emperor. He had proved not only his own worth but also the wisdom of a central figure best placed to avoid the ruinous infighting and national allegiances that had bedevilled politics back on the home planet. While no-one thought it would be perfect, in those dark times a strong, fair leader and a family bred for the task of leadership and continuity seemed the best system of governance, especially when compared to those that had failed so many times in the past.

Now that it was impossible for them to be followed, and safe in their colonies, the Doone family set about building a new civilisation amongst the stars from out of the ruins of the old. Josef's advances in genetic manipulation extended life three-fold, but unfortunately, it came too late for him, and he died peacefully, aged 105, surrounded by his family and friends.

Before dying, Doone had set out the future shape of his new Empire. Using the home solar system as the centre, the space around it was split up into thirty-six Sectors, each controlled by a Duke who reported directly to the Emperor. Planets were controlled by Earls who in turn reported to the Dukes. Planets were further sub-divided with Viscounts and Barons responsible for continents and major cities respectively. Senior Civil Servants could expect to hold minor ranks, such as Baronet.

Sector One would remain under the direct control of the Emperor and his family. For the other Sectors, the first Nobles were personally selected by Doone himself from amongst the ablest of his scientific team and loyal members of his commercial empire. The titles and responsibilities that went with the role would pass down to the first born child or named successor, subject to the Emperor's approval and their having reached twenty-one years of age. Thus began the first of several phases of rapid Imperial expansion, as the Nobility sought to increase their wealth and power bases for themselves and the Empire.

It would be several generations before a Doone returned to reclaim the ruined homeworld for their Empire.

Communication and travel between worlds in the Empire is straightforward. Ships travel through normal space from their home planet to the nearest Quantum Attraction transmitter and Customs Station, known as Jump Stations. These are always situated at the edge of a solar system, away from the sun's gravity and within a small area of space called the Jump Point. Larger suns tend to have more than one Jump Point, necessitating more than one Jump Station. Old, established Stations serving important star often grow to rival small cities in size, and all are heavily armed and armoured. Although primarily military in nature, they also house maintenance and repair docks, along with Custom and Trading Posts of the large Conglomerates and Imperial families. Also, those stations situated in systems on the edge of Empire are home to many citizens of the other races humanity trades, and on occasion, fight with.

On arriving at a Station and after a thorough inspection, ships are Jumped to the receiving station of their destination, then continue on in-system to the desired planet. Although Jumping from Point to Point is instantaneous, travel time within a star system is a function of whatever acceleration the occupants of the spaceship can tolerate and the size of the sun's gravity well. This also determines how far away the Jump Point is from the nearest habitable planet. Depending on the size of the system and the location of the planet in its orbit, travel time to or from a Jump Station at one-G normally can take anything between ten and twenty days. The more massive the sun or gas giants are within a solar system, the longer the distance to the Jump Point.

These long distances through normal space-time make travel between systems a long and expensive business, suitable only for cargo or the very wealthy. As a result, it is prudent for individual star systems to produce everything they need to maintain their populations and level of civilisation. This limits off-world trade to luxury foodstuffs or trade goods such as works of art that are able to counter their high transit costs.

Minor systems, those newly discovered or not yet commercially exploited don't justify the expense of a Jump Station and are open to all.

The Imperial family keep a tight grip on the manufacture and servicing of QA machinery and maintain Custom Posts at all Jump Points. These ensure Customs Duty is logged or paid and almost completely eliminates smuggling. An Imperial Tithe is taken on the value of any trade, although private citizens can travel without the levy, the only restriction on them being the high cost of travel. The sums raised by the Tithe pay for the upkeep of the Jump Stations and contribute a significant sum each year to the Imperial Treasury.

Unlike their civilian counterparts, larger or specialised Naval Vessels can generate their own QA field internally and do not rely on the Quantum transmitters at the Jump Stations. However, they cannot work outside of a Jump Point. Providing the Quantum Signature of the destination is known, the ability to independently Jump enables them to bypass the often long queues at Jump Points. As a courtesy from the Emperor, the private vessels of each Duke or Duchess are traditionally allowed their own QA drive.

As another important lever of control, the manufacture and servicing of all QA Jump engines remain an Imperial monopoly, with all profits going to the Crown. To be in possession of an unlicensed Jump capable ship is a treasonable offence. To further retain control, the ability to map a Quantum Signature remains restricted to the Imperial Navy.

Using QA, communication between Jump stations is instantaneous but relies on light speed to get relayed intra-system, making real-time conversations impossible between planets.

There is an exception, however, kept hidden from everyone by the Imperial family. Towards the end of his long life, Josef, the first Emperor and inventor of QA, devoted himself to the development of instantaneous communication. Although it took him nearly twenty years, shortly before his death, he managed to solve the problem of QA communications within a gravity well. This breakthrough led to solving the problem of Quantum Attraction Jumping **within** a gravity well without the need to use a Jump Point. However, this discovery had the potential to destabilise his newly formed Empire. If travel, communications or transit taxes couldn't be controlled and monitored, the State would quickly lose its grip on the levers of power. By reserving the use of instantaneous communication and travel to just the Emperor or Empress, the Crown would retain these levers. The advantage of always knowing the news a day or two before anyone else maintained the illusion of Imperial foresight and gave unparalleled advantages to the user in matters such as trade and finance. For these reasons Josef never divulged the discovery to anyone other than his son, Richard, and to this day remains a secret known only to the Emperor and Vimes.

Printed in Great Britain
by Amazon